MW01115748

RESTORE ME

J.L. SEEGARS

Copyright © 2022 by J.L. Seegars

All rights reserved.

No part of this book may be reproduced in any form or by any electronic or mechanical means, including information storage and retrieval systems, without written permission from the author, except for the use of brief quotations in a book review.

Fiction

This novel is entirely a work of fiction. The names, characters and incidents portrayed in it are the work of the author's imagination. Any resemblance to actual persons, living or dead, events or localities is entirely coincidental.

Moral Rights

Janil Seegars asserts the moral right to be identified as the author of this work.

External Content

Janil Seegars has no responsibility for the persistence or accuracy of URLs for external or third-party Internet Websites referred to in this publication and does not guarantee that any content on such Websites is, or will remain, accurate or appropriate.

Designations

Designations used by companies to distinguish their products are often claimed as trademarks. All brand names and product names used in this book and on its cover are trade names, service marks, trademarks and registered trademarks of their respective owners. The publishers and the book are not associated with any product or vendor mentioned in this book. None of the companies referenced within the book have endorsed the book.

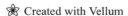 Created with Vellum

For Doodle: My one great love.

"Rarely, if ever, are any of us healed in isolation. Healing is an act of communion."

— bell hooks

AUTHOR NOTE

Please be aware this story involves sensitive topics such as spousal loss, grief, miscarriage, domestic violence, alcoholism, and mention of suicide. Although many of these situations are referenced in the work and happen off-page, I still advise you to consider your own health and well-being before diving into Sloane and Dominic's story.

THE PLAYLIST

01./ A Little Bit Yours by JP Saxe
02./ Strange by Celeste
03./ I Want You Around (Remix ft. 6LACK) by Snoh Aalegra
04./ All I Ask by Adele
05./ I Guess I'm in Love by Clinton Kane
06./ Say it First by Sam Smith
07./ ghostin by Ariana Grande
08./ When it Ends (ft. JORDY) by Avery Lynch
09./ Chicken Tendies by Clinton Kane
10./ pov by Ariana Grande
11./ Ghost by Justin Bieber
12./ nasty by Ariana Grande

1

PROLOGUE

Then

S he smelled like heaven.
 A fruity, floral cocktail that swirled in the late August air around her and carried the heady mixture straight into his nostrils. Flooding his senses until everything in his world was her. The sway of her hips. The graceful curve of her neck. The curly black strands that grazed her shoulders, brushing over golden skin, caressing her in places his fingers longed to touch. He couldn't help but think that was how she wanted it. His entire being awestruck, his soul stunned into silence while she imprinted herself on his skin with her very existence.

Why else would she have come out *here*?

To the back porch of the frat house where he was the sole occupant. He was the only person who needed a break from the music pounding through the speakers, the stench of alcohol he wouldn't drink seeping into his lungs, the overwhelming swell of people packed into the living room turned dance floor, trying to enjoy the first party of the year.

It seemed every person who'd opted to move onto New Haven

University's campus early had come out to party, but he had only come out here to get away from *her*.

To make sense of the magnetic pull that locked into place the moment their eyes met. She had just walked in and was surveying the crowd, and he—well, all he could see was her. The face of an angel with a body made for sin. She was even wearing white. A mini dress that hugged all of her curves and was probably what caught his attention in the first place. And now he knew she didn't just look like an angel, she smelled like one too.

After working the room with her friends, and sparking the most irrational flares of jealousy in him every time she danced with someone else, she was now standing in front of him. One hand on her hip and the other holding a cup he knew was filled with the same mixture of Jack and Coke she'd been drinking all night.

"I've been looking for you."

The sweet notes of her perfume or shampoo mixed with the smoky flavor of the liquor on her breath. Even though he never drank, he didn't mind the smell on her. His stomach wasn't turning the way it usually did when he smelled alcohol. And before he could delve any deeper into what that meant, or respond to her perplexing statement, she sauntered over and perched herself on his lap.

He couldn't help the surprised grunt that escaped his throat when her weight settled against him. She wasn't heavy. He was just caught off guard by how right it felt to have her body against his. The soft curve of her ass nestled against the hard muscles in his thighs. The slight brush of her curls against his bicep when his arm came up to rest against her back. Her eyes were wide and a bit glazed over as she blessed him with a smile. She was buzzed but still very much aware of what was going on around her.

"Why?"

She blinked slowly, pupils dilating as the sound of his voice washed over her and heat crept up in her cheeks. He studied her. Fascinated by the sight of someone being so affected by so little of him. If she was this responsive to his voice, he couldn't help but wonder how she would be underneath him or with his face buried between her thighs....

"You look like trouble, and that's exactly what I need to get into."

Her words interrupted his train of thought, startling him with their honesty. She called him trouble. It wasn't the first time someone had said that about him. Hell, it wasn't even the first time a girl had sat on his lap and admitted to being drawn to his darkness—that ugly, twisted part of him crafted by years of abuse and neglect at the hands of a narcissist—but it was the first time he'd ever felt like the person asking to dance with his shadows had some of their own.

His eyes roved over her face, and she held still, serenity lining her delicate features as he confirmed the presence of his twin flame dancing behind the golden flecks in her hazel eyes. And he was caught between the burning need to hold her to him and never let go, and the raging desire to find the person who shaped her darkness and destroy them with his bare hands.

In the end, he knew his choice was simple. He curled his arm around her waist, pulling her deeper into himself.

She smiled and tossed back the rest of her drink. "Well, are you?"

"Am I what?"

"Trouble."

"That depends, angel."

Shit. He hadn't meant to let the nickname slip. He didn't even know her real name, so it was strange to already be giving her one. There was something overly familiar and possessive in his tone that should have scared them both, but he could only think about how right the word felt on his tongue and how pleased she looked when he said it.

She bit her lip. "On?"

"What kind of trouble you're looking for."

In an instant, the dark flame in her eyes started to burn brighter, calling to the fire that was always ablaze inside of him and daring him to come and burn the world down with her. His breath caught, and he knew at that moment it didn't matter what kind of trouble she was looking for because he'd be it.

He'd be whatever she needed him to be.

2

SLOANE

Now

Dramatic exits have never been my thing. My mother, who's quite literally the queen of storming off, has told me repeatedly that jumping up to leave a room when things aren't going your way is the most undignified thing a woman can do.

Temper tantrums aren't attractive, Sloane Elise.

Unless, of course, she's the person throwing one, but in that case, it's always justified since Lauren Carson can do no wrong. Typically, I don't make a habit of heeding my mother's advice. In fact, a large part of my life—starting with my first party as a college freshman—has been dedicated to throwing every word she's ever said to me about how to conduct myself in public out the window. I've gotten quite good at overriding her voice in my head, but today....today I suck at it.

And it's all *his* fault.

Dominic Alexander.

I turn my head to openly glare at him, not caring for one second that James Robinson, my best client, is sitting across the desk from us looking confused about my clear hostility towards the man he's trying to introduce me to. *Please, Sloane.* His eyes plead with me from across the desk. *Don't screw this up for us. He's saving our asses.*

Your ass, James. I narrow my eyes at him. *He's saving your ass.*

Because this is all James' fault. He's the one who ran off Issac Hayes, the contractor we'd only been working with for two months. Issac was the *third* guy to sign on to handle the renovation of La Grande Nuit —the boutique luxury hotel in downtown New Haven that James hired me to design — and the third one to quit on us. We've been working on this project for over a year, chipping away at the old building, updating the exterior to look more elegant, transforming the interior by mixing in modern elements with the handful of original aspects I pressed James to keep.

All while going through contractors like cheap underwear.

I knew things with this project would be difficult when James insisted on personally overseeing every aspect of it. Having a client involved in all the decision-making always grates on my nerves and rubs the contractors the wrong way. And it doesn't help when that client is a man like James, who delights in giving outrageous deadlines and is as mercurial as they come. One minute he's in love with the antique French doors I spent weeks hunting down, and the next he's shouting about them feeling *too old.*

It's a lot to take.

Which is why I wasn't surprised to get the call from Issac this morning saying he was quitting even though his team was scheduled to start the final phase of the project—the demolition and subsequent renovation of the seventh and eighth floors where all of the high-end suites are— on Monday.

I was, however, surprised to get a follow-up call from James telling me to come by his office after lunch to meet the new contractor he'd already hired to complete the last leg of the project. And that surprise turned into shock when I walked into his office and found him sitting here with Satan himself, laughing and chatting like old friends.

Shock.

That must be why my brain went into autopilot as soon as I saw Dominic. It's the only thing that can explain why I walked in and sat down in the chair beside him. Why I didn't say anything about both of his long legs being spread out wide and making it impossible for my knees not to brush against his hard thighs as I settled in my seat and skimmed over every one of his infuriating features. The dark eyes and neatly trimmed beard. The square jaw and full lips. The deep bronze skin that's sometimes clearer than mine.

Annoying. Annoying. ANNOYING.

"Sloane, this is Nic Alexander. Nic, this is…."

"I know who she is."

The bastard doesn't even try to hide the boredom in his tone as he waves one of his big hands in my direction, a dismissive gesture if I've ever seen one, and throws James a friendly smile. But he makes no move to explain how we know each other, leaving me with the awkward task of explaining our…connection.

"Dominic was Eric's best friend and business partner," I explain to James, shifting in my seat to try and find a position that keeps my knees from coming into contact with his muscular legs again. The jolt of electricity that zipped down my spine when I touched him the first time unnerved me, and I need all of my faculties to fully understand what's happening here. Especially if it means talking, no matter how briefly, about my late husband.

A muscle in Dominic's jaw ticks. A tell-tale sign of his annoyance that's always overly active when I'm around, especially when I call him by his full name. James' inquisitive eyes bounce between us. No doubt wondering about the animosity bristling between the two of us. I can see the wheels turning in his mind as he tries to parse out the issue between a dead man's wife and his best friend.

Good luck working that one out. I think to myself. *Your guess is just as good as mine.*

I smile brightly at James and hope it doesn't look as brittle as it feels. "What's Dominic doing here? Did he help you find the new contractor?" The urge to cringe at my ridiculous question is strong, but I fight it back. I'm being deliberately obtuse, and as much as I hate it, nothing in me is going to accept the reality of working with Asshole

Alexander before it's necessary. Dominic turns to me, a hard look of incredulity heating the side of my face.

"You could say that."

James squints at me, confused by the question. "Nic is the new contractor. We've just taken care of the paperwork, and he says he can start next week."

"My team will be picking up right where *your* contractor left off."

The words are silky and dark, so smooth I almost miss the note of accusation. The one that suggests Issac pulling out of the project at the last minute is somehow on me. Our gazes collide as I turn to face him. My outrage at his statement is apparent in the frustrated huff of air that passes through my lips before I can clamp them shut. I can't decide what's worse: him taking such a cheap shot at me or the fact he's doing it in front of a client.

He holds my stare, waiting patiently for my response. His dark eyes glitter with amusement and some other emotion I can never name even though it's present whenever we argue, which is every time we're in a room together. I square my shoulders, ignoring the triumphant curve of his lips that tells me how much he's enjoying getting a rise out of me.

"You've been misinformed, Dominic." I bite out. "Issac is an independent contractor. He has no affiliation with Studio Six outside of the work we've done on La Grande Nuit. Any of his failings in terms of his contract are his and his alone." I smooth my skirt and turn back to James who is watching our exchange with a furrowed brow. "Are you sure this is the direction you want to go in?"

Something that sounds a lot like a growl comes from Dominic, but I keep my eyes trained on my client, silently pleading with him to walk this back. Even though it isn't a part of my job, I can find us another contractor because working with this man is not an option.

To my dismay, James nods. "Yes. Nic has a stellar reputation. His company does great work, and he's promised to personally supervise the team who will be completing the project."

Oh, great. That means I'll be seeing him on the regular.

An indelicate sniff of acknowledgment escapes me. It's all I can muster. James, who's known me long enough to realize when I'm not happy with one of his decisions, gives me a tight nod and turns back to Dominic to say something. The content of the statement—or question, it could have been a question—is drowned out by the ringing in my ears. Heated blood rushes to all of my extremities, making my vision go blurry with anger.

How the fuck did this happen?

By the time the meeting is over, I'm fuming, and the sound of my heels slapping against the gold-veined marble floor echos through the empty hallway as I march out, leaving James and his new best friend to think of new and exciting ways to ruin my life for the next ten weeks.

Any other time, I would be ecstatic to hear we've replaced a contractor so quickly, over the moon to know they can send in a team immediately. I should be sailing out of James' office feeling nothing but relieved that the opening date for the hotel is safe. Instead, I have a ball of dread sitting in the pit of my stomach that I know won't leave until this project is done and I can go back to only seeing Dominic at my mother-in-law's house for Sunday dinner.

Ridiculous, angry tears spill from my eyes as I fling myself into the driver seat of my car and tap out a message to Mallory Kent, my business partner and sister-in-law, to let her know how the meeting went.

> Sloane: The meeting is done, and I'm heading home for the day. I can't take any more bullshit right now.

> Mallory: K.

> Mallory: What exactly went down? Don't tell me the new contractor pulled out too?!

> Mallory: James needs to get his shit together. He keeps running off contractors and getting pissed with us when the deadlines aren't met.

> Sloane: No. The new contractor is good to go. His team will pick up where Issac's left off. They're going to start next week.

> Mallory: Okay? So what's the problem?

I stare at my phone, debating on telling Mal why I'm so upset and ultimately deciding not to because I know she'll just call me a brat and tell me to get over it. I throw my phone into the passenger seat and reverse out of my parking spot, ignoring the 'ding' that tells me I received another message.

Not returning her text is childish, especially since she is going to find out anyway, but her being pulled into the loop eventually doesn't mean I have to come to grips with reality just yet. I make a left out of the parking lot and head home. The headache I'm sure to be dealing with for the foreseeable future is already pounding behind my eyes. I rub at my temple with one hand.

"I'm going to murder James Robinson"

* * *

I PULL into my driveway about twenty minutes later and roll my eyes when I see Mal's car parked in my usual spot. *The girl has no chill whatsoever.* I'm not surprised she beat me here. The office for Studio Six, our interior design company, is only about ten minutes away from the suburban neighborhood my two-story Craftsman is nestled in. She probably left work as soon as I stopped answering her messages, intent on getting her answer one way or another.

When I walk through the door, balancing my purse and the bottle of wine I stopped at Whole Foods to pick up, I find Mal stretched across my sectional talking on the phone. Her long, black knotless braids are draped over the arm of the couch like a throw blanket and the sandals she paired with the coral wrap dress she wore to work today are lying haphazardly on the floor.

If it were anyone else, I would be beyond annoyed, but with Mal, this is par for the course. As soon as it became clear me and Eric, her twin brother, were going to be a real thing, Mal started giving me what she called 'the family treatment.' She made it sound special, but I quickly realized it just meant she could come over to my house and make herself at home whenever and however she liked.

And even though it's been four years since Eric died, she still acts the same. I'll never tell her, but I appreciate getting the family treatment. Since I grew up an only child, Mallory's the closest thing I've ever had to a sister, and I wouldn't trade her for the world.

One glance at her pinched features tells me whoever is on the other end of the line is grating on her last nerve. I move past her and into the kitchen, attempting to give her as much privacy as the open concept living area will provide.

"Listen, I've got to go." Mal's voice is cold, sharp even. She isn't happy to hear from this person. "Don't call me again."

There's no hiding my shock as I watch her toss her phone on the couch and move into the kitchen to take a seat at the island. I push the glass of wine I poured her across the island and arch a brow. "Who was that and what did they do to you?"

"No one you need to worry about."

She takes a long sip of her wine and throws me a fake smile. It doesn't touch her eyes and neither of the dimples in her cheeks pop out of her smooth mahogany skin. Something is clearly wrong, but I decide not to push because I know she'll tell me when she's ready to.

I shrug. "Fine. Did you at least order food when you decided to break into my house?"

"It's not breaking in if you have a key, Sloane." She rolls her eyes, a faint smile tugging at the corner of her lips. "But yes, I got us some sushi, teriyaki chicken, and fried rice from Roku. It should be here soon."

A moan of appreciation escapes my lips at the mention of my favorite restaurant. "That sounds amazing. It's about time something good happened to me today."

I toss back the rest of my wine and pour myself another glass, ignoring Mal's questioning stare. *Maybe if I stay quiet long enough, she'll forget she's here to interrogate me about my meeting with James and the contractor from hell.* It's a ridiculous thought. The girl is like a dog with a bone when it comes to stuff like this. Unlike me, she doesn't understand the concept of letting something go.

She crosses her arms and leans back in her chair. "Fill me in on this meeting with James and the contractor. You never said who it was, and I need to know....for business purposes."

Her eyes are sparkling with mischief. The little witch is enjoying seeing me all riled up. Granted, me being upset enough to leave work early *is* rare. Most days, you can't pay me to leave the office early, but today is different. There are extenuating circumstances, and Mal getting a kick of out my aggravation makes me want to smack her.

"No one you need to worry about," I repeat her words back to her.

Mal scoffs. "I'm your business partner, girl. I literally need to worry about who we're working with. I mean it's kind of hard to do my job without having their name or contact information."

She's right.

I put my wine glass up to my lips and take another long sip to buy myself some time. Mal waits patiently, her perfectly arched brows raised in anticipation and amusement. She's enjoying this a little too much. I sit my glass back down on the cold quartz and roll my eyes, making it known how annoyed I am.

"The new contractor is Dominic."

The words feel like gravel in my mouth. Disbelief and shock swirl in my belly and the headache that was fading a few minutes ago decides to kick back up in full force. Saying *his* name in relation to my project makes it all too real. I'm officially working with Satan himself.

Mal tosses her head back and lets out a loud howl. Her obnoxious laughter bounces off of the walls in the kitchen and rings in my ears. *I knew she would get a kick out of this.*

"It's not that funny, Mallory."

She's doubled over now, clutching her belly and trying to stay upright on the barstool.

"Oh, Sloane. It really, really is." She sits up and swipes a finger under each eye to wipe away the tears that fell while she was laughing in my face. "From the way you were acting, I thought James had hired someone *awful.* Like some kid who just got his license or that one guy who kept looking at your breasts every time y'all went over building plans for the Allister's house, but it's just Nic."

She's oversimplifying the issue and she knows it. Of course, working with an amateur or the perverted guy from the Allister project would have sucked, but working with Dominic will be *worse, s*o much worse. Because he hates me, and he always has.

It doesn't matter that we've known each other for over a decade or that my husband was his best friend and business partner. He just doesn't like me, and anytime we're in the same room, which is a lot given his relationship with the family I married into, he makes it clear.

He gives everyone else the warmth of his sunshine—full-blown smiles that reach his dark eyes and tight hugs that make his biceps bulge when he wraps his arms around the people he cares about—while I get nothing but ice. Cold indifference that sometimes slides into burning, white-hot anger when other people aren't around. I should be disturbed by those moments, but truthfully, I prefer his anger. It's better than being treated like I don't exist, and it gives me something to fight back against. Eric used to find our disdain for each other amusing, and clearly, Mal still does, but it's easy to be entertained when you aren't the one being hated for no reason other than you dare to exist.

When Eric and I got engaged, I stayed up all night trying to picture a future with Dominic as a permanent fixture and nearly had a panic attack when the images flashed through my mind.

Dominic standing beside Eric at our wedding, his dark eyes glittering with hatred for me.

Our kids running into his arms and screaming "Uncle Nic," so happy to see a man who can't stand their mother.

Christmases where he came over to our home and waited until I was alone just so he could give me the full rundown on everything he thought I'd done wrong that day.

Overwhelmed, I turned over and placed my head on Eric's chest, nestling into his warmth and firing off questions about how to get his grumpy, moody, asshole of a best friend to like me. The only advice he'd given me before falling asleep was to stop calling him by his full name.

"He hates when people call him Dominic, babe."

It was the worst advice Eric had ever given me. Just the idea of using one of his nicknames made my stomach lurch. I couldn't call him Dom or Nic like everyone else did. Not when he looked at me like I was gum on the sole of his favorite pair of Nikes. Nicknames indicated warmth, friendship, intimacy, and we had none of that.

Dominic treated me like an outsider. An unwelcome force that slithered into his inner circle, fell in love with one of his best friends, and enamored herself to the other. I was nothing to him but an inconvenience he had to deal with to spend time with the people he loved.

And nothing—not even losing Eric four years ago at the hands of a drunk driver — has changed the way he views me.

I pin Mal with a hard glare. "Do I have to remind you the man hates me?"

I don't. She's well aware of the state of my relationship with Dominic.

"He doesn't hate you, Sloane." She gives an exaggerated roll of her round eyes when I arch a questioning brow at her. "So you guys don't get along. I've seen you work with tons of assholes and still manage to get the job done. Hell, it's not like James is a walk in the park either."

That's true. James is young, handsome, rich, and used to getting everything he wants: cars, clothes, properties, businesses, women, and the like. He can be a jerk, but he's never one to me. Sometimes, he can be a little *too* friendly. A longing look here, a lingering touch there, posting pictures of us from events we both happened to be at on his Instagram with captions that made it seem like we didn't just run into each other.

He's even asked me out on dates before, and every time I turn him down he just smiles and says 'Next time.' I've never mentioned any of this to Mal. Even though me going out on a date is rarer than me leaving work early, she can still be pretty sensitive about it.

"You're right, he's not a walk in the park, but he also hasn't spent the last twelve years alternating between glaring at me from across the room or completely ignoring me at every family function."

Mal tosses her braids over her shoulder and purses her lips. "But see, that sounds like more of a personal issue. *This* is a professional matter. You're both there to do your jobs and get paid. You don't need to be friends to do that."

"Yes, but every working relationship requires mutual respect, and the only thing Dominic and I agree on is that we don't have any for each other."

"Well, you better find some!" She wiggles her brows at me and smirks. "The opening for La Grande Nuit is in ten weeks, and I'm not listening to James whine about having to bring in another contractor."

The finality of her statement is punctuated by the ringing of my doorbell. Mal jumps up and sprints towards the door. As soon as it swings open, the smell of sushi and fried rice waft towards me. My stomach grumbles at the heavenly scent.

While she settles up with the delivery person, I run upstairs to my bedroom to change clothes. The black heels I wore all day are the first thing to go, and the rest of my outfit follows in quick succession. I breathe a sigh of relief when I unhook my bra and toss it on the bed. After the stress of the day, it feels good to relax. I'm even thankful to have Mal here. She's messy and always telling me things I don't want to hear but being annoyed by her is better than being alone.

After four years of being a widow, I should be used to being by myself, but I'm not. I still miss Eric's presence in my life and usually at the oddest times. Like when my feet are cold at night or I cook too much food for one person to eat or days like today when I'm worried about his best friend making it impossible for me to finish the last leg of a project I've been working on for months.

Standing in front of the full-length mirror next to my bed, I wrap my arms around my middle, trying to imitate the way my husband would hold me after long days. I close my eyes and imagine his warmth enveloping me. The smell of his cologne flooding my senses and making me feel safe, loved and at home.

"Sloane!" Mal's voice rings out, breaking me out of my reverie. "Get your ass down here. The food is getting cold."

My eyes pop open and heat rushes to my face at the sight of the lonely woman staring back at me. She looks tired and worn down. Like someone who's had her heart shattered and completely given up ever being whole again because she knows those pieces are lost to her forever — floating around in the universe with the love of her life, never to be seen again.

I reach into the top drawer of my dresser and retrieve the shirt I sleep in every night, slipping it over my head before pulling on a pair of sweat pants. The cotton is soft as it settles on my skin. Years of wear have made the material feel like a warm hug. I rub the frayed hem between my fingers and wish it still smelt like Eric. Mal calls for me again, threatening to eat my dragon roll if I don't hurry up.

"I'm coming, girl."

She's already settled on the couch scrolling through my Netflix account with her plate in her lap when I come back down. She glances at me over her shoulder.

"Grey's Anatomy reruns?"

I shake my head as I move into the kitchen to grab the plate she fixed for me. "Hell no. I don't have time for Shonda's nonsense today."

Mal pulls a fake pout as I plop down on the couch beside her. "Please, Sloane."

"Fine." I toss a piece of sushi in my mouth and sit back. The opening credits for the episode start rolling and then Meredith Grey is asking how I would want to spend my last day on Earth. "Mal! Is this the bomb episode? You know this one always makes me cry."

Particularly on a day like today when I, much like Meredith, have had my whole life blown up unexpectedly at the hands of irresponsible and eternally selfish men with no care or concern for the damage done by the bombs they've dropped at my feet.

Mal can say what she wants, but I *know*—with an absolute certainty I can feel in my bones—working with Dominic Alexander is going to be the death of me.

3

SLOANE

Now

Here's the worst thing about having an enemy: they're always in your head. Not in a good way. No. It's more of an angry, unhealthy obsession. A think about every word they said and everything they did that pissed you off kind of madness. And once you give in to it, it doesn't stop. Your brain just keeps going, flipping through every interaction and breaking down every minute into endless seconds that are bursting at the seams with new reasons for you to hate them.

That's exactly what is happening to me right now. It's a Saturday night and I'm *trying* to work on the reconfiguration of a master bathroom for a residential project a couple of streets over from the home Eric and I shared before he died, but Dominic Alexander and his infuriating face refuse to leave my mind. I can't stop picturing that smug look he gave me when I walked into James' office and found him sitting there like he belonged.

And the headache that started with the rage-inducing curl of his lips is still slamming against my forehead over twenty-four hours later, making getting anything done impossible.

I glance down at my sketch and cringe when I realize I put two toilets in the water closet. My mind is not in the game at all, so I turn my tablet off and get up from my desk. I wander around the house restlessly for a few minutes before going to my room and grabbing my phone to text Mal and see what she's doing.

She stayed over last night and left early this morning to take Mama on her weekly errand run. I usually go with them since errand runs with Annette Kent generally end with a home-cooked meal and desserts from scratch, but I didn't want to risk running into Dominic. He always stops by on Saturdays to check in on her and fix things around the house. The way he takes care of her is honestly his one redeeming quality, but I'll never give him the satisfaction of knowing I like something about him.

I'm stretched out on my bed scrolling through social media to keep my mind off of my arch-nemesis when Mal's reply comes through.

> Mallory: I'm at Club Noir! Are you coming to get drunk with me?

Alcohol and dancing until my feet hurt sound like the perfect remedy for my restless body and treacherous brain that won't stop conjuring images of Asshole Alexander staring me down in James' office. My fingers fly over the keyboard as I jump off of my bed and head to my closet.

> Sloane: Yep. See you soon! :)

* * *

CLUB NOIR IS a black-owned nightclub in the heart of downtown and just a few blocks away from James' hotel. They have the best DJ in town on retainer and specialize in signature cocktails that cost twelve dollars apiece and can put you on your ass in five seconds flat. Needless to say, it's extremely popular with working professionals who want a place to blow off some steam without running into drunken college kids.

Mal is pacing by the entrance when I arrive. The heels of her gold stilettos move soundlessly over the black tile floors as I cross the threshold and call her name. She squeals with excitement when she takes in my outfit: a lacy red bodysuit with halter straps I paired with a black leather mini skirt and sky-high black heels. My usually wild curls are pulled up into an artfully messy bun with a few tendrils hanging to frame my face.

"You sure you didn't come to catch a man?" Mal teases playfully, looping her arm through mine and pulling me into the darkened entrance of the club.

"Trust me, the last thing on my mind right now is a man. I just wanted to look good. I thought it would make me feel better after yesterday."

I stood in my closet searching for the most scandalous pieces of clothing I owned. In the end, there were three contenders: a white mini dress I've had since college, a backless sage jumpsuit Eric liked to peel off with his teeth, and this outfit. It took me twenty minutes to decide which one made me feel the most powerful, sexy, and in control, and when I left the house, I felt confident I made the right choice.

Judging by the look of approval in Mal's eyes, I did.

Arm in arm, we traipse down a dimly lit hallway that spills out into the heart of the club. The dance floor is packed. A sea of bodies moving as one while a Drake song blasts through the speakers. I can feel the bumping of the bass in my chest. The vibrant energy of the crowd is contagious, reverberating through me in an instant.

"Let's get a drink!" Mal grabs my hand and pulls me towards the bar. We claim two empty seats and place our order with an overly attentive bartender who seems to only have eyes for Mal and refuses to take her money. Her dimpled cheeks are red when she turns back to me. "So, how are you feeling about the whole Nic and James situation?"

I frown, confused by her question. Mal never wants to talk business when we're out. I wonder if she senses that my invasive thoughts of Dominic are the reason I'm out tonight.

"I mean I'm still not thrilled about working with Satan's spawn, but I guess I'll have to get over it. Why?"

"How over it are you? Like on a scale of one to ten? One being 'If I see him before our scheduled meeting on Tuesday, I'm going to lose it.' Ten being 'I can be cordial as long as he stays far away from me.'?"

"Given my history with the man, I would say I'm always hovering around a one. Why?"

She glances over my shoulder with wide eyes, focusing on something on the opposite side of the club. I start to turn, curious about what caught her attention, but she grabs my arm.

"We need shots! Don't you want a shot? I *need* a shot!" She waves her hand in the air, getting the attention of the bartender once again and mouthing at him to bring us two shots of tequila.

"I don't want a shot. We just ordered drinks." I try to twist in my seat again, but her fingers grip me tight, keeping me from moving. "What's going on?"

Her frantic energy has me on high alert. I eye her suspiciously, but her gaze is trained on the bartender who is now sidling towards us with two glasses. Mal thanks him for the drinks, fists the shot glass in her hand, and then tosses the amber liquid down her throat. She doesn't seem remotely phased by the burn. I take a sip of my mixed drink and shake my head when she offers the other shot glass to me. When she throws mine back as well, my eyebrows shoot up.

Something is definitely going on with her.

"Why are you acting so weird?"

Mal pales at my question. "I'm not acting weird! I'm just drinking. Isn't that what you came to do?"

Her voice has gone up an entire octave, making the words sound more like a screech than anything else.

"Cut the shit, Mal. You're acting strange. You have been since I got here."

As soon as I say them, it dawns on me how true the words are. Suddenly, pieces start to click together. Her pacing while she waited for me at the front of the club like we haven't been here multiple times. The way she pulled me over to the bar to get drinks instead of ordering from the waitress circulating the room at a table like we always do. The sudden interest in the Dominic and James situation. Her downing tequila shots like they're going out of style. Her wide, frantic eyes as she glanced over my shoulder and posed hypothetical questions about seeing him.

He's here.

"Please don't tell me…." I spin around in my chair, narrowed eyes scanning the room, searching for him.

"Don't be mad!" Mal pleads. "He showed up right after you texted me to say you were on your way. I swear."

She's standing now, her voluptuous body, which is wrapped in a black mini dress, blocking my direct line of sight. I stand too, clutching my tiny handbag under my arm, prepared to leave.

"You could have texted and told me to turn my ass around! I came here to get my mind off of him. Not to stare at his smug face while sipping overpriced drinks!"

"It's nice to know you've been thinking of me, Sloane."

That voice. A smooth rasp with a dark lilt to it that makes the hairs on the back of my neck stand at attention. The way a doe's ears perk up when she realizes too late that a hungry wolf is closing in on her. Teeth bared, ready to attack.

I spin in the direction of it, my face already schooled into a look I hope conveys just how unhappy I am to see him while giving away none of the embarrassment I feel at him hearing me say he's been on my mind.

But I move too quickly, and grossly underestimate his proximity, because suddenly I'm colliding with him. Well, with his chest to be exact, but it might as well be a wall of concrete for how hard and unforgiving it is. My drink sloshes in my hand, the fruity contents spilling over the rim of the glass and turning my fingers into a sticky mess.

A soft grunt of surprise comes from Dominic as his hands fly to my waist, steadying me. His long, warm fingers dig into my flesh and give a tiny squeeze before releasing me. Then he takes a step back and glares at me. The inky black depths of his eyes flickering with the special cocktail of annoyance and impatience he reserves just for me. I glare back at him. Hating how I have to tilt my head back to meet his gaze.

"Don't get too excited, Dominic. You're always at the front of my mind when I'm contemplating murder."

Both of his dark brows raise, reaching for his razor-sharp hairline. His lips tilt in a sarcastic smirk. "Funny. Not sure you could manage to pull off a murder though, seeing how the minor task of walking is a struggle for you."

I sit my glass back on the bar and retrieve a napkin to wipe the alcohol and fruit juice mixture from my hand. "You'd be surprised what a person can do when they're properly motivated. All sorts of things that *should* be impossible become possible."

Mal's head swings back and forth between us. Her glossy lips twisted in anxious frustration. "Can you guys stop? Just this once, can we have a fun night out together. I mean, when's the last time we did that?"

Dominic and I both throw her an incredulous look. For once we seem to be on the same page about something. Mal knows good and damn well *we* have never had a fun night out together.

Her, Eric, and Dominic? Yes.

Me, her, and Eric. Absolutely.

Her and Dominic? Of course.

Me and her? For sure.

But fun isn't a word I'd ever use to describe an outing where Dominic and I *have* to interact, and I'm certain he feels the same way since he always gives me a wide berth anytime we happen to be in the same place. Only interacting with me when I happen to invade his space, which is usually an empty room or dark corner he's claimed as his own. And even then, he always has an insult or disarming look ready to fly. Some hurtful or below-the-belt quip meant to bring my claws out, so he can drag me down to the pits of hell with him. It's a sweet little tradition he started at the very first party I attended with him, Eric and Mal.

"I wouldn't have pegged you for an attention whore, Sloane. I

guess it's not enough for you to have my best friend wrapped around your finger, you gotta make sure everyone else has their eyes on you too, huh?"

I shake my head, trying to free myself from the memory and the way his twelve-year-old baritone washes over me like a wave of vengeful fire, turning everything it touches into ash. Mal's wide eyes are still bouncing between the two of us. Ill-advised hope shining in the amber pools and tugging at my heartstrings. I can do this for her. Give her this one night of fun where she doesn't have to worry about me ripping the man's head off.

Besides, it'll be good practice for the next ten weeks when I can't physically attack him without losing my job and putting my reputation as a consummate professional at stake.

"Fine." I concede, a ripple of satisfaction zinging through me at the surprised look on Dominic's face. He didn't think I would agree. He expected me to storm out of here in a blaze of fury like I did at the end of our meeting with James yesterday. *Not today, buddy.* My lips curve as I tip my head back and smile up at him sweetly. "Dominic can stay, as long as he promises to hold my purse."

Before he can answer, I pull the sparkly clutch from the safety of my arm and place it in his big hands. He doesn't say a word, but the waves of hostility rolling off of him are palpable. Mal laughs and puts her bag in his hand too, but the look he gives her isn't half as heated as the one he fixed me with.

The one that scorches my back as Mal and I weave through the crowd, parting the sea of bodies with our linked hands. We find a relatively empty spot on the dance floor and smile at each other like fools before breaking out into fluid movements that match the rhythm of the song spilling through the speakers.

"I'm so glad you didn't let this shit with Nic ruin your night!" Mal shouts, leaning close to me so the words aren't drowned out by the music.

I smile at her, even though I'm breathing the same air as Asshole Alexander, I *am* having a good time. "Thanks for encouraging me to stay."

She winks at me, but her response is replaced by a gasp when a tall, bald man with mocha skin and a full beard comes up behind her and grabs her by the waist. He's handsome, and a slightly lopsided smile takes over his face when Mal glances at him over her shoulder then grips his hands to hold them to her body.

It's universal club speak for *why yes, fine stranger, you can just grope me on the dance floor without so much as a hello.*

Mal wiggles her eyebrows at me conspiratorially and chucks her chin at something behind me. I turn and see another man moving through the crowd with his brown eyes set on me. I freeze, the strongest sensation of dread seeping into my bones as I absorb the meaning behind his look. Any woman in the club would probably be glad to have his attention on her. I mean he's nice-looking—if you like tall men with smooth skin and a fresh fade.

In another life, he'd probably be an option for me. Someone to smile and dance the night away with. Someone to take back to my empty house and hop into bed with. Someone to run his fingers over my skin and tell me how beautiful I am right before he strips me naked with his teeth and worships my body with his. Unfortunately for him, and maybe for me, I'm not like any of the women in this club or the girls who used to follow Dominic around in college.

I am, for lack of a better word, uninterested. Not in men, per se, just in their attention and expectations. I have no desire to know them or connect with them physically, emotionally, or anything in between.

And I know that because of my past I never will.

I just can't find it in me to get excited about getting to know someone else, and the idea of small talk, first dates, and learning all the little things about someone new just makes me sick to my stomach. It feels like a cruel joke to have to go through it all over again, especially when I already had my great love. My person whose arms felt like home, whose heart beat in time with mine.

I'm not crazy enough to believe it will happen for me twice, and I certainly don't deserve it, not after the way I hurt Eric—letting the poison bubbling inside of me spill out and into our lives, eating through all of our happiness and joy until there was nothing left. Not even him.

Less wallowing, more moving.

I bolt before the smiling man can take another step in my direction. My legs are steady and sure as they carry me off the dance floor and deposit me on the edge of the room, right in front of the black leather booths Mal likes to sit at when she comes here. Walking the length of the wall, I search for anything that might indicate which one she laid claim to before I arrived.

My answer comes in the shape of Dominic's large frame folded awkwardly over the small table where he's sat our drinks and purses. The hard lines of his face are pulled into a grimace as he stares down at his phone. I can't tell if he's reading an email or having an issue upgrading his Pornhub subscription, and I don't care as long as he isn't focused on me. Mal asked for a fun night, and I'm doing my best to give her that, but if he starts with his smart-ass comments I can't be held responsible for my actions.

"Had enough of the dance floor already?" He doesn't even look up from his phone. Thick fingers flying over the keyboard in rapid succession.

I pick up one of the three bottles of water on the table and crack it open before putting it to my lips and taking a long pull. The cold liquid is refreshing, reminding me of how draining dancing and drinking can be.

"Sure," I say coolly. "I can rest easy now, knowing everyone in this club has had their eyes on me. You know how us attention whores *need* to be seen."

I'm not sure why those specific words come tumbling out of my mouth. Maybe it's the memory of his first insult so fresh in my mind or the frustration from him butting into my project with James, but for some reason, I want to bait him. To remind him that even though I agreed to play nice tonight for Mal's sake, I haven't forgotten that he didn't.

That in all the years I've known him, he never has.

But the reward for my unprovoked jab is exactly what I didn't want: his full attention on me. The steely, midnight stare with a barely contained fire raging in its depths, the full lips pressed into a sharp, flat line. And of course, the *tick-tick-tick* of the muscle in the hard set of his jaw. Elements for a perfect storm that make my heart start to smack against my rib cage.

I've woken the beast.

4

DOMINIC

There are three things you need to know about Sloane Kent.

One: She's annoying as fuck. No, really. Everything about her is annoying. From the superior cadence of her voice to the way she scrunches up her nose when she's trying to make a point to the way she insists on calling me Dominic even though no one who's known me as long as she has does.

Two: She's good at her job. I'll never tell her that though cause it'll just go to her head, and the last thing I need is to hear Mal and Mama crying to me about her head inflating to three times the size of her body and carrying her away Harry Potter style. I mean, it wouldn't bother me one bit to be rid of her, but they certainly would be lost without her. And even though I'm an asshole, I don't want to see the women I think of like my little sister and second mom, suffer. Not after Eric.

Three: She *likes* fighting with me. More than once, she's accused me of getting some sick satisfaction out of arguing with her, *I'll plead the fifth on that one,* but it has always been evident to me that she enjoys the verbal sparring too. Especially in moments like this when she has actively sought me out to pick a fight.

Granted, I probably would have jumped at the opportunity to antagonize her had she not started with me first, but that doesn't matter. Not when she's thrown the first punch, spitting my words from a lifetime ago back at me like they were fresh in her mind. Did she remember everything I said to her in the brief moments I'd caught her alone over the years? *Maybe.* The possibility of my words sticking to her, swirling around in her mind does something to my chest.

You really are a sick bastard, Dom. The voice in my head quips, and I can't argue with it. Only a sick bastard would get a kick out of insulting his best friend's widow and take note of all the warning signs of her blazing anger with anticipation swelling in his chest. I know all of Sloane's by heart: the darkening of her hazel eyes, the curling of her tiny hands into useless fists, the crease between her brow getting deeper, and her cheeks growing red with unleashed heat.

I could push her further if I wanted to, get her so worked up she storms away from this table and leaves me free to breathe air that isn't filled with her scent, but right now I'll have to settle for a heated exchange I can't put my full heart into since Sloane promised Mal we'd have fun tonight and the two of us getting into it in the middle of a nightclub would only be fun for me.

Placing my phone on the table, I turn towards her, noting the hard glint in her eyes and the stubborn tilt of her chin that tells me she's ready for my response. I run a thumb over the rim of the tumbler in front of me. The dark liquid inside swirls around, and Sloane tracks my movement with her eyes. That surprises me. Usually, she can't be bothered to notice anything I do unless I'm insulting her.

"I guess your thoughts of me went a little further than plotting my murder. Sounds like you took a nice little trip down memory lane too."

Her gaze snags on mine. My pulse jumps with something that can only be described as anticipation. She takes another sip of the water she hasn't thanked me for ordering. Her mouth is pursed in contemplation when she sits it back down.

"Maybe I was just reviewing my list."

I arch a brow, intrigued. "Your list?"

"Yeah, the one I started to keep track of the many reasons I have for wanting to kill you." She shrugs as if discussing my murder in a nightclub is a natural thing to do. Considering our history, it isn't that far-fetched. "I figured it would be helpful…"

"In proving it was premeditated," I cut in, finishing her statement for her. My interruption wins me an annoyed scowl. I want to laugh, but I can't trust her not to throw a drink in my face, and I like the shirt I'm wearing.

"Or proving I was driven to the point of insanity by years of verbal abuse and…." She pauses, searching for the right word to describe our toxic banter, which she happily participates in. "Bullying."

A dark laugh rips free from my chest. I take a sip of my drink to shut it down. "Bullying? That would be your defense?"

I want to say more. To tell her she's far too intelligent to have to stand trial for murder. Especially when she works on several construction sites where she could easily hide a body, even if it's mine.

She blinks. No doubt surprised by how tame this conversation is by our standards. I sure as fuck am. "It worked for Betty Broderick, why not me?"

"Hmm. I could think of a few reasons why that wouldn't work for you. First, I'm not your husband. Second, I'm pretty sure the correct word to describe what her husband did is gaslighting. Third, she didn't get away with it."

Her plump lips roll inward. "Right. I guess I could always dispose of the body and avoid a trial altogether."

Smart girl. I think, but in reality, I say, "And how would you go about doing that?"

Sloane crosses her legs, drawing my attention to the smooth skin of her thighs which are on full display thanks to the short leather skirt she's wearing. I swallow then force my eyes to look anywhere else. I'm not about to be labeled a pervert on top of being an asshole.

She leans forward. The sudden movement jostling her breasts inside the flimsy lace of her top. It's clear she isn't wearing a bra. *Not that I'm looking.* The hand resting on my leg balls into a fist as I will my gaze to stay on her face.

"Do you think I'm dumb enough to tell you, a potential victim, where I'd hide your body?"

"*A* potential victim?" I lean forward too, liking the spark in her gaze as she processes my proximity. "Are you planning more than one murder, Sloane?"

Her lips part. The tiny crease in between her brows growing deeper. Music pulses in the air. Drunken patrons dance less than six feet away from us. But it feels like we're the only people in the room. Arguing with her, even in the mildest sense of the word, seems to take up all the space in my mind, making everyone else disappear from my focus.

"Maybe." She sits back in her seat, crossing her arms underneath her breasts. "James is high on my list after the stunt he pulled yesterday."

There's a new heat to her words. The playful teasing from a second ago is a thing of the past. Absently, I wonder if she did this on purpose. Lured me into a seemingly playful conversation, just to bring it all back to James fucking Robinson and his overpriced hotel.

I should have more polite thoughts for my new client who's paying through the nose for me to bring a team in at the last minute to complete the last two floors of his hotel renovation, but two things are stopping me from doing that.

First, there's the issue with the contractor. Yesterday, I suggested him quitting with only ten weeks left in the project was somehow Sloane's fault, but that was just me trying to piss her off. It was evident to me from the moment I met Robinson that he's the cause of the issues plaguing his hotel venture, and speaking to Issac, the former contractor, only solidified that fact for me. The guy is rich, demanding, and unrealistic when it comes to timelines.

And then there's the issue of the way he looked at Sloane when she came strutting into his office yesterday. His hungry eyes devoured her from head to toe in a split second. Like he knew what she looked like naked.

My vision went red. Burning rage creeping up my throat that I had to push back just so I could form a coherent sentence. Anger seeping beneath my skin as a question I had no right to ask bounced around my brain: What the fuck is going on with them?

The real question, the voice in my head reminded me, *is why the hell do you care?*

And I didn't have an answer for that question, or at least not one I could admit to myself, so I pushed the entire thing out of my mind. Now, she's forcing me to think about it again. His name falling from her lips hits me in my gut. Coaxing the anger I fucked into Kristen last night right back to the surface.

"Plotting on your boyfriend? Now *that* you might get away with." I toss the rest of my drink back, returning the heat of her question with my own fire.

Sloane's brows dip inward and then she rolls her eyes dramatically. "James isn't my boyfriend, Dominic. Maybe you two can work something out when you're sharing a grave though. You know, since he's your best friend and all."

She tosses her head to the side and arches a brow at me. I want to laugh in her pretty face. James Robinson will never be a friend of mine. Especially if he keeps saying her name like she's a goddess whose altar he worships at every night.

Why do you care how he says her name? She doesn't belong to you.

I exhale roughly. Thinking about her and Robinson is making my fucking chest tight, but the nagging voice in my head is right again. Sloane Kent does not belong to me, and I shouldn't give a damn about who she is or isn't fucking. Technically, she's a single woman, and we aren't friends. Hell, with Eric gone, we aren't even sort-of family.

Then let it go, Nic.

"Is it going to be like this for the next two and a half months?"

She glowers at me. "It doesn't have to be. You could call James tomorrow and tell him you're no longer interested in the project."

Something that looks a lot like hope edges into her eyes. Too bad for her, I'm about to stomp all over it. Lifting my hand, I wave the waitress over and place an order for another round of drinks. When we're alone again, I turn to her.

"Not happening."

Her shoulders sag a bit. It's a small movement, one another person wouldn't catch, but I do because I've spent a long time watching her. Acquiring an intimate knowledge of her facial expressions, body language, and the things that make her tick. Knowing all the right buttons to hit, that's what makes fucking with her so much fun.

"How did he even find you?"

"He didn't." This is the bomb I've been itching to drop on her. "I called him and offered my services."

Sloane's mouth falls open. "What? Why would you do that?" She's sputtering in the most un-Sloane-like way. "How did you even *know*?"

I lean back and stretch one arm across the back of the booth. Fingers drumming on the sleek leather as I consider her. "New Haven isn't that big, Sloane. Word travels fast, and when your contractor quit, I got a call from a mutual friend about the situation. I happened to have an opening in my schedule, and James was happy to use me."

Liar.

"To get on my last nerve," Sloane grumbles, taking the freshly mixed drink the waitress is offering her.

I accept my drink and wait for the starry-eyed girl to leave us alone. She's been flirting with me all night. Brushing her fingers against mine while she hands me drinks, batting her eyelashes when she asks if there's *anything* else she can do for me. The innuendo is clear, but I'm not interested. My days of taking random women home from the club are long over.

"To finish a job you couldn't do without me." I correct, getting a kick out of the fury in her eyes, swimming around with the flecks of gold in her irises.

"Business must be pretty slow if you're calling around begging for jobs." She shifts in her seat. The piece of fabric she calls a skirt slips up her thigh.

Now, *that* is funny, and I don't even try to stop the amused sound that escapes my chest in a huff. Who cares if I end up wearing the fruity pink concoction she's sipping?

"You and I both know my business is doing *very* well."

I don't need to elaborate. The regular deposits I make in her bank account prove Archway Construction, the company Eric and I started together, is doing just fine. We certainly aren't hard up for work. I had to move several projects around just to be able to personally oversee the hotel job. Alex, my assistant, was livid when I told him what needed to be done. No one in the office understood why I'd taken a special interest.

Hell, I can't even admit the answer to myself, but looking at Sloane now, all pissed off and on the brink of throwing something at my head, makes the aggravation worth it.

Okay, so I *do* get a sick satisfaction out of fighting with her. Is it really that surprising?

Sloane opens her mouth to respond, but before the words come out Mallory slides into the booth accompanied by the random I saw groping her on the dance floor. Their sudden intrusion forces Sloane to slide down and around, following the curve of the booth until she's right beside me. Her thigh touching mine, and her elbow brushing my ribs since I haven't moved an inch. I'm crowding her out. She tucks her arms into her body and tries, but fails, to put some space between our legs. A decent man would have noticed her discomfort and shifted to give her room, but I'm not a decent man.

Not where she's concerned.

"Are you guys playing nice?" Mal asks, in an annoying sing-song voice she only uses when she's drunk.

I glance down at Sloane. Her back is ramrod straight, hovering over the part of the seat my arm is resting on. "For once, yes. Sloane's been on her best behavior."

"Was that before or after I threatened to murder you?" Hard hazel eyes meet mine. A perfectly arched brow cocked at me like a loaded gun. She never knows when to holster her weapon. And I know if I give her cause, nothing, not even her promise to Mal, will stop her from pulling the trigger. I hold her gaze, letting her see I'm more than willing to make a mockery of her word if she is.

Mallory and the random laugh, and the drunken sound breaks our trance. Sloane snaps to attention, clearing her throat and laughing too.

She doesn't feel it though. I can tell because her body doesn't vibrate with the sound, and the smile never reaches her eyes the way it does when she's really amused.

That's part of the problem with knowing your enemy so well: becoming familiar with the information you never have a reason to use like how to make her eyes shine with happiness or the right thing to say to entice her lips to pull into that dazzling smile she gives to everyone but you.

"Nic? Did you hear Chase? He was asking what it's like to work in construction." Mal's voice filters through my reverie, pulling me back to reality. Everyone at the table is staring at me, including Sloane. My face warms where her hard gaze settles. Her scent, something sweet and fruity, is clinging to the air between us, and her bare thigh is still pressed to mine. Even through the fabric of my jeans, I can feel the heat coming off of her.

And it's distracting as hell.

I clear my throat, making eye contact with Chase for the first time. The guy doesn't look like he gives a fuck about construction. He's just being nice to Mal's friends in hopes of talking her into sleeping with him.

"The money's good and the hours are hell." The words sound rough and agitated, even to my ears. The pleasure I felt at crowding Sloane out just a moment ago is gone. Replaced by my confusing reaction to her proximity. I take another sip of my drink. "But I like what I do. Getting to be my own boss isn't too bad either."

Chase's head bobs up and down with feigned interest as he mutters something about entrepreneurship being cool before turning his attention back to Mal. Greedy eyes bouncing from her lips to her chest and then her legs like he can't decide which part of her he wants to look at most. It's annoying to watch.

Just annoying, huh? Where's the outrage from yesterday?

My heartbeat is a fierce and insistent pounding behind my rib cage. Exacerbated by the question posed to me by my own fucked up brain and Sloane's nearness. I almost pass out from relief when my phone starts to light up on the table, alerting me to an incoming call. I snatch it up quickly, barely even noticing Sloane's quick intake of air when my hand sweeps across the curve of her bare shoulder.

"Excuse me, I've got to take this." I don't *have* to, but I still hit accept on the call and stride away from the table before anyone can say anything.

Not that a single person at the table would have protested my departure. Mallory and Chase are eye-fucking each other, and Sloane is…well, Sloane. She never actually *wants* me around.

And that would be fine if, despite my best efforts and the promise I made to myself years ago, I didn't spend all of my time craving her infuriating presence.

5

SLOANE

The relief of having Dominic out of my personal space is immediate and intense. My body was in danger of short-circuiting from the zips of electricity and heat passing between us. They were so similar to what I felt in James' office when I sat beside him, only more concentrated. I assumed it was from the prolonged contact. Our legs pressed together and my body nestled into his side, despite my repeated attempts to put space between us. I couldn't pull in a breath without touching a part of him, and he refused to move.

A man as big as Dominic knows when he's crowding someone out. He's like six-seven for crying out loud! It should be instinct for someone that big to always be aware of the amount of space they're taking up and adjust accordingly. I mean it's just proper etiquette, but the man has proven time and again that when it comes to getting under my skin, he's all too happy to throw etiquette, morals, and decency out the window.

I roll my shoulders and my eyes when Chase takes Dominic's exit from the table as an invitation to maul Mal. Within seconds of his departure, they're both moaning into each other's mouths and smacking loudly every time their lips collide. It's sickening.

"I'm going to the restroom," I mumble to no one in particular since the two people at the table certainly don't hear me. The backs of my thighs are stuck to the leather seat, so it takes longer than it should to slide out of the booth, but I still manage to escape before Chase's wandering hands venture into indecent territory.

For the first time, I'm dismayed to find only a handful of people are waiting outside the bathroom. I go through the line in record time, and while my bladder is happy, I'm dreading going back to the table with Mal and Mr. Tall, Bald and Handsy. *And Lord help me*, if Dominic is back, I'll find myself smashed between his big body and the most inappropriate couple in the club. Since I have no interest in *that* particular seating arrangement, I head towards the bar.

I'm cutting through a group of girlfriends who give me the stink eye for interrupting their girl-on-girl dance routine, that's meant to draw the attention of every man in the club, when a sweaty hand grabs my wrist. My steps skid to a stop and then I'm moving backward, being pulled into an aggressive erection that hits me right in the center of my lower back.

"What the fuck?"

"Dance with me, baby." The man pants in my ear and the stench of Cognac on his breath makes my stomach roll. "You ran from me earlier, but I've got you now."

I wouldn't have thought it possible, but my spine stiffens even more as I twist around and catch a glimpse of his face that confirms he's the guy I ran from earlier. He flashes me a nasty smile, and I try to pull away again, but his grimy fingers dig into my waist, and it feels like he's ripping through the lace of my bodysuit.

"Let go of me!" I'm shouting, but the words are drowned out by the music. In the dark shadows of the club, we must look like every other couple on the dance floor losing ourselves in each other because no one looks our way.

"You smell so good, baby." His nose is in the crook of my neck and then I feel a rough scrape of teeth on my skin. A wave of nausea sweeps through me. "I'm not going to let you get away from me again, not when I've been waiting all night to get you alone."

Panic grips me as he starts to walk backward, pulling us deeper into the shadows where there are significantly fewer people. I score my nails into his hands, hard enough to draw blood, but he doesn't flinch.

"Please." I plead, but it falls on deaf ears.

Frantically, I search the crowd, looking for Mal, Chase, or even a friendly stranger that can stop me from being dragged into a dark corner to get groped by a drunken stranger.

"Don't worry. I'm going to take *very* good care of you."

I pull in lungfuls of useless air as my brain screams at me to fight, yell or drop to the damn ground, but I'm frozen. Shock rendering all of my limbs useless as a sick acceptance trickles down my spine.

This is happening.

Then my eyes land on Dominic. A hulking figure advancing towards me with danger and violence gleaming in his eyes, and for once it isn't aimed at me. My heart stutters to a stop and when it starts again, it's beating twice as fast. I've never been so happy to see him.

"Get your fucking hands off of her."

But he doesn't give my captor a chance to move. Instead, he catches my hand in his and yanks me towards him. I crash into his chest. Somewhere in my mind, I note that he smells nice—a warm and spicy scent that calms my racing pulse.

"What the hell, man? Get your own girl, she's mine." The drunken man is leering at me. Staggering as he reaches out to grab me again. Dominic puts his hands on my hips, shifting me around his body so I'm standing behind him, safely out of my stalker's reach.

Too bad for him, it puts him face to face with an avenging angel.

"Yours?" Dominic growls, taking a step forward. "You think someone like her could ever belong to a piece of shit like you?"

"Take it easy, man. It's plenty of ass out here for everybody." He leans to the side trying to get a look at me. I shrink back, hiding behind the wall that is Dominic's back. "You had all night to shoot your shot. She doesn't seem interested."

A strangled sound leaves the drunk, his voice breaking on the last word. I peek around just in time to see one of Dominic's fists connecting with the man's jaw for what I can only guess is the second time. The man stumbles, but Dominic catches him by his throat. Long fingers wrapping around his neck and squeezing.

Gasps ring out around us. All of the patrons who couldn't be bothered to pay attention when I was being assaulted are now riveted by the scene unfolding in front of them, but I can't think about them now. I watch in horror as the hands that were just digging into my flesh clutch Dominic's forearm, staging a rather flimsy attempt at breaking his hold.

"Dominic! Stop. Let him go."

His heavy gaze finds mine, and I falter. I'm not sure what I was expecting to see, but it isn't this. A deathly calm. Every muscle in his face is still, except for his lips which are curled into a snarl, like a rabid animal who's just been interrupted in the middle of its meal. When no other words come from my lips, he turns his attention back to the man in front of him.

"What she is"—he says brusquely—"is someone you will never touch again. In fact, you won't even think about what it was like to touch her. If you do, I'll find you and I will *fucking* end you."

And with nothing more than a flick of his wrist, Dominic releases the man, letting him fall to the ground in a wheezing heap. He turns around and his eyes are pools of molten darkness and heat. Almost like he's mad at…me?

I swallow. That can't be right. Even he isn't asshole enough to blame me for the actions of a drunk. Somewhere in my mind, I know that to be true, but I'm struggling to make sense of the events of the last few minutes. The man grabbing me. The scrape of his teeth on my neck, his fingers digging into my flesh. Dominic coming out of nowhere. The relief I felt at seeing him.

And *the rage*.

His rage and the way it coated the words he said to the man. Words that dripped with a pure animal urge to protect, to defend what was his. *Except I'm not his.* Dominic takes a step towards me, and my instincts tell me to take two steps back, shrinking away from the dangerous look that's spearing me.

"Alright folks, that's enough. Break it up or I'm going to have to call the cops."

A burly white man with red hair breaks through the crowd. He's wearing a black shirt with the club's logo embroidered on the sleeve and is holding a walky-talky in his hand. A security guard. *Of course, they would come when everything is over.*

He ambles over to me and places a hand on my shoulder. Dominic glowers at him, and he removes it. "Anybody want to tell me what happened here?"

Dominic speaks first. "What happened here is you've got paying customers on the floor doing your job while you're sitting on your ass letting predators run loose!"

Holy fuck, is he angry. It's more evident now. In the slant of his brows, the flare of his nostrils, and the heat in his eyes that's charring everything his glare touches. And right now it's focused solely on the security guard whose skin is now as red as his hair.

"None of my guys saw anyone doing anything *predatory*." He spits the last word out like it's an affront to his character to even say it. "They did see you punching another paying customer not once, but twice, and then choking him half to death though."

A dark, sarcastic smile tilts Dominic's lips. He takes two steps toward the guard, moving over the heaving man on the floor and looking like committing another act of violence in such a short time frame would mean nothing to him. "Are you—"

I step forward, putting myself between the two men. "Dominic, please don't."

My hand is on his chest, but I'm not fool enough to think I could stop him if he made a move for the guard. Slowly, as if he isn't sure he actually wants to, Dominic looks down at me. The muscle in his jaw is ticking again.

"I'd listen to your girl if I were you, pal." The guard laughs, bending down to help my groper up off of the floor. "If you're not out of here in five minutes, you're going to be spending the night in the drunk tank. Might even find yourself facing a drunk and disorderly conduct charge."

"You're *really* not helping, sir," I say sternly, resisting the urge to tell him to shut the hell up. I mean who thinks it's a good idea to antagonize a man who's just left another gasping for air? "Dominic, let's just get Mal and go."

With one last withering look at the security guard, Dominic nods his head then turns to walk away. It isn't until I'm running to keep up with his long strides that I realize he's holding my hand. His palm is rough and warm, and his fingers cradle mine in a grip that's firm but gentle.

"Stop. You don't need to…" I fight against his hold, barely slowing our progress as he parts the crowd with the sheer force of his will.

He glances back at me, disbelief marring his features. "Do you want me to go to jail, Sloane? Because that's exactly what's going to happen if I let you go and another fucking person in this shit hole touches you tonight."

"What? I—"

Words fail me. Disbelief and alcohol have made my brain sluggish, and Dominic uses my delayed processing skills to his advantage, tightening his grip on my limp hand and barreling back towards the booth where Mal and Chase are still sitting.

Her mouth drops when she sees us, and I can only imagine what we must look like. Me, shell-shocked and disbelieving, being dragged around by Dominic who looks no worse for wear after his physical exertions, but still has murder in his eyes.

"Sloane, what's going on?" She shrieks, attempting to stand.

Dominic gestures for her to sit back down. He's still holding my hand, using his free one to grab my clutch from the table. "We don't have time to go over all the minute details, Mallory. We have to go."

I grab my purse from Dominic and glance at Mal, who's looking more confused by the second. "Some drunk guy got a little handsy with me when I was heading to the bar. Dominic saw and—" Six eyes land on me, watching me struggle to find the right word for what my supposed enemy did for me. Turns out, there's only one.

"—*saved* me. But things got a little violent, so we've been asked to leave."

"Oh, shit. I guess that means..." Chase trails off awkwardly, standing to free Mal, who is scrambling out of the booth.

I can't believe he's leaving an opening for Mal to invite him back to her place after hearing her sister-in-law just got groped. And from the look of disgust on Dominic's face, he can't believe it either. I'm increasingly aware of his skin on mine. He's applying steady pressure to my wrist. Like he doesn't want me to forget for one second that his hand is there.

As if I could.

"Chase, honey. I'll give you a call tomorrow, okay?" Mal's voice is sugary sweet, but I can tell she's been rubbed the wrong way by his lack of consideration too. She presses a kiss to his cheek then smiles at me and Dominic. "You guys ready?"

I nod. I'm more than ready to get the hell out of this club. Mal waltzes over and takes our hands in her own, breaking the contact so she can step in between us and link our arms together. She looks up at Dominic, ready to fire off a thousand questions at him as we walk out.

Warm summer air caresses my skin as we step onto the sidewalk. It's late, at least two in the morning, but the street is still buzzing with people. Groups of friends who are staggering into another club. Their laughter filtering through the night. I'm staring a little too hard at a couple devouring each other on the corner when Mal finally lands on a question.

"Anyone want to tell me what the hell happened?"

Dominic fixes her with a hard stare. It's clear to me he's still pissed, that there's reckless anger still simmering in his veins, but Mal doesn't seem to register it.

"Not now, Mal."

It's a clipped, gruff response. Something I've rarely seen him give her. Usually, when she speaks, he's all warm indulgence and brotherly annoyance, but I guess he doesn't have the capacity for it tonight. Not when he still has violence swirling in the inky depths of his eyes.

Mal must realize it isn't smart to push him any further because she lets go of his arm and turns to me. Her soft, brown eyes assessing. "Are you okay?"

A mixture of guilt and concern has her brows furrowed. It tugs on my heart and brings my need to reassure her to the surface. I give her arm a gentle squeeze and nod. "Yeah. A little shaken up, but okay."

Or at least I will be. As soon as I get home and scrub my skin raw, so I can no longer feel the man's hands on me.

"I should have been there with you. I would have kicked the bastard in the balls."

The image of Mal sinking her red bottoms into that man's crotch makes me smile. I know in my heart of hearts she wouldn't have hesitated to do that. Just like Dominic didn't hesitate to put the man on his ass the second he saw his hands on me.

"Of course, you would have." I smile over at her, letting her see she doesn't need to worry. "But I think what Dominic did to him was a lot more memorable than a kick to the balls."

I chance a glance at him to see if he heard me, but he's walking ahead of us now. Hands shoved in his pockets, spine straight as a board as he leads us away from the club. I have no idea where he's going but I'm not about to question him.

This night is just full of surprises.

Mal gives me an impressed look. "Shit. Did he actually hit the guy?"

"He punched him. Twice." I'm whispering. Hyper aware of Dominic's presence in front of us. I don't know if he wants me to give Mal a play-by-play of his heroic efforts. "And then he choked him. I think the guy might have passed out."

She stops walking. "He did *what?*"

Her shrill tone makes me glad I didn't mention the part where Dominic threatened to find and kill the man if he ever thought about what it felt like to touch me. Just thinking about the dark thread of danger that was his voice when he said those words makes my knees weak.

"It was bad, Mal. He was so angry, and the guy just wouldn't stop talking. Then the security guard came and instead of helping, he just made it worse. I had to stop Dominic from knocking him to the ground."

"Nic? Our Nic?" She throws an astonished glance up the street to him. He's stopped walking too. The picture of impatience as he taps his foot on the sidewalk, silently telling us to come on. Mal starts moving again, pulling me along with her.

"Yes. Why do you sound so surprised?"

"I've never seen him throw a punch. *Ever.*" She purses her lips like she's searching her memory to make sure her statement is accurate. "You know how he grew up. He's not exactly a fan of physical violence."

That's right. Somewhere in the back of my mind, where I store all of my knowledge of Dominic, a file on his tumultuous childhood pops up. It's full of facts shared with me by Eric or Mal in their crusade to help me understand him better. The most important fact is highlighted in neon yellow: Dominic's father was an abusive drunk.

An angry man who lied, cheated, and beat his wife and son every chance he got. The only good thing Gabriel Alexander ever did was allow his son to spend time at the Kent home. Where he learned not everyone used their fists to express their feelings and decided he would never be the kind of man who did.

But tonight, he abandoned all of that. *For me.*

"Right…I guess that kind of goes out the window when you see a woman being dragged into a dark corner by a creepy stranger."

We're catching up to Dominic now. Only a few steps behind him as he turns into a parking lot. His strides are quicker now. Smooth, quick steps that eat up the pavement as he approaches his car, a midnight black Range Rover that matches his eyes. Mal leads me to the passenger side.

"Do you want to get in front, Sloane?" It's a question, but she already has the back door pulled open and one leg in the car.

I hesitate. "Umm, actually I think I'll—"

What? Wait in a dark parking lot for an Uber? I'm not sure what I was going to say, but the thought of sitting in the front with Dominic gives me pause. The palm of my hand is still tingling from being exposed to his skin in the club. His scent is still clinging to me, reminding me of the firm, unforgiving planes of his chest. I'm not sure I can survive being in such close proximity to him.

Not when my heart is singing with overwhelming gratitude for him.

But the alternative is quite ridiculous, and apparently, Dominic thinks so as well. He prowls around the car, keys jingling in his hand as he approaches us, looking like an exasperated father who's having the damnedest time getting his unruly kids in the car. Mal swings her body into the backseat and slams the door shut. I roll my eyes internally. *She's such a little coward.*

Dominic sighs. "Get your ass in the car, Sloane, or I'll put you in there myself."

He wouldn't really do that, would he? A day ago, my answer to that question would have been a solid, resolute no because Dominic never touches me, but now, I'm not so sure. Can't be when the feel of his hands on my waist is still fresh in my mind. He touched me with a familiarity and possessiveness that wasn't at all in line with the non-existent relationship we have.

I study him, looking for an answer to my unspoken question. The hard set of his jaw tells me yes, he actually would use his bulging biceps to lift me off the ground and place me in the vehicle. And his dark expression suggests he might enjoy it. My cheeks grow hot.

"No need for the caveman act, Alexander. I'm going." I scramble for the door, somehow knowing my body can't handle another encounter with his.

"What the hell is that?"

He closes the distance between us in the space of a heartbeat. Heat sparks in his gaze, which is focused somewhere along the spot where my skirt hugs my waist. Dominic reaches for me, his fingers gentle as they caress the skin of my hip. I look down, shocked at the contact and the warm rush of recognition dancing down my spine. Like my body knows him, like it recognizes his touch.

"Dominic."

I push his hand away and try not to think about the swell of disap-pointment that springs in my chest when his warmth fades from me, revealing a tear in my bodysuit. Now I understand the murder in his eyes.

"Jesus, fuck." He tosses his head back and releases a string of low, angry curses before looking back at me and pointing at the passenger door. "Get. In. The. Car. Before I go back in there and tear that man apart with my bare hands."

I swallow the snarky remark that pops into my mouth. Nothing in his tone suggests he's in the mood for an argument, and for the first time—probably due to a fear of watching him get arrested—I fight against my need to antagonize him.

Without another word, I climb into the car and shut the door. Dominic is in the driver's seat in a flash, peeling out of the parking lot before I can pull my seat belt on all the way. The force of his turn onto the busy street sends me flying into the console, and my elbow bumps his shoulder.

"Slow down, Nic!" Mal hisses from the backseat. "Are you trying to kill us?"

Glancing over at Dominic, I wonder if he should be driving. Mal and I both caught an Uber to the club, anticipating being too far gone to operate a vehicle. Of course, I feel relatively sober now. The shock of the last twenty minutes burnt through every bit of alcohol I managed to consume.

It's strange to me that Dominic would drive here knowing he was going to drink. I saw him toss back at least three tumblers full of a dark liquid I could only assume was liquor. Even if the surge of adrenaline from getting into a fight had cleared his head and steadied his motions, should he be driving us home? I open my mouth to ask him but lose all train of thought when his slow, heavy gaze turns on me.

"I had three Jack and Cokes, minus the Jack." He turns his attention back to the road like it's completely normal for him to be reading my mind.

He wasn't drinking.

That, I suddenly remember, is another byproduct of his upbringing. Satisfied we aren't actually in danger of crashing, I decide to try and relax. My head sinks into the buttery leather of the headrest, and

Dominic's spicy scent tickles my nose as my eyes fall shut. The quiet hum of the engine lulls me into a state of relaxation. I don't realize I've fallen asleep until I hear the low murmur of a voice in my ear.

"Sloane, wake up."

My exhausted mind is struggling to leave the fuzzy confines of sleep. A hand cradles my face, one thumb stroking over the line of my jaw. It's such a warm and gentle touch, I can't stop myself from nuzzling into it. My lips brush against rough skin, and a hiss rings out. Like someone just sucked in a painful breath through their teeth.

The sound pulls my sleepy brain back into the realm of reality. My eyes pop open, and I find Dominic's face a whisper from mine, worry creasing his brow as he studies me. His eyes rove over my features for a few seconds before he settles back in his seat and crosses his arms.

I look around, completely disoriented by the quiet in the car. "Where's Mal?"

"I dropped her off twenty minutes ago." He breathes, running a thumb over his bottom lip with his eyes still on me. "She asked me to text and let her know I got you home safely."

One glance out of the windshield of his SUV tells me he's done exactly that. Driven me home while I slept soundly in his front seat, and woke me up with gentle whispers and caresses that still have my skin tingling.

"Well," I clear my throat, looking anywhere but him. "Thank you for the ride and—"

"Don't mention it." He cuts me off, saving me from the awkward-ness of expressing my gratitude for his capacity to be violent on my behalf.

"Got it." I grab my purse and pull my keys out. "I do appreciate it though."

He nods but says nothing as I hop out of the car. I'm acutely aware of his watchful gaze on me as I walk to my house. When I glance over my shoulder, his dark figure is barely visible, obscured by a glare caused by the streetlight slicing across his vehicle. I reach my door and wave awkwardly from inside before I close it, breathing a sigh of relief as I turn the lock and abandon my shoes by the front door.

My body is aching. The stress of the night pressing down on me until I feel ready to break. Tears spring to my eyes, and I let them fall freely as I make my way to my bedroom and turn on the light. Bright light illuminates the room, and I hear a faint squeaking of brakes ring out. I pad over to the window and open the blinds just in time to see Dominic's tail lights as he drives down my street.

Surprised, I watch him drive away. He must have waited for me to get upstairs and turn on a light to make sure I was okay. It's such a kind, caring thing to do. Something you do when you want a person to know they're safe and loved. I'm not used to anyone doing things like that for me anymore. Not since Eric died.

In a moment of pure appreciation, I take my phone out of my purse and pull up his contact information. The message I send is short and does nothing to convey the riot of emotions coursing through me.

> Sloane: I know you said don't mention it, but I have to say it again. Thank you.

It isn't until I am freshly showered, safely ensconced in my bed, and on the brink of sleep that it occurs to me he didn't bother to text me back. Doubt trickles through me. I can't even be sure I have the right number for him, and I don't remember the last time I had a reason to call or text him directly.

I flip over on my stomach and close my eyes, reminding myself no matter how grateful I am for what he did tonight or how my pulse flutters when I recall the feel of his skin on mine, Dominic Alexander is not my friend.

And the fact I don't even have the right number for him, even though we've known each other for years and share a slight obsession with people whose last names are Kent, proves it.

6

SLOANE

I wake for the second time on Sunday morning to the sound of my phone ringing, and my mother's beautiful face flashing across the screen until I finally pick it up off of the nightstand and accept the call.

"Hello, Mother."

I stifle the yawn threatening to obscure my greeting. If she catches it, she'll launch into a long-winded lecture about me still being in bed at this time of day.

"Sloane." The disapproving way she says my name lets me know I've failed. "Please tell me you're not still in bed. It's almost noon for goodness sake."

It's only a little after ten, but my mother is not to be argued with. Lauren Carson is perfection personified, which means she is well-versed in identifying and pointing out everyone else's shortcomings, especially mine.

"I'm not feeling well." I sit up, resting my back against my headboard.

"Wallowing in bed won't make you feel any better will it?"

There it is again. Disapproval, where there should be maternal concern or, at the very least, the kind of surface-level care you would give a stranger, but caring for another person has never been my mother's thing.

Whenever I would get sick as a kid, she'd just pawn me off on one of the three nannies she kept on staff to take care of me. And when I would cry for her, she'd pat my head and tell me she just wasn't suited for this part of motherhood. I spent half of my life waiting to find out which part of the endeavor that was parenting she *was* suited for and gave up when I was sixteen and realized the only plausible answer was none of it.

Unless criticizing your only child until they second guess every decision they've ever made counts, and if that's the case, the woman belongs in someone's hall of fame.

"No, it won't," I sigh. "I was just about to get up and put on some clothes."

It's a lie, but that's what I do with my mother: lie to appease her and apologize when the lies aren't good enough, and her ego has to be assuaged some other way.

"Perfect. Then you'll come over for brunch. Your father wants to see you."

I close my eyes and try not to focus on the way she specified my father wants to see me. Not your father and I. Not your loving parents. Not we. Just your father. It's a testament to the unnatural dynamic between the three of us. The hands-off, narcissistic mother. The doting father who tried to fill in the gaps. And the broken only-child who let her childhood trauma ruin the best thing in her life.

"Mom, I can't come over today. I'm having dinner with Annette and Mallory, and I'm heading over in a few to help them cook."

Like I have every Sunday for as long as I can remember. I don't bother to point it out though because she already knows. She just doesn't care.

She scoffs. *Scoffs.* Like attending a regularly scheduled dinner with people I care for is a foreign concept to her. It probably is since the only regular appointments she has on her books are facials, massages, and lunch with the minions she calls her friends.

"Surely you can afford to miss one dinner, Sloane. It's not like the woman is cooking anything you haven't eaten already."

"And it's not like I can't see you and Dad another day!"

She gasps. "There's no need to speak to me that way, Sloane Elise. Is it such a crime for your father to want to see you?"

"Mom." I'm clinging desperately to my last shred of patience. "I'm sorry for raising my voice, but I can't come over today. Maybe later this week?"

The apology feels all wrong in my mouth, the words twisting their way out as if it's a fight for my tongue to form them. *It is.* I'm always the one apologizing even when I've done nothing wrong.

"Fine." She snaps, sounding distracted and annoyed. In my mind's eye, I can picture her: sitting at her vanity, touching up her makeup, and spritzing herself with perfume she doesn't even like the smell of but wears because one five-ounce bottle costs more than most people's rent. Her long black and gray curls framing her thin face, calling attention to her hazel eyes, perfectly arched brows, and high cheekbones.

No one has ever laid eyes on my mom and called her anything less than exquisite. Strangers say her beauty is only matched by the kindness and warmth she exudes. They rave about her welcoming smiles, the long embraces, and encouraging words she freely gives to everyone she meets.

I've never met that woman though. Never had her eyes shine with anything but cold criticism when she looks at me. A never-ending catalog of my faults and shortcomings reflected in her irises. Constant suggestions, about how I can be something more than a disappointment who shares her face but none of her grace and perfection, falling from her lips.

"Thank you for being so understanding, Mom." I rub at my temple, praying the headache that's been threatening to bloom at the front of my skull doesn't take flight. "Did you need anything else?"

"No. Please text your father and let him know you won't be able to make it today."

I bite back a bitter laugh. Of course, she can't be bothered to pass along the message.

"Okay. I'll let him know as soon as I hang up with you."

"Great." She huffs. "And Sloane?"

"Yes, Mother?"

"Please make sure to let us know which day you decide to grace us with your presence. I have several engagements scheduled this week, and I won't be happy if I have to miss them just to accommodate your lack of planning."

My mouth drops open. Did she just say that to me after calling me with some last-minute plans about brunch? "Got it. Talk to you later, Mom."

The faint clinking of glass lets me know my earlier thought about her sitting at her vanity was correct. It was a common sound in my childhood. One that punctuated the rare moments I spent with my mother in her bedroom before she promptly dismissed me.

"Goodbye, Sloane."

When she hangs up, I tap out a quick message to my dad apologizing for breaking our non-existent brunch plans and promising to call him tomorrow to make dinner plans this week. His response is immediate.

> Dad: No worries, bean! I'd be happy to see you whenever you have time. Dinner later this week sounds amazing. Maybe I'll put some steaks on the grill? :)

The smile his message puts on my face almost makes up for the fact he gave me Cruella de Ville for a mother.

> Sloane: That sounds perfect, Daddy! I'll come over on Friday.

With my promise kept, I decide to take my mother's advice and get out of bed. Thirty minutes later, I'm freshly showered and dressed, sitting on the couch sliding on a pair of shoes when my doorbell rings.

Surprised, I pad over to the door and open it to find a smiling Mal on the other side holding two cups of iced coffee in her hands. I move to the side to make space for her to pass through the doorway, and she shoves one of the cold plastic cups in my hand.

"Good morning, sunshine!"

"Morning." I take a sip of my iced caramel macchiato. "What are you doing here? I thought we were meeting at Mama's."

"We were, but I wanted to check on you first. You know," she gives me a significant look. "After last night."

I walk over and pull her into a short hug, leaning back to look into amber eyes that are a little too similar to the ones I miss more than anything in the world.

"I'm fine, Mal. I promise."

It's not a lie. As scary as last night was, I know it could have gone completely different. The scenario Dominic rescued me from has played out in huge, life-altering ways for far too many women in the world. My heart beats a little harder at that knowledge, and gratitude I expected to have dissipated a bit by now, swells in my chest for him again, turning my thoughts to the man who appeared in my dreams all night.

His lips. His eyes. His hands on my skin.

"Good!" Mal chirps brightly, pulling my wayward mind back to her. "In that case, let's go. Mama has already sent me a list of things she needs from the store."

I grab my purse, keys, and phone and follow Mal out of the door. "Didn't you just take her to the store yesterday?"

Mal throws her hands up in exasperation as she unlocks her car. I laugh, knowing from the one small gesture that Annette has been riding her daughter's nerves since early this morning. Once upon a time, those calls would've been coming to Eric's phone. Waking us up at the crack of dawn with reminders to stop by the store and pick up milk, eggs, flour, or another ingredient she needed to make dinner that day. Now, those calls go straight to Mal, and Mama doesn't care if her daughter is asleep, hungover, or snoring in the arms of a naked stranger: she still calls.

Mal backs out my driveway. "How was the ride home last night?"

"You tell me. I slept through the whole thing."

She purses her lips. "I didn't want to leave you, especially when you were asleep, but Nic insisted on dropping me off at my place first. Did you freak out on him when you woke up?"

Unbidden, thoughts of Dominic's gentle touch and warm breath caressing my skin as he nudged me awake pop into my mind. Freaking out on him was the last thing on my mind, and judging by the contents of my dream last night....I shake my head, trying to set the thought free. Thinking about my inappropriate dreams next to Mal feels wrong.

"Nope. You should be proud of me. I was nice to him."

"Nice?" Mal hums her approval. "I wasn't aware you knew how to be anything other than bitchy where Nic is concerned."

"Let's not make him sound like a victim, Mallory. Even though you and Mama love to make him out to be some sort of angel, he deserves every shot I take at him."

She scrunches her nose at me. "No one has ever called him an angel. Honestly, both of you get on my nerves with the constant bickering. It was nice to see the two of you getting along even if some drunk in the club was the reason."

The ill-advised hope that shined in her eyes last night is back, coating her words and making her sound like a small kid hoping her parents will finally stop fighting and say they love each other again.

I bite my lip. "Yeah. I guess you're right. Don't get used to it though."

Mal laughs. "Oh, honey. I wouldn't dream of it."

* * *

Two hours and three stores later, Mal and I are carrying last-minute essentials into Mama's kitchen with no help from any of the ten other people scattered throughout the yard and house waiting to scarf down the fruits of our labor. We find Mama in the kitchen chatting with her sister, Mary, while they clean collards and chop peaches for what I'm sure is going to be a delicious cobbler.

"About damn time!" Mama shouts, wrapping us in hugs that make us forget how annoyed we were with her just moments before. "I thought I was going to have to send Nic out to find you two."

"Cut the dramatics, Annette." Mal laughs, slinging the bags in her hand on the counter and heading towards the table to take a seat by her aunt.

Mama pops her on the butt as she walks away and starts unpacking bags by my side. We work together to put up everything she claimed she needed to make her meal today, and I shoot her a disbelieving look when everything but one bottle of barbecue sauce ends up in her cupboards.

"Thought you needed all of this stuff for dinner."

She winks at me. "I did. Just not for dinner today."

I shake my head at her, stifling the laughter that's always ready to spill out when I'm around my mother-in-law. She's so different from the woman who birthed me. Where my mom treats parenting like a hardship meant to be endured, Mama has always made it quite clear that being a mother is one of the great joys in her life.

Anytime her children are around, she glows with love. I can't remember a single time I've seen her look anything less than thrilled to have her children, me and Dominic included, around. Hence the reason she's always hosting dinners at her home or calling each of us throughout the week just to check-in.

"Mal's going to be so mad when she realizes you only needed that bottle of barbecue sauce." I bump her with my shoulder, returning her warm smile with one of my own. "We had to go to three stores to find your White Lily flour. She wanted to give up, but I told her I wasn't coming in here without it."

"Good girl." She beams at me, and the corners around her rich brown eyes crease in the best way.

For a moment, I just stare at her, taking in the soft lines of her face, and the black and gray whirls of curls that are pulled into a fluffy bun at the top of her head. My heart swells with love for her. For the way she looks at me. For the easy smiles and not-so-secret jokes. For the warmth of her arms and the strength of her love. A love that saved me from the depths of my grief even when her own must have been threatening to crush her.

"Sloane, baby," Mary calls, beckoning me over to the table with a wave of her hand. "Come on over here and help Mallory cut up these greens."

Before I can answer, she gets up from the table and gestures to her vacated seat. Mama shakes her head, muttering something about lazy sisters as she moves to the stove. I know better than to argue with any of the elders in this family, so I take a seat beside Mal and start cutting up greens. We fall into a comfortable silence as we each work on our tasks. Nothing but the sounds of pots simmering, spoons stirring, and knives chopping fill the small kitchen that's seen more than its fair share of family gatherings.

As I chop, my mind wanders and thoughts of Eric are at the forefront, the way they always are when I'm in his childhood home, basking in the love of the people who raised him. People who rallied around me and kept me close in the face of their own heartbreak and despair. I'm endlessly thankful for each of them and the way I've always been treated like someone who belongs by everyone lucky enough to be born into a family full of love and acceptance.

Except for Dominic.

Who up until last night, approached interactions with me in the exact opposite way. I'd be lying if I said I didn't spend a large portion of the time I wasn't dreaming of him last night wondering if things will be different with us now. If him saving me in the club and showing that he's capable of treating me with something resembling kindness is an opportunity for us to turn over a new leaf.

Heavy footsteps clunking up the steps of the back porch ring out, breaking me out of my thoughts. I look up just in time to see Dominic pull off his sweaty t-shirt, wipe his face and neck with the soiled fabric and then toss it on an empty chair on the back porch. Leaving the bronzed skin of his shoulders and bulging cords and veins in his arms on full display. His chest and midsection are barely covered by a black tank top that clings to his abs and highlights his sculpted pectoral muscles.

He looks up at me, a heavy gaze that burns into mine, and there's no hiding that I've been staring at him through the glass of the screen door. I bite my lower lip and turn my attention back to the cutting board in front of me. A second later, he breezes through the back door and presses a kiss to Mal's cheek before catching Mama up in his arms for a hug that has her giggling like a teenage girl.

When he releases her, he moves over to the fridge and pulls out a bottle of water. Taking a long pull before leaning back against the counter and burning the side of my face with the heat of his stare. It's the only indication he sees me. The only way he acknowledges my presence. Because he doesn't say a word to me.

Not while he's talking to Mama about the shed she wants him to build in her backyard. Not while he tells Mal about some old friend he ran into that, judging by the disgusted sniff she responds with, she doesn't want to hear about. Not while he washes his hands and helps Mama roll dough for the cobbler crust. And not when I get up to leave the cramped kitchen with my hands clenched into fists and a flimsy excuse about needing air on my lips.

So much for turning over a new leaf.

7

SLOANE

Then

"Your mom sounds like a real sweetheart."

I scrunch my nose at Eric as I slide my phone back into my pocket. The sarcasm in his voice is as evident as my aggravation with my mother and her sudden interest in parenting. After eighteen years of ignoring me and pawning me off on every nanny, housekeeper, and seemingly competent person within a five-mile radius, she's decided that now—when I'm living on campus and trying to carve out some semblance of an independent existence—is the time for her to get in touch with her maternal instincts.

And all you had to do to get her attention was cut loose for one night.

One night where I did what I wanted when I wanted. One night where I made decisions and didn't worry about how it reflected on my family or what it said about my worth as a woman in society. One night where I was free and blissfully unaware of the ramifications I would still be facing months later. And all of the aggravation and nagging would've been worth it if I could remember more than a few bits and pieces of it.

I toss myself back on Eric's bed and frown up at the ceiling. Phone calls with my mom always leave me agitated and spoiling for a fight, and I don't want to direct any of that at him. "She's a monster."

"True, but that doesn't mean you have to let it ruin your day."

He lays down beside me, forcing me to turn on my side to accommodate his wide frame on the twin-sized mattress, and an easy grin stretches across his face. It's all dimples and straight white teeth surrounded by full lips that make me want to spend all my time kissing him.

We've only been dating for a few months, but I already feel safe and at home with him in a way I never have with anyone else. He just has this calming energy around him. A serene aura I want to soak into my bones until letting things roll off of my back comes to me as easily as it does to him.

"You're right." I scoot closer to him and tip my mouth up for a kiss, which he happily gives. "I'd much rather spend the rest of my afternoon kissing you."

"Mhmm. That sounds like a plan." He gives me another short peck before breaking the kiss to look at his phone. "One we'll have to make a reality as soon as I get my clothes out of the dryer. I'll be right back."

He's off of the bed and bounding out of the door before I get the chance to sit up all the way. The door snaps closed behind him, leaving me with nothing but silence and the leftover agitation from my mom to keep me company. I lay back down and close my eyes, hoping to shake off the last vestige of irritation before Eric gets back. A few moments later, when my breathing has evened out and I feel as close to chill as I'm going to get, I hear the key in the lock and the faint sounds of the doorknob turning that let me know Eric's back.

His heavy footsteps ring out against the tile floor, stopping short at the foot of the bed. I can't stop the goofy smile that takes over my face as I imagine him standing over me.

"Are you just going to stand there or are you going to finish what you started before you abandoned me for laundry?"

"Wrong guy."

My eyes fly open, and I sit up when I see the tall, male figure looming over me. A deep frown marring his features as he watches me process his words with rapt curiosity. His voice is still ringing in my ears when I swing my legs over the side of Eric's bed and stand. I regret the move instantly.

The walkway between the beds is narrow, and his big frame is already taking up most of it. He stares down at me, and for a second he looks like he isn't going to do the proper thing and back up a little but eventually he does. With his eyes still on me, he takes a seat on the bed on the other side of the room.

"Oh my God." I hold my hand over my racing heart and try to arrange my body in a more suitable position. "You scared the hell out of me."

"All I did was walk into my room."

"Yes, but you could have announced yourself."

He crosses his arms over his chest. "Why would I do that? This is *my* room."

His room. Of course. My startled mind finally catches up to reality, recalling the sound of the key in the door and the confident way he moved around the room. This must be Dominic. Eric's best friend and roommate, who I haven't so much as laid an eye on since we started dating. The only thing I know about the guy is he became friends with Eric and his twin sister, Mallory, when they were young and they've been joined at the hip ever since.

Usually, this information would be enough to make me change course and try to make a good impression, but there's something adversarial about his tone that lets me know it won't matter.

"Right, but there's always the possibility your roommate could have company."

He rolls his eyes. "My roommate has spent more time in your bed than his own in the last few months, so I tend not to worry about who I might find in a room I usually have to myself."

The mention of the time Eric has spent in my bed is accurate since, thanks to my mother, I'm one of the only freshmen on campus with a single dorm, but his words still make me blush. They seem to be dripping with equal parts innuendo and disdain. Like he's intrigued and disgusted at the idea of his best friend spending time with me.

"I-"

"Nic!" Eric yells as he walks through the door, dropping his basket of freshly laundered clothes to go hug his best friend. "I thought you were in class, man."

"I was supposed to be," Dominic says, clapping Eric on the back with his eyes still on me. "My lab got canceled, so I came back here."

"Lucky bastard, my labs never get canceled."

Eric crosses the room and wraps his arms around my shoulders, hugging me to him and pressing a kiss to my forehead that makes Dominic's eyes flare. *God, what is this guy's problem?*

"Yeah." Dominic lifts both of his eyebrows. His gaze darkens as I lean into Eric's touch. "*I'm* the lucky one. You're the one spending the whole afternoon laid up with…sorry, what was your name again?"

"Stop being an ass." Eric laughs, flashing me a reassuring smile. "He knows who you are, babe. I guess spending too many nights alone in this room has made him forget his manners."

"Right." *Or maybe he's decided to hate my guts based on a five second interaction.*

Except that sounds kind of dramatic, so I push the thought down and force myself to smile back. It must be a little shaky though because Eric spins us around, turning his back on his friend and facing me with concern etched in his features.

"What's the matter? Your mom didn't call back again did she?"

"No. I'm fine."

I can't stop myself from looking over Eric's shoulder at Dominic to see what he thinks of this little exchange. I half expect him to be fighting back a laugh or on the verge of telling me I'm not good enough for his best friend, but he's not paying any attention to us. His long legs are stretched across his bed, his feet kicked up and there are headphones in his ears as he scrolls through his phone.

When I look back at Eric, he doesn't look convinced but thankfully doesn't press further.

"Alright, let's go back to your room then."

"Okay."

It takes us all of five minutes to pack up our things, and Dominic ignores me the whole time. He makes small talk with Eric about the trip they're planning to make to his mom's house this weekend and doesn't even blink in my direction until right before we're about to walk out the door when he pins me with a hard stare and says:

"Nice to *meet* you, Sloane."

8

DOMINIC

Now

Sloane: I know you said don't mention it, but
I have to say it again. Thank you.

I run my finger over the screen of my phone. Tracing the words of the message Sloane sent me on Saturday night. The ones I've read a thousand times since my phone pinged and my heart stopped when her name flashed on my lock screen.

I was at a red light less than five minutes away from her house when the message came through. My fingers were still aching from the memory of being in contact with her body, and that ache intensified as I held the phone in my hand and read her message. Shock slipped under my skin, quelling the fire that was still raging inside of me when I thought about what could have happened to her if I hadn't been stalking her from across the room.

The light turned green, and I pushed the gas, throwing the phone in the passenger seat like it had burned me. She never texted me. Mama was the only reason I even had her number saved, and I knew that was true for Sloane too because I was there when Mama made us promise to keep each other's contact information up to date. It was one of those requests she made after Eric died neither of us had the heart to deny even though we both knew we had nothing to say to each other that required an exchange as personal as a text. *Apparently, now she feels differently.*

Or at least she did four days ago.

Now, it's Tuesday and her text sits unanswered in a fresh message thread that haunts me with possibilities I can never consider. Possibilities that paralyzed me after leaving her place knowing there was a hole in her top the size of a grimy finger that belonged to an asshole I wanted to track down and kill.

And that was another problem.

The white-hot rage I've always known was inside of me but have never acted on out of fear of feeling too much like my father—a man who used his fists to hurt rather than protect, to break things down instead of building them up. And he's the last person I want to be like. I could almost forgive myself for bearing his name and looks, for having his large hands and the same charming smile that made my mom forget the bruises around her throat when he brought flowers. I told myself none of it mattered since I wasn't like him in all the ways that mattered.

The fundamental difference being my ability to keep my fucking hands to myself. To use my words to handle issues and to walk away when things moved past the point of discussion.

But every bit of that went out the window when I saw the panic in Sloane's eyes. Letting the rage take over was a conscious choice. Hitting the man not once, but twice and then choking him—*choking him*—felt like the most natural thing in the world to do because it meant protecting her. But I didn't know it also meant unleashing the darkest part of myself; the part I've spent my whole life trying to suppress.

Bitter.

Jealous.

Wrathful.

Violent.

And Sloane's message just....made it worse somehow. It fed the rage, and told it to make itself at home in my veins. And it listened. I watched in horror as it kicked up its feet and turned the power boil it was on down to a low simmer, so it could get comfortable with another substance that had infused itself into my blood: desire.

The two meshed together, mixing with her scent that was still lingering in my car. Haunting me. Making me remember things I should definitely forget when it came to my best friend's wife. Like the golden inches of skin that glistened under the lights when her skirt rode up her thigh. The way the curly tendrils at her nape clung to the curve of her neck like a passionate kiss.

Then there was the way she looked at me when I pulled her away from that asshole. Like I was her savior. Like I was someone she trusted to care about and take care of her. She let me touch her, leaned into me instead of pulling away. Used my body as a shield and believed with a fierceness that shined in those soft hazel eyes I wouldn't let any harm come to her. The worse thing about it? I wouldn't.

Club Noir would have been razed to the fucking ground if it wasn't for her tiny hand on my chest, covering my heart and reminding me of an angel in a white dress I'd given up finding a lifetime ago. And as much as I'd like to believe the rage thrumming in my blood would have been ignited in the same way if it was any other woman in that situation, I know it isn't true.

That's why the text and everything else that happened Saturday night—including a sleepless night full of dreams of her—has me so fucked up. Fucked up enough that I've tuned out everyone in the boardroom in favor of re-reading a message I have no idea how to respond to. It's probably too late to do it anyway.

Sliding my phone into the inside pocket of my jacket, I drag my gaze to Sloane. She's been sitting across from me for the last hour, tapping the tip of her pen on the table in front of her, eyes on the next man I'll have to strangle if he puts a hand on her. James shuffles the papers in front of him and wraps up a speech about deadlines that's supposed to be aimed at me, but he's looking directly at her. I would be upset if my eyes weren't on her too.

All of her beautiful curls are perfectly defined, shining like a black halo around her head, which is fitting since the daggers flying from her eyes every time she deigns to look my way could rival any angel of death. Then there's the black silk camisole that's tucked into a pair of high-waisted black slacks and paired with a—you guessed it—black blazer with lines sharp enough to cut you if you touched her.

Anyone else would look at the outfit and think she's just leaning into the monochromatic fad, but I see it for what it is: a suit of armor. It reminds me of the outfits she favored right after Eric died. When she was probably so raw emotionally just the thought of exposing herself to the world chafed against the cavern of grief that was her heart. I saw my mother do the same thing after my piece of shit father finished taking every inconvenience from his day out on her body.

Looking at Sloane reminds me a little too much of watching my mom slinking out of her room cloaked in cardigans, turtlenecks, and pants that swam around her ankles. I pull in a tight breath, forcing my eyes away from her and ignoring the need to ask if she's okay that's expanding in my chest. Is she hurt physically?

I did my best to examine her that night, but I can't be sure how reliable my eyes were when my vision was covered in red. Clenching my fist, I consider the possibility her wounds are more emotional. Shock isn't uncommon when it comes to sexual assault, even if it was a near miss, and Sloane had practically been vibrating with fear when I found her.

James glances at me. He's just finished talking and judging by the expectant look on his face, the words I've been ignoring were still being aimed at me.

I give him a curt nod. "Sounds good."

The vague response must be exactly what he's looking for because he turns his attention back to the papers in front of him and declares the meeting over a few minutes later. Everyone files out of the room, chatting about lunch plans and how their weekend went. I take my time vacating my seat, pretending to be engrossed in an email from my assistant as I watch James approach Sloane. She's still sitting, so her head tilts back when she looks up at him. A friendly, but vacant, smile curving her full lips.

James touches her shoulder and leans closer to her. His words are hushed and intimate, putting me on fucking edge. I hit reply on the email from Alex and type out a lengthy response, ears trained on the voices flowing to me from across the room.

"That sounds lovely, James. I just have a ton of work to get through today. Maybe another time?" Sloane's eyes flick to me as she pushes back from the table.

Am I keeping her from making plans with him? A flare of annoyance runs through me as the knowledge that she really could be seeing this asshole hits me like a physical blow to the chest. They're both moving towards the door. His hand is on the small of her back, and I can't stop myself from pushing to my feet and following them down the hall.

"Sloane," I call out, bringing both of their steps to a halt. She turns around and hits me with those daggers once again. "I need to speak to you for a moment."

One perfect brow raises, and I know a smart-ass response about me ignoring her message and entire presence at Mama's on Sunday is pinging around her head. But instead of letting it pass through her lips, she purses them and turns her attention back to James.

"Can we finish this discussion later?"

He smiles down at her. Rows of straight white teeth I want to knock out of his mouth gleaming with pleasure at the idea of speaking to her again. My hands clench into tight fists as he leans down and presses a kiss to her cheek.

"Sounds good, love. Give me a call if you change your mind about dinner."

Sloane frees herself from his hold, looking slightly uncomfortable. I track the motion with my eyes. Some part of my brain writes the discomfort in her eyes in the 'they are definitely not fucking' column, and I bristle at the realization that I'm keeping track. Then get even more annoyed when it dawns on me that her letting him touch her and kiss her cheek has to be tallied into the 'this asshole has probably seen her naked' column.

I take a few steps forward, using every inch of my frame to shatter their moment into pieces. James casts me a cursory glance before giving Sloane's elbow a final squeeze and making his way down the hall. As I watch his form disappear down the corridor, I wonder once again how much Sloane told him about me. About us. If they're sleeping together, and he knows how heated our spats can get, why would he just leave her alone with me to fend for herself?

Not that she needs any help on that front.

The sole of her red bottom taps on the marble floor, calling my attention to the stiletto that brings her eye-level with my mouth. "What do you want, Dominic?"

I push my hands in my pockets to dull the throbbing in my fingers. Did they have to choose this exact moment to recall the feel of her skin on mine?

"As I stated less than a minute ago, to talk."

"Right." She snaps her fingers like she's grateful to be reminded why she's standing here with me. "And what exactly do we need to talk about?"

My eyes rake over her body, assessing her from head to toe with a pointed glare that answers her question with no words.

Sloane shakes her head. "I'm not talking about that at work. Especially not with *you*."

The emphasis on the word 'you' makes me want to laugh. A few hours around her boyfriend and suddenly I'm not worth the time it takes to confirm her well-being or lack thereof.

"Is that how it is? You seemed much more grateful on Saturday night."

I take a step forward, closing the distance between us and not giving a single fuck about the flames dancing in her eyes when my words sink in. The corners of her eyes transform from soft lines to hard ridges. Hazel is charred by dark flames that lick at me as she fixes me with a disgusted stare.

"And here I was thinking you hadn't paid your phone bill. I guess being an asshole trumps decency every day of the week in your world."

I bite back a smirk, feeling way too comfortable with falling into our familiar pattern of verbally eviscerating each other until someone limps away to patch up their wounds. Going word for word with her feels a hell of a lot better than wondering how she manages to smell like a tropical smoothie every fucking day.

"Well, they don't call me Asshole Alexander for nothing."

Sloane bites her bottom lip to hide her surprised expression. I didn't intend to make my awareness of her nickname for me known but seeing her flounder for a response makes the premature reveal worth it.

"Do you think it's wise to take on another nickname at your age? It might start to confuse the other personalities you have floating around in there."

A vague gesture towards my head causes the sleeve of her blazer to roll back, exposing her wrist and the angry purple bruise I didn't notice when I saw her on Sunday. My hand flies forward, catching her wrist in the fingers of one hand while the others work the sleeve down her arm. There aren't any other blemishes on the smooth honey of her skin.

Surprisingly, Sloane doesn't make a noise as I examine her. Her breathing is shallow and her eyes are on the ceiling like she doesn't want to look at me. I realize too late that this must feel like an incredible invasion of her privacy, especially after Saturday, but she doesn't pull away and I don't let her go.

"Look at me." I drag my thumb over her pulse and watch in fascination as her pupils dilate when her gaze meets mine. "Does it hurt?"

"No. Not anymore."

The idea of her experiencing even a moment of pain when I could have prevented it makes my chest burn. I study her face looking for any indication that she's lying. She doesn't waver under the intensity of my stare, and I want to smile. Sloane never wavers.

I take a deep breath, inhaling the sweetness of her scent. This close I can finally discern notes of coconut, mango, and tangerine. Three simple fruits that wouldn't mean a damn thing to me in any other context, but on her, it's fucking intoxicating. One small pull on her arm and I could bury my face in her neck. Breathe in her scent until it's permanently imprinted in my brain. *Does James know how amazing she smells?* The unwelcome thought sets my blood on fire.

"Good. I guess it won't get in the way of your dinner plans with James then."

Her brows dip inward. "James and I don't have any dinner plans tonight."

"Right," I murmur, eyes riveted on the crease in her forehead. "You haven't had the chance to finalize them. Have you, *love*?"

Sloane makes a disgusted noise in her throat at my use of Jame's pet name for her and pulls her arm out of my grasp.

"Do you need anything else, Dominic? I have to get back to my office."

"It's noon. Shouldn't you be making lunch plans with Mal right now?"

"Mal took the day off." She admits. "So I'll be eating lunch at my desk while I work on the changes James requested in the meeting."

I nod like I know what she's talking about. She doesn't need to know that any requests for changes made during the meeting went right over my head. There isn't a single word written on the pages of the notebook I brought with me to the boardroom. Given my profession, distracted isn't something I can afford to be, but all of my attention was focused on the woman standing in front of me now.

"We should discuss them over lunch."

I don't know where the words come from, but they're out there now. Hanging in the air between us, waiting for Sloane to scoop them up or slap them down. She worries the plump flesh of her bottom lip between her teeth like she's actually considering the offer. Something that can only be described as petty triumph balloons inside of me. It doesn't even matter if she says no now. Because James' dinner invitation didn't get half as much consideration as my off-the-cuff lunch offer has.

9

SLOANE

Now

I must be in an alternate universe. Somewhere between leaving my house this morning, after another night of inappropriate dreams featuring Dominic, and exiting the board room a few minutes ago, I must have fallen into a black hole and been transported to another reality.

That's the only thing that can explain my continued participation in this exchange with him. Letting him brand me with his touch again when I still haven't fully recovered from the last time he touched me. Answering his ridiculous questions about my well-being. Telling him about my sad plans to eat lunch at my desk alone.

And worst of all, seriously considering his random offer to share a meal that doesn't include Mama or Mal. I tilt my head to the side, a little too aware of his darkened gaze on my mouth where I'm still biting my lip. Releasing the flesh from my teeth, I struggle for an answer. Part of me wants to say no—it only seems fair to turn down the man who made a point of ignoring me on two different fronts when all I did was thank him—but another part of me, the one that's developed a slight obsession with the Dominic from Saturday night, is screaming yes at the top of its lungs.

"Fine." I shrug, attempting to appear indifferent. "But you're buying."

If he's surprised I accepted his offer, Dominic doesn't let it show. Instead, he *smiles* at me before gesturing for me to lead us down the hallway. My steps feel shaky as the weight of his curved lips settles like a brick in the pit of my stomach. I can't recall a single instance in which the man has directed a smile at me. Not once in the time I've known him.

Before Saturday, you couldn't recall a time when he touched you either. And now he's made a habit out of it.

As if on cue, Dominic's hand presses into my lower back, steadying my wobbly stride. I'm slightly annoyed that something as simple as his smile can impact my ability to walk, but the feeling is quickly wiped out by the hum of awareness dancing up my spine. Radiating from the warmth of his hand that I shouldn't be able to feel through three layers of clothing.

Moments later, we're stepping out into the humid August air, and I'm massively regretting my choice of outfits. All black had felt like a good idea this morning when I was standing in my closet looking for a clothing option that would put some much needed space between me and the world, but now I'm close to melting out of my skin. I pause in the middle of the parking lot and slip out of my jacket. Dominic stops beside me, releasing me from his hold for a moment and then settling his palm against the silk of my camisole when the blazer is gone.

I toss it over my arm and glance at him. "Awfully quiet there, Alexander. The voices in your head aren't giving you too much trouble are they?"

Amusement flickers in his gaze, but he says nothing as he pulls out his keys and unlocks the doors of his SUV, ushering me over to the passenger side and opening the door. I pause, realizing too late he intends to drive us to lunch. Memories of the last time we were alone in his car flood me. His gentle murmurs, the soothing caress of his fingers on my skin. The embarrassing way I nuzzled into him like a cat in heat. Dominic's dark eyes are dancing with humor as he assesses me.

"Do I need to threaten to physically place you in my car again?"

"If you do, I'll scream bloody murder."

"It's adorable that you think you'd be able to get a word out before your ass hits the seat."

When I don't move, he releases a low growl and swoops down, lifting me off the ground with ease. His large hands grip my waist securely, but his touch is gentle as he twists to place me in the seat and slams the door. Suddenly, I'm drowning in a mixture of his scent—warm, spicy, and inherently male—and buttery leather.

Briefly, I consider hopping out and making the short trek to my car, but images of him hauling me back like the caveman he apparently is stop me. The last thing I want to do is make a scene in the parking lot. So when he finally opens his door, flexing his fingers like they're injured, I fix him with a withering glare. One that would be enough to make any one of the contractors I've worked with before cry, but Dominic doesn't even flinch.

Instead, he reaches over and pulls the seat belt across my chest, inadvertently brushing my breasts as he does, and I suck in a breath, refusing to acknowledge the tightening of my nipples at the small amount of friction or the wave of guilt and self-loathing that follows. It's a feeling I'm all too familiar with now that I've spent the past few nights dreaming of Dominic doing things to me I shouldn't be associating with my husband's best friend.

It doesn't help that a lot of those dreams start with me in this very seat. Letting him snake those large hands up my skirt, push my panties to the side, and sink one thick finger into my soaking wet core while he swallows my moans with his lips.

I try to slap his hand away. "I know how to put on my seat belt."

"That's funny." He chuckles but continues his ministrations. "Up until now, I didn't think you had the slightest idea how to get into a car let alone secure yourself in one."

The seat belt clicks into place, punctuating his last word. Dominic tugs on the belt to annoy me further and finally removes himself from my personal space. I breathe a sigh of relief.

"You're an ass."

Dominic makes quick work of his seat belt and starts the car before reversing out of the parking spot. "What can I say? You bring out the best in me."

He handles the large SUV with ease. The long fingers of one hand grip the steering wheel while the other shifts the car into drive. Then we're moving forward. The engine purring quietly as he turns onto the street.

I force myself to turn away from his hands and look out the window. Lunch hour traffic is in full swing. Cars are pouring into the street, and business professionals are spilling out of their high-rises in search of a quick meal before heading back to the office. While I'm trapped in a car with a man who loves pissing me off.

"I'm starting to think I should have stuck with my original lunch plans."

He releases an amused huff. "Missing your stapler and office plants already?"

"Not really. I just prefer the company of inanimate objects over you."

"Better conversation?" He counters drily.

"Something like that. At least when they ignore me, I can attribute it to their inability to talk back." *Why the hell did I just say that?*

Dominic looks at me, but I keep my eyes trained on the passing buildings as we weave in and out of traffic. I can't look at him because I don't want those pools of obsidian to mock me for being upset about an unanswered text message from someone I didn't expect anything from a week ago. While my brain was busy torturing me with explicit images of the man in my dreams, it didn't seem the least bit concerned with finding a reasonable explanation for how bothered I am by his silence in real life.

Well, at least not one I can live with anyway.

He turns his attention back to the road. "I didn't know how to respond."

"Don't tell me 'you're welcome' are the only two words in the English language you don't know how to say."

I shift in my seat and hope the movement will dislodge the lump his confession has placed in my throat. Something that feels an awful lot like relief springs in my chest, and I don't know if it's because I'm glad he doesn't hate me enough to leave me on read when I'm trying to be nice or because my message shocked him enough to keep him silent for four days.

We make a right down a familiar street and I realize I haven't even asked where we are going for lunch.

"Three words."

I drag my gaze back to him. "What?"

"You're welcome. Technically it's three words." He glances at me, a smug smile tugging at the corner of his lips. "You *are* welcome."

I give an exaggerated roll of my eyes. "Right, I guess you don't know anything about contractions either."

"Of course I do." He makes a left turn, swinging the vehicle into the parking lot of my favorite cafe. "I also know being corrected makes you irritable."

I nod my head, pretending to understand his logic. "And it's easier to ignore or irritate me than it is to text me back or acknowledge my presence. Got it."

He puts the car in park, and my gaze flicks down to his hands on the gear shift. When I look back up at him, he's already watching me. Damn, if I'm going to make a habit of staring at the man, I need to learn how to be more covert. *Good thing none of my plans involve doing that.*

"Well," He shuts off the engine. "If I had known it was going to mean so much to you, I would have texted you back immediately, but let's not forget about the part where I told you <u>not</u> to thank me."

And there it is. A sharp gaze cutting into me like a blade laced with poison. Anger swimming in their endless depths.

I narrow my eyes at him. "You're mad at me for saying thank you?"

"Yes." He states simply. Like it's natural to be offended when someone thanks you.

"Please, tell me how that makes sense in your head."

His gaze hardens, and I almost regret letting the words slip past my lips. I don't know if I can take another second of him looking at me like I've asked him for something far more insidious than an explanation.

"You're an intelligent woman, Sloane. Do you need me to spell it out for you?"

"Yes. It would be extremely helpful since I'm not in the habit of reading minds." A ball of frustration expands in my chest when amusement creeps into his otherwise dark expression. My hands itch with the urge to wipe the look right off of his face.

Dominic considers me for a moment before he speaks. "You already know the answer. Mal has a lot of gifts, but whispering isn't one of them."

My stomach clenches as I remember Mal's words from Saturday: violent acts aren't Dominic's norm. Hell, even I know he prefers verbal warfare. What he did to that man took him way out of his comfort zone and probably made him feel more like his father than anything else.

I swallow, realizing for the first time that my text, while well-intentioned, highlighted behavior he's ashamed of. I can relate to that. Sometimes at work, I open my mouth and my mother comes out. Snarky, impatient, and unkind words slicing into my team when my patience is thin and time is precious.

Unlike my mother, I always apologize for my behavior, and I've started talking to Dr. Williams, my therapist, about better ways to handle those situations, but I always feel like shit for being anything like her.

"Dominic, I—"

He waves a dismissive hand at me. "Don't. I'm starving. Let's go eat."

He pushes his door open and hops out without giving me a chance to respond. I grab my purse, so we can go over the notes I took during the meeting, and follow suit. Dominic waits for me then places the same hand he just used to dismiss me on the small of my back when I get to his side. Once again, I can't help but note how comfortable he feels touching me today.

I look up at him. "You might be surprised to hear this, but I manage to walk, get into cars and hook seat belts all by myself daily."

Dominic glances down at me as we cross the parking lot, confused by my random statement until I cast a pointed look at his arm snaking around my back.

"It might surprise *you* to hear this, but my mom didn't raise me to be an asshole. And she would be very disappointed in me if I let someone as clumsy as you walk through a cobblestone parking lot in six-inch heels without any assistance."

My heel chooses that exact moment to get caught between two stones. I wobble for half of a second before righting myself and being subjected to Dominic's laughter. Even with his entire body shaking from manly chuckles that reverberate through me, he manages to slide his hand around to grip my waist in a secure hold.

I swat it away and spin out of his reach. "That could have happened to anyone."

"Sure. If you keep this up though, I might have to start carrying you everywhere."

Choosing not to dignify that with a response, I continue towards the entrance of Twisted Sistas. Dominic follows behind me, his silent smirk burning a hole into my back.

The bell on the door dings loudly when I pull it open, announcing our presence to the sisters and co-owners, Maya and Asia. They both shout a warm greeting and then go back to filling lunch orders for the handful of patrons who are scattered about the eclectic cafe.

Music plays softly from invisible speakers somewhere in the ceiling as I step up to the counter and read the specials for the day. Dominic's presence is a steady thrum of awareness at my back. Once again, he's crowding me out, taking up all of my personal space when he doesn't have to. Warm breath caresses my neck as he leans down, putting his lips right at my ear.

"Tell me what's good here."

My brows fall together; his question makes no sense. He brought us here, so why wouldn't he know what's good? I turn around, intending to ask him exactly that, but he just stares at me like I've grown two heads.

"Everyone knows this is one of your favorite spots, Sloane, so tell me what you like."

For the second time today, the man has stunned me into silence. I'm blushing at the innuendo my mind casts over his words when Maya skips over to us and smiles at me.

"Twice in one day, Sloane! You must be in love with one of us."

A forced and awkward laugh springs free from my chest. *Okay, so I do come here a lot.* But that doesn't make it common knowledge. Certainly not common enough for it to be on Dominic's previously non-existent radar for me.

"Now, Maya, you know I took an oath never to fall in love again."

She gives me a knowing look as she types her employee code into the tablet they use to ring up orders and process payments. Maya lost her husband almost five years ago to cancer. Like me, she swore off men and romance and focused all of her energy on starting a business with her baby sister. Now, they have three different locations sprinkled throughout the city.

It takes her a moment to register Dominic looming behind me, but when she does the widow solidarity look transforms into a where did you find him and are there more where he came from gape. I roll my eyes, maybe Maya has changed her stance.

"Right. Right." She drags her eyes away from Dominic who's completely oblivious to the woman gawking at him. "What can I get you two?"

When I look back at Dominic, he's pulling his vibrating phone out of his pocket. I arch a questioning brow at him as he rejects the call with a tap of his finger and looks at me.

"Just get me whatever you're having."

I turn back to Maya. "Two chipotle chicken and avocado melts with water, please."

"And a slice of your double chocolate cheesecake," Dominic adds, reaching past me to hand Maya his card.

"Good choice." Maya beams at him. "That happens to be Sloane's favorite."

I step to the side to give Dominic space to sign the receipt Maya is handing him. He makes short work of it, leaving a tip that's well over the twenty percent I usually do, and hitting Maya with a heart-stopping smile.

"So I've heard." He winks at her, and she giggles. *Giggles.*

Rolling my eyes at the two of them, I move down the counter where Asia is fixing our drinks and dishing up the slice of cheesecake Dominic ordered for me. I'm starting to seriously consider that he can read minds. Or he's just super observant and saw me eyeing the chocolate decadence when I was pretending to be engrossed in the menu. I pick up the two cups of ice water the younger sister has just put on the counter.

"Hey, Asia!"

She rubs her pregnant belly and arches a brow at me. "Don't 'hey Asia!' me. We just saw each other four hours ago, and we have more interesting things to talk about."

With a pointed look at Dominic who's still being interrogated by Maya, she tries to lean over the counter towards me then gives a frustrated huff when her belly stops her.

I can't help but laugh. "There's nothing to talk about. He's Eric's best friend, and we're just grabbing a bite to talk about work."

The panini press sizzling on the counter behind her beeps, letting her know our sandwiches are ready. She spins around and dishes them up on two plates before placing them on a serving tray. Sliding the tray towards me, she looks thoughtfully at Dominic.

"*He's* the one you don't get along with?"

I nod. Though a part of me feels like that statement might not be exactly right anymore. Things are shifting. We aren't best friends, not by a long shot. He's still infuriating, but between the events of Saturday night and his apparent knowledge of my likes and dislikes as far as food, I'm starting to think there might be hope for us to be something more than enemies.

Acquaintances. Colleagues. Associates. Maybe even....friends.

Dominic walks over to me and gifts me with another smile. It happens in slow motion. A slow and easy curving of his lips that exposes his straight white teeth and makes warmth flood my chest. I can't ignore the rush of satisfaction I feel at finding myself on the receiving end of two of his smiles in one day.

Relax, Sloane. It's a smile, not a peace treaty.

He takes the tray from my hand, managing to send another zip of electricity up my spine when his fingers brush mine. "Maya suggested we sit over there."

I follow the direction of his tilted chin to the cozy-looking sofa facing a mural of Black poets and flanked by two oversized armchairs. It's notorious for being used as a make-out spot for couples who frequent the cafe. Behind me, I hear Maya and Asia whispering conspiratorially, holding back snickers as they stare at us. I make a mental note to strangle them both the next time I come in for a coffee and cinnamon roll then turn to Dominic.

"Sounds good."

10

SLOANE

On Friday afternoon, I leave work and head straight to my parent's house. The long drive from Studio Six to Walnut Grove—the upscale country club neighborhood my parents have lived in since before I was born—usually wears me out, but today I'm thankful for the time to think after a week of Dominic and James wreaking havoc on my nerves.

Since lunch on Tuesday, things with me and Dominic have been friendly, which has been confusing for me after years of being on guard around the man, but it's James who seems bothered the most by it. Even Mal, who probably has the most to gain from our tentative truce, isn't as interested as he is.

First, it was the weird look after Dominic brought me back to the hotel to pick up my car. James was standing outside talking to a new group of valets when we arrived, and his brows pulled together in clear confusion as he watched Dominic open the passenger door for me. He then proceeded to spend the rest of the afternoon peppering me with questions about our lunch with an irritated look on his face.

Then on Wednesday, when I stopped by to discuss tile choices for the fireplace in the Presidential Suite with Dominic, James came strolling into the construction site to interrupt us. He looked completely ridiculous in his three-piece suit and Italian loafers. Especially in comparison to Dominic and his men who were all wearing variations of the same outfit: steel-toe boots, rugged jeans, and form-fitting t-shirts. I could have sworn I saw a flicker of annoyance cross Dominic's face when James walked into the room and pressed a kiss to my cheek.

And yesterday, I had to come up with yet another excuse to get out of another one of James' dinner invites. This time, he'd asked me to accompany him to a gala that was happening in two weeks. I lied and said I had a family reunion scheduled for that weekend. And I was so caught off guard by his attempt to make plans with me weeks in advance, I even broke down and told Mal about it. To my surprise, she laughed and said I was being ridiculous for turning him down. I just rolled my eyes and kept my mouth shut because there was no point in telling her about my decision to never pursue a romantic connection again.

But today? Today took the cake when Dominic, with his annoying habit of being aware of every move I make, strode into James' office just as he was planting an unexpected, and completely unwelcome, kiss on my lips. He'd prefaced it with a speech about his feelings for me and his hope for us to be something more than friends, and I was searching for the right thing to say when he grabbed me by the shoulders and pressed his lips to mine.

Which is how Dominic found us.

When I heard the door open, I pushed at James' chest with both of my hands to put some space between us. I spun around to face the person who'd interrupted us and almost dropped dead from the darkness filling Dominic's eyes. It was a living, breathing thing. Pouring out of him and slithering into the room, wrapping its tendrils around me and squeezing like a vice. My breath left me in a shallow wheeze, but James wasn't phased. He moved around me, clapping Dominic on the shoulder and ushering him back into the hallway. The heavy mahogany door fell shut behind them, leaving me frozen in place.

The look in Dominic's eyes haunted me for the rest of the workday.

And it's still in my mind when I park behind my mother's sleek sports car and cut my engine. I lay my head back and fight the urge to skip this dinner altogether and go home. My stomach is in knots. A mixture of guilt and anxiety over the entire situation has me feeling nauseous and being around my mother when I already feel like crap never goes well. I eye the tall and opposing Craftsman skeptically, wondering what's waiting for me inside the strategically placed vines of ivy and white brick exterior. Nothing in me believes I'll find comfort in the marble floors, art-covered walls, or mahogany cabinets filled with crystal and china no one ever eats off of.

"It's more of a museum than a home."

That was Eric's first thought when I brought him here to meet my parents, and he was right. Compared to the small, but intimate, confines of Mama's house, which is constantly brimming with people and laughter and love, the house where I grew up feels cold and unwelcoming. It's more of a shrine to luxury and excess than anything else, and that's the way my mother likes it. If I thought about it long enough, I could probably link my obsession with making homes cozy and functional back to my mom and this house. *Hell, I can link most of my issues back to her.*

A knock on my window startles me out of my thoughts.

"What the hell?!" I twist in my seat to find my father's handsome face smiling at me. The knot in the pit of my stomach loosens a little when our eyes meet. "Daddy!"

I open the door and throw myself into his arms. He drops his briefcase and wraps both of his surprisingly muscular arms around me, lifting me off of the ground a bit. I squeal like a little girl and squeeze him a bit tighter. My dad, Mark Carson, is one of my favorite people in the world, and he's the only reason I survived having a real-life Disney villain for a mother.

"I've missed you so much."

I let him go just enough to allow him to put my feet back on the ground and stare into his face, taking in all of his features. The slight wrinkles around his round eyes are a little more evident now, but he's still as handsome as ever. All clean-shaven chestnut skin with sharp and soulful eyes that always make you feel comfortable and safe.

He plants a kiss on my forehead and laughs. "I've missed you too, bean. You don't come home enough."

"I know. Work keeps me busy, but I have to make more time to see you."

He studies me for a moment, and I notice a few gray hairs sparkling in his otherwise black eyebrows. "Sloane, you can't spend your whole life at that office. Tell me Mallory gets you out of there at a decent hour most nights. "

I scoff as I close the car door. "Did I just hear Mark 'I invented the term workaholic' Carson tell me I can't spend my life at work?"

"Yes, you did. And you should listen to me. "

He bends down and picks up his briefcase then wraps one arm around my shoulders. "Because you're my dad?"

"That's one reason. The other reason is a little more selfish: I want some grandbabies to spoil before I become old and decrepit."

I roll my eyes to hide the pain that twists through my heart at the mention of grandbabies. "Wow, laying it on pretty thick there, sir. You're nowhere near old and decrepit." Like at all. The man runs three miles every morning and is probably the only partner at his law firm who is over fifty and has abs. If he ever becomes a grandfather, he'll be the best looking one on the playground.

Just put the man out of his misery. You know you have no intention of ever giving him grandchildren.

As random and unfair as the thought seems, I can't argue against it. Once upon a time, coming over here with a couple of babies in tow felt like a forgone conclusion. Eric and I wanted kids; we dreamed up a whole life where we were surrounded by little curly head cuties with his smile and my eyes, but fate had other plans for us. Hurtful, destructive plans that tore us apart at the seams long before he left this world and took my hope of ever creating a new life with him.

My dad doesn't have to know that though.

He's still smiling as he leads me into the house, regaling me with stories about his day. I listen intently, remembering the days in my childhood when I would wait by the door for him to come home and talk to me just like this. A lot of the time, it would be the first conversation I'd have all day with someone who wasn't paid to be around me.

"Mark, darling, I didn't realize you would be home so early!" My mother's voice floats across the foyer to us, the sound of heels echoing along with it. "I was just about to call Sloane—"

She stops short when she sees me standing next to Dad who's already loosening his tie. He puts his briefcase down and walks over and envelops her in a tight hug. "Call Sloane for what?"

"To see if we could reschedule." She says, slipping out of his embrace and waltzing over to me. I resist the urge to cringe as she embraces me. Her bony fingers dig into my flesh and her perfume floods my nostrils. "Sloane, honey, you should have called before you came over."

My spine stiffens. "I didn't think I needed to call, Mom. Dad and I made these dinner plans on Sunday at your request." I pull back to look at her face. Her mouth is drawn tight, lips pressed into a flat line as she releases me.

"Yes, I know." She spins around on her heel and heads deeper into the house. Dad and I trace her steps to the kitchen. "But things with my schedule change so quickly. It would have been nice to have a reminder, dear. "

There it is. The subtle shift of blame. She probably agreed to attend some dinner or charity event instead of having the dinner she forced me to schedule. Of course, it's not her fault though. The great Lauren Carson could never be guilty of something so classless as double booking. I suck in a deep breath and swallow the urge to apologize to her. I didn't do anything wrong. Sure I could have called ahead and let her know I was still planning to visit, but what kind of mother forgets her child is coming over for dinner?

Mama never does. She spends hours in the kitchen preparing for me, Mal, or Dominic to visit her.

But the differences between my mom and my mother-in-law are so vast it makes my head spin just thinking about it. Until I met Mama, I had no idea what it felt like to be loved and cared for with so much deference. She can be overwhelming and nosy as all hell, but it's all born out of the selfless, life-altering love she has for her children. And for me.

"I'm sure Sloane was just excited to get home and see us, Lauren." Dad presses a soft kiss to her temple and hugs her from behind. Her hazel eyes soften, and I let out a sigh. Maybe dinner with Cruella won't be so bad with Dad here. Even as a kid, it was never lost on me that his presence had a calming effect on her—while my every breath only seemed to annoy her.

"Of course," she pins me with a hard look, letting me see how annoyed she is before twisting around in Dad's arms and planting a soft kiss on his lips. "I'll just call Ella and let her know we can't make it."

"Sounds great, Mom. Thanks for changing your plans for me."

It's a fight to keep the bitter sarcasm burning in my throat from coating the words. The last thing I want to do right now is fight with her in front of my dad. His blood pressure is already high—he says it's due to stress from his job—but it would kill me to know I contributed to it in any way.

"A relaxing evening with my two favorite girls sounds like a dream." Dad smiles at me over Mom's shoulder. He truly does look pleased by the prospect of spending the evening with us, even though I'm sure he has a ton of work he could be getting done right now. I smile back, hoping it doesn't look as fake as it feels.

"Yeah, sounds amazing."

"Yes, it's great we can have this time together." Mom chimes in, smiling as she picks up her phone and taps out a quick message—probably letting her minions know they have to suffer through a fabulous dinner without Her Royal Highness to tell them what to think, do and say.

Dad opens up the refrigerator and starts rummaging around. "Are we still good with steaks on the grill? Bean, you and Mom can rustle up a salad and some baked potatoes. It'll be just like old times."

Before we can answer, he spins around and places a pack of rib-eyes on the island. He looks over at me and grins like a Cheshire cat, which makes my heart swell in my chest with love for him. "That sounds awesome, Daddy."

It takes us less than an hour to get dinner done, and by us, I mean me and Dad. Mom conveniently got a call that needed her immediate attention just as the steaks hit the grill, leaving me to prepare all the sides on my own. With anyone else, I would have been annoyed, but when she floated out of the kitchen and up the stairs, I was only relieved I didn't have to spend thirty minutes listening to her complain about having to cancel her dinner plans.

I was hoping she wouldn't come back down at all, but that ship sails away when she comes waltzing onto the patio just as Dad is setting the steaks on the table. She looks stylish and refreshed in a cream wrap dress and a pair of designer sandals. Her long curls flow over her shoulders and down her back, nearly hitting her hip.

"Oh, dinner's done already?" She takes a seat next to my dad, who's still in his work clothes sans tie, and places a napkin in her lap. "I didn't think my call was going to run that long. Ella wanted to know if I was going to be able to make lunch tomorrow. I assured her I would unless Sloane comes over to see us again."

Her eyes are on me, waiting for me to react, but I don't give her the satisfaction. She wants to goad me into a fight, and I'm not in the mood. "I have plans with Mal tomorrow, so your lunch with Ella should be safe."

I take a sip of my wine—a crisp, sweet Zinfandel Dad pulled out of the cellar while the steaks were resting—and shoot her a sickeningly sweet smile. This time, I hope it looks as fake as it feels.

"How's work going, sweetie?" Dad asks, his eyebrows pulled together in concentration as he cuts and plates our steak.

"It's good. All of our projects are actually on schedule." I shift in my seat, turning my body towards the one person at the table who cares about what I'm saying. "I forgot to tell you, James hired another contractor, so the hotel renovation will be done on time."

I don't mention Dominic's name since I can't say it without the knot in my stomach clenching tight. Anxious guilt wrapping around my intestines and turning them black. Like the pools of darkness that swallowed me whole when he looked at me.

"James Robinson? I think we know his parents. Isn't that Rachel and John's son, Mark?" I bristle at the interruption, but I'm hardly surprised. My mother always finds a way to bring the conversation back around to her.

My dad nods. "Yes, John and I play golf together at the club. James is their oldest son."

"Interesting. And you're working with him, Sloane?"

For the first time today, or probably in my whole life, my mother looks interested in what I have to say and I haven't the slightest idea why. I clear my throat to hide my annoyance. "James and I have worked on several projects together, Mom."

"Must have been a relief to have a new contractor come in so quickly." Dad hands me my plate, which is now almost overflowing with food. He's even gone to the trouble of dressing my baked potato just the way I like it. I smile over at him and he pinches my cheek, love shining in his eyes.

"Yes, that's amazing." Mom drawls, her hazel eyes dancing with excitement that doesn't make sense to me until she continues. "Sloane, please tell me you're seeing James outside of work as well. In a more *personal* manner. "

I nearly choke on my wine. Leave it to her to suggest I sleep with a client based solely on the fact his parents are members of the same country club. It doesn't help that James was suggesting the same thing just a few hours ago.

"No, Mom. I'm not seeing him in a more *personal* manner. James is just a client."

She takes a dainty bite of her steak. "Oh, don't be ridiculous! The Robinsons are a very powerful family, and as the oldest son, James stands to inherit John's CEO title when he retires in a few years. You would be a fool not to align yourself with someone like him."

So that's why she's so interested in this conversation.

I set my fork down and level her with a glare. "My relationship with James is, and will continue to be, strictly professional. Why can't you just be proud of your daughter for being a talented designer who's known for her ability and professionalism?"

"Professionalism won't get you a husband, dear. And neither will shouting at the dinner table."

My mouth drops open. *Did she seriously just say that to me?* I look over to my dad for backup, but he's just sitting there looking disappointed that his relaxing evening with his girls is about to turn into a WWE smackdown.

I stand up from my seat, nearly knocking over my chair with the abrupt movement. My hands are balled into fists at my side, but I manage to speak evenly. "I had a husband, Mother, or did you forget attending your son-in-law's funeral? Maybe it's all a blur for you, lost in a sea of the pointless dinners and charity events you use to fill up your empty life?"

"Sloane." My dad places a hand on my arm, silently asking me to back down. As always, he's focusing on the wrong person. I didn't start this fight and I won't apologize for participating in it.

My mother looks up at me, taking in the anger that's flowing off of me with sick pleasure. She lifts her wine glass to her mouth and takes a long, victorious sip before addressing me. "I remember Eric's funeral well. I'll never forget the spectacle you made of yourself, shouting and crying at the top of your lungs like the world had ended—embarrassing everyone there. I also remember that it was *four years* ago, which means you've had more than enough time to put away your pity party decorations and move on with your life. Hopefully this time, you'll choose someone in your league."

Several emotions run through me at once. Shock. Anger. Frustration. Hurt. They all swirl around inside of me, taking a hold of the knot already there, as I stare at her. Waiting for something, anything to happen. I know she won't take it back. She never apologizes because she never says anything she doesn't mean. And somehow knowing she *really* believes all of the things she just said to her own daughter makes it so much worse. The world seems to stop as we stare at each other—even the cicadas have stopped singing—and I don't know how much time goes by before my dad breaks the silence.

"Lauren." He rubs at his forehead roughly, his shoulders drooping in defeat. "You need to apologize. *Right now.*"

Her head snaps back as if he struck her, but her lips remain pressed together in a tight line. She's not going to take it back. Angry tears spring in my eyes and I swear hers gleam with a renewed sense of triumph. Destroying someone in a verbal sparring match is one of her favorite things to do; it doesn't matter if the person she's cutting with her words is her flesh and blood. Before I even realize what I'm doing, I'm moving. My legs carrying me around the table, past my dad's shocked face, into the house to grab my keys and purse and then out of the front door to my car.

The whole time tears are flowing freely down my face, and they don't stop until I pull into my driveway and find Dominic Alexander sitting on my front steps.

11

DOMINIC

I nsanity. Pure insanity. That's the only thing that can explain why I dropped every single one of my plans for tonight to show up at Sloane's house without an invitation or the slightest clue how to keep her from thinking someone died because the last time I came to her house alone was four years ago when it was Eric and both of our worlds were split open.

Most of that day is still a blur for me, but the shit I do remember still fucks with my head. *Driving to a job site and coming across a crash that had traffic backed up to hell. Texting Eric to tell him he should take a different route, so one of us could get there on time. Finally moving around the wreckage, seeing the Archway Construction logo on a crumpled door and knowing....*The rest is just blank until I saw her face.

"Dominic, what are you doing here?"

I look up and find Sloane standing over me. Both arms crossed over her body in a protective stance. It takes me one second to note the redness around the rims of her eyes, and the black smudges of mascara caked up around the corners. Her hair, which was a cloud of loose curls that framed her heart-shaped face earlier today, is pulled up into a messy bun on the top of her head, drawing attention to the fresh tears that have just cascaded down her cheeks. *Fuck, she's upset.* I push to my feet and go to her, every one of my protective instincts roaring to life, demanding I find the person who made her cry and plant a fist in their face.

Bonus points if it's the asshole I saw her kissing today.

I would bet my life that's not it though, especially not after the conversation we had in the hallway once we were away from Sloane. I'd taken the hand he had on my shoulder, the one he'd just used to hold her body to his, and twisted it up and back until pain wiped away the smug smile on his face. Then I told him if he ever touched her again, especially without her permission, I would gladly make him disappear.

At first, he looked shocked at my volatile reaction, but then understanding dawned on his face, and he apologized profusely for coming on to my best friend's wife. Muttering something about not knowing it would matter since it's been four years. If it hadn't been for the red clouding my vision and the angry beast snarling in my chest, I would have laughed.

I wish my issue with them kissing had something to do with Sloane being Eric's wife. It would make my reaction a hell of a lot more honorable.

"What's wrong?"

It's a challenge to keep the rage out of my voice, and the tears shining in her soft hazel eyes make it even harder. Sloane blinks up at me. For a moment, she looks ready to spill her guts. Vulnerability isn't an easy thing for Sloane. Especially not with me, and I know why. Being cordial for less than a week doesn't negate years of gutting each other verbally, but now more than ever, I wish it did because the urge to hold her is so strong I have to physically restrain myself from doing so.

I see the exact moment she decides I can't be trusted with her pain and watch in awe as a carefully constructed mask falls into place. She schools her features into passive submission and then wipes the tear tracks on her cheeks away with a flick of her hand.

And just like that, the transformation is complete.

"Nothing." She shifts her weight from one foot to the other. The movement makes the hem of her dress swish around her knees. "Did you need something?"

The name and location of the person who put those tears in your eyes.

I scrub a hand over my face to buy some time to make up an excuse. The truth is, I have no idea why I'm here. I should be meeting up with Chris, Mal's ex from college who's just moved back to the city, but instead I'm standing in front of Sloane and choking down the questions I have about her and James. That kiss. His hands on her skin. The indecipherable look in her eyes when she turned around and saw me standing there.

None of your fucking business.

"Yes." I lie smoothly. "My assistant lost the contact information for the stone vendor. The guy who has the marble you chose for the Presidential Suite. I wanted to call him and get an estimate for another project I'm working on."

Sloane frowns, and a small crease pops up in the center of her forehead. "Oh. You didn't have to come over here for that. You could have texted me, and I would have sent it again."

"You're right." I put my hands in my pockets. "Except I needed the information immediately, and we don't have a great history with text messages."

She laughs, and it's a sweet, simple sound that works at the flame in my chest that started hours ago when I barged into that office just because I knew she was in there. Alone with him. "Speak for yourself, Dominic. I have a perfect text message return record."

Does she? I probably fucked up my only chance to find out when I left her on read last week. I doubt she'll be giving any second chances.

"Text message return records." I suppress the smile pulling at the corner of my lips. "If there was such a thing, you would be the kind of person to keep track of it."

She raises her chin. The sadness in her eyes is chased away by a glint of playful stubbornness. "Of course, I would. I'm detail-oriented. Unlike you and your assistant, who somehow manages to lose the information I sent in an email. How does that happen?"

I shrug. "No idea. Alex must have deleted it by accident."

He would hate me for lying on him like this. The man never loses anything. He's more detail-oriented than the arrogant woman standing in front of me. Sloane shakes her head and digs her phone out of her purse. When she taps on the screen, it refuses to come on since it's dead. *Guess she missed that detail.*

"Damn. I forgot to charge it on the way to my parents."

Her parents? Pieces start to fall into place at the mention of the wealthy older couple I've only met a few times. From what I can remember of them Mark is open, personable, and completely in awe of his daughter. He looks at her like she hung the moon, but his wife is a different story. Beautiful, like her daughter, with none of the softness in her hazel eyes.

As far as I can tell, the only person who pisses Sloane off more than me is her mom, and I get it because that woman could give Cersei Lannister a run for her money in the cold and ruthless department. The queen would at least soften for her children though. I don't think Lauren Carson knows how to be anything but glacial when it comes to Sloane. On the day of Eric's funeral, she spent the entire service frowning at Sloane's tears. Like she was morally opposed to a show of real, human emotion.

Is that what happened tonight? Did Lauren spend the evening berating her daughter for not being a heartless bitch? I search Sloane's face, wishing for a crack in her mask, a peek at the emotions I know are brewing beneath it, but all I see is what she allows me to.

"You must've been too busy keeping track of *other* details to notice."

It was supposed to be a joke, but the moment the words leave my lips I hear the note of bitterness in them. The indirect reference to the kiss burning my tongue like acid. Sloane catches it too, and her eyes flash with emotion. Going from surprise to guilt before landing on indignation.

My brain chooses to ignore the last emotion, opting instead to focus on the way her pulse is fluttering at the base of her throat. A slight incline of my head, and I could press a kiss there. Breathe in the sweet, fruity smell of her. Feel every beat of her heart against my lips.

Why the fuck did I just think about that?

Probably for the same reason I can't stop dreaming about her. It all has to be a byproduct of spending so much time around her this past week. Time where we were getting along, and I found myself looking forward to seeing her. Anticipating talking with her. Teasing her without the goal of making her mad enough to walk away.

Sloane moves around me, and her arm brushes my shoulder as she walks to her front door. "Yeah. Like the proper way to store an email, so I don't lose the pertinent information it contains."

The key turns in the lock, and her door swings open. She glances at me over her shoulder, toying with the idea of inviting me in. This would be new territory for us. Me inside her home without Eric there. And I feel it. Her brain whirling, trying to decide if it's worth it to shift us out of the weird space between what we are now and what we could be.

A faint light spills out from inside of the house, framing Sloane's silhouette in the doorway. Illuminating every curve of her body, and calling up the memory of a girl I never got to know.

The bright fluorescent light spilling from the cracked door of the bathroom connected to her dorm room, bathing her body in its warm glow. Her drunken giggles slipping under my skin as I help her to bed. The sheets smell like her—tropical fruit and the nectar of the sweetest flowers. I kiss her forehead and make her promise to call me in the morning.

"Dominic," Sloane calls from the open door. "I asked if you wanted to come in?"

My feet start moving towards her before my brain fully processes the question. I take the steps two at a time, eyes glued to the bare soles of her feet that are now padding across the hardwood floors that run throughout the entire first floor. Closing and locking the door behind me, I absorb every detail available to me. Greedy for a glimpse into the sanctuary of a woman who still feels like a mystery to me sometimes.

This isn't the home she shared with Eric. She moved out of there a year after his death and bought this place. And it's everything you would expect the home of an interior designer to be—open and airy with perfectly coordinated colors and textures. Furniture that's stylish but functional. And just the right amount of pillows and throw blankets.

It feels like her.

A little too much like her. Almost like she never shared a home with another person at all. I grit my teeth and run through a thousand different scenarios that could make the glaring absence of Eric in this house sit right with me and come up empty. Yeah, it's been four years but is that really enough time to just completely erase someone from your life?

Is it enough time for you to be thinking about kissing her throat or dreaming about tasting her on your desk?

I close my eyes and count to ten, hoping for a calm that refuses to come. It makes no sense for me to be judging Sloane on how she chooses to represent her husband in her home after letting my mind go off the rails for the last week. The fact of the matter is, Sloane is single. And her choosing to put away her past to make room for a different kind of future is exactly what Eric would have wanted for her. I'm just glad he isn't here to see bastards like James Robinson drooling all over her, and I'm even more thankful he won't ever know how close I am to breaking every rule in the book whenever I'm around his wife.

Although, sometimes a part of me can't help but feel like he broke them first.

Sloane's phone is plugged up and charging on the island when I finally make it into her kitchen. She's tapping her nails on the white quartz counter and watching me with faint curiosity as I take a seat on one of the stools across from her.

"I like your place," I say, meeting her curious gaze with my own questioning one.

"Thanks. It's kind of weird having you here. You know, without Eric."

I rest my arms on the island. "I was just thinking that too. But it feels slightly less weird since he was never—"

"Here." She cuts in, tilting her head to one side. "Yeah. I suppose that does make it a little less weird."

"Might also help that you're being nice to me these days." I tease and get rewarded with the gift of her smile.

"I don't think I'm the one who has a problem with being nice."

I arch a brow. "Are you suggesting I'm the one with the problem?"

"No." She says coolly. "It's a fact, not a suggestion. You're always starting with me. From the moment I started coming around, you had an issue. If I wasn't so delightful, I would think *I* was the problem."

"Maybe your delightful-ness is the problem," I state simply. Spine stiffening at how close the statement is to revealing my true issue with Sloane. The one I won't ever say out loud because it won't change a damn thing. Not for the better anyway.

"I see." And for a second I think she does. Her eyes sparkle with a serene sense of clarity that stops my heart from across the room. "You thought everyone was going to like me more. That my delightful-ness, as you put it, would make Eric and Mal think twice about the whole hanging out with a grumpy, broody asshole thing?"

"Hilarious. Please tell me you're considering a career in comedy if interior design ever falls through."

Her lips roll inward as she considers me. "I'm only halfway joking, Dominic. Did you think I was trying to edge you out or something? That's the only reason I could ever come up with for your…."

The sentence breaks off as Sloane's attention is pulled to her phone, which has just switched back on. I fully expect her to move over to it, send me the email Alex never lost, and push me out of her door, but she surprises me by turning those thoughtful hazel eyes back on me.

Eyes that have probably glazed over numerous times trying to figure out why I didn't like her when everyone else did. I never knew she thought about it, and the admission almost makes me want to tell her the truth. Jumbled words crowd on the tip of my tongue, ready to push their way through, but I swallow them down. She isn't ready for that and probably never will be.

"No. I didn't think you were trying to edge me out. Eric and Mallory have been my family since we were in diapers. A random girl wasn't going to change that."

Sloane flinches at the use of the word random. I get it. It doesn't even begin to capture what she was to Eric and Mal. Or me. I clear my throat. "I'm sorry. That wasn't the right word."

She recovers quickly, crossing her arms over her body again. Right under the swell of her breasts. Pushing the lush curves up until the thinnest sliver of skin peeks over the sweetheart neckline of her dress.

Don't stare, Nic. Don't fucking stare.

But it's too late. In the grand scheme of things, it's not a lot of skin. I've seen more of a woman working out at the gym without it conjuring a reaction. Hell, the skimpy outfits Mal wears to Sunday dinners at Mama's house show more than Sloane is right now, but it's still a fight to stop myself from taking it all in—the way each soft globe presses against the cotton of her dress, leaving the slightest impression of her nipples. Two perfect buds that are probably the same color as her lips, visible for anyone to see and feel if she happened to press against them.

James definitely felt that when he kissed her today.

Red clouds my vision, and I will the crystal clear image of knocking the man's teeth loose with one hand while the other squeezes the air from his lungs to go back to whatever depths of depravity it came from. I need to get my fucking head checked.

"It's okay." Sloane shrugs. "I know what Eric and I meant to each other. Nothing you or my mom say can change that."

Ouch. Now I'm being compared to the Ice Queen who forbid her from marrying someone without a trust fund? I lean back and cross my arms, turning her words over in my mind. I decide it's best not to tell her I'm nothing like her monster of a mother. To remind her that I helped her husband pick out the ring she still wears on her finger and stood up beside them while they promised each other forever with a boulder on my chest and a smile on my face.

Because she made him happy. And he—well, he was everything she deserved. They made sense together. His calm, protective and gentle nature meshing perfectly with her sharp edges. Sanding them down until it was safe to hold her close enough to see the treasure that was her heart.

The clue Sloane's just given me for her mood earlier glitters like gold in the crater her words have just left in my chest, and I grasp it with both hands. Letting it pull me out of my thoughts about why she and Eric were made for each other. Of all the good things about him, that brought the good out in her. Things I don't have inside of me, whether by nature, nurture, or just the sheer dumb luck of having Gabriel Alexander's blood running through my veins.

I flex my fingers, feeling the grind and pull of tendons moving over bone. There's a faint soreness there. Leftover from slamming them into the hard jaw of the man who dared to touch her, to attempt to lay claim to her when she was....

What? Yours?

I shake the thought free. Forcing myself to fill the silence hanging between us even though Sloane doesn't seem to mind it. "Sounds like dinner with your parents didn't go too well."

"That"—she turns on her heel and walks over to the refrigerator to grab two bottles of water—"is the understatement of the year."

I catch the bottle she slides across the island without taking my eyes off of her. The mask is slipping now, fracturing around the crease in her forehead and letting the faintest stream of anger spill out. Sloane cracks open her bottle and takes a long sip of water while I wait for her to continue or change the subject. I'm not sure which is more likely since my experience with her venting habits is limited to being the person she needs to vent about. Her gaze slides over mine, and I think —*I hope*—I'm about to become familiar with them. For some idiotic reason, I want to be a person she trusts enough to vent to. My heart lifts at the idea of being that for Sloane. I can never be Eric: the man to lend her calm, comfort, or peace. But maybe...just maybe I can do this.

Offer her a listening ear.

Give her the gift of righteous anger that matches hers.

Be an avenging angel motivated by the wobble of her chin, driven by the shimmer in her eyes, galvanized by every beat of her heart.

Unbidden, images from the last week flash through my mind. Sloane's easy smile. The openness of her expression when she looked at me. The rich notes of her laughter when I made a joke she would have pretended not to hear less than a month ago. *And I want it.* I want to hear about everything that's bothering her, even if it's me. My heart beats a frantic tattoo, like the possibility of comforting Sloane is too much for it to bear, and then the possibility becomes a reality.

Sloane opens her pretty mouth again and lets it all pour out. With her arms flailing, fists clenched and nose scrunched, she tells me about her mom forcing her into scheduling dinner then trying to get out of it. When she gets to the part about her mom suggesting she see James in a more personal manner, she blushes, and I have to bite the inside of my cheek to keep from asking about the kiss.

"And then she said I embarrassed myself at Eric's funeral when I cried. Like I should have been concerned about what other people were thinking about me when I was *burying* my husband."

A fine sheen of fresh tears shines in her eyes and burns a hole right through me. I stand and round the counter. The need to hold her, to comfort her, driving me forward until I'm right in front of her with my arms open. Sloane gasps as I pull her to me and envelop her in a hug.

"You were perfect," I whisper against the messy bundle of curls brushing my nose, and it's the most honest thing I've said to her tonight. "The only thing anyone thought about you that day was how amazing you were. No one, not even your mom, could have gotten through burying the love of their life without shedding a tear, Sloane."

"Thank you."

She sniffles against my chest. Her arms are wrapped around my torso, and she's surprisingly relaxed in my hold. I almost smile; all those instances of being unable to keep my hands off of her have paid off in the most unexpected way: Sloane Kent is used to my touch.

My mind is swirling with the realization when she loosens her grip and looks up at me. Her head tilted back, lips upturned like she's asking for a kiss. A slow smile spreads across her face. And I return it without thinking about it.

"What?"

"You're being nice to me."

I roll my eyes. "Is that a problem for you?"

"No," she shakes her head. "I was just thinking if you keep this up, I might have to stop calling you Asshole Alexander."

I smile down at the angel in my arms and let the desire to be more to her than the asshole who reminds her of her mother bleed out of the cracks in the mask I've been wearing for years. The one that's hidden the shattered man who watched his best friend fall in love and build a life with the woman who already owned his fucking soul.

Because twelve years ago, on a warm summer night in August, not much different than tonight, I held an angel in my arms and let the shadows in her eyes—the ones that fit so well with mine—convince me trouble could be a good thing. A place where love could be forged in fire and not come out in a heap of ashes. A place where twin flames could exist together without burning everything around them down.

Her shadows were wrong, but I was too busy pressing a lifetime of hopes and dreams into the smooth creases of her skin with my desperate kisses and reverent touches to notice. I didn't know then that she wasn't mine to have.

Just mine to want.

To love.

To wish for.

To dream of while she belonged to my best friend, my brother. The one man I would never dream of hurting even though letting him have her felt like flaying myself open over and over again.

Careful, angel. I think silently. *You might prefer the asshole to what you've just awakened.*

12

DOMINIC

My plan for the next four years was simple: go to college, room with Eric, and graduate with a degree that would allow me to make enough money to never have to go back to living in a house with Gabriel Alexander again. The last part is kind of irrelevant given the sizable life insurance check that's been sitting in my bank account since last year when Mom died, but I'm still not taking any risks because ending up in a house with my dad would cost me what little sanity I have left.

The past twelve months have been hard enough but living with the piece of shit who might as well have put her in the grave himself, made it all unbearable. Listening to him weep over pictures of her and romanticize their history. Sitting through his attempts to try and walk me down a rose-colored memory lane like I didn't live through all of their dysfunctional bullshit.

The lies.

The cheating.

The slaps across her face.

The bruises from his hands around her neck.

It all slowed down when I got old enough to shield her body with mine. And then when she got sick, breast cancer in the advanced stages, it stopped altogether. He just transformed into this loving, gentle man who doted on his sick wife, tending to her every need with the kind of devotion he refused to give her for years. It was sickening to watch him, knowing all those years of abuse could've been avoided if he hadn't woken up every day and chosen to be a mean, heartless bastard.

For all of those reasons—and a few I'm probably not far enough along in therapy to fully understand—I have to stick to my plan. A plan that didn't include attending frat parties with Chris, the resident assistant on my hall, or being brought to my knees by the walking contradiction that is the woman sitting on my lap right now.

I came out here to avoid her. To get away from the white dress, long legs, and sexy mess of curls flowing down her back. To avoid the inevitable moment when the air around me was replaced by her heavenly scent and the sweet, fruity notes wafting up from her skin mixed a little too well with the smoky flavor of the liquor on her breath. I don't know how, but the moment I saw her I knew she would spell disaster for the plan. Probably because none of the bullet points included feeling this way about a stranger.

Except she doesn't feel like a stranger. She feels like home. She feels like the only person who has ever looked at me and known me in a single second. She feels like every dream I've ever had, every wish I've ever made, every oath I've ever sworn to keep all rolled up into one perfect being. All real, and all mine from the moment she sat her perfect ass on my lap and dared me to come and burn the world down with only her eyes.

Fuck the plan.

I curl my arm around her waist, pulling her deeper into me and inviting her to continue the conversation she started when she sat down and told me I looked like trouble. She smiles and tosses back the rest of her drink. "Well, are you?"

"Am I what?"

"Trouble."

"That depends, angel."

Shit. I didn't mean to let the nickname slip. I don't even know her real name, so it's strange to already be giving her one. There's something overly familiar and possessive in my tone that should scare us both, but I can only think about how right the word feels on my tongue and how pleased she looks because I said it.

She bites her lip. "On?"

"What kind of trouble you're looking for."

She leans forward and sets the empty cup on the window sill behind me. The movement causes her breasts to come dangerously close to brushing my cheek. I stay still, not wanting to startle her by nuzzling into the most inviting cleavage I've ever had the pleasure of being this close to. When she settles back into my hold, she sighs audibly and tilts her head back to look up at the stars.

"This is going to sound weird, but there's this girl who lives inside of me. She spends all of her time trying to be perfect and do everything right so everyone else can be happy with who she is, how she looks, and what she does. I've spent my whole life letting her drive the bus because I thought she knew what she was doing, but she doesn't. She *really* fucking doesn't."

In some ways, this whole monologue *does* sound weird, but somehow it also doesn't. I get what it's like to push down all of your true thoughts and feelings so people only get the most palatable version of you. Going through your life and only showing one part of yourself to the world seems exhausting.

"And now you're trying to make up for lost time by doing all the things she would never do."

Her gaze snaps to mine. "Yes. Exactly."

I consider her for a moment, trying to convince myself I'm not already caught up in her spell, like I won't do, or be, whatever she asks me to. And it's a waste of energy because I already know I will. I knew it the moment I saw her standing in the doorway over an hour ago. She was surrounded by a group of people coming into the party, but I could only see her.

My fingers flex, digging into the soft flesh at her side, and the fire in her eyes burns brighter.

"Why do you think I can help you with that?"

"I saw the way you looked at me when I walked in."

"You and your friends walked right past me."

She giggles and even the sound is heavenly. I want to soak it up, pull every note out of the air, and absorb it into my being. *Jesus, this girl is already in my fucking blood.* When she realizes I'm not amused, her lips push out into a faux pout.

"I'm sorry. They asked me to stay close until they tracked down the guys who invited us. Then they left me, and I came to find you because I knew you were the only person who could help me check the last two things off of my trouble list."

"What's on your trouble list?"

She shifts around and suddenly she's straddling me. Those long arms looping around my neck and the hem of her dress riding up her thighs as she makes herself at home on top of the erection I've been dealing with since she walked out the back door and set her sights on me. Both of my hands come up and grip her waist; she smiles triumphantly at me.

"I can't tell you until you say yes."

I shake my head in disbelief. I don't know if I'm more shocked by her audacity or the fact I'm considering saying yes even though I have no idea what she's going to ask of me.

"Who are you?"

She bites her lip, and for the first time tonight, she doesn't look so sure of herself. Her fingers ghost over the back of my neck, and my dick twitches. A small gasp leaves her lips, and I swallow the urge to capture the sound with my mouth.

"That's such a loaded question. I think I'm going to need you to be more specific."

My lips quirk as I fight back a smile. She's such a smart ass. "Let's start with something simple, like your name."

"*You* call me angel."

A jolt of electricity passes between us. Satisfaction swells in my chest, spurred by her repeating the nickname I gave her. "True, and I probably still will after you tell me what everyone else calls you."

She leans back and extends her hand. "Sloane."

Shaking her hand while the heat of her body is pressed against my erection is almost laughable, but the serious look on her face demands I do it anyway. Her hand is small and fits perfectly inside of my palm.

"I'm Dominic, but all of my friends call me Nic."

Her head tilts to the side, eyes sparkling with mischief. "Does anyone ever call you Dom?"

I can't stop looking at her mouth. "Nope, not until now."

The statement wins me another brilliant smile that hits me right in the chest and makes me wonder how I went through my entire life without this impossibly perfect girl looking at me like her shadows were made for mine.

"Good." She slurs, leaning in closer until her lips are hovering over mine and her breasts are grazing my chest. "Do you want to know what's on my list, Dom?"

"Yes."

"Number One: Get drunk for the first time. *Check.* Number Two: Wear a dress short enough to make a stripper blush and go to a party. *Check.* Number Three: Shake my ass for the sexiest guy at the party." An adorable, but undeniably drunken, hiccup escapes her as she wiggles her brows at me. "Number four: Go home with that guy and spend the night in his bed doing everything but sleeping."

"Sloane—"

"Do you want to dance with me?"

Everything in me is telling me to walk away right now, to run from her like I did earlier because her drunken recitation of the running list in her head proves that my instincts about her being a source of disruption in my life were spot on. Still, I can't bring myself to move. I'm too intrigued by her and the tangle of emotions swelling in my chest just from being close to her.

"Tell me one thing first."

Sloane blinks several times to focus. Her eyes have that glassy look to them that indicates major alcohol consumption, and I wonder exactly how much she's had to drink.

"What do you want to know?"

"Can't you just tell whoever pissed you off to go screw themselves?"

Her brows dip together. "What do you mean?"

"This list isn't about you. It's about proving something to someone else, so why don't you just tell them to go screw themselves and move on with your life?"

"She'd just see it as confirmation that she's been right about me all along. Her twisted mind will find a way to make her the victim even though she called her own daughter an ungrateful little bitch and a constant source of disappointment."

She says the last bit with practiced indifference, trying to make it seem like she doesn't care, but I see it for what it is: the source of her shadows, the reason for the restless flame that called to me before. And it sends anger slicing through me on her behalf. The idea that anyone could treat her that way makes me want to rip the world apart with my bare hands. My body tenses. Not just at the thought, but at the realization, I *would* do that for her.

"Your mom said that?"

"Among other things, but please don't feel bad for me. I should have given up trying to please her a long time ago. Now, are you going to dance with me or should I find someone else to help me check off the last two items on my list for tonight?"

I lift an un-amused brow at her, and she blushes as I stand with her in my arms. "Don't tease me, Sloane."

Both of her legs wrap around my waist, nestling the heat of her right along my abs. We stare at each other for a beat, and then our lips crash together in a fierce entanglement that's all lips, tongues, and teeth and punctuated by a feral groan that takes my brain a full second to realize belongs to me. Sloane giggles against my lips, and the sound of her laughter being swallowed by my mouth is so intimate, so exquisite my heart starts trying to beat itself right out of my chest.

"More, Dom." Sloane moans into my mouth. "I need more."

"I know, baby. I know."

I want more too. I want to peel this dress off of her body with my teeth. I want to kiss every inch of her bare skin and mark her with my scent. I want to taste her and tease her while she moans my name and leaves welts in my back because it all just feels so fucking good. But I can't give her more. Not while we're standing on the back porch of a frat house where anyone can see us.

And not while she's drunk.

The image of Sloane tossing back drinks is like a bucket of ice water being poured down my back, sobering me up even though I haven't had a drop of alcohol tonight. I pull back and look at her. She looks even more beautiful now with her lips swollen from my kisses and her eyes half-hooded with lust for me, but I can't keep going. I shouldn't have taken it this far when I knew she was drinking.

Although it pains me, I reach around and loosen the death grip her legs have on my waist. Sloane drops them to the ground, complying even though the furrow in her brows tells me she's a little confused.

"What are you doing?"

"Stopping this before we jump straight to list item number four."

"Oh, right." She pulls her dress down and casts an alarmed, but almost regretful, look at the erection tenting my pants. "We should head back inside."

"Yes, we should."

The moment the words pass my lips, Sloane starts walking without looking back to see if I'm following. She marches onto the dance floor, claims a spot, and starts to move. Her hands are in her curls, lifting them off of her neck, and the additional flash of skin has me damn near running to get to her. As soon as I'm behind her, she leans back into me, grabbing my hands and placing them on her waist while she sets a rhythm I'm all too happy to follow.

I don't know how long we stay like that, but I love every minute of it. Every roll of her ass into an erection I don't even try to control because she's so fucking happy to have it pressing into her. Every whiskey-laced kiss she gives me when she comes back from the kitchen with another drink in her hand. Every sultry smirk she throws over her shoulder as we work together to check off the third item on her list.

"You okay, Dom?"

She gives another swivel of her hips. The movement makes her scent waft up to me and tickle my nose. I don't answer. I'm too caught up in the graceful curve of her neck and the curly black strands that graze her shoulders, demanding that I touch her there.

I obey. My fingers gliding over soft, creamy skin the color of honey. Sloane shivers at the touch and throws yet another lazy smirk over her shoulder. My heart does a flip in my chest as I realize why I couldn't walk away even when I thought I wanted to: s*he fucking owns me.*

The knot of emotions in my chest digs in deeper, making themselves at home right behind my rib cage. I can't even begin to name them all, but I know they're there and I know what they mean. Know it the same way I know whatever my parents had wasn't love. I mean, the abuse and the cheating made that clear, but I also never saw them look at each other the way I know I look at Sloane.

Gripping her waist and pulling her back into a roll of my hips, I ignore the doubts running through my mind. The ones that tell me falling in love with a girl at the first college party I've attended is not only dumb but a terrible cliche.

It can't be love.

The voice in my head shouts at me, searching for something, anything to explain away the thing happening to me. But no matter how hard I think about it, how long I wait, the tangle doesn't go away.

I glance around the room. Bodies writhe all around us. Moving together to the beat of the music blasting through the speakers. Every one of them can blame the shameless bumping and grinding they're doing on the liquid sloshing around in their red Solo cups, but I'm not drunk. I never get drunk, so it has to be something else.

Something real.

Something more than alcohol-laced lust masquerading as love. And I know I'll only find out if I get us out of here.

I brush her curls to the side, liking the way she shivers when my fingertips skim her shoulder, and lean forward to whisper in her ear.

"Do you want to get out of here, angel?"

She spins in my arms and nods. Her pupils are blown, hazel giving way to pools of molten gold that burn into me. "Yes, *please.*"

* * *

To my surprise, and relief, the absence of other people only seems to intensify our connection. Sloane grabs my hand, pulling me down the street and back towards the path Chris and I took a few hours ago when we walked over, which means she must stay on campus.

We take our time walking back, a slow stroll that gives me time to pull her into my side, feel the warmth of her body melting into me and notice how much the moonlight loves to caress her skin. Dancing over the elegant features of her face, illuminating the curls cascading down her back. Making her look even more like a celestial being that came down on a cloud from heaven just to capture my heart.

If that celestial being was drunk and stumbling over nothing the entire way back to her dorm.

When Sloane nearly falls for the third time in a row, I ignore her protests and pick her up, cradling her in my arms while she gives me directions back to her building, which is on the nicer side of campus near the cafeteria and student life center.

Everything around us is quiet without the gold heels she's wearing click-clacking on the sidewalk, but I don't care because she's looking up at me with those soft eyes I know will bring me to my knees one day.

"What?" I ask softly, trying to hide how affected I am by the swirl of emotions I see on her beautiful face.

She shakes her head. "Nothing. You're just a little too nice for a guy that screams trouble."

"And you're an exceptionally shitty planner for a girl who came out just to find it."

"What's that supposed to mean?"

"You came to a party for the sole purpose of drinking and hooking up. And you were probably already drunk when you walked across campus with your friends wearing—" I nod vaguely at the dress hugging her curves. "—*this*."

"Don't be dramatic. I wasn't drunk, and we didn't walk." Her chin lifts defiantly. "My roommate drove us. She's the designated driver for the night."

Knowing she wasn't walking around the dark campus in this dress makes it a little better, but she still came to the party, drank like a fish, and lost track of the only people she knew there, one of which was her ride home.

"This the same roommate who ditched you after she found the guy she was looking for?"

She rolls her eyes. "Yes, but I also left her to come find you."

"And what if we hadn't met? How were you planning on getting home?"

I can't even stomach the possibility of any other guy being the one to walk her home tonight. Someone who wouldn't care she was drunk and would have taken her mile-long legs, golden skin, and full lips as an open invitation regardless of what she said.

Sloane taps on the thin strap of the cross-body bag she's been carrying all night that's now sitting in her lap. It's a small rectangle that's barely big enough to hold a tube of lip gloss, but she manages to pull a phone out of it.

"See this? It's called a cell phone. You can use them to get in touch with people who aren't in the same place as you. Ever heard of one?" Her nose wrinkles as she waves the phone around in my face, letting me see that the device she hinged her entire rescue plan on is dead.

"Do you happen to have a charger in that Ziploc bag you call a purse?"

She frowns. "No. Why?"

"Your phone is dead."

"No, it's not."

I balance her weight on one arm just so I can pluck the phone out of her hand and flip it around to let her see the screen is black. She curses and snatches it out of my hand, which makes me laugh.

"It's okay, angel. You must have forgotten to charge it when you were downing wine coolers."

Sloane slaps me on my arm. "Shut up! They weren't wine coolers."

There's no heat in her eyes when the blow lands, only playful annoyance and a slight glassiness that reminds me of her current condition. A happy silence stretches between us as we approach the door to her building. I stop outside the doors to set Sloane on her feet.

She pulls a set of keys out of her purse and sways a bit as she uses her student ID to let us into the building. I reach out to steady her.

"Thanks."

Her smile is all perfect teeth and full pink lips, so tempting I have to look away or else I'm not going to be able to do what I need to do, which is see her to her door, maybe kiss her goodnight, give her my number and leave.

Luckily, she's staying on the first floor, and I'm treated to a prime-time view of her hips swinging as I follow her to her room. As soon as she unlocks the door, I release a long breath.

Sloane pushes the door open and glances back at me. "You okay?"

"Yeah. Looking at you is just making it hard for me to do what I need to do."

A knowing smile tugs at the corner of her lips. She leans against the partially open door. The room is dark, except for a sliver of light coming from somewhere inside. The beam spills out into the hallway and illuminates Sloane's silhouette. I stare at her, so caught up in her beauty, I almost forget she's drunk.

That is until the door swings out from behind her and sends her stumbling into the room.

I reach for her, but I'm too late. Her body hits the floor with a dull thud, and then she's flat on her back laughing at the ceiling. The sound reminds me of just how far gone she is.

"Well, that should make this next part a lot easier on you."

All at once, I'm shocked by how gracefully she managed to land and charmed by her sense of humor in what has got to be an extremely embarrassing moment for someone as confident and self-possessed as Sloane.

I step into the room, bend over her prone form and extend a hand. "Actually, it makes it harder since now I have to consider whether it's safe to leave you when you might have a concussion."

I pull her up and as soon as her feet touch the ground, I scoop her up into my arms again. Our faces are mere inches apart, and I brush my nose over hers, leaving her eyelids fluttering when I pull back and stare at her some more.

"I need to brush my teeth."

"Where's your bathroom?"

She points at a partially open, and well-lit, doorway on the other side of the room with a perfectly manicured finger. I follow it just like I've followed her all night long. Like I plan to follow her for the rest of my life. The tangle of emotions in my chest hums its assent.

Crossing the room takes no time at all, even with Sloane in my arms. When we enter the small bathroom, I drop her on the countertop by the sink. "Where's your stuff, angel?"

She indicates her toiletries with a flick of her finger and then watches with a dazed look on her face as I place a tiny dab of toothpaste on her toothbrush, run it under water and bring it to her lips.

"Open."

The order lights a spark in her eyes, and I know she intends for me to take it as a non-verbal challenge, but I don't. I'm not sure why I need to do this, but nothing is going to stop me from taking care of her.

Something in my expression must tell her this isn't a battle she's going to win because she gives a dramatic roll of her eyes and opens her mouth. With a triumphant grin on my face, I brush her teeth, making sure to be thorough, so the taste of Jack Daniels and any other alcohol she consumed is no longer in her mouth.

When I'm done, and she's finished glowering at me, I try to pull her into my arms again.

"I let you brush my teeth, but I draw the line at your carrying me around like I'm incapable of walking two feet without running into something." I raise a skeptical brow at her, and she rolls her eyes. "Dom, I'm fine. And I could use a minute with the uh—"

She gestures towards the toilet, and I get the hint. "Shit. Sorry. I'll just wait out here."

I hook a finger in the general direction of her room and step out of the bathroom. The lock clicks behind me, and I fold myself into a desk chair. One look at the contents on the desk tells me it's Sloane's. Her smiling face peers up at me from a silver frame, and I pick it up to get a closer look. It's a recent photo of her alongside an older man with medium brown skin, a bald head, and streaks of gray in his neatly trimmed beard. This must be her dad.

When I sit the picture back down, my eyes light on a colorful square of sticky notes lying beside a cup of pens. Plucking up a pen, I write a short note to Sloane on the pad then slide it to the edge of the desk closest to her bed. I finish up just as she comes slinking out of the bathroom, slowly walking past me, like she doesn't believe she can make it to her bed without falling or bumping into something.

"You okay?"

She braces herself with one hand on the desk. "Yes. Just a little dizzy."

"Almost there." I rise to my feet and come up behind her, placing one hand on the small of her back. She sways into me, her hips brushing into my groin. The erection I've been fighting back since we left the party, springs back to life.

Sloane wiggles her hips. "Someone's happy to see me."

"Behave." I smack her on the ass and walk her forward until her knees hit the frame of her bed. Reaching past her, I pull her cover and top sheet back. They smell like her already. "Alright. Up you go."

She hops up on her bed with a pout on her full lips. "Is this how the night is going to end? With you tucking me into bed instead of climbing in with me to complete list item number four?"

"Yes." I lean forward and press a kiss to her forehead. "But there's always tomorrow night."

And all the nights after. You can have me every night if you want.

Tired eyes blink up at me. "Stay. Please."

I shake my head, but my resolve is wavering. Going back to my room to sleep alone sounds like the worst idea ever when I have an angel inviting me to her bed.

"Your phone is still dead, so I wrote my number down for you. I'm leaving it right here. Call me in the morning, okay?"

"Mhmm. Hmm." Sloane's eyelids flutter once, twice and then they're closed.

With another soft kiss to her forehead, I slip out of her room, making sure the door is secure before I go. Leaving her feels wrong, but I force myself to do it anyway because she's drunk, and I don't know how much of this she'll remember in the morning when her mind isn't sluggish from alcohol. Hopefully, everything. And if not, I know the note I left will fill in the blanks, which means I'll hear from her tomorrow.

Tomorrow.

I pull out my phone and see it's a little after 2:00 a.m., which means technically it's already tomorrow. So today. Today, I will hear from my angel and find out if the solid knot in my chest feels any different in the light of day.

A loud ding from my phone lets me know I've just received a message. Even though I know she's fast asleep, a part of me hopes it's Sloane. Instead, I see Eric's name flashing across the screen. He's finally replying to a message I sent earlier about the beds in our room.

> Eric: Both of them look like they sleep like shit, but if you've got the better one we might have to square up for it. Otherwise, I might have to tell Mama I'm staying home after all. Lol.

I laugh at his message but don't bother replying for two reasons: 1. Eric would rather sleep on shards of glass for the next four years than give up the freedom that living on campus is going to give him. 2. If things with Sloane go the way I think, sleeping in any bed that isn't hers will be the least of my worries.

13

SLOANE

Now

"What the hell is *that*?"

Mal eyes the contents of the plate in my hand like it's a grenade with a pulled pin. I glance down at the offending plate, examining it closely to see what the problem is, but all I see is the red velvet cake Mama made for dessert.

I turn to her. "Uh, a piece of red velvet cake?"

"No shit, Sloane. I was right here when Nic handed it to you."

"Then why are you acting confused?"

She slides to the edge of the sofa where we've been sitting since Mama shoved us out of the kitchen and angles her body towards me. "*Nic* brought it to you, and the bastard didn't even bring me one."

"Oh my, God." I laugh. "I'm sure he'll be happy to bring you a slice if you ask him."

Like clockwork, Dominic appears with another slice of cake in his hand. He hands Mal the plate and plops down on the sofa beside her, stretching one of his long arms over the back of the chair and stretching his legs wide, like a king holding court. I don't realize I'm staring at him until he winks at me with a wolfish grin curving his lips.

Shit. How many times is the man going to catch me staring at him?

Mal looks between the two of us suspiciously, catching his smile and my blush but nothing else. "Are you two getting along?" Dominic stares at her but says nothing. The grin is gone now, replaced by an I-know-something-you-don't-know smirk that has Mal focusing her attention on me.

I wrinkle my nose at her. "I wouldn't go that far. He's just moved down a space or two on my murder list."

That's a lie. I'm not entirely sure Dominic is even on my list anymore. It pains me to admit it, but I'm finding it hard to hate him. He still manages to annoy me sometimes, like right now when he's leaving me to answer all of Mal's questions about the sudden shift in our dynamic, but things aren't like they were before. My heart doesn't sink when I see him coming. My hackles don't rise with the inherent need to defend myself whenever he's around. Hell, I even sought him out just to say hello when I got here today.

I found him in the kitchen, posted up against the refrigerator giving Mama a rundown on the repairs he was planning on making to her house. Like always, I was hit with a rush of appreciation for him and the way he cares for her in all the ways that Mal and I can't, but instead of biting back the compliment, I said it out loud. The words rushed out of my mouth before I had a chance to stop them, and I don't know who was more surprised by the outburst: me, Dominic, or Mama.

Her face broke into a megawatt smile, pulling her soft features into an expression that was a mix of happiness and relief. Dominic laughed it off. His chiseled features schooled into the picture of nonchalance while his eyes burned holes into my face. I couldn't pinpoint the emotions that played across his face as he assessed me, but I think I saw surprise and maybe a little amusement when I was finally brave enough to meet his midnight gaze.

Honestly, I feel like I'm starting to see him as something other than an enemy, and it's kind of nice. Especially when the benefits of getting along with him include comforting hugs where I can rest my head against the hard planes of his chest and listen to the deep rumbles of his voice when he's saying something that's not meant to insult me. I want more of it. Especially if it means getting first dibs on a piece of Mama's red velvet cake without having to move a muscle.

Mal takes a bite of her cake. "Well, I guess that's nice."

"I'm glad you think so," Dominic says. "Considering it's exactly what you asked for."

"I know I asked for it, but I never expected it to happen. And I didn't expect it to mean you'd bring *Sloane* cake before you brought me some."

She pouts at Dominic who rolls his eyes with all of the annoyance of a big brother who has made the grave mistake of spending years spoiling his little sister. "You're ridiculous, you know that? You got your cake less than five seconds after she did. Now shut up and eat it."

"Don't tell me to shut up, *Dominic*."

"Stop whining like a child, *Mallory Pearl*."

"You're such an ass. Bringing my middle name into this is such a low blow."

She sticks her tongue out at him, and he rolls his eyes. I watch the whole exchange in silence, knowing from years of watching Mal, Eric, and Dominic bickering that there's no real heat or hurt in their words. This is just something that they do. An added benefit to growing up with siblings—or in Dominic's case, people who treated you like one.

"You started it. We both know how I feel about people calling me by my full name."

Mal opens her mouth to respond, but she's interrupted by Mama yelling for her from the kitchen. She floats off in a huff, leaving Dominic and me on the sofa alone. I look around, noticing that we're the only ones in the living room. Everyone else has either gone home or is outside in the backyard for the basketball game that happens every Sunday after dinner. Eric and Dominic always played, and most weekends Dominic still does.

Weirdly, he's not out there today.

I flick my gaze over to him only to find he's already looking at me. I blush and hope he wasn't watching when I took that last bite of cake because I'm ninety percent certain I have icing on my face.

"Thanks for the cake," I say, feeling awkward now with his dark eyes glued to mine.

He shrugs, tapping his fingers rhythmically along the back of the sofa. "Don't mention it."

"Oh no." I sigh dramatically and turn to face him. "Is this the part where you get upset with me for thanking you instead of just saying you're welcome?"

Dominic winces. The muscle in his jaw starts to do that little *tick, tick, tick,* and panic slices through me as I wonder if maybe it's too soon in our friendship—using that term very loosely—for me to be making jokes like that. But then a slow, lazy smile pulls at his lips.

"You're welcome, Sloane." He says my name slowly, drawing out the one syllable until it sounds like the slow glide of a zipper racing down the back of a woman's dress at the hand of her lover.

I swallow and drag my gaze away from him. It doesn't matter though. The image of his mouth curving around my name is seared into my brain. "I'm glad to know you *are* capable of forming those words with your mouth."

"I'm capable of doing a lot of things with my mouth."

What did he just say? Have we made it to the part of our fledgling friendship where we make bad jokes riddled with sexual innuendo already?

I rack my brain to try and find an acceptable response. One that toes the line just in case I completely misread his words and the panty-dropping smile was all in my head. Dominic-based delusions aren't exactly a rarity for me these days. The vivid dreams and the very real, but highly inappropriate, responses to his touch are proof of my mind's ability to impart brow-raising suggestions on just about everything the man does.

"Right." It's an effort to push the word past my lips. "I'm sure Kristen is more than satisfied with your…. mouth's capabilities."

Oh, hell. I send up a silent prayer, hoping for someone to summon me from another part of the house or for the ground to just open up and swallow me whole. Why the hell did I bring up Kristen? I don't know anything about his ex-girlfriend besides what Mal told me a few months ago about them ending their relationship just to turn around and become friends with benefits. Somehow my brain retained the information without me even knowing it, updating the mental files I've always kept on Dominic but never had a reason to use.

Up until now. When I am so desperate for a comeback I have no problem sliding into this completely uncharted territory with him. The only upside to mentioning the woman he's currently sleeping with is that it's exactly what I need to stop my brain from ticking off the number of things his mouth has done to me in my dreams.

Dominic slides down the sofa, and the heat of his body envelops mine the instant he closes the distance between us. Our thighs touch. A muscular, denim-clad leg pressing into the skin bared by my sundress. Rough fingers grip my chin, turning my head and making me face the amused expression that's taken over his entire face.

"Probably just as satisfied as James is with yours." He murmurs, his eyes on my mouth.

I shake my head, ready to rid him of any notions about my relationship with James, but all I get out is a strangled noise before he swipes a thumb over the corner of my mouth and pulls back with a fleck of cream-cheese icing smeared across the pad of his finger. I watch shamelessly as he brings the digit to his mouth and, with a flick of his tongue that sends an arc of electricity down my spine, sucks it clean.

My mouth hangs open as my brain struggles to process what I've just witnessed. Dominic smirks at me, and I don't know how to stop the heat from creeping up my neck and into my cheeks. He sees the whole thing, because of course he does, and it only makes me blush harder.

"Yo, Dom!" A voice calls out from outside, and I almost jump out of my skin when I turn to see Eric's younger cousin, Julian, standing on the front porch. He pulls the door open and peeks his head through. "We need another person for this pick-up game. You playing?"

I look down at my hands and send up a silent prayer that Julian missed the entire icing exchange. He can't go a day without gossiping with his mom on the phone, and the last thing I need is for Aunt Mary to be shouting to the high heavens that Dominic and I are having an affair when we *absolutely* are not. I would never do something like that to Eric. Not with his best friend, and especially not in his mom's house.

Right, so what exactly does it mean when you let a man lick icing off of your face?

I blanch. *That really happened.* I sat here and let my husband's best friend do that without so much as a protest. The same way I didn't protest when he held my hand in the club, hugged me in my kitchen, or placed a light, but possessive, touch to the small of my back, which he's prone to do every time he happens to be walking beside me lately.

My stomach twists into guilty knots with the realization, and I'm overwhelmed with the need to get away from this man whose touch makes me forget things I should be holding on to with both hands. Like where I am, who we are to each other, and the fact that just a few weeks ago we couldn't stand the sight of one another.

"Yeah, man," Dominic says to Julian. "Let me just grab my stuff out of the car."

"Alright! I'll go let everyone know we got a game."

The screen door slams shut, and as soon as Julian's head disappears, I jump out of my seat, sending the plate in my lap flying to the floor. Dominic catches it with one hand and rises to his feet. He's still so close to me. Close enough that I can feel his abs flex when he sucks in a breath and looks down at me. His lips part, and I know without a doubt that I don't want to hear anything he's about to say, so I hold up a hand to stop him.

"Don't."

Surprisingly, he stops. He presses his lips into a hard line and watches me quietly as I take the plate and push past him, but I only make it a few steps before his hand flies out and grips my arm gently. His heated gaze stays on my face, and for a moment we just stare at each other. Then his grip is slipping down my arm. *Down, down, down.* Slowly ghosting over my wrist, then my palm, and finally my fingertips.

Every inch of skin that's been exposed to his touch is on fire, and the whisper of a smile playing on his lips as he leaves me standing in the living room with a half-eaten slice of red velvet cake tells me that was his intention.

I just have no idea why.

* * *

Rivulets of rain run down the window of my office, and I watch them fall because pretending to be the lead in a late 90's R&B video seems to be the only task my frazzled brain can complete. I didn't see Dominic at work at all, which is good since I'm still reeling from yesterday. Replaying the scene on Mama's couch and the moments that followed over and over again. No matter how many times I turn it over in my mind, I can't figure it out.

I've never claimed to know Dominic all that well, but lately the things he does make no sense to me. At first, I was glad for the changes the night in the club forced on us. We were getting along, becoming something close to friends. I was even getting some semblance of control over my body's reaction to his touch. Hours upon hours of thinking about it, and a hypothetical conversation with Dr. Williams after lunch with him last Tuesday, helped me pinpoint exactly what was to blame for my body's reaction to Dominic.

Skin hunger.

That was the term she used, and apparently, it's a normal reaction to not receiving the amount of loving, human touch you desire for an extended amount of time. In my case, going four years without letting any man who isn't my dad so much as shake my hand has made me unfamiliar with being touched with intention and purpose. It was a good explanation, and honestly who cared if it didn't begin to cover why Dominic's fingers trailing down my arm unlocked something in me I'd convinced myself I could live without when Eric died?

I *was* working through it.

I was well on my way to convincing myself that my inane sex dreams about him, and the hum of awareness that roared to life every time a part of his body brushed against mine, were a misguided byproduct of my touch starved skin. Something I could work through on my own. Something I needed to get a handle on immediately since it was all in my head.

Then Icing-Gate happened, and I was slapped in the face with the possibility that I'm not the only one who feels it. The current of desire rippling between us, like an invisible string linked to the curve of Dominic's lips and tied directly to the coil of desire that's been lying dormant in the pit of my belly since the last time my husband touched me. You'd expect these things to have some sense of loyalty to the man I promised my heart and life to, but no. Here it is, unfurling like a lazy cat waking from a nap, purring for a man I'm still not sure I can call my friend.

Part of me wishes I could talk to Mal about it, but I can already see that conversation going left. Her round, whiskey-colored eyes going wide with surprise and then darkening with accusation. *The same way Eric's did the morning of his accident.* My heart lurches in my chest, and I force my brain to shift gears. Tacking on thoughts of Eric on the tail end of my internal monologue about Dominic feels so wrong. No. It doesn't just *feel* wrong, it *is* wrong.

Dominic is Eric's best friend, and I'm his wife. Nothing, not even four years of life without him, will change those facts. Who cares if I'm touched deprived and halfway attracted to the man? Who cares if he seems to be attracted to me too? None of it matters. None of it changes who we are and what we can never be. But it *can* change how I've been operating for the past four years though.

Swearing off men and romance for the rest of my life sounded like such a smart idea when I was still drowning in grief and more than ready to accept a lonely life with nothing but hugs from family and friends and orgasms provided by my vibrator to get me through, but this thing with Dominic has me rattled. It's made me realize a twenty-six year old, grief-stricken widow had no business making declarations for a healthy, vibrant thirty-year-old with a need for physical connection and a lot of life left to live.

Smiling, I lean back in my office chair and decide right then and there to be thankful for the whole situation with Dominic. If it wasn't for him, I would have never been brave enough to make this choice. To step outside of my grief and finally focus on the part of myself I've been neglecting for years: the strong, sexy Sloane who wants orgasms and post-coital cuddles even if she doesn't deserve the things that usually come along with it.

On a whim, I grab my phone and type out a text to Mal. She left the office with the rest of our team at five sharp, leaving me to sit in my office for hours and pretend to work while my brain ran itself ragged trying to figure things out. It's almost nine now, and the relief I feel at finally thinking things through is quickly swiped away as uncertainty swirls in my gut. I don't know how Mal is going to react to the content of my message, but she's the only person I can trust to walk me through this particular minefield. Before I can chicken out, I squeeze my eyes shut and press send.

> Sloane: I've decided to start dating again, and I want your help. Only if it's not weird for you though....

A few seconds later, my phone vibrates in my hand. I release a breath I didn't know I was holding as I read her responses, which chime in one after another. *The little drama queen can't be bothered to put everything in one response.*

> Mallory: Babeeee!
>
> Mallory: I'm so excited for you, and it's not weird at all.
>
> Mallory: You deserve to be happy, Sloane. Eric would have wanted that for you.
>
> Mallory: When do we start? I know SO many sexy ass men who would die for a chance to get at you.
>
> Mallory: Wait! What about James?! The man is in LOVE with you.

I scrunch my nose up at the mention of that name. Mal still doesn't know about the kiss, and I don't want to tell her since she might threaten to kick him in the balls the next time she sees him. Shaking my head, I decide it's best to keep it to myself until I've had a chance to let James know once and for all that I'm just not interested in something romantic with him.

> Sloane: First off, I love your dramatic ass so much. Thank you for not freaking out about this. Second, please don't try to give me any of your thirsty throw-aways who can't get over you. Third, James is a no. I'm not mixing personal and professional relationships.

Three dots pop up immediately, letting me know she's working on her response. While I wait, I clear my desk and lock up the office so I can finally head home. For the first time in a while I feel good, excited by the prospect of a future where I'm not in danger of ruining all of the important relationships in my life with inappropriate attraction, and the knot of guilt and self-loathing that's been lodged in my gut is starting to dissolve.

I smile as I crank my car. Confident that Mission Defeat Sloane's Skin Hunger is exactly what I need to make that knot, and the feelings that created it, disappear completely.

14

SLOANE

Now

"I didn't *say* I don't like it. I *said* it's not right for this room."

James pulls the box holding a brass crane bathroom faucet out of my hand and frowns at it. The same way he frowned at me an hour ago when I stood in his office and told him I didn't think it was smart for us to have anything other than the friendly, but professional, relationship we've had for years.

It was such an awkward conversation to have, and I was more than proud of myself for getting through it without stumbling over my words, but a bubble of panic rose in my throat when a frown tugged his mouth downward. To his credit, he recovered quickly and pulled a tight smile out of thin air before telling me he understood what I was saying. He even apologized for the kiss and told me he hoped his actions on Friday didn't change things between us, which sent a flicker of agitation through me.

Why do men think they can do things that change everything and then lay the burden of voicing exactly what it changed at our feet?

Of course, I didn't say that to him. Instead, I let my years of socialite training kick in and flashed him a fake smile I knew looked sincere then lied smoothly about the kiss not making me see him differently and changed the subject to the bathroom fixtures that'd just arrived. The conversation led us upstairs to the Presidential Suite, where Dominic and his team were hanging drywall, so James could see the fixtures in the room. His request made absolutely no sense to me, given there isn't anything here besides drywall, boxes of tile, and another man I need to have an awkward conversation with.

I glance at Dominic, who's leaning against the partially installed vanity of the master suite with a flat expression on his face. He hasn't said more than a handful of words since we barged into his construction zone, and James has only thrown a few nervous glances his way. There's a weird vibe between them that wasn't there before, but I don't have the energy to care because I've been arguing over the merits of a brass faucet for the better part of an hour and just want to go home.

"James," I pinch the bridge of my nose and pray for patience. "It's hard to get the full picture when you're standing in a room that's still being put together. Faucets and cabinet pulls are finishes. As in, meant to be installed and viewed when everything else is *finished,* so you can get the full effect."

The explanation comes off a little more condescending than I intend it to, but I can't even find it in me to be sorry. We chose these finishes together weeks ago. I had to send a freaking gift basket to the manager of the supply store just to get them in on time, and now he's looking at me like I brought in some builder-grade fixtures instead of a stylish, contemporary faucet that will go perfectly with the luxurious ambiance we're creating for this room.

He tosses the box on the unfinished top of the vanity. "I know what finishes are, Sloane. Just like I know this isn't the right finish for my bathroom. Find something else."

And without another word, he storms out of the room. Leaving me and Dominic staring behind him. I pull in a long breath through my nose and hold it for a second before exhaling. There's a dangerous mixture of anger and murderous intention swirling in my veins, and when I look at Dominic his expression is a mirror image of what I'm feeling inside.

"Does he make a habit of speaking to you that way?"

I don't know what calls to me first: the quiet darkness curling around his words or the thoughtful thumb rubbing across his lower lip as he considers me. Whatever it is, it hits me right in the pit of my stomach. Stroking the coil of desire there until it unravels into a continuous, undulating line that spells his name.

Fucking skin hunger. I think to myself, but even I can't miss the fact that he's not touching me right now. The reaction my body is having to him is caused completely by the muscle in his jaw that's raging with righteous anger for me.

I blink slowly then shake my head. "No. James is being a nit-picky asshole, which is the exact reason Issac felt like he had to quit on the last leg of the project, but he'll get over it. We had a....disagreement before we came in here."

"Lover's quarrel?" Dark eyes search my face.

"The opposite actually. I told him I didn't want anything more than a professional relationship with him." I pick at an invisible piece of lint on my skirt, willing to do anything for a break from the molten gaze burning into me, pulling words I don't want to say out of my mouth with no effort. "I thought he was okay, but the temper tantrum makes me think differently."

Dominic scoffs. "You think a man could know how your lips taste and not be mad about being told he'll never get to have that again?"

A ghost of an emotion moves across his face, darkening his expression for a moment, but it's gone in an instant.

"And his feelings are *my* problem? That seems a little unfair considering I never offered them to him in the first place."

His eyebrows raise, and his expression goes from dark anger to genuine surprise. The sudden change makes me realize, not for the first time, that Dominic thought James and I were a thing. And the idea makes him—Angry? Jealous?

"No." Dominic says softly, pushing off of the wall. "His feelings aren't your problem at all. Men who take things from you without your permission don't deserve their next breath let alone your consideration."

"Does that include you?"

He takes a step towards me. Now there are only a few inches of space between us. "No, Sloane, that doesn't include me."

I have to tip my head back to look at him. He's staring down at me, and this close I get the full effect of his eyes. They always look so dark to me, black pools with the faintest hint of bronze, but now I can see they're more of a rich, dark brown.

"It should."

"Why is that?" He cants his head to the side. "What have I taken from you without your permission, angel?"

The nickname pings around my head, crashing into the walls of my skull and ringing with a familiar sense of deja-vu I don't have time to fully explore because Dominic is leaning down now, mere inches from my face and my lips that tingle with the need to be kissed when his gaze falls on them.

I search my brain for an answer to his question and come up blank. There's no way to tell him his habit of touching me has stolen my resolve to maintain a solitary existence. There's no way to describe his role in discovering my skin hunger, and the subsequent plan to alleviate it, without sounding like a complete weirdo, so I latch onto the only real thing he's taken from me and hope for the best.

"On Sunday at Mama's...you touched me. You touched my mouth."

I hate the way I'm stumbling over my words. Hate how breathless I am while I'm trying to make it sound like I haven't spent the last forty-eight hours replaying every second of our encounter in my head. Dominic's lips quirk.

"I did do that, but I don't think it counts."

"*It counts*. I didn't give you permission to touch me." *Didn't give you permission to ignite a fire in my veins no amount of time with my vibrator can put out.*

"You're right, but I think there's a difference between me and James."

The air between us is thick, and it's a struggle to pull in a full breath. "And what would that be?"

"I'm your friend."

Any other day I'd be laughing at the declaration. The idea of being friends with Dominic has always felt impossible to me, and it feels infinitely more impossible now that his heated gaze is telling me the word 'friend' might mean something different to him than it does to me.

"You are?" I sound desperate and needy. Like the one thing I want more than anything in this world is for this man to say we're friends.

"Yes." He nods slowly. "Now ask me why that makes what I did to you on Sunday different from the clumsy lip attack James subjected you to on Friday."

What I did to you... Those words, combined with the finality of his command, send waves of desire coursing through my veins and straight to my clit. I shuffle on my feet as I feel the evidence of my arousal pooling in my core. God, I need to get away from this man.

I press my lips together. There's no way in hell I'm going to obey his order. It doesn't matter if my brain is screaming at me to do exactly that. Dominic's eyes glow with triumph like even my resistance satisfies him.

"Go on, angel. You know you want to know."

The use of his new, but somehow familiar, nickname makes my toes curl.

"Just tell me, Dominic." I blow out an unsteady breath.

He chuckles darkly. "Well, I think you know that at its most basic level friendship is about taking care of one another, and that's what I did on Sunday. I took care of you."

A shiver runs down my spine at the double entendre. "You wiped icing off of my face. Let's not make it sound like you saved me from a burning building or something." *Or like you gave me back-to-back mind-blowing orgasms with your wicked mouth because that only happened in my dreams.*

"I saved you from the embarrassment of walking around with icing on your face." His grin is wolfish. "I think that falls quite comfortably in the 'taking care of a friend' column."

I shake my head. "Stop saying it like that. You make it sound—"

"What? Tell me how I make it sound, Sloane." His words are playful, but his tone is the exact opposite. It's rough, husky, sinful to match the wicked curve of his lips.

"You know what it sounds like, Dominic."

"I do." He reaches up, brushing the same thumb that was just skating across his lower lip over mine. "I just want to hear you say it."

I glare at him. "Dirty. It sounds dirty."

His other hand comes up and now he's cradling my face, hungry eyes steady on my mouth. My lips are tingling, and I know my skin is flushed. I can feel the heat creeping into my cheeks, burning up underneath the rough skin of his palms.

"Is that a problem for you, angel?"

"Yes." *No.*

"Why?" He licks his lips, and the quick swipe of his tongue sends my mind into a free fall. Vivid images of all the obscene things he could do to me with that tongue bombard me, and another warm rush of arousal slips down my spine.

"We're not like that, Dominic. We can't be like that." *Can we? Please say we can.*

He takes another step forward and steals every bit of air from my lungs when his erection presses into my stomach. And *oh, my God,* the feel of him. Hot and hard, against me has me biting my lip to stifle the moan clawing up my throat. My eyes fall closed on their own accord, but I can still feel his gaze on me.

"Stop biting your lip and look at me, Sloane."

But I can't do it. I can't look at him. He releases my face, and his hands glide down my neck, coasting over my shoulders and arms. It's like he can't stop touching me, and nothing in me wants him to. His fingers feel exactly how I imagined: rough from years of physical labor and hot enough to brand me.

"You've thought about what it would feel like for me to touch you?"

Fuck, I said that out loud?

My eyes pop open, and my reward for the delayed response to his command is diving headfirst into two liquid pools of pure desire and *need.* A look so raw and carnal I want to look away again because if I don't, I'm going to explode right here in James' unfinished bathroom. I start to turn my head, but his hand comes up and catches my chin between two long fingers—forcing me to look at him, to bear witness to the unexpected desire pouring off of him.

"Answer me, Sloane."

Another command. One that matches the heat and severity of his gaze. My lips part but the words won't come. I don't know how to tell him his touch has been in my mind for days on end, that I've dreamed of him touching me just like this except with a lot less clothes between us. Putting those words into the world would make them too real, so I settle for a small nod. His answering smile makes my knees weak.

"I want to kiss you. I need to know if you taste as good as you do in my dreams."

What? The confession is a low growl, one that has me squeezing my legs together in a laughable attempt to quell the ache between my thighs. Before I can say anything, he dips his head and presses his lips to mine, rendering me motionless. Warm and wet lips work against my stiff and stunned ones. I can't remember the last time I've welcomed a kiss from a man, but damned if this doesn't feel amazing.

Dominic's kiss is hungry yet gentle. Both of his hands are back on my face, tilting my head so he can slant his full lips over my mouth. A moan rings out, and it takes a second for me to realize it's mine. He laughs, and it's a sensual, dark sound full of promises I shouldn't want him to keep. "Quiet, angel." He whispers against my lips. "Do you want everyone to know what's happening in here right now?"

His words should scare me. The idea of any member of his team walking in on us like this—with Dominic's dick pressed into my stomach and my body soft and pliable against every hard inch of his—should be like having a bucket of ice water poured over my head, but it just intensifies my need, making it a tangible thing in the room.

I want to feel his skin under my hands and find out if my touch affects him as much as his affects me, so that's what I do. I run my hand down his face, over the hairs of his beard that are tickling my face. And then, when it's not enough, I fist his shirt in my hand, tugging hard to bring him closer to me. Dominic releases a groan of satisfaction. And then that wicked tongue swipes over my bottom lip, coaxing me to open for him. My body obeys his command without any direction from my brain.

Suddenly he's tasting me, groaning into my mouth like a starving man who's just had the first bite of an amazing meal. I want to laugh at the way he's disregarding the warning he just gave me, but a shiver rolls down my spine at the sound. *It's so damn sexy.* Dominic traces the path of the shiver over the thin fabric of my blouse, and that familiar zip of energy races through me. Somewhere in the back of my mind, I'm screaming at myself to stop—telling myself it doesn't matter that my body feels alive under his touch or that I'm so turned on the evidence of it must be soaking through the lace of my thong—because this isn't right.

I pull back. "Dominic."

"*Sloane.*" He draws it out. It's similar to the way he did on Sunday when the sight of his mouth curling around my name set my soul on fire. His lips move to my neck, and he takes a deep breath, inhaling my scent before dropping more kisses down my throat to my collarbone. My pulse pounds in my ears, stealing all of my thoughts.

"Dominic, please…" The desperate plea hits the air, and Dominic freezes. He pulls back to search my face, and I wonder what he sees there—desire, hunger, panicked need that matches his own.

"What is it?" Another kiss to my lips. Soft and quick like he knows he'll have the chance to do it again. "Tell me what you want, angel."

My eyes fall closed when he pulls my bottom lip between his teeth, bites it, and then releases it. Suddenly, I'm all sensation, trembling in the hands of my husband's best friend. Dying for his lips to coast over mine again. For his hands to touch me, to do something about the incessant need that's like a heartbeat between my legs. Why am I stopping this again?

Oh, yes. We're at work, and this is Dominic 'Asshole' Alexander. The man who has spent more than a decade insulting me, glaring at me, taking every chance he got to let me know just how much he disliked me. "You don't like me," I whisper. "We don't like each other. Why are we doing this?"

Another dark chuckle rumbles in his chest as he rolls his hips into me, letting me feel how turned on he is. His dick is a bar of hot steel against my stomach. I moan—a strangled, erotic purr I've never heard myself make.

"Every time I'm around you lately, I have one of these. Just from being near you, breathing in your scent, seeing your smile, and now just from kissing your pretty mouth."

My cheeks heat at his words. I had no clue I affected him this way. Something close to feminine pride swells in my chest.

"I think, we're well past the point of discussing whether or not I like you. As for how you feel about me...." He starts moving, forcing me backward until my back collides with the wall. "Well, you could say you hate me right now, and I'd still want you to sit on my face."

"Dominic!" I gasp, slapping him in the chest and trying to sound horrified instead of turned on at the thought of his face between my legs. I don't know why I even bother. It's clear to me how thrilled I am at the idea of Dominic liking me. Wanting me. That dangerous swell of feminine pride in my chest expands. Encouraged by the heat of his body soaking into mine, mixing headily with a need so intense it has my nipples tightening into hard peaks I know he can feel pressing into him. I can't tell if I'm devastated or relieved that he can't feel the way my clit is throbbing, begging for his attention. For a release I somehow know only he can give me.

How can I be so certain of that?

Dominic sees right through my act. His sinful mouth curls into a devilish grin before swooping down and sealing over mine again. He dips his tongue into my mouth with imploring strokes that mimic the way his hips are subtly thrusting into me, branding me with the evidence of his desire. Both his hands slide down my body and reach around, gripping my ass and then lifting me up. He pins me in place with one powerful thigh wedged between my legs and the pressure is *exquisite*. I roll my hips, rocking shamelessly against him to chase the familiar building of pressure that promises an earth-shattering release.

"Fuck, Sloane, *look at you.*" He whispers hoarsely, breaking the kiss to take in the sight of me riding his leg. His eyes are narrowed and full of heat; the set of his jaw tense and the muscle in it ticking in the most familiar way. I lean forward, intent on scraping my teeth across that infuriatingly beautiful muscle, but Dominic pins me to the wall with one hand on my hip. His fingers are rough as they dig into my waist, but I don't care because now he's directing my movements. Urging me to angle my hips forward, so the demanding bundle of nerves is rubbing against his leg with every swirl of my hips.

And the idea of us working together like this—as a unit, a team—with my pleasure as its sole focus has me half-crazed with wanting him. Dying for more than his powerful thigh between mine, his commanding hand at my waist, and his reverent lips on my skin. Even as my orgasm builds, I'm hyper-aware of the empty ache inside of me. Of the hungry clenches of my walls that won't be satisfied this way.

"Dominic, I need—"

"I know, angel." He brushes his lips over mine, tasting my plea. "But I can't give you that now. Not here."

The promise of another moment like this with him sends a wave of panic through me, but it's quickly swept away as his other hand comes up to grip my breast and nimble fingers tease my nipples. Plucking and strumming them until I'm panting and frantic with the need to come. *More.* My body screams. *More. More. More.*

As if he can read my mind, Dominic tightens his grasp on my waist. Moving me in slow, intentional swivels that have me whimpering desperately into his mouth while he presses his leg harder against me.

"You're so beautiful when you're about to come." His gaze is hot on my face, molten lava that burns me up from the inside out. "I can't wait to have you like this again, but next time you'll be coming on my dick. Do you want that, angel?"

I can't answer, but he doesn't care. He doesn't need a verbal response because my body is telling him everything he needs to know. "I know you do." He leans forward and plants a hot, wet kiss on my collarbone. "This feels amazing, but it's not enough for you is it, baby?

Next time we'll have hours. I'll strip you down with my teeth, so I can see every inch of you while I fuck you against the wall."

My pussy ripples around the empty pressure building in my core. The image Dominic paints of us with his words pushes me to the brink. I lean forward, burying my face in his neck and biting hard to muffle the strangled noise being ripped from my throat as my orgasm shatters me, slamming into me until I'm nothing but tiny fragments of lust and desire, and the only thing holding me together is Dominic's large body caging me to the wall. His rough voice, reverent and worshipful, as he runs his hands up and down my back.

I come back down slowly, shivering into the crook of his neck and trying desperately to pull in a lungful of air that isn't obstructed by the lump in my throat. I swallow several times in hopes of clearing it out, but the sinking feeling in the pit of my stomach lets me know it's not going anywhere.

Not before it destroys me.

Panic grips me first. Rooting me in place so guilt and shame can latch onto me with ease, washing away every remnant of the thrill and exhilaration I felt just moments ago. Without the fuzzy haze of lust clouding my mind, I can't hide from them. I can't beat them back or shut them down, and I feel like I'm being eaten alive.

My heart starts to pound. Tiny beads of sweat dot my hairline. And I *still* can't fucking breathe. I'm vaguely aware of my arms dropping from Dominic's neck, of my hands at his chest pushing him away from me while tears slip down my face.

Stay calm. You're okay. You are okay. The rational part of my brain croons, but the other part—the part screaming for me to get far away from this man so I can cry my eyes out—is louder.

And I have no choice but to let it win.

15

DOMINIC

Now

S loane's desperate pants ringing in my ears are the only thing tethering me to Earth. I'm vaguely aware of the praises spilling from my mouth and skating across her skin, but even I don't know what I'm saying. I just can't stop talking to her, can't stop thanking her for giving me all of the things I resigned myself to never having the moment I saw her smile at Eric with the whole world shining in her eyes.

I'll never forget walking into our dorm that day and seeing her sprawled out on his bed, a goofy smile curving her perfect lips, and a question about finishing what I'd started hanging in the air between us. Except none of it, not the question or her smile, was meant for me. It shouldn't have hurt—weeks of listening to Eric talk about her and seeing pictures of them together on social media should have prepared me—but in that moment all I felt was pain.

Pain that increased tenfold when Eric walked in on us arguing and turned the scowl she was giving me into a smile that made her eyes glow in a matter of seconds. And that same smile killed all of the hope I'd foolishly held onto for months died because out of all the things I saw shimmering in the dapples of gold the night we met—joy, wonder, lust, intoxication—she never looked at me like that. Like I was everything good and right in her world.

Eric's presence soothed her. His touch smothered the flames of the fire I was all too happy to ignite. Watching them together was hard at first. Knife sliding into your heart and twisting deeper and deeper with every breath until your body is nothing but a gaping wound, hard. Leaking blood, spilling hope, love, and any desire for happiness on everything you touched, hard.

And then the dreams started, glimpses of the future I forfeited flashing through my mind on an endless loop. All of them starring my best friend's wife: the woman I pretended to hate in the light of day but made love to in the darkest corners of my mind every night.

I *should* have felt guilty. Eric was my brother in every sense of the word and coveting the love of his life should've been more than enough reason for me to hate myself. But in true Alexander fashion, I didn't. Instead, I rationalized. I told myself the dreams were okay because Eric got to have *her*. He got her smiles, her laughs, her soft moans, and breathless pleas for more. He got everything.

When those thoughts still weren't enough to assuage the guilt, and I could barely look myself in the mirror, I went dark, telling myself we should both be glad I wasn't more like my father. A man who would have never stepped aside and settled for dreams when there was a chance he could have the real thing.

Somehow, probably just to spite the strands of Gabriel Alexander's DNA coursing through my veins, I managed to survive. Living off of scraps that were unsatisfying and apparently inaccurate because even the most explicit ones couldn't hold a candle to what just happened between me and Sloane in this bathroom.

My heart is pounding in my chest, smacking against my rib cage while every drop of blood aches painfully inside the erection I still have pressed against Sloane's stomach. Another bead of precum leaks out of my tip, and I know I have less than a minute to disentangle myself from this woman before I lose my shit and take her against the wall.

Sloane doesn't give me the chance to move. Her hands come up to my chest and start pushing. Gently at first, and then with more force, like she can't wait to put some distance between our bodies. I pull back, expecting to see her flushed and sated, eyes still hazy and soft with lust for me. Instead, I find tears streaming down her face and a sullen expression marring her beautiful features.

Shit.

She's still shoving at my chest, so I lower her gently to the ground with a slide of my leg. The empty look in her eyes and the deafening silence in the room makes moving from between her thighs awkward as hell. Once I'm free, my hands bracket her waist just long enough to make sure she's steady on her feet, and then I drop them.

It hurts to let her go.

Especially when she looks like she could use a hug like the one I gave her on Friday when she was upset about that fight with her mom. But today it seems like I'm the source of her tears, which makes my chances of being the person to comfort her significantly lower. I probably have a five percent chance of not having my head bitten off if I try to touch her right now, but I'm willing to take the gamble if it means getting rid of the storm cloud that's gathered over her head.

I reach out, putting my hand gently on her forearm. "Are you okay?" She shrugs me off before my brain even registers our bodies have touched. The tears are flowing freely now, rolling like waves while she looks everywhere but at me.

"What's the matter?"

It's such a dumb question because anyone looking at the panic creeping into the corners of her eyes and the dejected slump of her shoulders would know what I'm too scared to hear her admit: she's ashamed. The guilt of what she just did, and who she did it with, is threatening to eat her alive.

I know that's what it is because I feel it too. A millstone around my neck that's never really gone away but gets a bit heavier every time I see her and my heart skips a beat just to remind me she's the only person who's ever truly owned it. It started in on me the second she walked in the room with James today, looking all annoyed with him but blushing every time I glanced at her. I wanted her then, even though I had no reason to hope she would let me have her.

And now that she has, she regrets it.

Why wouldn't she? It's not like you're Eric. You're not the man she swore her life and love to. You don't make things better for her. You just make them more complicated.

"Sloane—" I start, but she shakes her head. Both of her hands are working at her clothes, trying to straighten the wrinkles on her chest where I kneaded her breasts only moments ago. My gaze darkens. I want to beg her not to erase the proof that this moment happened, but I fight the urge because I know it'll only make the situation worse.

"Can you please turn around?"

Her voice breaks on the last word and tears fall steadily down her face. The last thing I want to do is turn my back on her, but I can't deny her request. I turn and stare at the drywall, ears primed and listening for any sound that comes from her. There's a slight rustle of fabric as she shifts her skirt back down. A gasp as she smoothes her fingers over her curls, and then sniffles. First, they're small, so faint I think I'm imagining them, but when they turn into sobs I whirl around to face her.

Her clothes are straight now. All evidence of our encounter is gone, save for the puddle of liquid arousal she's left on my leg. It's soaked through the denim of my jeans, so it's not visible at all, which is good because it would probably only add to the great, heaving sobs wracking through her body. She's got a hand clamped over her mouth, trying, and failing, to stifle the broken sounds pouring out of her.

My heart twists. *Fuck, does she regret what we just did that much?*

I move towards her, and she turns away from me, shrinking further into herself. I take another step, my front pressing to her back, and wrap my arms around her. This time she doesn't move away, and relief floods me when she relaxes into my hold. But it only lasts for a second before it transforms into something more destructive while I listen to her cry.

Her tears seem to go on forever, each sob bleeding into another until I can't tell where one begins and another ends, and I don't move or breathe because I'm too scared to remind her I'm the one comforting her.

When they turn into soft sniffles, I put my hands on her hips and turn her around. I need to understand what went wrong and how I can stop it from happening next time—*if there's going to be a next time—* but she still won't meet my eyes.

"Sloane, I—" I don't know what to say because there's nothing I can say to relieve her of the burden of her guilt and grief. "It's okay, angel. Please don't cry."

Her back goes ramrod straight and then she's pulling away from me. Our gazes lock, and I wish like hell she wasn't looking at me because there's nothing masking the absolute devastation playing across her features and nowhere to run from those watery eyes, flushed cheeks, or trembling lips threatening to destroy me. It breaks my heart to see her like this, to know being with me in the most basic way did this to her.

"Don't." Her chin wobbles. "Please don't call me that."

This is the sickest form of confirmation, undeniable proof of just how wrong I've always been for her. It doesn't matter how long I've wanted her or how much I loved the girl I met all those years ago, I wasn't right for her then and I'm sure as hell not right for her now. *Why did I think I ever could be?*

I knew better than any other man that might pursue her what I was up against: the memory of her perfect husband who was funny, kind, and loved her beyond belief.

Eric never raised his voice at her or intentionally provoked her to anger. He wouldn't have taken more than a kiss from her while she was working, and he damn sure wouldn't have pushed her to the edge when she was barely recovered from a fight with yet another person who wanted things from her she didn't want to give.

But I'm not Eric.

Honestly, right now I feel a lot like my dad. Reckless and self-serving with a nasty habit of disregarding other people's needs in favor of his selfish desires. My stomach hitches, protesting at the thought of being anything like my father, but the proof is right here looking at me with defeated hazel eyes.

"I have to go," Sloane whispers, more to herself than to me. "I have to get out of here."

When she pushes at my chest a final time, I don't have it in me to stop her. I watch her walk out of the room on unsteady feet, teetering on heels that make no sense for a construction site. Her head hung low and her chin tucked into her chest.

And seeing that—her entire body bowed and broken with regretting me—finally destroys me.

I don't know how long I stand in there, wrapped in shame and already missing the warmth of her body, but when I finally start moving, my feet are blocks of cement. Only two of my guys, Malcolm and Jason, are still working in the interior of the suite. They're both too focused on the piece of drywall they're installing in the space that will serve as the living room to pay any attention to me, which is fine because my mind is on Sloane.

On the hurt in her eyes and the defeat lining her features. Those heart-wrenching sobs tearing through her like a thousand tiny knives puncturing my chest. I don't have to go out looking for her to know she's left the building. I can feel her absence in my bones.

In another life, I would go after her, hold her in my arms and make everything okay, but if the past few minutes have taught me anything it's that my hands are not a source of solace for Sloane. As fucked up as it is, I wish Eric was here, so I could tell him how I screwed it all up. He would know exactly what to say to her, exactly how to fix the mess I've made, but unfortunately for both of us, he isn't.

If he was here, she never would have let you touch her. And you would still be pretending to hate her guts to keep everyone from seeing how much you love her.

God, this is all so fucked up.

It's the kind of mess only an Alexander man could make, but unlike my bastard of a father, I don't plan on leaving Sloane to pick up all of the pieces on her own. She won't let me comfort her, and I can't give her Eric, so I'll make sure she has the next best thing. Grabbing my phone, I type out a quick message to Mal.

Dominic: Can you go check on Sloane? She didn't look well when she left the hotel a while ago.

There. It's the vaguest message I've ever sent, but I know it'll be enough to get Mal moving. She's too much like Eric not to jump into action when someone she loves needs her.

Mal: I was just wondering why she wasn't back at the office yet. I'll swing by the house and check on her.

That's the Kents for you. Caring. Selfless. Loyal to a fault. Knowing Mal will be with Sloane soon, taking care of her in a way I now know she'll never let me, does nothing for the crack in my chest, but I can't find it in me to care.

I deserve this pain. I practically begged the universe for it the first time I touched her skin after years of holding her at arm's length with nothing but my words, so it's on me. All the hurt I feel, all the pain Sloane feels, lies squarely on my shoulders, and I'll bear it because that's what you do for the people you love.

You put their needs before your own.

You take the rain, so they can dance in the sunshine.

You place a bandage over the gaping hole in your chest, so blood doesn't spill on their shoes.

I've done it for her before, and it might take time, but I'll do it again. Really, it was so stupid of me to think she would ever want more from me. Her enemy. Her husband's best friend. A man who was so caught up in his desire he didn't even think about what would come after the spell broke.

She deserves so much better than that, and the best thing I can do is get out of her way and give her a chance to find it.

Tossing my phone back in my work bag, I square my shoulders and let the resolute vow to leave Sloane Kent the fuck alone wash over me. I don't expect it to bring me peace, but I'm caught off guard by the ferocious way my body rejects the old promise made new.

My skin tightens, and my fingers ache at the thought of never holding her again. My shoulders grow tense and another pound is added to the millstone around my neck. I pull in a deep breath and push it out slowly, willing my body to give, begging for the pressure to let up *just a little,* but it doesn't happen.

Frustrated, I turn and walk towards my guys that are still working. I grab another ladder and position it underneath them then climb up to hold a corner of the large drywall slab in place. With my help, the job is done in minutes, and we all silently agree to move on to hanging the next slab.

After the ceiling is completely covered, I tell the guys to take a break and start taping the seams myself. It's tedious work, but the monotony is exactly what I need to get my mind off of losing Sloane before I got the chance to have her.

* * *

Every muscle in my back is coiled tightly, protesting the excessive amount of work I put in today, as I hop out of my pickup and walk into my apartment building. It was close to eight when I called it quits at the hotel, and by the time I left, every inch of drywall we'd cut for the Presidential Suite was installed, taped, and ready for mudding—a job I decided to leave for Andre, my second in command.

I *should* be happy, but I'm not because throwing myself into work didn't do a damn thing to ease the pain of existing in a world where the one woman I want can never be mine. At this point, it feels like all I do, *all I've ever done,* is get over her, and I'm exhausted at the prospect of having to do it again.

The lobby is surprisingly empty when I make my way to the elevator and press the call button. The car comes quickly, and I let out a sigh of relief when I step inside and find it empty. My neighbors are friendly enough, but most of them feel compelled to engage in small talk during elevator rides, and I'm not in the mood.

I tap my fingers on my thigh impatiently as the car shoots to the tenth floor, anxious to get home and wash this day off. *Well, some parts of it.* Other parts I want to ink into my skin and keep with me forever.

The taste of Sloane's skin, the sweet smell of her desire curling in the air around us, my name on her lips.

Stop thinking about her.

It's a useless directive. One I've issued to my brain multiple times today because it won't get the damn hint. Instead of erring on the side of self-preservation, it's chosen to focus on the few minutes of heaven I got to experience today, stretching every second into immeasurable units of time until I can't be sure how long the actual encounter lasted.

And when it was done, it lingered on the moments that followed, obsessing over the tears that slid down Sloane's face and the sobs that rang out around us while she cried in my arms.

It's been damn near impossible not to reach out to her just to find out how she's doing, but I've managed to stop myself every time the urge to text or call her prickled at my fingertips. I know she doesn't want to hear from me. Hell, for all I know she's pissed I sent Mal to check on her.

Mal.

Now there's someone I *could* contact and get all the information I want and some I don't. The girl is a chronic over-sharer, and that's never been limited to details about her life. My heart lifts at the prospect of exploiting my only viable option for figuring out what's going on with Sloane. I'll have to be careful though, keep my phrasing vague and be sure to sound uninterested because if Sloane didn't tell her what happened, I sure as hell won't be the one to let it slip. With my decision made, I pull out my phone and text Mal.

> Dominic: Hey. Was everything okay with Sloane? We can't afford to lose our lead designer at this point in the project.

There. Let it sound like I only care about her well-being as far as it relates to her job. *Asshole Alexander, indeed.* The elevator doors part and I exit, thankful my door is only a few steps down at the end of the hall. I waste no time getting inside, toeing off my boots and leaving them by the door so I don't track any worksite debris onto the hand-scraped hardwoods I just installed last year.

I make a beeline for my bedroom with my phone in my hand. I toss it on the bed, so I don't spend the rest of my evening desperately waiting for a message from Mal, and strip down before heading into the bathroom and starting the shower. With the water on the hottest setting, I step inside. Steam billows around me, enveloping my body and making a futile attempt at easing the tension in my muscles. I let the scorching water run over my muscles for long moments before accepting that relaxation just isn't in the cards for me and scrubbing myself clean.

When I emerge from the bathroom, clean but as tightly coiled as ever, my phone screen is lit with text notifications. I scoop it up and see three notifications: one from Kristen, one from Angie, my dad's nurse at the assisted living facility, and another from Mal. The gallop of my heartbeat demands I bypass Kristen and Angie's messages in favor of getting a small update on Sloane, and I obey it without question.

> Mal: She's fine. Don't tell her I said this, but I think she's just freaking out about the date she has on Friday. I keep telling her Eric would want her to be happy but....

The rest of Mal's overly expressive message blurs in front of me as red tints my vision. Sloane is going on a *date*. Unbidden, the moments we shared play back in my mind—Sloane's eyes half-hooded with lust, her breathy little moans, the way she bit her lip while she used me to find her release—and my blood roars in my ears.

Just the thought of someone else seeing her like that has bile rising in my throat. And the moments after... *Jesus*. I can't even think about some random asshole making her feel like shit because he doesn't understand what giving her body to someone else means to her.

Rage, white-hot and consuming, fills me, and without thinking I send my phone flying across the room. It hits the wall with a satisfying crack as the glass screen splits into tiny shards that refuse to let go of each other even though they're shattered.

I pull in shallow breaths, feeling the rise and fall of my chest even though no oxygen is making it into my lungs. This isn't happening. There's no way in hell this is happening.

And what are you going to do to stop it?

Before I can think of a response to the question that doesn't involve threatening bodily harm to every man that so much as looks at Sloane, my doorbell rings. Twice. And it's the second ring, the one following the first one so closely it might as well be one and the same, that has dread swirling in my gut because only one person rings my doorbell that way, and she's the last person I want to see right now.

Pulling on a pair of gray sweats and a black tank, I leave my shattered phone on my bedroom floor and head back into the living room, turning on the lights as I go. At this time of night, the moonlight mixes with the endless city lights and filters through the floor-to-ceiling windows of my living room, casting a romantic glow over the entire space. It's not the vibe I'm going for.

When I pull the front door open, Kristen is holding up a bag of food and wearing a smile that stretches across her face. Even in my sorry state, I can appreciate her beauty – the high cheekbones standing proud against flawless, tawny skin and accented by almond-shaped brown eyes that are always sharp and focused. Once upon a time, I lived to see a smile on her face, but that was before, back when making myself believe I had to live without Sloane was as crucial to my survival as my next breath.

"Kristen," I say, unable to keep the impatience out of my voice. "How nice of you to drop by completely unannounced."

She flips her long black hair, that's always bone straight, over her shoulder with a flicker of annoyance crossing her face. "I texted you. You never answered."

"Because I'm not in the mood to talk."

I also didn't get to read your message before I shattered my phone against the wall.

"Most people don't consider responding to a text message talking."

I frown at her. *Most people* don't take a lack of response as an invitation to come over. Especially not when the person they're texting called off their friends-with-benefits arrangement weeks ago. Which is exactly what I did after that fucker grabbed Sloane in the club and my hands remembered that nothing compared to the feeling of holding her.

"What do you want, Kris?"

"Can I come in please?" Tears shine in her eyes as she clutches the bag in her hand like a lifeline. "I had a really bad day at work and could use a friend right now."

Completely unnerved, and unwilling to play a part in shattering another woman today, I take a step back and gesture for her to come in. "Of course."

She breezes past me, and I pinch the bridge of my nose as I shut and lock the door behind us. I don't know how I ever let Kristen talk me into being anything other than friends after our three-year relationship ended.

We had a clean breakup, which was a miracle considering things started to deteriorate when she began dropping hints about wanting to get married and have kids in the next two years. I wasn't exactly opposed to the idea of marriage and a family, but I couldn't shake the feeling that she only wanted those things because she thought she was *supposed* to have them. Like tying your life to another person and bringing children into the world were just two more things for her to cross off of her checklist of a life.

Nothing about that sounded appealing to me, so I called it quits and hoped in time she would find someone who would give her the things she wanted. Then in early April, about a month after our break-up, she showed up on my doorstep in nothing but a trench coat and proposed a casual arrangement because her career as a defense attorney didn't leave her time to start something new.

Foolishly, I agreed and inadvertently turned a clean breakup into a minefield of messy expectations and blurred lines.

"I got all of your favorites, so I hope you're hungry," Kristen says as she kicks off her heels and leaves them beside my work boots on her way to the kitchen.

I stare at them for a moment, taking in the familiar and domestic image that hints at the life she wanted us to have together. The sight makes my gut wrench because the only person I've ever wanted a life like that with is Sloane, even when she was living it with my best friend. Even when I was committed to Kristen and trying my damnedest to love her like I loved Sloane.

Stop. Thinking. About. Her.

Shaking my head to bring my wandering mind back to reality, I focus my attention on the woman in my kitchen, unpacking the Chinese takeout she brought over and moving around with a familiarity that attests to the years we've spent together. Something—probably the part of me that feels guilty as hell for stealing years of her life to try and soothe the part of me yearning for the one woman I could never have—softens towards her a little.

"I'm starving," I say as I join her in the kitchen.

She bumps me with her shoulder as I set out plates for her to slide the food onto. Her eyes are dry now, and her smile is huge while she talks about her day. And even though my heart and mind want to continue to obsess over Sloane, I force myself to focus on the details of Kristen's stressful new case and the partner offer she'll get if she wins it.

"I don't think I've ever wanted anything this bad, Nic." She peeks up at me through her lashes. "Except for….well, you know."

"Kris."

My flat tone has her hands flying up in surrender, but there's still a suggestive tilt to her lips that tells me she's not taking me seriously. "I'm sorry! You know how I get when I'm under a lot of stress."

I set my fork down. "I do, but what I told you on Saturday still stands."

"You're no fun anymore, babe." I bristle at the term of endearment and rise from the table, picking up my half-eaten food and carrying it back to the kitchen. Kris is hot on my trail. "You never even told me why you wanted to end things, Nic. Did you meet someone else?"

"Does it matter?"

She crosses her arms and leans back against the counter. "Yes, it matters."

I round on her as the irritation from earlier in the day catches fire in my veins. The last thing I want to do is argue with Kristen about our 'relationship' when there's a gaping hole in my chest where my heart used to be. I scrub a rough hand over my face and search for an answer. Even if Sloane hadn't walked out on me, even if there was a chance we could be something, I wouldn't tell Kristen because she has a jealous streak a mile long.

Yet another reason why I should have never said yes to this arrangement.

"There's no one else."

She pins me with a hard stare, examining me with the same expression I know she uses to read her clients for the truth, and I stare back at her because I don't have anything to hide. There can't be someone else when you aren't actually in a relationship, and the person you want just walked out on you.

"So we're just done with the friends-with-benefits thing?"

"Yes."

"Okay."

Relief courses through me, washing out some of the irritation as Kristen and I smile at each other. Not being at odds with her right now feels nice, and it gives me hope for some kind of resolution with Sloane that'll keep her in my life as something between what we are right now and what I've always hoped we could be.

16

SLOANE

Now

The week after Eric died was the longest of my life. Seven days of emptiness. Seven days of guilt gnawing away at me, eating me alive from the inside out. A week of tears and rage, of drinking and crying and cursing my existence. Of questioning God and, at my lowest point, praying for the strength to remove myself from this world because I didn't want to live without him. *If my mother thought I was being dramatic at the funeral, my behavior during that week would have given her an aneurysm.*

It was in that week that I made myself face the hard truth about what my future would look like without Eric: a quiet house, a lonely bed, no hand to clasp tightly in my hardest moments, no arms that felt like home, no kisses to my forehead while I slept

A solitary existence. That's what I was in for, and funnily enough, it was exactly what Eric was convinced I wanted when he walked out the door that day, and I let him believe it because I was scared. It all seems so pointless now: the fight, my fear, his hurt. I could have spared us all if I had just been brave enough to tell the truth, but instead, I let my fear keep me rooted to the spot while I watched my husband walk out of my life for the last time. That day, when my ability to be brave mattered more than anything, I was a coward, and, four years later, I still am.

Just in a different way.

For the last few days, my fear has had me in constant motion. Whirling in and out of La Grande Nuit like a short-lived tornado because the thought of ending up alone with Dominic after what happened on Tuesday terrified me. It'd taken an emergency session with my therapist and a full-blown breakdown in front of Mal—where I lied and said I was feeling guilty about going on a date—just to pull me out of the pit of despair I was plunged into when the post-orgasm clarity hit me, and I wasn't willing to go back there for anything. Not even for another endless moment with the delicious heat of Dominic's body pressed against mine or the intoxicating feel of his fingers digging into my flesh.

I just couldn't risk it.

So I spent the week running, caught somewhere between desperately wanting Dominic to seek me out and tell me my erratic behavior was completely understandable and hoping he never looked in my direction again. Ultimately, I landed on hoping he never looked in my direction again, and that's exactly what I got.

In the rare moments that we were in the same space, meetings with James or passing each other in the hallway he looked right through me like I didn't even exist. Having my silent wish granted shouldn't have hurt, but it did because it took me back to the time before our weird friendship happened and made me realize I had no clue what it meant to truly be iced out by the man.

For years I hated him for the way he treated me, thinking his glares and hurtful words were the worst he could do to me, but this was different. This was stepping out of the safety of a warm car and having the cold bite into your skin. This was reopening a wound you thought was on its way to healing. This was a swell of dark clouds after weeks of sunshine. This was....the closest thing to heartbreak I've known since Eric died. Only it makes no sense to be heartbroken over a man I should hate myself for wanting.

Should being the operative word.

After the incident, I thought I hated myself, but the longer I sat with my feelings, the more I realized I didn't. Sure I was embarrassed about the way things went down, but ultimately I had to accept that I didn't *do* anything wrong. My husband is gone, and the vows I swore to him on our wedding day were intact when his heart stopped beating. All of the promises I made to him had been kept well past till death do us part. And like Mal has pointed out several times since I said I wanted to start dating again, Eric would want me to be happy.

Would she still be saying that if she knew you were the reason Eric was on the road that day? Would she still be so supportive of you dating if she knew you were dreaming of Dominic taking her brother's spot in your bed?

Now *that* I don't know. Okay, yes I do. I don't need to ask Mal to know she wouldn't be happy about any romantic developments between me and Dominic. This is the same woman who got mad at him for bringing me a slice of cake first, so I think it's safe to say all hell would break loose if she found out about Tuesday. There would probably be tears, accusations, and a stain of betrayal on our relationship that would never go away.

Just the thought of it makes me sick to my stomach. Thankfully, I don't have to wonder about whether the chemistry between me and Dominic is worth it—*it's not*—because he has iced me out so quickly and efficiently, my head is still spinning. *I just wish I knew why...*

"It doesn't matter," I whisper to myself as I search for the perfect shoes to pair with the outfit I've laid out on my bed in preparation for my date. That's right. I'm going on a date. Tonight I'm going to have dinner with a handsome man whose romantic interest doesn't threaten to implode my entire life, and I'm going to like it.

Okay, I'm going to try to enjoy it, but I can't make any promises.

"Sloane, why aren't you dressed yet? Ash will be here in twenty minutes." Mal storms into my room just as I'm exiting my closet with a pair of nude heels that make my legs look incredible. She has both hands on her hips and wrath shining in her amber eyes as she glares at my robe. "Please don't tell me you canceled."

"No, I didn't cancel. I just needed to find some shoes to go with my outfit."

I gesture towards the red satin dress I bought yesterday to get excited about this date with Ash Strickland—a former NBA star who dominated the court for some team on the west coast until he tore his ACL two years ago and was forced to retire at thirty-two. All the information I'd gleaned from the short Google search I ran on him last night told me he wasn't letting the massive blow to his plans slow him down at all. He went from owning the court to conquering the New Haven real estate scene in a matter of years.

Oh hell, now I'm quoting article headlines like a groupie.

"Great choice. Your boobs are going to look incredible in this."

Mal throws herself across my bed and smiles at me. I try to smile back, but it feels like more of a grimace because her comment has me thinking about Dominic kneading my breasts with just the right amount of roughness while he licked into my mouth with hungry strokes of his tongue.

"Thanks," I say weakly, spinning my wedding ring around my finger absentmindedly. Light catches the diamonds in the pear-shaped setting, sending luminescent shards glittering throughout the room with every revolution. She tracks each spin with her eyes but doesn't say anything for a long moment.

"Are you going to take it off?"

Our eyes meet, and I see an uneasiness there that I've been expecting for a while now. She's been going out of her way to be cheerful and supportive of me dating, but I know this has to be difficult for her. I move over to the bed and lay next to her, taking her hand in mine.

"No. I'm not taking it off even though I probably should. I mean it'll make the whole dinner thing awkward, but I don't want to be with anyone who doesn't understand what Eric meant to me. What he'll always mean to me."

Relief smoothes over the lines in her forehead. "It's weird right?" She turns her head and looks at me. I raise a brow, not understanding her question "Me being sad about you dating….it's weird." My lips part, ready and willing to dole out some reassurance, but she shakes her head. "Don't lie and say it isn't. We *both* know it makes it seem like I don't want you to move on even though I do." Her fingers thread through mine, and she gives my hand a light squeeze. "I *do* want you to find some happiness, Sloane."

"I know that Mal."

And I do, she's been my biggest cheerleader through this whole process. Hell, I would still be skimming through the prospects on Tinder if it wasn't for her. She nods, and I can tell my words have soothed her a little, giving her just enough strength to say the last part.

"But being here with you, seeing you get ready for a date, it just makes him being gone so…"

"Real." I finish for her, understanding exactly what she means. It was the hardest part about Tuesday. Realizing I didn't do anything wrong because the only person I could have technically betrayed was no longer here to be hurt by my actions. I glance at Mal. *Well, maybe not the only person.*

"Yeah," she breathes. "It makes it all too real."

"I don't have to do this if you're not ready yet, Mal." I sit up slightly, so I can look her in the eyes. She searches my face, amber eyes roving over every one of my features to gauge my sincerity. If we weren't having a rare serious moment, I would be annoyed that she's doubting me. Doesn't she know by now I would do anything to keep her from hurting? Including, but not limited to, canceling this date with Ash.

Doing so would bring Mission Defeat Sloane's Skin Hunger to a grinding halt, but I don't think it matters now that my attraction to Dominic is no longer an issue. *Okay, the attraction is still there, but it's not like I'm ever going to act on it again.* Maybe him acting like I don't exist is exactly what I need to put this thing to bed; if his touch ignited the flame, maybe his ice is enough to kill it.

A tiny bubble of hope springs in my chest, but bursts immediately when I catch sight of the drawer of my nightstand. It's not closed all the way, which means when I used my vibrator last night after waking up from a particularly explicit dream about Dominic I was too blissed out to secure it properly. The view is all I need to accept that my skin hunger, and treacherous brain, are still alive and well.

Fine. That just means I'll have to find a way to handle it that doesn't hurt Mal.

"No!" Mal shoots up from the bed and stands over me. Her hands are back on her hips, and the blonde bob she's been sporting since she took out her braids swings from the motion. "You said you wanted to do this, and I said I was going to help you, so this is happening." She grabs my hand and yanks me up onto my feet before continuing. "Plus, Ash is sexy as hell, and I happen to know for a fact he's amazing in bed."

I scrunch my nose. "How do *you* know that? Please tell me this isn't one of your left-over one-night stands, Mal." She laughs mischievously, and I pin her with a hard glare. If she's slept with Ash, then we might as well call him right now and tell him to stay home. I'm not planning on having sex with the man tonight but having dinner with him seems like a waste of an evening if there's no chance of it happening at all.

"Relax, will you?" Mal smacks my arm. "You were clear about not dating one of *my* exes." I narrow my eyes at the emphasis she placed on *"my."* The bit of tension I've been carrying in my shoulders all week increases tenfold when I realize Mal never told me how she knew Ash. I know it's not from college because I would have met him too, and it can't be from work because Studio Six doesn't deal with anyone I don't know.

"Mallory Pearl Kent."

"Oh my, god!" She rolls her eyes. "He used to date Jasmine. You remember her, right? She was my suitemate freshman year."

The name is familiar, but I can't picture the girl's face. I didn't even know she and Mal were still in touch, let alone swapping exes. *Lord, do I really need to do this?*

"Yeah," I mutter, twisting my ring around again. "I remember her."

Mal pads over to me, stilling my fidgety hands with her surprisingly steady ones. "Don't freak out, Sloane. They broke up right after he got injured because she didn't want her name attached to a washed-up athlete. Her words, not mine."

I shake my head, suddenly remembering the snooty, rail-thin girl with resting bitch face who was preoccupied with marrying rich. Throwing a man to the side as soon as he wasn't useful to her anymore sounds on-brand for her, but it's too bad she didn't have the foresight to hang in there for Ash's second act.

"She sounds like a dream."

Mal snorts. "Please, she's a money-hungry bitch who lacks empathy and basic decency, but her loss is your gain tonight, babe. Now get dressed because your date will be here soon!"

At that exact moment, my doorbell rings, and Mal's eyes go wide with a surprise I thought I was going to feel when my date showed up. I actually feel fine. Nothing but a little flutter of nerves that's easily tampered with a deep breath.

"Get dressed!" Mal hisses while she's running out of my bedroom. "I'll let him in."

I nod but say nothing as I watch her go. The door clicks behind her and everything goes quiet around me. I know I won't be able to hear anything going on downstairs, but I still try to listen. After a few moments, I turn to the full-length mirror and shrug out of my robe.

Smiling at my reflection, I admire how perfectly the black lace lingerie set I picked up yesterday fits. I adjust the garter belt and the lacy black cuffs wrapped around my thighs then grab my dress off the bed and slip it on. Zipping the back to the top without help is a bit of a challenge, so I wait for Mal to come back up to do it. I slip into my heels and walk over to the mirror to fasten my earrings and pick out a necklace. I'm clasping it on when Mal walks back in with the biggest smile on her face.

"Sloaneeeee!" She squeals when the door closes behind her. "He looks so good, and he's even nicer than I remember."

"That's great, Mal. Are you sure *you* don't want to go on a date with him?"

"Nah. I'm good. I already have plans for the night."

She zips up the back of my dress and smacks me on the ass. I shoot her a death glare.

"Oh, yeah?" I turn to face her. "You didn't tell me about any plans."

"I'm telling you now." She straightens my necklace and smiles at me. "Plus, I didn't want you to cancel on Ash to come with me, especially when I'm going to Reign."

The mention of the popular nightclub makes my pulse kick up a bit. She's right; I might be nervous about my date with Ash, but I don't think I'm ready to be in a nightclub right now either.

"I could have canceled and stayed right here in my bed."

"Sure, but your vibrator needs a break, babe."

Mal starts pushing me towards the door, and I choose to let her comment about my vibrator slide. When we reach the landing, Ash is standing at the bottom of the stairs waiting with a huge smile on his face. Mal was right. He does look good—over six feet tall, with light brown skin and curly hair that he keeps short. A muscular frame poured into a black polo and slacks. His brown eyes are warm as they take me in, raking over my body with a subtle look of appreciation before he steps forward to offer me his hand.

"Wow. Sloane, you're breathtaking."

"Right?" Mal exclaims from behind me. "I told her that dress makes her boobs look incredible."

Ash flushes and clears his throat, making a show of keeping his eyes on my face, and I can't help but laugh. "Thank you, Ash. You look nice tonight as well." He smiles pleasantly at me, giving my hand a light squeeze before letting it go.

"Are you ready to get going?"

"Yes, just let me grab my purse."

"Already got it!"

Mal pushes my bag, keys, and phone into my hand and shoos us out the door like she owns the place. Ash and I step out into the thick night air, and as we walk down the driveway towards his car, a sleek Audi convertible, his hand finds its way to the small of my back. I hold my breath, waiting to feel something besides the weight of it. A zip of electricity. A tingle of awareness. Something to indicate an underlying current of attraction between us, but there's nothing.

Ash opens the passenger door for me, and I slide in. The inside of his car smells nice—like sandalwood and vanilla. It's a good mix, but it doesn't compare to the warm spice and buttery leather of…. *Don't do that.* Ash rounds the car and gives me an easy smile as he slips into his seat and watches me secure my seat belt.

"All set?"

"Yes. I'm good to go."

"Perfect." He runs a hand over his hair, and I wonder if he's nervous. "I made reservations for dinner at Hill House. Have you ever been?"

Fancy. Hill House is one of the most exclusive restaurants in town. My parents like to go there for special occasions, and I think the last time I ate there was on my mom's birthday a couple of months ago. They don't require reservations, but I appreciate Ash going the extra mile to make one. It's a thoughtful gesture, especially for a first date. *Who needs sparks and electricity when you have thoughtfulness and intention?*

"Yes." I smile at him, surprised to find it's genuine. "I love their truffle fries."

"Ah. A woman who likes to eat. I think we'll get along just fine."

And we do. The ride into downtown flies by with us talking about my work and his. We discover that we have some mutual friends beyond Mal and his hideous ex-girlfriend, who I don't dare bring up because talking about past relationships isn't a smart thing to do on a first date when you're a widow. Ash is friendly and open, talking to me like an old friend rather than a virtual stranger, which helps the conversation flow easily. By the time we reach the restaurant, I'm relaxed and happy I didn't cancel on him.

Hill House is busy—even for a Friday night—so despite our reservations, we have to spend twenty minutes at the bar waiting for our table. Ash orders water for himself and a glass of white wine for me. I'm wrestling with my feelings about him ordering for me when I hear a familiar voice call my name from somewhere over my shoulder.

I turn around, surprise stamped across my face, and find my parents standing behind me. My mother's angular features are alive with delight as she takes in the picture of me standing next to Ash. I haven't seen or talked to her since that awful dinner last week, but you would never know it from the tight hug she envelops me in while my dad shakes Ash's hand.

"Darling." Mom purrs in my ear. "You didn't tell me you were seeing *Ash Strickland*. The man is even more handsome in person." I curb the urge to roll my eyes and paste on a fake smile as I disentangle myself from her arms.

"There's nothing to tell, Mother. We're on our first date."

Ash and my dad are beaming at each other like two old friends, and I can't tell if it's because they're both overly friendly people or if they know each other.

"Mom. Dad. This is Ash Strickland." I say, wondering if there's a point in making introductions when my parents already know who he is. "Ash, these are my parents." My dad smiles as he pulls me into a quick hug.

"No need for the introductions, Bean. Ash has been a client of mine for the last year."

Huh. I guess that makes sense. Dad's been a highly sought-after real estate lawyer for most of my life. His firm works with most of the major real estate developers in the state, including James' parents. And Ash, apparently. *This is rich. Running into my parents on my first date in years only to find they knew the man before I did.*

"Mark—" Ash clears his throat. "Uh, your dad, recommended this place for our date tonight." My skin prickles and heat blooms in my cheeks at the idea of my dad inadvertently choosing the location for my date tonight.

"But I didn't know the lovely young lady you were taking out was my Sloane." Dad looks between us, his face stretching into a wide grin.

Ash laughs."Yes, well, with the different last names, I didn't put two and two together."

The comment has my stomach twisting with panic, but I don't

know why. I know Mal told Ash I was married before, so it's not like I need to explain why my last name is different from my father's.

"Here's your drink, miss."

The bartender places a glass of white wine at my elbow. I smile thinly and thank her for it before taking a long sip. Everyone's eyes are on me, so I force myself not to chug the entire thing. My mom shoots me a pointed glare. It's a non-verbal warning. *Don't screw this up.*

"Mark, we should get going. I'm sure Sloane and Ash want to get back to their evening, and you owe me dessert."

She links her arm with Dad's and gives him a dazzling smile. The kind he's always helpless to resist, and for the first time, I'm thankful she knows all of his weaknesses. Dad smiles down at her. "Of course, my love. Sloane. Ash. I'm afraid this is where we'll have to leave you. Enjoy your dinner."

Thank God.

We say our goodbyes, and the panic bubbling in my chest doesn't subside until they're out of the building. Ash is quiet beside me, sipping the glass of water the waitress just slid his way, while I attempt to gather my thoughts.

"So," he says. "That was kind of awkward, but at least we know your parents like me."

I burst out laughing at the sheepish look on his face, and all of the awkwardness falls away. To my surprise, it stays that way for the rest of our evening. I tease Ash about my dad threatening him with bodily harm at their next meeting, and he makes a point of calling me 'Bean' while we wait for our entrees. By the time the bill comes, we've developed an easy banter that feels nice to have with someone who isn't Mal or Dominic—even though that lasted for all of two seconds.

Don't think about him.

Ash takes care of the bill and then offers me his hand. I take it and try to ignore the glaring absence of electricity between us. His grip is firm and comfortable, and it's *nice* to hold his hand, but it's not exactly stimulating. There's an attraction there but no real heat between us. No fire in my belly. No pinpricks of awareness skating across my skin.

And when he lets my hand go to give the ticket to the valet, I don't
mourn the loss of his warmth.

God, how I wish I did.

"Are you up for a nightcap?" Ash asks, his eyes slipping over my
body.

It's the third time I've caught him checking me out. I know I
should feel flattered, but it feels a little awkward having his eyes on
me. I mean, I appreciate his appreciation. After all, I bought this dress
just for tonight, so it feels good to know he likes what he sees. But
something is just....missing. Like the final piece of the puzzle that is
my desire is lingering at the edges of my brain, waiting to be clicked
into place.

Maybe it's just the awkwardness of the first date, or the whole
running into my parents thing, that's holding it at bay. Maybe we just
need a change of scenery, something more intimate and freeing than
the stuffy scene of the restaurant.

Ash waits patiently for my answer, and fire or not, I can appreciate
a man who knows when to talk and when to listen. That in and of itself
wins him a little bit more of my time tonight. Time to get used to his
eyes on me and maybe, just maybe, have the last piece of the puzzle
click into place.

Please, God.

"A nightcap sounds good, and I know the perfect place."

* * *

"THIS PLACE IS NICE. How'd you hear about it again?"

Ash's lips brush my ear every so slightly as we look out at the
packed dance floor of Reign. Being inside a nightclub after what
happened a few weeks ago was a little off-putting at first, but I figured
if I was facing my dating fears with Ash I might as well kill two birds
with one stone. Plus, being here with a date has me feeling marginally
safer.

He's standing close to me, one arm draped on the bar behind my
back while I scan the crowd for Mal. I texted her to let her know Ash

and I would be joining her, but she hasn't responded yet. Searching for her is proving to be a pointless task because she could be anywhere in the thick crowd on the first floor, where Ash and I stand, or living it up in one of the private booths on the second.

I turn towards him and lean close. "Mal told me about it. She said she was coming here tonight with a few of our friends."

That's not exactly the truth. Mal didn't say who she was coming out with, but I'm sure I'll know whoever it is. It's probably just a few girls from work or one of her many sorority sisters. Hopefully, she isn't on a date.

"Ahh." Ash nods like I've just cleared something up for him. "And you wanted to round out the evening by putting me on the chopping block for your friends. Got it."

"What? No, I—"

"It's fine. *It's fine.*" He wraps his arms around my waist and pulls me to him. "This will be the first time I've ever met the parents *and* the friends all in the same night, but I'm game." He smiles down at me, warmth and playfulness shining in his eyes, and I can't help but smile back. My breasts are pressed into his chest, and he gives them a cursory glance before honing in on my lips.

Then he's leaning forward, and I know he's going to kiss me.

Maybe. My heart screams, hoping against all hope for sparks, fireworks, or something in between. *Maybe.* My soul whispers as my eyes fall shut because that's what they're supposed to do when a handsome man is about to kiss you.

"Sloane."

The voice comes from behind me, and I would know it anywhere— the raspy, dark lilt that hasn't spoken my name in days but promises me pleasure and all-consuming desire every night in my dreams. Except tonight it's different somehow, laced with thinly veiled anger and the promise of danger.

Dominic.

I open my eyes and turn my head, trying to locate him in the group of patrons ordering drinks at the bar. It only takes a second. Our eyes meet at the exact moment that Ash's lips collide with my cheek. His eyes are still closed, and they pop open suddenly, surprised at missing their mark. I catch all of this out the corner of my eye because the majority of attention is on Dominic who's now standing in front of us with murder in his eyes.

"Uh, Sloane. Do you know this guy?" Ash asks, clearly put out by the apparent stranger interrupting us.

"Dominic," I murmur, still in shock at his sudden appearance. Both men look at me, probably wondering why I'm whispering in the middle of a loud ass club, and I clear my throat before trying again. "Ash, this is Dominic Alexander. Dominic this is Ash Strickland."

Shit. Why is introducing my date to Dominic more awkward than him meeting my parents? Ash steps forward and holds a hand out to Dominic. He's a few inches shorter than him, so he has to tilt his head back a little look him in the eye.

"Nice to meet you, man."

Dominic stares at his hand for a long minute before giving it a firm shake and letting it go. Ash steps back and curves an arm around my waist. Dominic tracks the movement with increasingly dark eyes before looking back at me.

"What are you doing here?"

He tilts his head to the side as he questions me, and I flush under the weight of his stare. This is the most he's looked at me since Tuesday when his eyes were positively feral with want. *Do. Not. Think. About. Tuesday.* I take a sip of my drink and hold his gaze.

"Ash and I are having a nightcap. What are you doing here?"

That's a dumb question. He's probably here with Mal because the chance of them both being at the same club by coincidence is pretty low. *Then again, so is running into your parents on your first date, but that happened.* Before Dominic can answer, a slender hand with perfectly manicured fingers slides around his torso in a show of possession. Then, just as suddenly as her hand appeared, Kristen is standing beside him.

"Please tell me you've already ordered the drinks, Nic." She beams up at him with a hungry glint in her eyes that makes my blood boil.

Dominic is still looking at me. His eyes are hard with an emotion I can't name, and his body has gone stiff under her touch. It does nothing to soothe the bitterness curling around the base of my spine at seeing her touching him. I half expect Dominic to throw her hands off of him, but he doesn't move a muscle. Kristen turns her focus to me and Ash, her long hair swishing with the motion. She blasts us with a smile that shows all of her teeth but doesn't reach her eyes.

"Sloane! I haven't seen you in forever!" Her voice is an octave too high, trying too hard to sound friendly when I know for a fact she can't stand me, as her gaze slides over Ash's hand around me. "It's so nice to see you out, and dating again *so soon.*"

Our interactions have always gone like this, the fake smiles and friendly tone used to disguise the backhanded compliments, but my back still stiffens at the patronizing pout she gives me when she says that last part.

"Yes, it has been a while hasn't it? I think the last time I saw you was in March when you came to dinner at Mama's." *When you were still Dominic's girlfriend and not just the woman he fucks from time to time.*

I keep my tone friendly, but I know she catches the implication when her smile thins out and turns into more of a grimace. I'm being catty, and I don't care because it's fully justified. There's no way in hell I'm going to let a woman who's never liked me make me feel like crap for being on a date four years after my husband died.

"That's right. We had so much fun that day." She stretches out a hand to Ash who takes it graciously. "Sorry, we're being so rude. I'm Kristen Newman."

"I'm Ash—"

"Strickland." Kristen finishes for him. "You don't have to introduce yourself, everyone in New Haven knows who you are."

Ash releases her hand, an uneasy smile tugging on his lips. He seems a bit taken aback by her declaration. "I don't know about that, but I guess I'll take your word for it."

Kristen preens, looking very satisfied for a woman who's creeped out a grown man. "Are you two going to be staying? We've managed to snag a private booth on the second floor, and I'm sure Mal would be happy to have you."

Spending another moment watching Kristen drape herself across Dominic like a throw blanket is the last thing I want to do. I'm just about to make our apologies and drag Ash out the door when he answers for me. "Of course, we're staying. This beautiful woman was all too eager to hang out with you guys tonight. Right, Sloane?"

He bumps me gently with his shoulder, and I give him a weak smile. "Yeah. Sure."

Dominic's gaze burns into me, and I don't have to wonder whether he hears the hesitation in my voice because of course he does. I accepted a while ago that when he's paying attention to me, there's not a lot he doesn't hear or see.

"Great!" Kristen exclaims. "I'll show you guys up to the booth while Nic orders our drinks. Is that okay with you, babe?"

Babe. The use of the nickname makes me arch a brow. I don't even care if doing so means letting Dominic know I'm feeling some type of way about him being here with Kristen. He doesn't see the look though, because he's back to being the picture of cool indifference. Features hard as granite. Eyes still and assessing. Shoulders relaxed, stance wide. Like a bored king waiting to be entertained.

"Sounds good." He shrugs her hand off of him and moves towards the bar. Giving us all a view of his broad back while dismissing us from his presence.

Asshole.

Ash moves his hand to the small of my back and starts to move forward to follow Kristen through the crowd. I take a few steps, but I stop short before we break into the crowd. Flashbacks of being pulled through a sea of bodies just like the one in front of us bombard me. My pulse kicks up, and the air around me starts to feel too hot. I turn to Ash.

"I think I'm going to hit the restroom first." I hook a thumb over my shoulder to the arched doorway off of the bar where the bathrooms are. "You guys go on up without me."

His eyebrows dip inward. "No. I'll go with you. We can head up together."

"Ash, it's fine. I'll only be a moment. I just want to freshen up a bit."

"Okay." He agrees reluctantly. "Just promise you're not ditching me."

"And miss a chance to see you on the chopping block?" I joke weakly. "Never."

He chuckles and gives my hand a light squeeze before continuing through the crowd with Kristen. While they head up the stairs to the second floor, I make a beeline for the bathroom. Thankfully, there's no line. I push the door open and breathe a sigh of relief when it closes behind me.

I walk over to the sink and run cold water over a paper towel, patting it over my face and neck to cool my overheated skin. A second later the door swings open and slow, but steady, footsteps carry a familiar frame into the room.

"I don't know what's worse: you coming here with a date or you leaving that date to wander around another club with no one watching out for you."

17

SLOANE

Now

I'm not a person who's easily surprised. Something about receiving the most shocking news of your life at the tender age of twenty-six just steals your ability to be caught off guard by regular everyday things like flat tires, screwed up tile orders, and increases in insurance premiums.

But nothing, and I mean nothing, could have ever prepared me for the sight of Dominic Alexander standing in a women's bathroom looking every bit like a wrathful god with his dark washed jeans, well-fitting button-down, and rolled-up sleeves showing off his deliciously corded forearms.

Did you just call his forearms delicious?

He prowls towards me, and my instincts scream for me to back up. To get far away from him and the dangerous glint in his eyes, but two things are stopping me from doing that: the shock slipping down my spine and the bathroom sink, which my ass is already pressed firmly against.

All of which means, I can't go any damn where, and I'm not entirely sure I want to.

"Why did you let him bring you here?"

Dominic is standing mere inches away from me now, so close I could reach out and touch him if I wanted to. *And damn do I want to.* I raise my chin, determined to not sound like a breathless idiot while I answer his question. A question he has no right to ask, by the way.

"Ash didn't *bring* me anywhere. Coming here was my idea. I wanted to have a nightcap before he took me home."

I catch the potential implication in my words a second too late. Dominic's eyes glitter as he takes another step towards me, and the tips of his shoes bump into the toe of my heels. I'm glad I wore them tonight because they keep me from having to tilt my head back too far to meet his gaze.

His hands go to my waist, gripping the fabric of my dress and bunching it up. My breath catches in my throat, and I feel *it*. The last piece of the puzzle clicking into place with just his touch. And all of a sudden, my fruitless search for it makes sense. I wouldn't have been able to solve the riddle of my desire with Ash, or anyone else for that matter, because the moment I let Dominic Alexander touch me, it stopped belonging to me.

When the fabric of my dress is above my knees, Dominic groans at the sight of my garter belt then lifts me up and places me on the counter. He nudges my legs apart to make room for the span of his hips, and I don't do a thing to stop him.

"You wear *this* for him—" He snaps one of the straps connecting the lace cuffs on my thighs to the belt around my torso, and I gasp. "—And he's upstairs sipping drinks with strangers while you're down here by yourself. He couldn't even be bothered to wait for you and make sure no other drunken asshole got his hands on you?" His fingers are on my neck. They run up and down the column of skin with soft strokes. "I guess I'm the only one who's concerned about your well-being."

Irritation slides down my back at his words, but I can't hold on to it. Everything he makes me feel, anger, regret, frustration, irritation, is all overridden by need the moment his skin touches mine. Somehow I think he knows that and is using it against me, which tells me I need to get his hands off of me immediately.

Both of my hands come up, landing on Dominic's chest and extracting a surprised hiss from his lips as I shove him. He backs away, and I don't even bother feeling triumphant at breaking the moment because I know I was only able to move him because he allowed me to. I pull my dress down as much as I can before glaring at him.

"You don't give a fuck about my well-being. If you did you wouldn't have spent the better part of the week acting like I didn't exist after… "

"After you ran out on me."

His words are vicious, biting into my skin with their truth. I did run out on him, but that doesn't mean it's okay for him to ice me out. "I was upset, and anyone with eyes could see that. I mean is there some rule against being embarrassed about not having a handle on my skin hunger and losing it at work with my husband's best friend of all people? God, Dominic—"

"Not having a handle on your *what*?"

His brows furrow as he stops me mid-rant, and I feel myself turning the color of my dress when I realize what I just said. Talking about my skin hunger with him, or anyone that isn't my therapist, feels like a new kind of nightmare. We stare at each other, and I know he's waiting for an explanation just as surely as I'm waiting for him to be enough of a gentleman to forget I ever said those words. One look at him tells me that's not going to happen though.

"Skin hunger," I repeat, steeling myself for the moment when he bursts into laughter and makes me feel like even more of a fool. But it doesn't come. Instead, Dominic looks at me expectantly and gestures for me to continue. "My therapist said it's also referred to as touch starvation, and it's something a lot of people struggle with when their spouses die, and they go from having regular physical contact, like hugs, cuddles and sex, to not having any meaningful touch for long stretches of time."

"I see," Dominic says quietly, his fingers flexing like my admission is his personal call to action and he's barely containing the urge to put his hands back on me. "And this is something you struggle with?"

"Yes. Hence the whole dating thing." *Goddammit, Sloane!* It's like I can't keep my mouth closed. Dominic's eyes darken at the mention of my date and the suggestion that I'm using Ash for cuddles, or worse, sex. "I didn't mean it like that. I mean, it's not like I'm using him…"

"Use me."

"What?" I sputter, even though I heard him loud and clear. "Use you? For what?"

"To take care of your needs. You said your skin is starved for touch. Use me to sate your hunger." He starts to move towards me again, but I hold my hands up.

"Dominic, no."

"Why not? We already know we're attracted to each other, and I've got to be a better option than some random guy Mal scraped up for you. I know you, angel." His eyes glitter dangerously, and I can practically see his synapses firing as he lists off all the reasons I should use him, the man who started this problem in the first place, to fix it. "After Tuesday, I understand what even the most basic physical situation means to you, and I'll make sure you feel comfortable and safe going into it. Can you honestly say you'd trust someone else to do that for you?"

For a second I'm captivated by the certainty lining his features. It's contagious, spilling into the air and wrapping around my lungs. But then I remember his reaction to what happened between us and come back to reality.

"No, but I don't think I can trust you to do that for me either."

He frowns. "Why not?"

"Because you regret what happened on Tuesday."

That was the only plausible explanation I could come up with when I noticed how cold he was being the next day, and it made perfect sense to me that he might have felt that way. Eric was like his brother and being with me must have felt like betraying him.

While I'm lost in my thoughts, Dominic closes the space between us, and I don't make a move to block him. In the blink of an eye, he's back between my legs, cradling my face in his hands and staring down at me with raw, brutal emotion.

"Sloane, the *only* part of Tuesday I regret is not thinking about how you would feel after the moment passed." He gives me a rueful grin. "I know it might make me sound like a bastard, but the rest of it is inconsequential."

"You're not a bastard."

A dark chuckle rumbles in his chest. "Oh, but I am, angel. If I wasn't I wouldn't be considering ripping your panties off, eating your pussy until you scream the walls down, and sending you back to your date with the juices of your orgasm running down your thighs."

My heartbeat drops between my legs. A delicious swirl of anticipation curls low in my belly at the thought of Dominic's tongue gliding through my wet folds. Unfortunately, it's quickly followed by panic. Not about someone walking in on us or facing Ash after letting this man have his way with me.

Though those are somewhere on the list.

But at the possibility of losing it in front of Dominic once I come down from whatever heights his wicked mouth sends me to. He presses a soft kiss to the corner of my mouth.

"Don't worry. I'm not giving you another orgasm until I can tie you down and make damn sure you can't walk out on me again."

"And what's going to stop you from ignoring me again?"

"The thought of you in another man's arms." He nips a line down my neck, scraping his teeth across my skin and then sucking gently on the abused flesh. "I want to kill Mal for setting you up with that fucker."

A moan climbs up my throat, but I bite it back. "Ash is nice."

Dominic pulls back and the loss of contact has protest flooding my veins. "*Ash* is a dead man if he lays another finger on you."

"He's my date, Dominic. And you—"

"And *I* am the only man that's allowed to touch you, angel. I'll give you a pass for tonight since you came here with him, but after that, all bets are off."

Fury rolls through me. Leave it to Dominic to be making declarations about what I can and can't do with my date while he's here with a woman he's fucked countless times. I shove at his chest again and hop down from the sink to fix my dress when he moves away.

"Does that go for you and Kristen too, or am I supposed to join your little situation-ship with a smile on my face?"

A smug smirk curves his lips as he stares at me without saying a word. I shake my head in disbelief, wondering why I was even considering taking him up on his offer. I move past him, intent on leaving him and his infuriating face standing in the middle of a women's bathroom, but I've only taken a few steps towards the door when his hand wraps around my wrist and yanks me back into his arms.

Thanks to my heels, the curve of my ass is perfectly lined up with his crotch. He's rock hard, and when he rolls his hips into me, I'm certain it's just to make sure I can feel it. He smiles against the side of my neck.

"Jealousy is such a good look on you, I almost hate to tell I haven't fucked Kristen, or anyone else, in a month. You're the only person I want, which is why I'm offering myself to you so readily." His voice is a dark promise and a lullaby all in one. I could listen to him whisper in my ear like this all day. "I'll do whatever it takes to have you, including letting you use me to fulfill every need and desire you have, but that kind of privilege comes with some rules. Do you want to hear them, angel?"

"Yes," I murmur, because of course I want to hear his fucking rules.

"I'll tell you at dinner tomorrow if—" He drops a kiss behind my ear as one of his hands coasts overs my breast and down my torso before coming to a rest on my lower belly. Just a few inches above the part of me that's slick with need for him.

"If?" I whisper breathlessly, knowing I probably won't like this next part, but accepting that I'll do anything he wants me to.

"If you go out there and tell your date you're not feeling well and need to go home."

My mouth falls open on a moan when he presses a hot, wet kiss to my neck with an open mouth. "Dominic…"

"I'm not going to sit by and watch him touch you when I can't. Trust me, angel, this is the only option that doesn't end with my fist in his face."

"And what about Kristen?" The words taste like acid on my tongue, laced with an ugly jealousy I'm not proud of.

"She's not an issue, Sloane. We're just here as friends, and she knows it." He gives me another hot kiss to my neck that makes my knees weak. I sway back, and Dominic supports me with ease. His long fingers are splayed on my stomach, pressing me into his erection. I spin in his arms and offer him my lips because I want his mouth on me more than I want my next breath. Dominic acquiesces immediately.

His lips crash into mine with a hungry, yet practiced, finesse that drives me crazy. Unlike the last time we kissed, when he caught me off guard, I'm ready when his lips hit mine. I open for him immediately, letting him explore and taste as much as he wants because I'm doing it right back.

My hands are all over him, touching his face, running down his chest, slipping under his shirt to feel the sculpted muscles of his abs, scoring my nails into his back when he drags his teeth over my bottom lip. Every cell in my body is singing for him, demanding more. More of his tongue. More of his touch. More of *him*. Dominic growls as he breaks the kiss and releases me like I've just burned him.

"Jesus, Sloane. Do you *want* me to fuck you in this bathroom?"

I blink up at him. My brain is so sluggish with arousal and need it takes a moment to really see him. The tension lining his shoulders. The smoldering look in his eyes. The prominent bulge in his pants I was just pressed against.

He looks like a man at the end of his rope, barely holding on to the control he usually has a firm grip on. And knowing I've done that just by responding helplessly to him, sends another rush of desire through my veins.

Lord, help me.

Dominic adjusts himself inside of his pants, and I watch, riveted. The act is as intimate as it is erotic, and I'm practically salivating at the sight. Ever watchful, Dominic catches me staring at him, his eyes darkening further as he pauses his movements.

"You're biting your lip, angel. I hope that means you're going to say yes to my offer."

A million things run through my mind all at once; thoughts and images that have tortured me for weeks now slamming into me forcefully, begging me to say yes, so Dominic can make them all a reality. I already know what my answer is going to be, but I want to keep him in suspense for a little while longer. With a slow smile spreading across my face, I start backing away, inching closer to the door as his eyes track my steps.

"I'll consider your offer and let you know my answer tomorrow at dinner."

The last thing I see before I slip out of the door is the devilish smirk on Dominic's face and his hand still in his pants, palming an impressive hard-on I can't wait to see in person.

* * *

"Are you sure I can't get you anything?"

Ash's concern is palpable as we stand on my front porch underneath the moonlit sky. Getting him out of the club was a major feat, Kristen was clinging to him with a wild determination that made no sense because he was there with me and she's still very clearly into Dominic.

In the end, Mal ended up physically removing her hand from Ash's arm, so we could leave. By the time Ash and I cleared the second floor, Dominic still hadn't made it back with the drinks. If it struck anyone as weird that he and I were missing from the group at the same time, they didn't let on, which was good because I don't want anyone knowing about this arrangement between us yet. *Or at all.*

I guess that's something else Dominic and I will have to talk about at dinner tomorrow. *Dinner.* I'm going on an actual date with Dominic Alexander. But first, I have to politely dismiss the handsome and kind man currently regaling me with a list of his many care-taking skills. None of which I need at the moment.

To say I feel bad about flaking out on this sweet man would be an insult to the ball of dread chilling my stomach. I meant what I said to Dominic in the bathroom: Ash is a nice man, and he deserves better than a date who can't bring herself to kiss him but jumps at the chance to make out with someone else.

Well, not just someone else. It couldn't have been any other man in that bathroom with me. Even if I don't understand it, I know it's true. Dominic is the only man who can arouse and infuriate me in the space of a heartbeat, and I'm fairly certain he's the only one who can satisfy the demanding need thrumming underneath my skin.

"Ash." I place a light hand on his forearm. "I'm fine. I think I just got a little overheated in the club."

Understatement of the year.

Ash gives me a small smile that doesn't quite reach his eyes. He doesn't believe me, but he's too polite to say so. "Okay. I'll let you get some rest then. Have a good night, Sloane."

He leans in close and places a chaste kiss on my cheek. I offer him a tight smile when he pulls back and starts down the steps. "Thank you for dinner and the almost nightcap."

A small smile full of regret ghosts over his lips. "One day, when you feel ready—really ready—we'll have that nightcap, and maybe something more." Then he's gone. Shoulders back and head held high as he climbs into his car and pulls off.

The smallest bit of insidious doubt trickles through my mind as I unlock my front door and step into the house. Being with a man like Ash would be simple, uncomplicated, because anything that happened with him—good or bad—wouldn't pose a threat to the most important relationships in my life.

The same can't be said for this thing with Dominic, and I can't help but wonder if it's worth it. If giving in to the attraction blooming between us is worth hurting the people who mean the most to us. People that are only in our lives because of Eric. People I can't imagine losing.

My gut clenches at the thought, and my pulse leaps as panic tries to set in. But I'm determined not to let it. This thing with me and Dominic can be good, and it doesn't have to destroy everything. Not if we're smart about it. We could lay out some ground rules, put a date on this thing, so we aren't lying to the people we love for an indefinite amount of time. *I mean how long should it take to sate my touch starved skin?*

Leaning my head against the cool wood of my front door, I pull in slow, soothing breaths until my heart is no longer trying to leap out of my chest. And all of that work flies out the window when three hard knocks sound on the other side of the door making me jump back. I clasp my hand over my mouth to keep the scream clawing its way out of my chest from hitting the air.

A faint buzz rings out from my purse, which is clutched in my hand, and I dig it out quickly to silence it. Only pausing to see that my screen is lit with a text notification from Dominic.

Dominic: I'm at your door. Open up.

A wild fluttering of butterfly wings starts up in my belly, and my poor heart starts a rapid tattoo it can't possibly sustain. If it keeps going at this pace, I'll go into cardiac arrest before I get to see Dominic without his clothes. And I'll be one angry dead woman if that happens.

I unlatch the lock with shaky hands and lose my breath altogether when the door swings open and reveals Dominic standing on the other side. He's unfastened several of the buttons on his shirt, and I catch a glimpse of the exquisite pectorals I ran my hands across less than an hour ago. Raw, masculine energy vibrates off of him as we stare at each other. Me, breathing in his scent and trying desperately not to fall headfirst into the pools of liquid heat that are his eyes. Him, doing nothing to hide the desire pouring off of him.

"What are you doing here?" I breathe.

Dominic pushes past me, and I step back to allow him through the doorway. Electricity arcs between us as his shoulder brushes mine. I push the door closed again and turn to find him mere inches away from me. Both of his palms pressed flat against the door on either side of my head, caging me in. For the first time, I don't mind that he's the wolf and I'm the prey because I want more than anything to be devoured by him.

My breasts brush against his chest with every breath I take, nipples hardening at the delicious friction I'm desperate to have more of. Dominic brings his forehead to mine, his lips brushing over my mouth.

"You let him kiss you." He growls, nipping at my lips before raining kisses along my jaw and down my neck.

"On the cheek."

I tilt my head to give him better access, and he uses his new vantage point to bite down on the exposed tendon. It's a light bite, more pleasure than pain, but the scrape of his teeth on the sensitive flesh has me arching into him. Both of his hands come down, abandoning their post on the door to cup my breasts. He runs a rough thumb across each of my nipples through the fabric, and I cry out.

Then his fingers are dipping into the cups of my bra, freeing the swollen flesh from the restraints of satin and lace. Cool air whooshes across my skin, making my nipples tighten into peaks that are so hard it's almost painful when Dominic rolls one between his deft fingers.

"It doesn't matter." He dips his head down to take the bud into the wet heat of his mouth. My head falls back against the door with a moan. "I own your kisses now, which means you don't give them to anyone but me. You got that?"

His words send a shiver of satisfaction rippling through me. The most primal part of me responding to the claim he speaks against my skin. It's a declaration, a promise of possession and passion I thought was lost to me forever, that speaks the darkest parts of me. I'm ready to give in to him completely, but the idea of crossing this line with him before we've hammered out the details of our agreement is nagging at me.

"I haven't said yes yet."

Dominic pauses and pulls his mouth away from me with a reluctant growl. There's no mistaking the incredulous look on his face as his eyes search my face. "Your mouth hasn't, but your body has."

I flush as his heated gaze drops to my exposed breasts and move to try and cover them up. Dominic grasps both of my wrists in his hands and pins them to the door.

"Dominic…"

"Say yes, Sloane."

He dips his head and starts his assault on my breasts all over again. They're still restrained by the fabric, but it doesn't stop him from lavishing attention on them, kissing and suckling until my skin is chafed from the hair of his beard and my need for him is coating my thighs.

"Oh, God." I'm coming apart at the seams, panting desperately as my mind works overtime to hold on to the point I was trying to make. "You're not fighting fair."

When he pulls away from me this time, his smile is sinful. "I told you I was a bastard, angel. Are you really surprised?"

"No. I'm not."

He nuzzles into my throat. "Say yes."

It's supposed to be an order. A command. But somewhere underneath the stern timbre is a thread of desperation that feeds the fire he's stoked in my veins. The idea of him wanting me so badly, so desperately, that he's on the verge of begging sends a heady rush of power through me.

"Why are you doing this?"

The muscle in his jaw starts to jump. "Because none of the men you spend time with are worthy of being with you this way."

"And you are?"

A shadow passes across his face as if my words hurt him, and I almost regret asking the question. "No, but I'm not going to let that stop me from giving you what you need." His fingers dig into my wrists. "Say yes. Let me take care of you, even if it's just for tonight."

"No, I—" I pause to figure out exactly what I'm going to say, and his entire face falls as he starts to pull away. "I want more than a night, Dominic."

For a moment, he stops moving altogether, and we just stare at each other. Then he releases my hands and rough fingers snake around my back to find the zipper of my dress. I breathe a sigh of relief when the fabric gives, and Dominic's fingers brush over my bare skin. He takes my mouth again, sliding the straps down my arms. The satin rasps against my skin quietly until it finally lands in a puddle at my feet.

"Fuck." Dominic hisses through his teeth, taking a step back to look at me in nothing but heels and a lingerie set I didn't think anyone was going to see tonight. "You're so God damn beautiful, Sloane. Better than anything I could have ever dreamed."

This is the second time he's mentioned dreaming of me, and the words set a thousand butterflies free in my stomach. Their wings flutter madly as my heart pounds in my chest. Before I can speak, he drops down to his knees.

And the sight of him kneeling before me sends a mixture of pleasure and heat dancing down my spine. His face is upturned, and I get to see the dark brown of his eyes turn black. The golden flecks stand out in stark contrast, highlighting his blown pupils and the tender reverence in his gaze. He leans forward and presses a soft kiss to the center of my stomach. A shudder rolls through me. Both of his large hands go to my hips and run over the black lace at my torso.

"Were you going to let him see this tonight?" His eyes are narrowed, showing just how bothered he is by the thought, but his touch is still gentle—infuriatingly so—as I squirm under his ministrations.

"No."

"Good." He snaps the garter strap against my thigh and my back arches. The small bite of pain turns my blood into liquid fire. "Does that feel good, angel?"

It does, but I'm not sure why. I've never really been into pain with sex, but in the few times I've been with Dominic pain has always seemed to be intertwined with pleasure. The scrape of his teeth against my skin. The snap of the strap against my thigh. The rough pads of his fingers digging into my flesh. It all feels new but so damn good.

"Yes," I admit breathlessly. "But I don't—" I search for the words. The right way to tell him that this is new territory for me. That we don't have to go here if he isn't into it.

"You don't know why." He breathes, his lips moving against my inner thigh. "You don't have to know, it only matters that you want it. And if there's something you want—" Dark eyes flick up to mine, alight with danger and desire. "—I'm going to be the one to give it to you."

Lust clogs my throat, preventing me from answering, which is fine because Dominic doesn't seem to want one. His fingers find the band of my thong and pull it down my legs in one fell swoop. The evidence of my arousal glistens on the thin fabric, and he examines it closely before tossing it to the side. His hands go to my ankle, lifting my left leg and placing it on his shoulder before coming to rest on my ass. He's holding me in place so he can have an up-close and personal view of the bare skin of my pussy.

He groans, warm breath flowing over the sensitive flesh and making me shiver. "You're so wet. Who's all of that for, angel?"

Any other day, in any other situation, I would be annoyed with the question because he's only asking to remind me of the thing he's apparently always known, but I just found out in the bathroom at Reign: my desire belongs to him. I rock my hips forward, trying to force him to come closer to the spot where I desperately need him, but he pulls back and bites my thigh.

"Who is it for, angel?" His fingers dig into my skin with a delicious bite as his nickname for me sets sparks off in my mind. I still haven't figured out why it feels so familiar. "Sloane…"

His voice has an edge to it, a strain that wasn't there a second ago, and I realize he needs me to say it. He needs me to tell him how much I want him, and I don't want to deny him. Not when he's already given me so much.

"You. It's all for you."

A feral growl rips from his throat as he presses his face between my legs and inhales. He stays like that, breathing me in, for a second, and I'm desperate for him to move. My hips churn in tiny circles, and I'm about to beg when he opens his mouth against me. His tongue parting my folds with wet glides that send heat pulsing through my blood.

"Oh God, *yes*."

I rock my hips shamelessly into his mouth, meeting every lash of his wicked tongue in hopes of getting that perfect bit of friction on the bundle of nerves pulsating for him. When he finally sucks it into his mouth, my eyes roll back into my head. I put my hands on his broad shoulders while my leg flexes against his back, holding him close to my body even though he shows no signs of ever wanting to leave it.

Dominic releases his death grip on my ass and uses his free hand to hold me open for him. He lashes at my exposed clit over and over again before dipping inside of my soaked entrance.

"Shit." I hiss. My back arches off the door again, and Dominic uses the one hand he has on my ass to rock me back and forth onto his sinful tongue. He fucks me with slow, shallow thrusts until I'm shaking and crazed, the orgasm building inside my core threatening to tear its way through my body.

I'm so close. One brush of his finger, or lash of his tongue over the swollen bud of nerves Dominic is currently neglecting, away from coming apart on his hand. Every time he pulls his tongue out and pushes back into me again, my walls ripple around him, telling him I'm on the edge.

Dominic pulls back, licking my essence off of his lips before pressing a kiss to my inner thigh. I wiggle my hips, trying to get his mouth back where I need it, and he flashes me a devious grin. "Relax, angel."

On his last word, he sinks one long, thick finger into me. The look he gives me is scorching hot as he pulls it out and slides it back in accompanied by another. His fingers are huge and brutal in their intrusion. There's a bite of pain as he pushes deep inside me, stretching me out. It's the most action I've had with another person in years, so it takes me a second to adjust. My nails dig into his shoulder.

"Dominic...oh, god. Dominic."

"It's okay, angel. I've got you." He plants a soft kiss to my cleft. "Just relax."

I push out air through my nose and try to follow his instructions. Dominic dips his head down again and gives me a long lick with the flat of his tongue before circling my clit with his lips. Sucking gently and rhythmically while his tongue flutters over the engorged bundle of nerves with a relentless hunger.

Everything in my core starts to tighten. I squeeze my eyes shut, focusing on the orgasm that's hovering just out of my reach, spurred on by the exquisite fullness his fingers provide when my walls clamp down on them. Pleasure ripples through me when his fingers finally start to move inside of me. Slow glides that have my hips churning, pumping into his mouth with reckless abandon while the open flame inside of me turns into a full-blown inferno.

My orgasm is so close I can almost taste it, and every word from my lips is a plea. More. Harder. Deeper. Faster. *Please, Dominic. Please.* It's like my voice belongs to someone else. A mindless woman who's desperate for the brutal ferocity of the fingers spearing me, the wicked tongue lashing at my clit and lapping up my juices like liquid honey rushing out of me. Dominic pushes in deeper, curling his fingers back so they massage the ridges along the front of my walls with every stroke.

"I'm close. Oh, god. I'm so close."

"Let me have it, Sloane."

I'm all sensation. Lost to everything but the deep, hot pressure at my core, building, and building until finally—with a vicious flick of his tongue—I break apart. The orgasm washes over me in fiery waves, and I cry out, my legs growing weak as warmth spreads through my entire body. Dominic supports my weight with his shoulders, using his tongue and fingers to prolong my pleasure. When the final tremor fades, he pulls back, and his beard is soaked from my orgasm.

He licks his lips. "So much better than my dreams, angel."

Slowly, he places my foot back on the ground and withdraws from me. The little 'pop' his fingertips make as they leave my entrance is the only sound in the house. Dominic says something else, but I don't hear it because I'm too busy conducting a silent examination of my mental state. There's no lump in my throat or tears pricking my eyes, and only an infinitesimal amount of guilt and shame clawing at my chest.

So far, so good.

Dominic stands up slowly, studying my face with thoughtful eyes that have just a hint of wariness in them. It takes a moment for me to notice he's not touching me anymore. His body is still close enough that his scent floods my senses and his heat bleeds into my damp skin, but his hands are at his sides.

"Tell me you're okay," he orders quietly.

"I'm okay."

My legs are a bit wobbly, and both of my breasts are a little cold after being trussed up over my bra and exposed to the air for so long, but I'm delighted to find the words aren't a lie. He gives me one more second before he reaches for me, pulling me into his body with enough force to elicit a sharp gasp from me. Mainly because it presses me right into his erection.

"If you're not, you have to tell me. I know this isn't easy for you, but I'm here. And I'm not going anywhere. Do you understand?"

"Yes. Can I ask you a question?"

His fingers skate over my skin, drifting up my back to unhook my bra. "What is it?"

I almost forget what I want to say when his thumbs brush over my nipples. My skin is so sensitive. Still a little raw from being nuzzled and suckled by his busy mouth. "What happened to tying me down?"

He brushes a damp tendril from my temple and smiles. "Maybe next time. Right now, I want to get you to bed."

"Mhmm." I hum, delighted at the idea of having Dominic in my bed. "Maybe I can take care of this for you." I palm his dick in my hand and squeeze lightly. Emboldened by the flare of heat in his eyes, I move my hand up and down, stroking him through the denim of his jeans.

"Sloane." Dominic rasps, stilling the movement with his hand.

I blink up at him, confused. He's been hard all night and has already forfeited his pleasure to tend to my needs. I would have never pegged him for a selfless lover, and I want—no need—to return the favor. Why would he stop me from doing that?

"Because," Dominic says roughly, answering my unspoken question. "You're fine right now, but the last thing I'm going to do is fuck this up by pushing you too hard tonight. I'm going to take you upstairs, put you in the shower, and then the bed—"

I frown. The idea of going to bed without him bothers me a lot more than it should at this early stage in our….whatever the hell this is. Dominic continues, reading me like a book. "Where you're going to let me hold you in my arms until we both fall asleep."

I'm not even disturbed by how easily he reads my expression. He's spent more than a decade annoying the life out of me, and I know from experience that knowing how to push someone's buttons comes with the ability to see right through them. To read their minds through facial expressions and body language alone. Dominic has that ability because he's just addressed all of my concerns without me having to breathe a word. The thing he doesn't realize is, I have the same set of skills, and they only apply to him.

Which is how I know that no matter what his mouth is saying, his body is telling a different story. Blown pupils. Tense shoulders. Raging hard-on that's straining against the seam of his zipper. Molten eyes that blaze with lust for me. I bite my lip. Caught between the need to push him on this so I can show him how much I want him and the post-orgasmic exhaustion seeping into my bones.

Dominic leans down to kiss my lips just as a traitorous yawn tries to escape. I stifle it, but he still sees and kisses me anyway. "You're tired, Sloane."

I arch a brow. "I'm not *that* tired, Dominic."

And I'm not. I can rally. I can splash some water on my face and give some pleasure to the man who has given me more than he could ever know. I can….Another yawn breaks free, and Dominic gives me a laugh that tells me I can take my ass to bed and enjoy some much-needed, but not truly deserved, post-coital cuddles.

"Sleep, angel. That's the only thing happening in your bed tonight."

Then he's lifting me into his arms, cradling me to his chest as he heads up the stairs. When we hit the landing on the second floor, he heads straight for my closed bedroom door. He carries me across the threshold and into the adjoining bathroom before setting me on the double vanity. Before I can blink, he's kneeling in front of me again.

Pulling my heels off and massaging my feet one at a time. My head dips back.

"That feels *nice*." I don't mean for it to sound sexual, but it comes out as a moan.

Dominic's gaze flicks to mine. "Behave." He smacks my sole lightly before starting again, working out the tension with practiced movements that make me wonder where he learned the skill. Jealousy pricks at my skin like a thousand tiny needles at the thought of him doing this for someone else—namely a certain catty ex-girlfriend who doesn't want to accept that things are over between them.

Don't think about her right now. Feeling jealous of Dominic's time with Kristen is ridiculous. When they were together, I was determined to be alone forever and the possibility of me with anyone—let alone Dominic—didn't exist. And none of that would have changed if it wasn't for that night at Club Noir.

"Alright, up you go." He grasps my hands in his and tugs me off of the vanity so I'm standing in front of him.

Awfully bossy for a man on his knees.

"Isn't the person on their knees usually the one *taking* orders?"

"Is that something you want, angel?" He cocks a brow at me while his hands are busy unhooking the straps of my garter belt. "Me on my knees, taking orders from you?"

The idea of bossing this impossible man around brings a smile to my face, but I don't know how satisfying it would be in the moment. I would probably spend the whole time in my head, worrying about looking and sounding silly, instead of enjoying having him at my beck and call. I run my hand over his hair just because I can.

"One day, maybe. Right now, the only thing I *truly* want is for you to take your clothes off. You've seen every inch of me, and all I've seen of you are your forearms."

My statement is punctuated by the removal of the last lace cuff around my thigh. Standing there fully naked, I arch a brow and Dominic smirks at me before standing up. He's so tall. Without my heels, I feel small and feminine beside him. Without my clothes on, I feel exposed and vulnerable, especially when my nakedness forces me to acknowledge that he's remained fully dressed.

Again.

Each time we've been together, I've been the one putting it all out there: losing it on his leg, baring myself to him as soon as he crossed my threshold, and dissolving into a puddle of mush every time he put his hands on me. All while he's held it together. Managing to walk away with nothing, besides the few changes only I notice, on his person indicating his world has just been turned upside down by my existence. And it's disconcerting.

Dominic lifts my chin, and I know from the moment our eyes meet that he sees it. All of my thoughts are on display for him. "Every time I touch you is a gift, Sloane. One I don't know if I'm going to get to keep, which means I want to rush this more than anything. I want to dive headfirst into your eyes and never come up for air. I want to use every part of my body to bring pleasure to yours, but—" His eyes fall shut, a pained expression crossing his features before he schools them into something less devastating. "—last time I pushed you too far and scared you. *Hell, I scared myself,* and that can't happen again. You need to be able to trust me, and if we do anything else tonight I'm not going to be able to control myself. You deserve more than that especially if this is the first time since…"

My head bobs up and down, letting him know I understand exactly what he means.

"It is. I haven't wanted this with anyone else, although, a part of me wishes I could. That's why I went out with Ash tonight, but I just… can't."

I finish lamely, ignoring the way Dominic's eyes darken when I say Ash's name. His hand goes to my nape, pulling me forward to meet his ardent mouth. He kisses me with a tenderness that's the perfect answer to my confession. I wrap my arms around his neck, sliding my naked body against him and wishing his clothes would just disappear. Dominic palms both of my ass cheeks in his large hands and squeezes before breaking the kiss with a reluctant growl.

"Is that what you call slow?"

I just stare at him and lick my lips. I love that my taste is still on his tongue. He takes a step back, eyeing me like a wild animal who might attack at any moment, which, in all honesty, is exactly what I am.

"Shower." He points a commanding finger at me and then at the walk-in behind me, and I almost laugh at the ridiculousness of him giving me directions to my shower. "I'm going to wait in the bedroom." He hooks a thumb towards the door that he's currently edging towards, and I'm hit with a sudden and strong sense of deja vu. Just like when he first called me angel.

The feeling Dominic and I have lived through a very similar scene sticks with me as I wash my face and shower. I towel off, lotion up, and throw my hair in a loose pineapple before slipping on a robe. All while trying to call up the full image that doesn't seem to want to come. I'm mildly irritated by my brain's inability to fully form the image, but it disappears the moment I walk out of my bathroom and find a man—naked except for a pair of black boxer briefs that were made for the sole purpose of accentuating the curve of his ass—pulling back the duvet on my bed.

The sight stops me in my tracks, and I don't know if I'm more shocked that there's a man in my room or that the man is Dominic, but I can't stop staring at him. Hungry eyes roving over smooth bronze skin, unblemished save for the small numerical tattoo on his ribs that I can't make out from where I'm standing, with muscles I've grown used to feeling pressed against my body rippling underneath.

Swollen pectorals with a light dusting of dark curls, abs that would make any woman in her right mind drool especially because the indentations on either side of his waist are like an arrow, directing you to the bulge hidden inside his underwear. I lick my lips and wonder if it's normal to feel jealous of cotton. Dominic catches me staring and a playful smile curves his lips as he takes in my stunned face.

"Which side do you sleep on?"

His question gets the wheels of my brain turning again. "I like the right side, but I'm happy to take the left if you'll be more comfortable there."

He shakes his head. "No need. I prefer the left side."

I smile at him then resume my trek to my dresser, slipping on a pair of boy shorts before opening the top drawer in search of a shirt to wear to bed. My fingers freeze as they brush over the familiar fabric of Eric's shirt, the one I sleep in every night, and I want to kick myself. In all my obsessing over getting a man in my bed, I hadn't stopped to consider what would happen when they got there.

Most men probably wouldn't notice if I chose to sleep in a threadbare t-shirt, and they wouldn't automatically assume it belonged to my late husband, but this is Dominic and a shirt Eric got as a part of his graduation kit when he was a senior at Lakewood High; the school they attended together. He'll recognize it right away and probably think I'm a crazy widow who can't let her dead husband go even when she's got someone else's arms wrapped around her.

I could just get another shirt to sleep in, or wear one of the many silly pajama sets Mama has gotten me for Christmas over the years, but that doesn't sit right with me. It feels too much like kicking Eric out of my bed because I've invited someone else into it.

"I can hear the wheels in your mind spinning. What's going on?"

18

DOMINIC

Now

Sloane turns around slowly, her face stricken with something between panic and guilt. Seeing that expression on her face when I'm practically naked in her bed has *me* feeling panicked, but understanding washes over me as my eyes settle on what she's holding in her hands.

A senior shirt from Lakewood High.

It's faded and threadbare from years of being worn, but I can still make out the emblem. There are only two places she could have gotten that shirt, and since I know her and Mal aren't in the habit of exchanging clothes, it has to be Eric's. I don't know what I expect to feel at the sight of his shirt in her hand, but all I do feel is understanding tinged with sadness.

For Eric. For me. For Sloane.

It's evident to anyone looking at her, that she still loves him. That she still hasn't quite recovered from losing him and probably never will. And as much as I want to own every part of her, every moment and memory, I've always known that wasn't realistic because pursuing anything with her means accepting the time she spent loving someone that wasn't me. Which is why I don't have to think twice about going to her and taking the shirt from her hands. Her eyes go wide, the golden flecks shimmering with fear and a hint of anger.

"Arms up, angel."

She lifts her arms, obeying my command without hesitation, and my dick twitches. Seeing her follow my orders without a contrary word from her pretty mouth turns me on, but now isn't the time for worrying about my lengthening dick. Now is the time for comforting my angel and letting her know I don't give a fuck about what she sleeps in, as long as she sleeps in it next to me.

I slip the soft cotton down her arms and then over her head. It ghosts over the curves of her breasts before settling around the tops of her thighs. Eric was taller and bigger than her, so it's a loose fit. I rub the hem of the shirt between my fingertips while tears brim in Sloane's eyes.

I press a kiss to her forehead. "Let's go to bed."

She scrambles up onto the mattress without a word. I turn off the lights and try to slow the pounding in my chest. The last thing I want is to die before I get a chance to hold this woman in my arms. When I slide into bed, Sloane gives me a second to settle before laying her head on my chest. I curve an arm around her waist, pulling her body closer to me until there's no space between us. She plants a kiss on my chest, and I don't need to see her to know she's looking at me.

"How did you do it?"

"Do what?" I rub her back, loving the small sigh of contentment that falls from her lips. My heart does a flip in my chest at the sound. For years, I've fallen asleep dreaming of having nights like tonight with her. Kissing her, holding her, burying my face in her sweet pussy, and tonguing her until she couldn't see straight. Now it's my reality.

"Stop hating me."

Her words make my chest tighten, but they shouldn't. After all, I'm the person who made sure she believed I hated her for all these years. The asshole who would rather go to war with her than find a way to live with his own fucked up feelings. Of course, she thought I hated her.

Rubbing tiny circles on her back, I search for the right words to say. A way to explain that I never hated her without revealing a truth she's not ready to hear. I turn on my side, so I can face her.

"I didn't." Her body goes stiff. "I never hated you, Sloane."

"What? But you—"

She tries to sit up, but I tighten my grip, anchoring her to me. I can't have this conversation with her. Not tonight. Maybe not ever. She won't believe me about everything that happened on the night we met, or what *didn't* happen the next morning.

"I know." My fingers slip under her shirt, coasting up her side until I find her breast, kneading at the soft flesh until a moan escapes her throat. "But that doesn't matter now, does it, angel?"

I pinch her nipple and smile when the bite of pain forces her to arch her back. Sloane's nails dig into my forearm. Moonlight filters through the blinds, turning her face into a luminescent silhouette. *So damn beautiful it makes my heart hurt.* She lifts her chin, offering her lips to me in sweet supplication. I swallow her next moan with my mouth, licking into her with a hungry determination that has Sloane tossing her leg over my hip and grinding against my dick. I can feel the soft heat of her right on my tip. It would be nothing to move her panties to the side and slide into her welcoming pussy.

She's already wet. The moisture gathering at her core soaks through her panties as she works herself over me. Greedy little whimpers fall from her lips when I rock my hips up, angling my thrusts so my dick collides with her swollen clit every time she comes down. I break the kiss just so I can see her face when the pleasure floods her.

"Oh, Dominic." Sloane moans into my mouth. "You make me feel so fucking good."

I have no words for what she's doing to me, so I just let the satisfied grunt at the back of my throat break free and focus on not coming in my briefs like a fucking teenager. Beads of precum are already leaking out of my tip, and my skin is stretched tight and flushed with a needy heat. *Why am I pushing the whole waiting thing again?*

Right. Because I might fuck this all up if I give Sloane too much too soon. Whether she knows it or not, she needs me to take this slow, because what I didn't tell her in the bathroom is that the moment I take her I'm never letting her go. And I don't think that's what she needs to hear right now.

"That's it, baby." I grab a generous handful of her perfect ass and squeeze, letting the words fall from my lips. "This is exactly what I meant when I told you to use me for your pleasure. Are you going to come again, angel?"

Sloane doesn't answer. She's writhing and moaning as she grinds against me, making me wish I was inside of her to feel the constant clenching of her muscles as her orgasm builds. I drop a kiss on her lips.

"Let me hear you."

A strangled groan escapes her, and my dick twitches in response. I've never been this fucking hard in my life. I grip her nape and pull her lips down on mine, so I can fuck her mouth with my tongue. Timing the strokes to match the thrust of my hips until she's falling apart around me. Her back arching and head thrashing against the satin-covered pillowcases that smell just like her as she screams my name.

"Fuck." I wrap my arms around her, pinning her to my side as I roll onto my back. "I could listen to that sound every day."

Sloane rests her head over my heart. A hum of acknowledgment is the only thing I hear before her breathing evens out and soft snores fill the room. I stare up at the ceiling, disbelief mingling with the helpless contentment bubbling in my chest until I can barely stay still. The only thing holding me in place is the sleeping angel wrapped around my body.

Years of waiting, wanting, and wishing for her, for a moment just like this, couldn't have prepared me for how this would feel. Like standing at the gates of Heaven and hoping years of being a bastard won't keep you from being let in. Like being forgiven for your biggest mistake after a lifetime of paying penance. Like finally coming home after a journey you didn't think you were going to make it back from.

I press a light kiss to Sloane's forehead, and she stirs a bit but doesn't wake up.

"I could never hate you, angel," I whisper against her skin. "I've always loved you too much for that."

* * *

WAKING up next to Sloane is the single best thing I've ever experienced in my life, or at least I think it might be. I don't get the chance to experience it because when I crack my eyes open the next morning, she's nowhere to be found. Only the muted, grayish-blue light of the early morning and the happy chirping of a bird somewhere outside greet me when I sit up and listen for any sign of her in the master suite.

The silence around me would be daunting if I wasn't certain Sloane wouldn't flee her own home just to get away from me. Waking me up in the middle of the night demanding I leave? Now that was a hell of a lot more likely, but she didn't do that, which means despite all odds she isn't losing it over spending the night with me.

When I was on my way over here last night, a trip that took longer than necessary because I had to drop Kristen off and she wanted to fight about why I came back without any drinks demanding we leave, I wondered how smart it was to come here. Sloane had agreed to have dinner with me and give me an answer to the offer I pulled out of the clear blue sky, but neither of us had discussed me coming over, let alone spending the night.

Making it through her door was a long shot. Getting the chance to taste her was a dream I was desperate to make a reality, but I didn't dare hope for it. And spending the night in her bed—well that was just an idea I floated out there and prayed she would grab hold of. *Okay, it was more of an order, but Sloane had to know she was well within her rights to show me the door if she wanted to.* To my surprise, she didn't want to.

She wanted everything I did.

The thought puts an embarrassingly huge smile on my face. One that sticks with me as I knock on the door of the master bathroom before entering and handling my business. When I spot a spare tooth-brush laying on the countertop between the sinks, the smile grows wider. Clearly, Sloane was thinking of me when she woke up this morning and went where ever the hell she snuck off to while I was still sleeping.

After I brush my teeth, I pull on my clothes from last night and head downstairs. It's quiet on the first floor too, but I see Sloane sitting at her kitchen island sipping a cup of coffee. Her curls are loose now, flowing freely over her shoulders, and she's exchanged the shirt she slept in for a gray t-shirt dress that hugs her curves while exposing the smooth expanse of her legs.

I clear my throat so she isn't startled by my sudden appearance in her living room, and delighted hazel eyes lift to mine, a shy smile curving her lips. My fucking heart stutters to a stop then starts pounding in my chest.

Sloane sets her cup down. "Morning."

"Good morning, beautiful." I close the distance between us with a few strides. The need to be close to her is a demand in my blood I don't have to fight anymore. Sloane watches me approach with an expectant spark in her eye that makes me want to laugh.

She's insatiable.

I snake a hand around her neck, grabbing a fistful of hair at her nape and tilting her head up, so I can kiss her beautiful lips. When I pull back, we're both panting and breathless. Before I release her, I brush my nose over hers three times like my mom used to do every night before she tucked me into bed and told me how much she loved me.

Watching Sloane's eyelids flutter rapidly in response to the motion transports me back to the night we met, when just being in her pres-ence compelled me to use one of the most loving gestures from my childhood to convey emotions I didn't dare put a name to, and she looked at me the same way.

So much has changed between that night twelve years ago and today, but all of the most important things have stayed the same: I'm still so far gone for this woman, captivated by her smile, devastated by the sway of her hips, shattered by the thought of living without her and willing to do anything to stop it from happening.

Last time I was unprepared, completely blindsided by whatever circumstances had conspired together to keep us apart, but I'm not letting that happen again. Not after living so long without her, not after finally getting the chance to taste her, not after letting a cozy-looking picture of her and James on Instagram fuck with my head, prompting me to strong-arm my way onto this project just to keep them apart.

My original plan for accomplishing that goal wasn't even fully formed by the time I accepted his offer to finish the project, and when Sloane walked out on me on Tuesday I thought it was all blown to hell. But then last night happened and all the pieces fell into place thanks to a condition I'd never even heard of and a proposition I couldn't stop myself from making.

Sloane runs a tentative hand down my chest and over my abs. "How'd you sleep?"

"Like a baby." I release her hair and take a sip of her coffee. It's still hot, but I only take one sip before handing it back to her with a frown. "Jesus, woman. Did you put *any* coffee in there at all?"

There have to be at least five spoons of sugar and half a carton of creamer in that cup. No one in their right mind would call this coffee, let alone sit around drinking it at eight in the morning.

She laughs. "That's what you get for putting your lips on my cup."

"Oh. All of a sudden you have an issue with where I put my lips?"

A flush creeps up her neck, giving her skin an adorable red tint that reaches her cheeks.

"Nope." She says, popping the 'p' with her lips. "I like everything you do with your lips."

I nod, my lips quirking. "You don't have to tell me, angel. Your moans last night were more than enough proof."

Sloane shoves my shoulder, but she's laughing as she pushes me away. "Shut up. Would you like your own cup of coffee?"

"I would love one. No diabetes for me though."

Her ass bounces as she hops up and prances over to the Keurig on the counter. Both of my eyes are glued to her, tracking her every move-ment. It's no surprise that watching Sloane do even the most mundane task is riveting to me. I could watch her do shit like this all day and not get bored. What's worse is, I *want* to.

A few moments later, she's sliding a hot cup of black coffee my way."Would you like some sugar and creamer or do you like it black like your soul?"Her lips twitch, suppressing the urge to laugh at her bad joke, and I sigh. This is the shit that breaks my heart. She's prob-ably made a thousand of these atrocious attempts at humor over cups of coffee, and I haven't been around to give her shit about any of them.

She had Eric though.

The reminder helps a little but makes it hard not to begrudge my best friend every morning he spent waking up beside the woman we both love. Drinking coffee that made his teeth ache and cracking corny jokes while they planned their day. Part of me knows I have no right to be angry with Eric for having Sloane while I was alone, trying to fill the hole in my chest with all the wrong women, but the smallest part of me does.

Sick shit right?

Being jealous of my best friend, coveting his wife, and stealing my way into the bed he'd still be in if he hadn't been ripped from this world far too soon. I would feel bad about it, but I've lived with the guilt of wanting her for years, and I'm past the point of regretting it, too far gone to feel bad enough to stop what's happening between us.

And if claiming my angel means I'm going to hell…well then, I'll be a happy inhabitant when my time comes.

I roll my eyes to mask the dark thoughts flipping through my mind. "I'll take some creamer if you have any left. I'm assuming you didn't use the *whole* thing when you made your cup."

She sticks her tongue out at me as she grabs the creamer out of the fridge. When she saunters back over to me with the carton in her hand, I just stare at her, amazed by how beautiful and relaxed she looks. No emptiness in her eyes, no slump to her shoulders, not a hint of regret or shame lining her features. It's the happiest I've seen her look in a long time, and my heart flips in my chest knowing I had something to do with it.

"What are you staring at Alexander?" She sets the carton down and takes a seat with her body angled toward me.

My eyes go to her legs, admiring the golden inches of skin left on display by her short cotton dress, before coming back to her face. "You. Always you, angel."

Sloane's eyes go soft with emotion. "Why do you call me that?"

The question punches a hole right through my chest because of course I can't tell her about the white dress that clung to her like a desperate lover and the magnetic pull that locked into place the moment our eyes met. I clear my throat, focusing my attention on pouring creamer into my cup, so I don't have to look her in the eye when I skirt around her question.

"You don't like it?"

Her brows furrow. "I didn't say that, Dominic. I just wanted to know why you chose that particular... term of endearment."

I bite back a bitter laugh and mix in the creamer. *Term of endearment*, my ass. It's not a nickname or some cute epithet used in the fit of passion when you don't want to ruin the moment by calling the woman you're balls deep in the wrong name. I call her my angel because that's what she is to me.

The promise of God's love in human form, a treasure from heaven walking here on Earth making the lives of every person she meets better. And that's what she's always been, even when her presence chafed against my skin and burned a hole in my heart.

All of those thoughts fly through my mind, mixing with thoughts of the night we met. In all the time I dreamed about being with Sloane, I never considered how hard it would be to suppress the relentless memories that want to spill out of me. The need to make her remember is a pounding beneath my collarbone, a demand that builds with every beat of my heart, but she's not ready.

I shrug, turning my gaze back on her. "Just seemed fitting."

Her lips part, but before she can say anything the sound of her doorbell ringing echoes around us. Surprise laced with panic has

Sloane's eyes stretching wide. It would be comical if she didn't look so afraid. Indignation unfurls in my gut, stoked by the disappointment of having my morning with Sloane interrupted.

Whoever is at her door can go to hell in a hand basket. For interrupting us and for putting that look on Sloane's face.

"Shit." Sloane hisses, jumping up from her seat. "I forgot Mal and I were taking Mama to breakfast today." Wide eyes flick from the door to me and back again. "Where did you park?"

I take a sip of my coffee, and Sloane's eyes nearly pop out of her head. "In your driveway, like the rest of your guests."

My voice is even. I'm going for nonchalance because if I start freaking out it will only add to the terror gripping her. The doorbell sounds again and all of the color drains from her face.

"Oh my, God." She turns to me. Hopelessness creeping into the corners of her eyes. "Mal can't find you here, Dominic. She can't know about this. She'll think….she'll hate me."

The last part is a broken whisper that etches itself into my skin and jump-starts the ferocious beast in my chest that exists for the sole purpose of destroying everything and everyone that's ever put that look on her face.

"Sloane, look at me." I keep my voice soft, gripping her chin to force her to focus on my calm expression. "It's going to be okay. Go let Mal in and act like everything is normal."

Skepticism pulls her brows together. "But…"

"Just trust me, okay?"

She nods, setting the cup on the island with shaky hands before smoothing over her dress. Then she's moving towards the door with leaden feet. While she's taking the world's slowest trek across her hardwood floors, I head over to the sink with my cup and spoon. Pouring out the coffee and rinsing the cup quickly while Sloane calls that she's coming.

I see her stuffing the thong and dress we left in a heap by her door in a basket where she keeps pillows and throw blankets as I duck under her kitchen sink and start fiddling around with nothing at all.

Less than a minute goes by before I hear Mal and Sloane heading back into the kitchen. Mal's tone is animated while Sloane's is more reserved, and I silently curse myself for not considering the ramifications of parking in her driveway last night knowing full well Mal makes a habit of showing up here without calling or texting in advance.

"Why is Nic's car in your driveway?" Mal is asking now.

"Uh…" Sloane hesitates, leaving an awkward and suspicious gap in the already stilted conversation.

"Because," I say, making a show of closing the kitchen cabinets and standing. Sloane looks even more panicked than her voice suggested. "Someone thinks us being friends makes me her on-call plumber. She called me at the crack of dawn complaining about a leak in her kitchen sink, and I came over."

Mal scrunches up her nose at me. "In the clothes you were wearing last night? Please, don't tell me you spent the night at Kristen's again, Nic. I thought y'all were done."

Shit. I forgot about my clothes.

"Yeah," I say, rubbing my neck. "We were. I mean, we still are. Last night was just a one-time thing."

Sloane's eyes flash, a furious and brilliant spark of anger and jealousy that I feel in my groin. I meant what I said last night: jealousy looks good on her. She sits back down at the counter and sips her coffee to hide it, but I still see it. And it makes me hard.

Mal rolls her eyes. "Yeah, yeah. You say that now, but that woman doesn't want to let you go. Every time you give her the D, you encourage her. Tell him, Sloane."

"Right." Sloane's shoulders go back, and her eyes land everywhere but on mine. "You shouldn't encourage her, Dominic."

There it is again. Possession coating the delicate lilt of her voice, curling into the air and wrapping right around my balls. They tighten fiercely in response, and I'm glad I'm standing behind the island where neither of the women in the room can see what's happening in my pants. *I have to get out of here.*

"Well, I think I've got the leak taken care of, so I'm going to head out."

"Thanks for the help, Dominic," Sloane says, finally looking at me.

Mal smiles, her eyes bouncing between the two of us with fascination. "Wow. I can't believe you two are friends. Eric would be so happy to see you getting along."

Yep, it's definitely time to get out here. The mere mention of Eric's name has Sloane's hands shaking. I want to go to her, to rub her back and kiss the crown of her head until she steadies, but I can't do any of those things right now.

Instead, I send up a silent prayer that the progress we made last night isn't about to be undone by Eric's twin sister standing here talking about how her brother would feel about us no longer wanting to rip each other's heads off.

Not heads. Just clothes. Mal has no idea how well I'm getting along with her sister-in-law, and judging by the look on Sloane's face she won't ever find out, but that's a problem for another day.

"Don't mention it."

I flash them both a smile and fish my keys out of my pocket as I head towards the door.

"Okay, I need all the details. How was your date?" Mal says just as my hand touches the doorknob. I resist the urge to linger, knowing that talking about her date with me around will only make Sloane more nervous.

"There's not much to tell," Sloane starts.

But I don't hear the rest as I step out into the crisp morning air. It's almost September, and eventually, there will be a slight chill in the air. The leaves will go from green to hues of orange and yellow. Subtle shifts in the world around us that will pale in comparison to the life-altering changes happening in my life.

I allow myself a moment to let the events of last night and this morning sink into my skin, happy that for once acting on instinct and selfish need worked out in my favor. When I came here last night, I had no idea things would turn out like this. I was just driven by the need to see Sloane, to get her to accept my offer so I could have a plausible reason to be near her, a real chance to claim her in all the ways I promised myself I wouldn't.

And she gave it to me.

I can't do anything to stop the shit-eating grin stretching across my face as I climb into my car and pull out of her driveway. There's a dangerous bubble of happiness swelling in my chest, giving me just enough hope to make it until tonight when I get to take Sloane out to dinner.

19

DOMINIC

Eric's fingers shake as he goes from fiddling with his bow tie to the lapels of his tuxedo, and I nudge him with my elbow to make him stop. We've been standing at the altar for almost fifteen minutes, and the waves of nervous energy floating off of him into the air around us are wreaking havoc on the ball of dread in the pit of my stomach.

I should be used to it now, after carrying it around for so fucking long, but today it feels extra heavy. Today the jealous, covetous poison sloshing around inside of me feels like enough to break open the floor and drag me down to the depths of hell where I deserve to be.

Because what kind of man stands beside his life-long best friend, his brother, knowing just twelve hours ago he was standing outside his future wife's hotel suite with a truth that would destroy everything gathered on his tongue?

A fucked up, bastard of a man.

I don't know how I pulled myself away from Sloane's door but walking away from her— choosing to suffer so the two people I love more than anything can be happy together—was the hardest thing I've ever done in my life. At least that's what I thought at the moment, but standing here with Eric right now, I know the pain has only just begun.

"What's taking so long?" Eric's panicked eyes meet mine. "You don't think she's having second thoughts do you?"

I shake my head. "About you? Never. I'm sure it just took them a little longer than planned to get ready."

"Right. You're probably right."

"I am. Now fix your face, you look like *you're* the one having second thoughts."

He laughs and turns his back to me. "Screw you."

"I mean I'm open, but I'm pretty sure your wife wouldn't be too happy about sharing you on her wedding day."

Eric coughs to cover up the shocked laughter shaking his shoulders, and for the first time today, I smile a real smile. I even manage to keep it up when the doors fling open and the bridesmaids walk in, but the moment the bride's processional starts it dies on my lips. One by one, the muscles in my body go slack and then turn rigid until I'm nothing but a living, breathing statue with stone features.

The door swings open again and everyone's eyes land on the angel at the end of the aisle. My heart stutters to a stop. I was prepared to see her in white again, it is her wedding day after all, but nothing I imagined could have done the floral lace bodice hugging her torso or the full tulle skirt swirling around her legs justice. Her father has his arm linked in hers, and she's already crying. The silent tears slipping down her cheeks make her look infinitely more beautiful as she stares at Eric the way she always does. With love, hope, and possibility dancing in the pools of hazel.

And not a fucking shadow, or single spark of the flame I thought matched mine, in sight.

It's all the reminder I need to tuck away my feelings and slide on the mask I'll be counting on to get me through the rest of my life. As soon as it clicks into place, I force myself to look anywhere but at Sloane as she closes in on the alter.

Since Eric's shoulders are in my direct line of sight, I decide to make them my focal point for the rest of the ceremony, only looking up from them when I have to pull Sloane's wedding band out of my pocket and hand it to Eric. When he turns around to grab it from me, his smile is the biggest I've ever seen, and I allow myself to take comfort in it.

My best friend is happy.

The woman I love is happy.

I can live with a shattered heart if it means theirs get to stay whole.

* * *

"Pop, I have to go. They're giving speeches, and I'm pretty sure I'm next."

It's a lie. My speech was over an hour ago, and right after I gave it, I abandoned the reception hall for the quiet comfort of the hallway where I don't have to try to hide the ache in my chest at seeing Eric and Sloane together.

It shouldn't hurt like this. I've watched them together for years now, and they've basically been living in the loft for the past few months, but there's something about the wedding bands flashing on their fingers as they hold hands and kiss at the table that makes it all more devastating.

And ending up on the phone with my dad is only making me more irritable. He never calls me, but it's fitting that he would come out of the woodwork on the worst day of my life.

"Still don't know why I didn't get an invite," he gripes. "Eric grew up in my house."

"That's not how I remember it."

"Well, we've already established we remember things differently."

Yes, because you keep trying to rewrite history.

"Can you just tell me why you called so I can go?"

He coughs roughly, and the sound grates on my nerves. "Damn, boy. You can't give your old man five minutes to let you know he's dying?"

The whole world stops spinning and a wave of emotions I don't understand washes over me. I wouldn't say I'm sad, but there's a definite note of melancholy lacing the feelings swirling around in my gut. Probably stemming from the childish part of me that still loves him even though he's never done a damn thing to deserve it.

I scrub my hand over my face. "What are you talking about?"

"Lung cancer, Nic."

A door opens from somewhere behind me, and the noise of the celebration going on in the reception hall spills out. The sounds hit the quiet hallway in a quick burst then go quiet again when the door slams. I turn my head, hoping no one has come looking for me, and lose my breath when I see Sloane walking down the hall.

"I've got to go, Pop."

I hang the phone up and put it in my pocket before turning to face her. By some twist of fate, we're the only two people out here, but I know it won't be long before someone comes looking for her. She's the bride after all. And the most beautiful one I've seen in my life. I press my lips together to keep myself from saying that, or anything else, to her as she walks past me.

The same way she did years ago when one look in her eyes changed my entire life.

Only this time, she stops in front of me and turns on her heel. There's a steely determination in her eyes when they land on me, and even though I know I'm in no condition to talk to her right now, I can't bring myself to look away. She comes to a stop in front of me, and her perfectly manicured fingers are on her wedding band, spinning it around in a gesture I can't help but read as nervous.

"I've been looking for you."

I recoil as if she's physically struck me, and she might as well have because hearing her repeat the first words she ever said to me makes it feel like someone's ripping my heart right out of my chest.

"Why?"

Her teeth sink into the flesh of her bottom lip. "I was hoping we could come to some kind of agreement about how to navigate our relationship now that we're….family."

The laugh blooming in my throat tastes bitter as hell. Of all the things I dreamed of being with her, family isn't one of them. At least not in the way she means. "I have no interest in being your family, Sloane."

She holds her left hand up, and the light catches her ring. "Kind of late for that."

"Marrying Eric makes you his family, not mine."

I watch my words kill all the hope she had in her eyes when she marched out here and wish I felt bad for the way they hurt her. Her shoulders sag, and her jaw tenses as a single spark turns into a full-blown flame. And standing there, with those soft black curls cascading down her back contrasting perfectly with the angelic white of her dress, she looks more like the woman I fell in love with than she has in years.

"So you plan to treat me like *this* for the rest of our lives?"

Both of my hands turn into fists, and I shove them into my pockets as I step into her orbit. Her scent floods my nostrils, the same fruity, floral notes from a lifetime ago making my stomach churn.

"*I plan* to do you a favor and forget you wasted my time with this pointless conversation. Let's just call it my wedding gift to you."

Her lips part, and I can see all the things she wants to say scrolling across her features like a billboard. Reading her is second nature to me at this point, like blinking or taking my next breath, and I know every word her response will contain before she says them.

"You're such an asshole, Dominic. I don't know why I ever thought we could be anything more than what we are right now."

With a swish of her skirts and a withering glare, she twists on her heels and marches away. I watch her go, wondering how I'm going to survive the rest of my life with the weight of all the things I dreamed of being with her threatening to crush me.

20

SLOANE

"There isn't anything to tell, Mom. You were there for half of the date! You saw how it went."

I'm speaking through clenched teeth as I slam my front door behind me, which can only mean it's time to hang up the phone because the next step is screaming at the top of my lungs that I don't want to talk about my date with Ash Strickland.

Not with Mal, who spent the entire day insinuating that I made Ash leave early last night because I wanted to jump his bones.

Not with Mama, who found out about me dating through her big mouth daughter and was surprisingly supportive even if there was a glimmer of sadness in her eyes.

And most definitely not with my mom, who still hasn't apologized for the horrible things she said to me at dinner last week.

Apparently, she thought seeing me out with Ash last night meant I was finally taking her advice and getting under a new man to get over my dead husband, and I've spent the entire drive back to my house dodging her invasive questions when I should have been using that valuable time to think through what I'm going to say to Dominic tonight when he picks me up for dinner in less than thirty minutes.

I planned on using the day to get my mind right and maybe call Dr. Williams to ask another hypothetical question about the best way to convince your husband's best friend to fuck you five ways to Sunday, but Mama and Mal decided to turn breakfast into a full day of activities: shopping, nail salon, lunch at Twisted Sistas and then an afternoon of massages and gossip.

We had an amazing time, but now I'm struggling to make it in the house and freshen up before Dominic gets here. I've only heard from him once today, a text to tell me to be ready at six and to leave my panties at home, and I'm more eager than I've ever been to be in his orbit again.

"Well forgive me for caring about your love life." My mother continues, ignoring the tension in my voice. "I didn't even realize you were dating again. Especially with the fit you threw at dinner the other night."

"Going on a date doesn't mean I can't be upset about you minimizing my grief over the death of my husband."

She scoffs. "Sloane, please stop weaponizing your therapy phrases to make me the villain. My comment about your behavior at Eric's funeral was simply my opinion. I can hardly see how that's relevant to our conversation about your date with Ash."

"We're not having a conversation, Mom. You're asking inappropriate questions and giving me advice I didn't ask for."

My phone buzzes in my hand. I pull it away from my ear to see a text from Dominic lighting up my screen, and my heart cuts a flip in my chest.

Dominic: Be there in 15.

"Sloane Elise! I don't know when you got to be so rude and unappreciative of me, but I am not going to tolerate it anymore. Please call me when you remember how to be the respectful young lady I raised you to be."

Now it's my turn to scoff. The closest this woman has gotten to raising me was raising her hand to sign the check for the revolving door of nannies she kept on staff so she didn't have to bother caring for me. Still, there's a note of pain in her voice that tugs on my heartstrings. The ones she knows how to pluck better than anyone else. I grit my teeth. I can practically feel the apology her tone has elicited gathering on my tongue.

Guilt trip activated.

"Mom." I sigh, pulling several deep breaths through my nose. "I'm sorry for being short with you, but I meant what I said. My love life, past or present, is not up for discussion."

The words burn as they tumble out. She owes me an apology, but here I am feeling bad about snapping at her. Just another day with Lauren Carson as a mother.

"Fine. I won't show any interest in my only child's life even though you're always complaining about me not caring about you."

I roll my eyes. "I have to go now."

"Of course." She sniffs. "You always have something better to do. Goodbye."

And so do you. We both know you only called to see if you'll have any juicy news to share with your nosy, money-hungry friends at brunch tomorrow.

"Bye, Mom."

Hanging up the phone, I take the stairs two at a time and rush straight to my bathroom to freshen up. Minutes later, I emerge freshly showered, shaved, and moisturized. I check my phone and see that I have less than three minutes before Dominic arrives. He's nothing if not punctual, so I know he'll be here on time, looking amazing, smelling good, and, hopefully, completely over the whole 'let's take this slow' thing.

I rummage through the shopping bag from the boutique Mal, Mama, and I went to earlier today. It was a cute little shop with an amazing selection and inclusive sizing. Mal picked up a ton of things, but I only managed to find one that caught my eye. A burgundy midi skirt with a slit up the side that's high enough to expose most of my thigh but not enough to be indecent.

With no time to waste, I run into my closet and grab a cream camisole and a pair of sandals. Getting dressed takes no time at all given the whole no panty order and the fact that my top doesn't require a bra. When I'm done, I give myself one minute to check out my reflection in the mirror, and shock courses through me as I take in the woman standing in front of me.

A brazen, wide-eyed woman with lust lacing her features. A woman who spent the night in the arms of a man after years of sleeping alone and is looking forward to doing that, and more, again.

My thighs clench at the thought. Last night was amazing, but I want more and I know Dominic does too. For whatever reason, and against all the odds, this man feels the same thing I do when we touch. And even though I appreciate his reasons for wanting to take it slow—reasons that come from a soft, tender place I never expected to witness from Dominic first hand—I don't have any interest in doing so.

The need to have him, and let him have me, is an incessant pulsing in my blood, growing stronger with every beat of my heart. I'd be lying if I said I understand it, but I'm well past the point of dwelling on it. The only thing that matters is it exists, and I'm going to do everything in my power to make sure the man that's awakened the greedy and desperate hunger inside of me takes care of it *immediately*.

After all, that's what he signed on for.

I smooth the fabric of my skirt and adjust my top one last time before grabbing my phone and purse and heading downstairs. My foot has just hit the last step when the doorbell rings, causing the butterflies that have taken up residence in my stomach to take off in a mad dash, their wings stirring the desire unfurling low in my belly.

When I open the door for Dominic this time my hands only shake a little bit, but my breath still leaves me in a soft *woosh* at the sight of him. He looks mouthwatering in all black: a simple but expensive t-shirt, jeans that hug his thighs and probably make his ass look amazing, and low-top Converses. He looks good, really good, but I almost want to laugh at the simplicity of his outfit. *Fashion is so easy for men.*

Dominic clears his throat, pulling my attention to his eyes. They're two pools of midnight that threaten to swallow me whole, and I'm crazy enough to *want* to be pulled into their heated depths.

"Hey." I tuck a curl behind my ear to stop myself from yanking him into the house and saying screw dinner altogether. "You look nice."

His lips curl into a smirk, and I know he has a pretty good idea of what I'm thinking right now. Knowing Dominic, it's probably more than a good idea. He seems to have an uncanny ability to read my mind these days.

"I wish I had the words to tell you how incredible you look right now. Do you have everything you need?" He waits for me to nod before grabbing my hand and gently pulling me out the door.

I pull it closed behind me and lock it quickly before turning to face Dominic. "Don't tell me you've forgotten how to say thank you again. I thought we had that whole thing with your mouth figured out."

The late August air swirls around us, but all I feel is the heat pouring off of him.

"Don't make jokes about my mouth right now, Sloane."

I give him my best pout, pushing out my freshly glossed lips and loving the way his expression darkens when he tracks the movement with his eyes.

"Why? Are you feeling sensitive about it?"

He tugs on my hand, and I step forward until my breasts are pressed into his chest. My nipples tighten almost instantly at the contact. Dominic's hands go to my hips. His fingers are warm, and they dig into my flesh, squeezing just a bit as he looks down at me.

"No, angel. I'm not feeling sensitive about it, but I *am* trying to resist the urge to pin you against your door and show you exactly how well my mouth works. I thought I showed you last night, but I guess you need a reminder."

Yes, please. My thighs clench, and I lift my chin, silently begging him to kiss me. I want to feel his lips against mine, to relish in the slide of his tongue as he tastes me. God, I don't know when this obsession with him got so strong, but I don't plan on doing anything to stop it.

"Mhmm." I fist his shirt in my hand. The fabric is soft and smells like him. "A reminder sounds amazing. Let's do that instead of dinner."

Dominic's lips skate over mine. "Trust me, Sloane. You're going to want to go to dinner. The payoff will most definitely be worth it."

His warm breath mixes with mine, smelling like mint and oranges, and the only thing I want to eat for dinner is him. But the suggestive promise in his words is too much for me to ignore. If getting through a meal is the only thing standing between me and a replay of last night, this time featuring a naked Dominic, then I'll happily scarf down my food. I stand on my tiptoes, hoping to get closer to him. I want him to initiate and control the kiss because if I do it, I'm going to maul him right here on my porch.

"For both of us?"

Because another sexual encounter between us without him getting anything out of it, besides me coming on whatever part of his body he's using to please me, just seems unfair. He has to be sporting a major set of blue balls by now, and I'm desperate to give him as much pleasure as he's given me.

Finally, his lips touch mine. It's a short, chaste kiss that makes me smile, but his eyes are serious when he pulls back to look at me. "Are you under the impression that what we've done together so far hasn't been worth it for me?"

There he goes again, reading me like a damn book.

"Maybe." I bite my lip, suddenly feeling shy about voicing my concerns about his pleasure or lack thereof. "I mean it's not like you've actually, uh…finished while we've been together."

He gives me an amused smirk. "Don't worry about me, angel. I've gotten *more* than enough pleasure from watching you come."

This time my pout is real. "Dominic, we both know there's only so much pleasure you can get from watching me, and besides I want to—"

I stop short because I honestly don't know what I was going to say, and the last thing I want to do is let one of the scenarios from my ridiculous dreams pass through my lips.

Me wide open and dripping for him. Dominic's hands gripping my waist, yanking me down the bed and straight onto his dick.

Him fucking me from behind, his rough hands fisted in my hair as he pounds into me over and over again. The sound of his balls slapping against my ass as he bottoms out inside me with every thrust.

His large frame covering me. Our skin sticky with sweat and desire as he presses a soft kiss to my shoulder and whispers, "Come for me, Sloane."

A shiver rolls through me as the images flit through my mind, reminding me exactly why I shouldn't finish my sentence. There are too many possible endings, all of which would be incredibly embarrassing to express to him. There are a lot of things I want to do tonight, but dying from mortification is not one of them.

Dominic watches me, and I feel an embarrassing blush creeping up into my cheeks. He knows exactly what I'm thinking, and I wonder if I'll ever be able to stop my wayward thoughts from flashing across my face like a neon sign.

"Let's go, angel." He places his hand at the small of my back and ushers me off the porch. I follow him on unsteady legs and thank God that I decided not to wear heels tonight. "You can tell me about all the dirty things you want to do to me in the car."

I don't answer—mainly because I still can't believe that he reads me so well—and Dominic's lips twitch with amusement. Thankfully, he doesn't say anything else as he opens the car door for me and I climb inside.

I'm just securing my seat belt when Dominic folds himself into the driver's seat. He's still fighting back a smile, but there's something tender in his eyes when he looks over at me. His gaze is like the caress of reverent fingertips, slipping over my features, down the curve of my neck, and straight to the bit of cleavage left exposed by my top.

"Why are you looking at me like that?"

"Because I've just realized I can say you're the most beautiful woman I've ever seen without you biting my head off or doing that sexy little scowl that makes your nose scrunch up like you've smelled something rotten."

My mouth drops open. "I don't scowl!"

"Is that all you got from that, Sloane?" Dominic shakes his head as he starts the car and backs out of my driveway.

Like a fiend, I watch as he uses one hand to turn the wheel and the other to grip the headrest on my seat. The movement causes the cords in his forearms to bulge slightly, and I can't tear my eyes away.

"You're scowling right now." Dominic continues, glancing over at me. "Or at least you were before you started staring at my hands. I didn't know you had a hand fetish, angel."

I force myself to meet his gaze. "I don't. Not usually."

And it's the truth. I can't remember ever being as captivated by a man's hands, not even Eric's. They did the same job, but their hands couldn't have been more different. Eric's fingers were long and slender. He always did everything with an easy, gentle touch. But Dominic's hands are big and rough. Thick, calloused fingers with a confident dexterity that forces you to watch everything they do.

Something flickers behind his eyes, but before I can catch it he turns his attention back to the road. We fall into a silence, that's not exactly comfortable but not as awkward as it could be, as he navigates us through the city closer to his side of town. After a few minutes, the heart of New Haven comes into view, and my heart starts to beat a little faster. Every bar, restaurant, and club is packed to capacity on Saturdays, and if last night taught me anything, we could run into anyone while we're out tonight.

I didn't feel the need to tell Dominic we should avoid places our friends and family frequent, but now that he's pulling into a parking garage underneath Cerros—one of the most popular hotels in town, revered for its rooftop bar and incredible luxury suites—I'm starting to think I should have.

I shift in my seat, angling my body towards him. "Where are we going?"

It's a fight to keep my voice even, to sound casual while panic curls around my breastbone. It's the same thing I felt when Mal showed up at my house this morning and Dominic was sitting at my island sipping coffee like it was completely normal for us to be spending the morning together.

I don't know why I bother trying to conceal it because Dominic sees right through me like he always does. He puts the car in park and reaches over to brush his knuckles across my cheek. My eyelids flutter closed for a second. The gesture is calming, settling the nerves in my stomach almost instantly.

"Hey. I've got you, okay? I know you're not ready for anyone to find out about this—" He gestures between us. "—just yet, and I'm not either. Not before we have a chance to lay all of our cards on the table."

There's a steady certainty to his words that makes it impossible for me not to believe him. In my heart, I know Dominic wouldn't do anything to jeopardize this thing between us. Whatever it is, it's as special to him as it is to me. Hopefully, tonight will help me figure out exactly why.

I breathe a sigh of relief. "Okay."

Dominic searches my face before gifting me with a smile. If I had on any panties, they'd be on the floor right about now. "Okay. Let's go then."

He hops out and rounds the car. When he pulls my door open, I have to squeeze my legs together to make sure I don't flash him. Dominic's hand goes back to my back as we walk to the elevator. We step inside the car, and when he presses the button for the rooftop, a bubble of panic starts to rise in my throat. I force it back down, focusing instead on the handsome man beside me, who's currently sliding his hand down my back and over the curve of my ass.

Deft fingers knead my flesh, searching for a panty line we both know he won't find. I expect him to stop when he realizes I obeyed his order, but he doesn't. With all the grace and fluidity of a panther, he moves behind me. Pressing the hand that was just on my ass to my stomach and pulling me back into him. Once again, I find him hard as steel, and it sends a jolt of pleasure down my spine.

The elevator dings, letting us know we've passed another floor. Dominic runs a hand down the front of my skirt and over my mound. A grunt of satisfaction rumbles out of him as his fingers slip through my folds and find me wet.

"You're insatiable, angel." His breath is warm, caressing the shell of my ear and sending a shiver down my spine. "Should I make you come before I feed you or after?"

My head falls back against his shoulder. "Both. *Please.*"

Less than five seconds of his hands on me and I'm already begging. This is what he does to me, dissolves me into a desperate, breathless mess of a woman who doesn't care about anything as long as he's touching me with those rough fingers that promise pleasure mixed with a hint of pain.

"Who knew you were such a greedy girl?" Dominic's lips curve against my skin. "Keep your eyes on the door, love. We wouldn't want anyone to see how badly you want me."

There's a tinge of bitterness coating his words, but I don't have time to dwell on it. Dominic uses one of his feet to shove mine apart, widening my stance and opening me up for him. He dips one finger inside the warm wetness gathered at my core, treating me to several shallow thrusts, before dragging it up to my clit.

I bite my lip and let a small whimper escape me as his fingers swirl around the swollen bundle of nerves, using firm yet gentle pressure to coax my orgasm forward. I can feel it building, gathering low and heavy in the pit of my stomach.

Another ding sounds. We've passed another floor. Our journey to the top of the building has, thankfully, been unimpeded thus far, but I don't know what I'll do if we stop to let another passenger on. I'd like to believe I would have the decency to stop, but with Dominic's hands on me, I can't be certain.

"You've got about thirty seconds, angel. Less if this elevator stops and someone else gets on. If that happens, I'll have to stop taking care of this greedy little pussy and you'll have to wait until after dinner to come. Is that what you want?"

"N-no." I breathe, barely containing the moan climbing up my throat.

"It's not what I want either, baby. I want to hear you scream my name while you make a mess on my hand." Dominic nips at my neck, dipping his fingers back inside of me before spreading my wetness over my clit again. "You're so fucking wet for me, Sloane."

Ecstasy unravels in my veins from his filthy words and his skillful handling of my sensitive flesh. I rock into his hand feeling the promise of my release curling around the base of my spine. His free hand comes up to my breast, rubbing at the pebbled skin of my nipples through the thin fabric of my camisole. My eyes roll into the back of my head as thousands of shooting stars fire off behind my eyelids. Dominic kisses my temple.

"Do you have any idea how beautiful you look when you're about to come for me?"

I hear his question, but I can't answer. All of the words that I know have disappeared from my mind. Pushed out by the blood pounding in my ears and the heat from my core threatening to consume every living thing around me.

But once again, he isn't bothered by my lack of an answer, taking my moans for an answer as he keeps working at me. Each swirl around my swollen and needy nub delivers the perfect amount of pressure, and I can feel my arousal dripping down my leg.

"Fifteen seconds, baby."

Two thick fingers slip inside of me, driving into me with shallow thrusts that graze my g-spot lightly with every glide. I'm so wet there's no resistance at all, and the elevator car is filled with the sounds of his fingers invading my body, stroking pleasure into my core.

Dominic's thumbs are busy. One pressing into my clit with a delicious, almost torturous friction, the other joining with his index finger to pinch my nipples. And it's that bit of pain that sends me tumbling over a cliff with a scream that sounds a lot like Dominic's name before it turns into an endless moan when he keeps working me over. Using his hands to draw out every second of my pleasure even though he said we were short on time. When the last tremble has subsided, my body goes limp in his arms. I sag against his body, and he holds me up, gently fixing my clothes and raining kisses from my temple to my jawline until I catch my breath.

Another ding sounds, and I see we've only got two more floors to go before we hit the rooftop. It'll be filled with people eating, drinking, and having a good time with no clue what we've just done in the elevator. Behind me, Dominic is adjusting himself in his pants, seemingly unphased by his neglected, but very impressive, erection.

I bite my lip, keeping my eyes on the elevator doors to give him some privacy. "That can't be comfortable."

"It's not." He admits, stepping forward to place a kiss on the top of my head. "But I'll live. You need more time to adjust, and I'm going to give it to you whether you want it or not."

My body stiffens. *Now that just makes me want to scream.* While I appreciate his thoughtfulness, I'm over being treated like a ticking time bomb. A girl has one breakdown after an orgasm, and suddenly she's unable to handle the intricacies of a....whatever the hell this is?! He hardly seems concerned when he's using every part of his body but his dick to whip me into a frenzy, so why is this so different?

"Dominic. You can't go from having what I assume was regular sex with your ex to abstaining completely."

"And yet, here I am doing exactly that." He reminds me coarsely, wrapping his arms around my waist and hugging me closer to him. "Don't argue with me on this, Sloane. We're going to take this slow."

His tone brooks no argument, and I don't push him. All I've wanted to do since he left my house this morning is be with him, and I don't want to ruin it by arguing about something he's determined not to budge on. It shouldn't even bother me. I should be delighted that the man I spent so many years calling my enemy cares enough about me to take things slow.

Except, I've never known him to be the take-it-slow type. When we were in college, Eric would spend the night in my room just to get away from Dominic and his ever-growing harem that consisted of girls he met at parties, girls he sat beside in class, girls who came up to him in the library asking for a 'study date', multiple girls from the cheerleading squad and, if Mal is to be believed, one very young adjunct professor. In all that time, I never heard of him saying no to any one of them.

Hell, I'm certain he didn't because if he had, Eric wouldn't have practically lived with me freshman year.

Don't get me wrong, the orgasms are nice, but it's hard to feel like this waiting period is *only* about me adjusting. Maybe he's delaying things because deep down he wants to renege on the offer he begged me to accept just last night. Maybe this morning made him realize being with me isn't worth the trouble. The guilt. The lying. The sneaking around and hiding from the world. The potential to ruin relationships with people he's known and loved all his life.

Since this whole thing started, I've spent a lot of time thinking about how this thing could impact my life, but I'd be lying if I said I thought about what it would mean for his. Probably because I know any fallout from this will have a longer, more lasting, effect on me. If anyone finds out about us, at best I'll be the lying whore who spent her whole marriage lusting after her husband's best friend and finally seduced him. At worst, I'll be the shameless slut who fucked her husband's best friend while he was still alive and kept up the affair after he was gone.

But Dominic?

He'll just be the best friend who got caught in my web. A helpless man that couldn't do anything to protect himself against my feminine wiles. He'll be forgiven by Mama and Mal, revered by all the men in the Kent family for getting me to open my legs for him and repeatedly propositioned by the younger female relatives who will be desperate to have a taste of what I got to experience before he dropped me like a bad habit.

Suddenly, I'm thankful we're going to dinner to talk things through because I know the first thing I want to discuss: an end date for our arrangement. A twinge of sadness goes through me at the thought of ending things before we've even really begun, but I know I have to do it. It doesn't matter how good it feels right now, or how excited I am about getting a handle on my skin hunger issue, I can't lie and sneak around with Dominic forever. The risk is too great, and my heart can't take too many more situations like the one we had this morning.

Plus, knowing there's a time limit on us might be exactly what Dominic needs to quit being so stubborn about this whole sex thing.

I square my shoulders, prepared to have one hard talk for a few weeks of Dominic in my bed and between my legs. I smile to myself as the elevator dings one final time. The doors slide open, and Dominic gestures for me to go first. His hand goes to my back as we leave the car and step out into a short hallway with walls covered in greenery and the hotel's logo shining from a lit sign nestled in the vines on both walls. There's a hostess standing at a booth to our right, a young white girl with long red hair and a bright smile who grabs two menus as soon as she sees us coming.

"Welcome to Cerros! My name is Sarah, and I'll be your server for the evening. Please follow me to your table." She saunters down the hall without even asking us what name our reservation is under.

My eyebrows fall together as I look up at Dominic. His features are schooled into a mask of indifference as we move down the uncharacteristically empty hallway. I've only been here once before, with a client who insisted on treating me and my team to dinner after a project wrapped, but it shouldn't be so quiet on a Saturday night. Even if we are here earlier than most people.

"Dominic, why didn't she ask for your..."

The rest of my question dies on my tongue as we come out on the other side of the hallway and step right into the empty dining area. My mouth falls open, and I gaze up at Dominic with an obvious, and questioning wonder. This is why he wasn't worried about anyone seeing us tonight.

"You rented out the entire rooftop just to have dinner with me?"

I can't keep the disbelief out of my voice. Just last night I was surprised that Ash made reservations at Hill House, but now I'm stunned. I couldn't have ever dreamed someone, let alone Dominic, would do something like this for me.

Dominic gives me a long and heavy look, and I swear I see something—some emotion I can't name—moving behind his eyes like shadows I can't pin down no matter how badly I want to.

His hands come up to cradle my face. He rubs small circles on both of my cheeks before leaning down and brushing his nose across mine three times. Then his eyes are locked on mine, burning into me with a seriousness I can't bear.

"Let's take a seat, angel. I want to spend the entire evening staring at your lovely face and enjoying being in your presence without having to pretend like I don't know what you sound like when you come."

21

SLOANE

Now

Heat rushes to my cheeks at Dominic's words. I'm starting to think the man gets off on making me blush. *Pretty sure it's the only thing he's getting off on these days.* Especially if what he said about not sleeping with Kristen in over a month is the truth. I have no way to confirm it, but for some reason, I believe him. I've known Dominic to be a lot of things, but a liar isn't one of them.

Sarah stands off to the side, waiting patiently for us to take our seats at the table closest to the glass panes lining the edge of the rooftop. There are fresh-cut flowers and lit tea candles in the center of the table. Dominic releases my face and grabs my hand, pulling me gently towards the table. I follow quietly, still kind of stunned by his words and the incredibly romantic gesture he's just made.

He pulls my chair out and makes sure to brush his fingers across my shoulders when I take my seat. I admire the way the denim hugs his ass as he moves around the table and folds himself into the chair across from me. Sarah sets a menu in front of each of us and takes our drink orders before disappearing, leaving us alone with the city of New Haven spread out before us.

"Dominic, this is…" I pause. "There aren't words to describe what this means to me."

His eyes are on my face, and he's looking at me like he wants to burn the image of my pleasure into his mind. And there it is again. That stupid blush creeping up my cheeks, making me flush like a teenage girl. I can't hold his gaze, so I focus on my menu instead.

He reaches across the table and lifts my chin. "I'd do anything to put a smile on your face, Sloane. Just say the word and it's yours."

"Anything, huh? I can think of at least one thing you won't give me even though I've asked for it repeatedly."

He runs a thumb across my bottom lip, amusement flickering in his eyes. "Patience is a virtue, angel."

"That's what they say." I agree, taking his hand in my own. I don't think I'll ever get used to having the right to touch him like this. I press a kiss to his palm, just because I can, before letting it go. "But it's never been something I've excelled at."

Dominic sits back in his seat and crosses his arms. The same thumb that was just running over my bottom lip is now skating over his.

"Why are you in such a rush?"

His gaze rolls across my features, studying me with the same relentless intensity I've seen him give the blueprints from James' architect. Suddenly I feel hot and uncertain about what I want to say. All the strength and resolution I had in the elevator falls away, stripped down by the heat in his tone.

I shift in my seat. "I just don't want us to run out of time. We have a specific goal we're trying to achieve, and I don't see the point in waiting. Especially when we don't know how long this is going to last…" Dominic's hardening expression makes me lose my train of thought. "Why are you looking at me like that?"

"Just trying to understand why you're talking about this ending before it's even started."

Both my shoulders go up in a gesture my mother would frown at. Lauren Carson doesn't believe in shrugging or slouching or any movement that makes you look anything but perfectly polished and sure of yourself.

"I'm not, but I know it's not realistic to think we can do this for an extended amount of time, Dominic. The lying, the sneaking around, the freaking out when Mal shows up at my house unexpectedly. You saw me this morning. I'm liable to have a heart attack before I ever see you naked!"

The last part of my rant makes the corner of his mouth tip up just a bit. He thinks it's funny that I'm obsessed with seeing him without any clothes on, and I can't blame him. If I wasn't the desperate one, I would probably think it was funny too.

I take a sip of my water just to keep anything else from coming out of my mouth. I don't know where this forward and brazen woman has come from. No one would ever describe me as shy, but I am not in the habit of harassing men about taking me to bed. But then again, I haven't dated in over a decade, and Eric never had a problem with dicking me down on the regular.

Eric. I nearly choke on my water when I realize I've just compared Dominic to Eric in the most unfair way. Eric is the whole reason he wants to take things slow. My hand shakes slightly as I set my glass down.

"You okay?" Dominic arches a brow, catching the tremble in my hand.

I nod. "Yes."

"Good." He leans forward, steepling his fingers as he regards me. "Do you remember the point of this dinner, angel?"

His voice is black velvet, the words sliding over my skin like a caress. My breath leaves my lungs and takes all of my coherent thoughts with it. "We're establishing rules for our—"

"Relationship." Dominic finishes for me, possessiveness flaring in his eyes.

Although I just had a sip of water, my mouth is suddenly dry. I lick my lips, "Yes, our relationship." I start to squirm in my seat, but the movement is immediately halted when I feel the evidence of my recent orgasm at the junction of my thighs. It's crazy how I can let the man kiss me at work, bring me to orgasm in an elevator, and spend the night in my bed, but hearing him say we're in a relationship makes me nervous.

And there's no doubt in my mind it's because of the vow I swore after Eric died. The one where I promised to never pursue anything even resembling a relationship because my last chance at happiness and love died with my husband.

Relax, it's not like he's asking you to marry him. He's probably just trying to help you feel more comfortable about using him as your personal sex toy.

I exhale through my nose. Yes, that makes a lot of sense. He knows I haven't been with anyone since Eric, I told him as much last night, and he probably thinks putting a label on it will make me feel safe and secure in this mess we're about to make.

Dominic opens his mouth to say something, but he's interrupted by the loud buzzing coming from his phone. It's face down on the table, so I can't see who's interrupting the conversation I've waited all day to have with him, but when he looks at the screen he frowns and hits decline.

The phone starts ringing again before he even puts it back on the table, and a flash of annoyance crosses his face as he stabs the decline button again.

"You can take the call. It must be important if they called two times in a row."

He waves a dismissive hand. "No, this is more important. Tell me what you need, Sloane, and I'll give it to you. This dinner isn't just about discussing my rules, and I *do* have rules, but I want to know what you need out of this. What you need from me."

"I—"

"Alright, you two. What can I get for you?"

Sarah is back with a bright smile on her face and a notepad in her hand. Dominic gestures for me to order first, but I have no idea what I want, reading the menu has been difficult with the most intense midnight stare burning into my soul. Dominic and Sarah wait patiently for me to decide, and I settle on wagyu beef sliders and a side salad. Dominic doesn't even glance at the menu before he orders a grass-fed New York strip with a side of roasted potatoes. As he hands the menus back, he orders a glass of Shiraz to go with my entree.

I arch a brow at him, and he smiles. "You'll enjoy it. Trust me."

"How do you know? You don't drink."

"True, but I do dine frequently with people who drink." His lips curve into a smile. "And they've said the wine goes well with the sliders you ordered."

My elbows rest on the edge of the table as I lean forward. "Tell me more about these people you dine with frequently."

Dominic shakes his head. "Letting the green-eyed monster get a hold of you again, angel?"

"No." *Yes. Maybe a little.* "Just making conversation."

"A few years ago, Cerros underwent a small-scale renovation. The scope of work included suites on the top floor as well as the rooftop conversion. Do you remember?"

I almost don't hear the question because I'm too caught up watching his finger trace the rim of his glass with the same finger that was inside of me when I came less than twenty minutes ago.

"Yes." I swallow. "Mal wanted us to bid on the project, but we'd just lost one of our senior designers, and I didn't want to be stretched thin."

"Right." He murmurs. "She was sad that we missed the chance to work on a project together."

My eyes snap to his face. "Archway handled the renovation."

"*I* handled the renovation personally, per the owner's request. He had been burned by contractors before and wanted to be sure his project was in good hands." He lifts a cocky brow as he says the last word, and a fire erupts in my veins. "Anyway, by the time we were done, he owed me a few favors."

Understanding seeps into my bones. *Owed.* As in the past tense. As in Dominic cashed in a valuable favor owed to him by a powerful man because he knew I would be worried about someone seeing us together. And not just *any* powerful man, but Sebastian Adler of Adler Holdings, the oldest son of the family who shocked the world when he decided to open a chain of hotels, luxury condominiums, and restaurants instead of taking the CEO title he was raised to hold in the family company.

"Dominic, you didn't..."

"I did, and I'd do it again just to see the look on your face when we walked in here and you realized the place was empty."

I tilt my head to the side, wondering if I'll ever get a handle on this man or the whirlwind of emotions he stirs up in me when he shows me his sweet side every now and again. "Who knew there was a heart under all that asshole-ish behavior?"

"Asshole-ish?" He laughs, and the sound is warm and rich, washing over me in waves. "All that private school education and you resort to making up words?"

I wrinkle my nose at him. "It's not a made-up word. It's an informal adverb that means 'to some extent.' You know like *Black-ish?* Kind of Black or, in your case, kind of an asshole."

He gives me a questioning look before treating me to a grin that I'm way more attached to than I should be at this point. "Damn. That was kind of sexy. I always hated English, but I could listen to you say shit like that all day."

Suddenly, I'm blushing again and a stupid giggle escapes my lips. I take another sip of water and wave him off. "Shut up."

"I'm serious though. When you say stuff like that or hand James his ass about looking at finishes in an unfinished room, it just reminds me how incredible you are. I haven't told you that enough, even though I've always thought it."

Even though I've always thought it.

I never hated you, Sloane.

Dominic's confessions ring in my ears, reminding me once again that nothing with him is as exactly as it seems. All these years I thought he hated me, barely tolerated my presence, resented every breath I took, but now he wants me to believe none of that was true.

And the worst part is: I kind of do.

Of course, I still have questions. Like if he never hated me, why did he always insist on treating me like the most annoying person on the planet? And if he thought I was so amazing for all these years, why couldn't he have told me? It surely would have saved us both a lot of time and aggravation. Not to mention the peace it would have brought to Eric, Mal, and Mama.

"You could have told me, Dom—"

Loud vibrations coming from his phone cut me off, startling me and chopping his name in half so it becomes an overly familiar nickname with all kinds of sexual innuendo attached to it. I blush furiously as he picks up the phone and moves to decline the call again.

"Don't!" I shake my head. "Whoever it is, they need to speak to you, so please take it."

"Are you sure? It's just Kristen and I can call her back later."

Hearing Kristen's name on his lips makes me second guess my suggestion but backing down now will only make me look petty and insecure. Two things I certainly am not.

"Yes. Take the call, Dominic."

He rises from his chair, phone in hand and a smirk on his lips. "I think I like it better when you call me Dom."

"I didn't call you Dom," I call out to his retreating back. "Your phone cut me off."

I roll my eyes and admire the way those tight, black jeans hug his ass and muscular thighs perfectly. His broad shoulders line with tension as he puts the phone to his ear. Nothing about his situation with Kristen makes sense to me. He says they're over, that their relationship and the friends with benefits situation has been done for quite some time, but she still touches him like she owns him, still calls him like he's supposed to be on his way home to her.

She's possessive of him, and it bothers me more than it should because Dominic isn't mine. At least not in a real way. Not in the way he belonged to Kristen when they were together. Not in the way Eric belonged to me when he was here. Whatever we have now isn't the same as what we shared with them, and I don't think it gives me the right to question why Kristen feels the need to call him back to back any more than it gives him the right to question why I sleep in Eric's shirt every night.

Not that he would ask. Apparently, Dominic doesn't struggle with the same jealousy issues I do when it comes to Eric. Other men, like Ash and James, are a different story altogether though. Seeing me with both men brought out the same green-eyed monster he accuses me of having on my back, and even though I've never admitted it to him, I *am* jealous.

Because Kristen gets to call him whenever she wants. She gets to run her greedy hands all over his body in public and call him 'babe' no matter who's around. And worst of all, she knows what it feels like to have him inside her. She's experienced the things I've only dreamed about doing with him firsthand, and it makes me want to claw her eyes out.

I take another sip of my water, hoping the cool liquid will soothe the ugly, hot envy burning inside of me that's aimed squarely at the woman who's currently monopolizing the time Dominic should be spending with me.

Over my shoulder, I hear Sarah's heels clicking on the concrete as she approaches the table with several plates expertly balanced in her hands and along her dainty forearms. Behind her, a stunning woman with rich ebony skin and eyes the color of whiskey waits patiently for the plates to be set with a glass of wine in her hand. One look at her perfectly tailored, designer pantsuit and the sleek, but sexy, ponytail her wavy tresses are secured in tells me she's not a server like Sarah even though their name tags are identical. Hers says Nadia, and she's probably Sarah's boss, which would make her the manager and the one person working who has better things to do than personally deliver a glass of wine. Still, she sets it in front of me with a smile before turning on her heel to leave.

Sarah wipes her palms on her apron and glances at me. "Does everything look good? Can I get you anything else?"

"No. I think we're okay for the moment. Maybe more water for him."

I indicate Dominic with my chin, and both of our eyes go to him. He's still on the phone but his back is turned to us, so I can't tell how the conversation is going. Judging by the continued tension in the line of his shoulders, it's probably not good.

"Of course," Sarah says breathlessly, and I resist the urge to roll my eyes at the red flush creeping up her neck. She clears her throat and drags her eyes back to me. "You're so lucky to have a boyfriend like Mr. Alexander. He seems like an extremely thoughtful partner."

Keeping the disbelief from lining my features is a challenge. *Were girls always this bad at hiding their interest in the man currently buying you dinner?*

"Yes." I agree, pinning her with a look I've seen my mother use on overly friendly women who faun over my dad at the country club. "Dominic is a very thoughtful man."

I don't feel the need to tell her he's not my boyfriend. The last thing this dinner needs is Sarah throwing herself all over Dominic while she refills his water glass. *If he ever makes it back to the table, that is.*

A flicker of uncertainty passes through her corn-flower blue eyes, and I only hate myself a little bit for channeling my mother to make her feel uncomfortable.

"Right. I'll be right back with that water."

I nod mixing the dressing into my salad without looking at her. "Sounds good. Thank you, Sarah."

The sound of her heels clicking back to the server's area ring out and then subside quickly, leaving me in near silence. Dominic's voice carries from the other side of the dining area as he turns his head to look at me. I feel his gaze, but I keep mixing my salad. Whatever they're discussing doesn't have anything to do with me, but my heart still lifts when I hear him tell her he has to go.

When his heavy footsteps are heading back towards the table, I finally allow myself to look up. His brows are pinched together and the muscle in his jaw is fluttering rapidly. Obviously, the phone call with Kristen has made him upset. I open my mouth to ask what's wrong, close it because my brain is screaming that it's none of my business. Then open it again because it kind of is my business since she interrupted our dinner.

"Is everything okay?"

Dominic sits down with a sigh. "Yeah. She's just..." He scrubs a hand over his face. "I don't know what's going on with her lately. There's this case she's handling at work that has her stressed out, and she's used to venting to me."

My lips roll inward as I try to school my features into an expression of understanding I don't feel. I want to give Kristen the benefit of the doubt because I can't imagine the stress she's under as a defense attorney. My dad just handles real estate law, and he's got high blood pressure directly related to his job, so I believe dealing with high-profile cases where people's lives are on the line can take its toll on you.

But I find it hard to believe Dominic is the only person in her life who can understand what she's going through. I mean, she must have friends from work, family members, or a therapist she can call on Saturday night when she's having a breakdown.

And who's sitting around thinking about work on a Saturday night? Not anyone I know.

I study Dominic as he takes a sip of water and fight the urge to tell him his ex-girlfriend is full of shit. She might be stressed at work, but that doesn't have anything to do with the back to back calls to his phone on a Saturday evening when most single, attractive men are either out on a date or preparing to go out and find someone to spend the rest of their night with.

It kind of feels like she's determined to get in the way of him moving on, and I can't help but wonder if she was the one calling him back to back that night at Club Noir. Judging by her behavior tonight, that seems extremely likely.

"It's nice of you to be there for her," I say before taking a sip of my wine to wash away the bitter taste of the lie.

Dominic's eyes burn into mine as he cuts into his steak. "You don't mean that."

What's the point of lying when the man sees right through me?

"No." I bite my lip and hold his eyes. "I don't."

His gaze drops to my mouth. "You never told me what you need from me, angel. We're not leaving this rooftop until we both lay out what we need to make this relationship work."

I blink, confused at the sudden change in direction. Dominic takes a bite of his steak and lifts a brow as he chews. He wants me to go first, but I don't know why. He was the one who wanted to use this dinner to tell me his rules.

I smooth my hands over my skirt. "I only have one thing I need, but judging by your reaction when I brought it up earlier, you're not going to like it."

He continues eating, but I'm suddenly too nervous to take a single bite of my food. Instead, I sip on my wine and try not to squirm under the weight of his silence. Finally, he swallows. The motion causes his Adam's apple to bob. *Damn, he even makes eating sexy.*

"You want to put an expiration date on us." Emotion flares behind his eyes before fading into unforgiving obsidian. "Tell me why."

I push the greens in my salad around. "Well, I don't know how long it'll take to solve my uh….problem, but I'm sure you don't want to be tied up in this—"

"Don't make this about me, Sloane, and don't lie."

"I'm not lying, Dominic."

"Yes, you are." His jaw tenses. "Now tell me the real reason."

I set my fork down and sigh. "Because the longer this goes on, the more likely it is that Mal or Mama will find out, and I don't think my relationship with either of them would survive that. They'll hate me, Dominic, and I can't lose them."

Several seconds tick by, and I watch Dominic weigh my words. Turning them over in his head with careful consideration. My heart pounds in my chest as I wait for him to say something, hoping he'll agree to the only condition I have because if he doesn't, I don't know what I'm going to do.

You're going to walk away. The voice in my head sneers and I hate to admit it, but it's right. If Dominic can't agree to this, then I'm going to have to walk away from him.

Even if the thought threatens to destroy my already shattered heart.

22

DOMINIC

Now

I'm becoming too familiar with the way Sloane's forehead creases and her beautiful hazel eyes widen when panic is coursing through her veins. It's a look I've seen more than I'd like to admit over the past few weeks: when that bastard had his hands on her in the club, when I walked in on James kissing her, when I burst into the women's bathroom last night and scared the shit out of her, this morning when Mal showed up at her house, and right now when she's waiting on me to respond to her suggestion that we put an end date on us.

Every cell in my body is screaming at me to shut the idea down. To lean over the table and tell her in no uncertain terms that she is mine. I've waited twelve fucking years to have her, and now she wants me to agree to what? A few weeks or months in her bed?

My hand clenches into a fist at the thought of getting so little of her even as I admit to myself that her reasons are valid. I know how much her relationship with Mal and Mama means to her. They're her family, and I can't say with any kind of certainty they won't react exactly the way she thinks they will if they find out about us.

But damn if this isn't fair. Twelve years of waiting just to be given....

"How long?"

Sloane flinches at the sharpness of my words, but she recovers quickly. "Until the renovation at La Grande Nuit is done. That should be long enough to get a handle on my skin hunger. Plus, when the project is done we won't have a reason to be around each other as much."

Right. I guess it doesn't matter that you've fucking owned me for twelve years, and I don't know how I'm going to survive you.

My jaw tenses as I do the mental calculation. My team has been ahead of schedule so far, which means barring any major changes from James, we have eight weeks left in this project. *Eight weeks.* I want to throw something.

"There are eight weeks left in the project. Is that all you want?" I set my fork down and study her. "Two months hardly seems like enough time for you to get comfortable with what's happening here."

Her nostrils flare, and I can see the irritation slipping over her features. She thinks I'm being patronizing, handling her with kid gloves, but I'm the only person at this table who knows how fucking broken she looked when she left me in that bathroom on Tuesday. So far we haven't had another one of those situations, and I want to trust that she's ready for more, but Sloane has no idea what it's going to mean for me and her when I finally claim her the way I should have all those years ago.

It's going to mean forever. It's going to mean no turning back. It's going to mean more than eight weeks in her fucking bed like a man on borrowed time.

"You don't think I'm comfortable?" Sloane hisses. "I let you finger me in an elevator on the way up here, and you don't think I'm comfortable with what we're doing here?!"

My dick twitches, her words making me flashback to the heady rush of having my way with her. When I rubbed her ass and found out she obeyed my command to leave her panties at home, it made me hard in an instant. It took every bit of restraint I had not to pin her against the wall and fuck her until she saw stars.

"We both know sex is different, angel." I reach over the table and grab her hand. She's still mad, but she doesn't snatch away. "Last night you said this was new for you, which I took to mean you haven't—" I search her eyes, hoping that bringing up Eric isn't about to blow this all to hell. "—I assumed it meant you haven't been with anyone since Eric. Was I right?"

Please, God, say I am. I don't want to have to waste a second of our time together hunting down every man she's been with and making him forget what it was like to have her.

"Yes." She answers softly, some of the stiffness leaving her shoulders.

I rub small circles on her skin with my thumb, and she lets out a sigh. "And we both remember what happened on Tuesday, so please stop trying to rush this. I know a lot of ways to bring you pleasure that don't include pushing you to the end of your limits and fucking this all up."

"Fine." She releases my hand and crosses her arms. "If you want to spend the next few weeks doing everything but the one thing we both want to do, that's what we'll do. But if I break my vibrator or die from sexual frustration because you refuse to give me some dick, that's on you."

I try to hold the laugh in, I swear I do, but something about the petulant little scowl marring her beautiful features and the seriousness of her tone when she mentions her vibrator, rips a loud laugh from my throat.

Sloane rolls her eyes at me and tries to hide the smile threatening to curve her lips by taking a bite of the salad she's been playing over since this conversation started. By the time I'm done laughing, she's moved on to her sliders and her eyes are rolling into the back of her head as she chews. I don't even try to hide that I'm watching her enjoy her meal.

"I want to spend a whole day feeding you, just to have the pleasure of watching you eat."

She takes a sip of her wine and raises a brow. "Is that your first rule, Mr. Alexander?"

There's a sultry curve to her lips as they wrap around the question, and it makes my dick throb. I've been hard since Sloane mentioned our little scene in the elevator, and the situation has gotten even more dire. I try to be subtle about adjusting myself in my pants.

"No, but I might be inclined to add it to my list of things I hope to get the chance to do over the next eight weeks."

Hopefulness smoothes the creases in her forehead. "So you're not fighting me on the end date anymore?"

"No." *Yes, just not in the way you think.* "You make some good points, and I don't want anything to get in the way of this." *Of me claiming your body and soul. Of me etching myself into your lungs until you can't fucking breathe without me.*

I take a bite of my steak and soak up the sunshine of her smile. There's no need for Sloane to know I plan on spending the next eight weeks making her need me as much as I need her. I've lived a lifetime without her in my arms, hating myself for wanting her, and now that I have her, letting her go is not an option.

"Thank you, Dominic."

"You don't have to thank me, angel. Do you have more cards to lay on the table?"

"No, I'm good. All of my cards are out there."

Great, so the only thing you need is a definitive ending to the best thing that's ever happened to me. Keeping the bitter thought from showing on my face is hard as hell, but I manage to do it. It's the only way to keep this conversation on track, and damn do I want to get this shit over with so I can take her home and bury my face between her legs.

"Perfect. Then are you ready to hear my rules?"

"Yes."

She's breathless like she was in the club last night when I ran my hands over her curves in that stunning red dress. But instead of leaning into my body, soft and pliable like putty in my hands, her back is ramrod straight. Her shoulders squared and her eyes thoughtful as they meet mine. Now, she's all business.

I tap my fingers on the table slowly, just to see if her business-like facade will break. My angel has a thing for hands. Specifically, *my* hands, which gives me more pleasure than it should. Sloane's gaze flicks to the table for less than a second, her tongue a flash of pink as it darts out to lick her lips. I give her a wolfish smile, and the sick satisfaction that stems directly from owning a part of her she hasn't given to someone else sends sparks of liquid fire down my spine.

"Let's get straight to it then. First things first, and I think this should go without saying, as long as there's an us, there's no one else. No James. No Ash. And no other asshole Mal thinks you'll enjoy spending an evening with."

Sloane pushes her empty plate away. "Fine. That also means no more Kristen."

"I've already told you Kristen and I aren't a thing."

"You should tell *her*. Because the back-to-back phone calls and the hand she was running all over your body at the club last night tells me she hasn't accepted that truth yet."

Fuck, jealous Sloane is sexy as hell, but she's also wrong. Kristen knows it's over between us. Yes, she did get a little friendly in front of Sloane last night, but that's just how she is when she's drinking. And tonight, well she was just freaking out about being passed over for partnership if she loses her current case.

"We're just friends, and before you ask, yes I meant it when I said I haven't slept with her in weeks."

Sloane's shoulders go back. "And you've been tested since then?"

There's something dangerous about those words coming from her —a sinful implication that coaxes the image of me spurting hot ropes of cum into her spasming pussy, right to the front of my brain. Thoughts of filling her up until it leaks out and runs down her thighs, covering our joined skin in the sticky evidence of my need for her has my balls tightening viciously. *Jesus. Will she let me have that?*

The hungry glint in her eye makes me think it's a possibility.

"Yes, angel. Even though I always use condoms, I make a point of getting tested regularly. I'm clean, and I don't doubt that you are."

"I am, and I have an IUD." She takes another sip of her wine. When she says the last part, she glances away from me, and I swear I see something close to shame passing over her features before she looks at me again. "So, no other men for me and no other women for you. What else?"

"I want you in my bed every night. We'll have to spend all day long pretending like nothing has changed between us when everything has, and while I understand your reasoning, I know the only way I can live through it is if I know you'll be coming home to me when the day is over."

Home to me. Let her continue to think this is temporary after spending every night sleeping in my arms.

Sloane bites her lip, and those worried little creases are back in her forehead. I search her eyes, hoping to find the source of the uncertainty flickering in their golden depths, but come up empty. Honestly, I didn't expect this to be an issue. She didn't complain about sharing a bed with me last night, so I don't get her hesitation.

"I can't do that."

"Why? I seem to remember cuddling being one of the things on your list of desired physical activities, and it certainly would help improve your quality of sleep, which I've read can be an issue for people who suffer from touch starvation."

Her brows lift in surprise. "You researched touch starvation?"

"I promised I would help you. I can't do that if I don't have all the facts available to me. Now tell me why we can't spend every night together."

"I don't have a problem with us spending every night together. I just can't stay at your place because it'll feel weird to be there with you after the nights I spent there with Eric when you two lived together." She sighs, her brows furrowing together as she fiddles with her wedding band. "I know that must sound ridiculous, but I just can't be there without thinking about him."

Of course. Eric spent a year in the second bedroom of my place—

which I turned into an office a few years back—because Mama forbid him from living with Sloane before they got married. It was a pointless declaration since they alternated between the loft Eric and I shared and the townhouse Sloane shared with Mal.

Mostly though, they were at our place. Laughing on the couch. Play fighting in the kitchen. Quietly making love when they thought I was asleep, the only indication they were doing anything at all being the light tapping of the headboard against the wall.

Thankfully, time and the structural changes I made when I took out a mortgage on the place, have helped me forget all about the months I spent avoiding my own home just to get away from them. Still, I should have thought about what it would mean for me to demand that she spend every night in my bed. It was an oversight on my part, and it won't happen again.

"No. You don't sound ridiculous, angel. I don't want you to be uncomfortable or worried when you're in my arms at night, but where do you suggest we sleep? Because waking up next to you isn't up for discussion."

She smirks. "That's usually what it means when you say something is a rule, Dominic."

"Are we back to Dominic now?"

"We never left it."

I can't help but smile. She's so beautiful and stubborn as hell. How she can insist on being so formal when I've had my fingers inside of her on multiple occasions is beyond me, but I won't press. As much as I'd love to hear her use a nickname for me—one that reflects the intimate relationship we now have and reminds me of our night together— I know it's not important in the grand scheme of things. She's agreed to every single one of my rules with no argument, so I can give her this one concession. Even if she doesn't understand what it means for me to do so.

"If you say so." I shrug, taking a final bite of my potatoes before pushing my plate out of the way. "Would you feel more comfortable sleeping at your place?"

"Yes, unless you think Sebastian Adler wants to put us up in the penthouse for the next two months," she jokes. "Though I'm pretty sure giving you this place for the night means *you* owe him one now."

An amused huff passes my lips. "Seb owes me more than one favor, angel, and I'd happily cash them all in for you. But, I don't think you want that. You want this new thing to happen somewhere you feel safe and secure, and that's what we're going to do, but tell me one thing."

The corners of her mouth tip up in a soft smile, and the urge to kiss her is like a kick to the gut. I love seeing her happy. Love being the one who made her that way. Her shoulders are relaxed, her cheeks are that perfect rosy color that indicates the presence of alcohol in her system. She's beautiful. The most incredible woman I've ever had the pleasure of sharing a meal with. The living, breathing embodiment of all of my wildest dreams, and s*he's mine.*

"What do you want to know?"

"What happens when Mal shows up unexpectedly and my car is in your driveway?"

She worries the plump flesh of her bottom lip between her teeth briefly. "You can park in my garage. No one ever goes in there, and I'll tell Mal to make a habit of calling before she pops up or I'm going to take my key back."

Of course, she let the nosiest person on Earth have a key to her house so she would be free to come and go as she pleases. Never in a million years would I give that woman the ability to pop up on me without a moment's notice, but Sloane and Mal are like sisters. They don't think twice about being in each other's space all the time. It's a small miracle Mal knocked on the door this morning instead of barging in like she owned the place.

"Sounds like you thought this through." *How to hide us. How to end this. How to make it out of this clean when I know there's no way in hell that's going to happen for me.*

"I have." She tips back the rest of her wine. "Now, are you going to fight me on this or are you going to take me home and let me thank you for this amazing dinner?"

My mouth goes dry as the image of Sloane on her knees in front of me with her pretty lips wrapped around my dick bombards me.

"Almost, angel."

I motion for Sarah to come forward. She rushes over, and her eyes flit nervously between me and Sloane as she clears the table in record time. I stand and walk around to Sloane, offering her my hand. She takes it with a smile, and I pull her close to me. One hand goes around her waist while the other grips her nape. I brush my nose over hers, breathing in her sweet scent, and she sighs.

"I've got one last rule."

Her breath skates over my lips. "What is it?"

"I say when." I hold her gaze, watching my words wash over her before continuing. "We're not fucking this up because you're dissatisfied with your vibrator. I take care of the things that belong to me, Sloane, and *you are mine*. Your smart mouth, your incredible mind, and your greedy little pussy." I study her face, hoping she catches the finality of my words. Hears how determined I am to not let her go. The rapid fluttering of her pulse under my thumb makes me think she does, even if it's just subconsciously. "Every part of you belongs to me, and I might not be worthy of the job, but I promise you I won't rest until all of your needs are met. All you have to do is trust me to take care of them. Can you do that, angel?"

Can you trust me to take care of your body and your heart?

Sloane nods. "Yes."

Her easy agreement sets something free in my chest, and I lean down to take her mouth in a rough kiss. Her lips part on a moan, and I take full advantage of her openness, slipping my tongue into the wet heat of her mouth and exploring like it's the first time all over again. Kissing Sloane is like floating in an ocean of relief, desire, hope, and the pure, unadulterated need that's been bubbling inside of me for years. I don't know if I'll ever get used to holding her in my arms, running my hands all over her ass, and caressing the generous dips of her hips.

When I finally release her, my dick is hot and throbbing against her stomach, and half-lidded eyes, hazy with lust, meet mine as she palms my erection with her tiny hand. I suck in a breath through my teeth and lay a hand over hers before she can do more than give it a light squeeze. Even as I hold her hand in place, I feel my skin tightening, a bead of precum dampening the front of my briefs.

This fucking woman.

"And that—" I thread my fingers through hers and bring her hand to my lips, kissing each digit before bringing them to rest over my heart. "—is exactly why you have to let me set the pace for this, angel. I fucking love how hungry you are for me, and I wish you knew how much I want you. How badly I need to bury myself inside of you and not stop until you beg me to." Sloane's eyes widen, and I can't tell if she's afraid of my words or turned on by them. "But I need to know that you're safe and comfortable more than I need anything else, so hear me when I say this: the decision about taking this to another level will be mine and mine alone."

"I hear you." Sloane pouts, standing up on her tiptoes to brush her lips over mine again. "But please don't think I'm going to make it easy on you."

"Oh, angel. I wouldn't expect anything less from you." I squeeze her hips and take her mouth again, pulling away before I give in to the urge to spread her out on one of these tables and give Sarah and Nadia a hell of a show. Sloane's eyes are bright with alcohol and arousal as she smiles up at me. "Let's get out of here, beautiful."

* * *

THE DING of the elevator announces my arrival on the tenth floor of my building and effectively snaps my mind out of thoughts of Sloane and the little pants of pleasure she made on our ride down from the rooftop as I kissed and sucked at her neck until she was attempting to climb me like a tree.

I couldn't stop touching her on the way over to my place, and I was thankful when she insisted on staying in the car while I ran up to pack a bag. The short break from her gives me time to breathe, to shore up my resolve not to take her home tonight and fuck her until neither one of us can walk.

No one's in the hallway as I rush to my door. Knowing that Sloane is waiting for me, breathless and a little tipsy, has me moving fast. So fast I don't pay any mind to the familiar vanilla and citrus notes lingering in the air or see the black trench coat thrown over the arm of my couch. In fact, none of those things register until I enter my bedroom and see Kristen sitting against my headboard, her usually bone straight locks curly and mussed in a way that kind of reminds me of Sloane's hair.

Except Sloane's curls are natural, soft black ringlets with hints of brown and gold that match her eyes and only show in certain light. Like the sunlight that filtered in through the window above her kitchen sink this morning. Kristen's are beautiful but obviously provided by a curling iron or those soft foam things Mal uses on her wigs sometimes. *Flexi-rods.* I think absently, surprisingly calm for a man who's just found his ex-girlfriend turned casual fling waiting in his bed, wrapped in his sheets and naked. Suddenly, I'm glad Sloane refused to sleep at my place because if she walked in on *this*, we would have been over before we even started.

Yes, this certainly looks like a woman who knows you're just friends.

"You're home." Kristen purrs, sitting up to let the sheet fall. It pools around her waist, exposing her breasts. She crooks a finger at me. "Come to bed. I've missed you."

I scrub a hand over my face, calling up the last bit of patience I have for the woman in front of me. Trying to remember that she's a friend, someone I care about who seems to be struggling a bit more than I initially thought. The call while Sloane and I were at dinner was worrying; she was all over the place on the phone, mumbling about feeling overwhelmed and needing me because her life was falling apart.

You're my rock, Nic.

I downplayed it because I was feeling defensive about Sloane implying Kristen was a blind spot for me, but I'm not just blind. I'm stupid too. Because I truly believed Kristen understood me when I said this was over.

"What are you doing?"

Her smile fractures a bit, the first vestiges of doubt wrinkling her brow. "I'm....do I need spell it out for you, babe?"

She pushes the covers away, revealing the rest of her slender form as she gets on her hands and knees, crawling to the edge of the bed and reaching for my belt. I take a step back.

"Jesus, Kris. You know that we're—" I pull in a sharp breath, biting back the harsh words crowding my tongue because they sound too much like my father did when he was berating my mother. No matter how annoyed I am right now, I won't turn into him.

It's too late for that. Stringing women along was Gabriel Alexander's bread and butter. A nasty voice whispers in my head. *How many women did he use up and throw away just like you're about to do this poor girl?*

"We're not doing this anymore." I finish finally, backing away to put some distance between us. I won't go back to Sloane smelling like Kristen's perfume.

"Nic." She pouts, stumbling off of the bed. "I need this. I need you. You never used to have a problem with helping me relieve stress from work. What's so different now?"

Everything.

"We're not together, Kristen. I told you I wasn't doing this with you anymore."

"You said that before, Nic, but you came back to me." She crosses the room to me, arms trying to close around my waist. I put my hands on her shoulders to stop her from coming closer. Undeterred, she runs a hand down my chest and smiles. "You can't deny that we're good together, baby. Come to bed with me. Let me remind you how good I make you feel."

"No." I ease her back gently.

Thankfully, she keeps her distance, but both of her brows pinch together, and her mouth turns into a thin line at my gentle rebuff. She crosses her arms over her chest in a protective gesture that makes no sense considering she's the one propositioning me in my bedroom.

"What's your problem? Everything was going so great with us until a few weeks ago. We were getting back on track! Working our way back to each other, back to where we were before you lost your fucking mind and broke up with me!"

She plops down on the edge of my bed and glances up at me with teary eyes.

What? In what world were we working our way back to each other? Having casual sex is nowhere near trying to reconcile.

I brace both hands behind my head, and my threaded fingers dig into my scalp. "That was never the plan, Kris. You said you wanted a casual situation after we broke up, and I was good with that for a while, but I'm not anymore. I want more for me and quite frankly *you* deserve more than I could ever give you."

"I don't want more, Nic. I want you!"

Tears spill over her cheeks as she searches the room for something to shield herself from the truth of my words. I hate seeing her cry, even more so while she's naked and vulnerable on my bed. I cross the room, turning my back to her while I rummage through my dresser and pull out a shirt and some shorts for her to put on.

My phone buzzes in my pocket, probably a message from Sloane wondering what's taking me so long, and frustration bubbles in my chest. I want to get back to her, to go back to the magic of our night together before Hurricane Kristen swept in.

Making your own storm and getting mad when it rains? The apple doesn't fall far from the tree, huh?

It takes everything in me not to look at my phone, to keep Sloane waiting again, but all of my attention needs to be on Kristen right now. Getting her calm. Getting her out of my apartment, so I can get back to Sloane.

The room is quiet as I make my way back to the bed. Kristen's unanswered confession hangs in the air between us. I place the clothes in her hands, and she stares angry daggers into the space above my head.

"I'm sorry," I say, backing away to give her some space. "Put the clothes on, Kris. I'll be in the living room."

A sarcastic snort leaves her as I walk towards the door. Then the sound of glass shattering on the left side of my head rings in my ears. I turn towards the noise just in time to see a framed picture of me and my mom clattering to the floor. Frozen, I stare at the glass shards scattered over the image. It's from the last birthday I got to celebrate with her before she died.

She recruited Eric to keep me busy all day, so she and Mama could decorate our small yard with balloons and streamers and other cheesy decorations for a surprise party. No one knew my dad had ruined the surprise earlier in the week during a rant about how worthless I was, so they didn't catch the disgusting smirk on his face when he watched me pretend I was surprised just for my mom's sake.

The picture laying on the ground was taken right after I walked in. My mom's frail arms are wrapped around my torso, and she's beaming up at me, looking beautiful even though her hair had long since fallen out and the treatments kept her rail-thin.

Annoyance flares in my chest, and it's narrowly beaten out by the shock simmering in my veins. I've always known Kristen had a temper, but she's never been violent or cruel like this. A triumphant grin twists her features as she comes back around to the foot of the bed. The clothes I just gave her lay discarded on the floor as she struts past me.

"A temper tantrum." I follow her out into the living room. "How mature."

Wary of having yet another one of my belongings thrown at me, I give her a wide berth. Tension rolls off of her in waves as she slides on her coat and fastens the belt.

"You're so full of shit, you know that?" She hisses at me. "You think you're such a fucking gentleman, such a good man, but you're just like every other asshole out there, Nic. Using women up, making them fall in love with you and then tossing them to the side when they aren't any good to you anymore."

I stare at her, keeping my expression carefully blank at her gross miscategorization of our relationship. We were never perfect—didn't have a chance to be when my heart was so damn wrapped up in Sloane it could never truly be hers—and it wasn't smart for me to agree to this friends with benefits thing, but I never used her.

The annoyance flaring in my chest expands to a dangerous level. "I never used you."

She snatches her purse off of the couch, and I marvel silently at all the indications of her presence that I missed walking in here because I was so eager to get back to Sloane.

"Keep telling yourself that. I'm sure the bitch you're seeing now will feel the same way in a few months when you're done stomping all over her heart."

The protective beast in my chest snarls, raging at the word 'bitch' being used in reference to Sloane even if Kristen doesn't know that's who she's talking about. My mind goes to the woman waiting for me outside of my building, and my jaw hardens.

"You need to go. Please leave my key on the table by the door." I return harshly, and then because I'm not a complete asshole. "Get home safe, Kris. I'll call tomorrow to check on you."

Her face crumples, sadness joining the misdirected anger etched in her features as she digs the key out of her purse and launches it at me.

"Fuck you, Nic."

23

SLOANE

The engine of Dominic's car purrs quietly as I scroll through social media on my phone in hopes of distracting the giddy butterflies swirling around in my stomach. The thought of having him in my bed again has my thighs clenching in anticipation and my heart beating triple time. I'm eager to get him home, but it's been over half an hour since he went inside his building, and he still hasn't come back down or responded to my text.

Worry tries to burrow its way into my chest, but I quickly dismiss it. No way is Dominic up there trying to find a way to tell me this is over. He's made it very clear that he doesn't regret this relationship, no matter how short-lived and ill-advised it may be, so whatever is keeping him probably doesn't have anything to do with us.

Closing out my social media, I open up my work email and respond to a few messages from clients who have been working primarily with my senior designer, Sasha. I've just sent her a private e-mail telling her how awesome she's doing when a tingle of awareness prickles across my skin. At first, I think it must be Dominic, but it's nothing like the zip of electricity I feel when he's near. This is something more creepy, like someone with less than good intentions is watching me from afar.

My head snaps up, scanning the front of Dominic's building for any sketchy guys looking a little too hard at the idling car, but there's no one out there except for a lone woman with bouncing curls in a dark trench coat marching towards the other side of the building where guests park.

"Relax, Sloane," I mutter to myself.

The door to Dominic's building swings open, and I smile like a fool when I finally see him emerge carrying a duffel bag as big as me in his hand. *He wasn't playing about spending every night together.* But then I meet his eyes and my heart sinks. They're dark and serious, and all of the playfulness he's had most of the evening is gone. I wonder if it has something to do with whatever kept him in his place for so long.

He tosses his bag in the back seat then hops upfront with me. I stare at him, examining every inch of his body for a clue to the sudden shift in his demeanor. My eyes linger on the band-aid sitting in the palm of his left hand. I stare pointedly at it, and Dominic shifts it from my view.

That's not suspicious at all.

"What happened to you?"

"Put on your seat belt, angel," he orders quietly.

Despite my current irritation at him evading my simple question, the demand still makes a wave of liquid heat pool in my core. Ignoring his order, and my own ridiculous response to it, I get on my knees and reach for his injured hand from across the console.

"How'd you cut yourself packing an overnight bag?"

"Put your seat belt on, and I'll tell you."

I roll my eyes. "Tell me and I'll put my seat belt on."

Dominic releases a frustrated growl, pushing me back into my seat and pulling my seat belt across my body as soon my ass hits the leather. I reach for his hand again, but he manages to secure the belt before I can get a good grip on him.

"Stubborn woman."

A sarcastic snort rips from my throat. "Well if it isn't the pot calling the kettle black."

He shakes his head and backs out of the parking spot. Surprisingly, my gaze stays glued to his face as he maneuvers us back onto the main road and heads towards my house.

"You sound like Mama."

"And you sound like a man who's avoiding a simple question."

He sighs, looking over at me with soft, but serious, eyes. "I cut my hand."

"Yes." I nod knowingly. "The band-aid kind of gave it away. What I want to know is how you cut your hand and why you're acting like it's classified information."

Three heartbeats pass, and I watch Dominic turn the truth over in his mind. Once. Twice. Three times before I *see* him decide to lie to me. I watch his lips part, disbelief twisting my stomach.

I hold up my hand. "Don't lie to me, not about something as simple as this."

The curt, dry look he gives me is meant to scare me off, to make me back down from whatever storm of emotions I've stumbled upon that he doesn't want me to see. Except I do see them. Etched into the ridge of his brow and swimming in his eyes. Something is wrong, and either he doesn't trust me enough to talk about it or the something wrong is….

Don't even go there! You know what he wants. He's told you that he wants this. How'd you go from a cut hand to him rethinking this entire arrangement?

But doubt is digging its way into the crack in my chest created by Dominic's silence, wrapping around my lungs like a vice and squeezing hard. Stealing the breath from my lungs and forcing me to admit to myself just how badly I want this relationship, how badly I want this man who holds more than the key to my desire in his hands.

Don't do it. The voice in my head warns, but it's too late. I'm already jumping headfirst into a pool of outlandish conclusions.

"Are you having second thoughts about us?" I swallow past the lump in my throat. "It's okay if you are. I mean this is hard for me, but

I don't have a clue what it's like for you." Dominic's gaze snaps to mine, brow furrowed in confusion. "Being with me." I clarify. "I don't know what being with me is like for you. You said you don't feel guilty, but I know how much you loved Eric, and you have to feel something about doing this with me." His frown deepens, but now that I've started, I can't stop myself from purging my emotions all over his car. "It's okay if that something is regret, Dominic. I mean I was hoping maybe the moments we'd have together would be worth whatever it costs you emotionally to help me, but if you don't think it is you can tell me."

Oh, God. Someone kill me now.

Dominic curses under his breath, reaching over to grab my hand. I thread my fingers through his and try not to think about the way my heart rate evens out as soon as he's touching me.

"I could never regret you, angel." He pulls our linked hands up to his mouth, pressing a kiss to my fingers. "Even when you break my heart by saying shit like you hope you're worth whatever this is costing me emotionally. Let's be clear, whatever the price is for being with you, I'll happily pay it. I'll give up my soul for a moment of your time. I'll sell everything I own for a night in your bed. There's no sacrifice I wouldn't make to hear you laugh, make you smile, or shield you from pain."

Everything inside of me goes still as Dominic's unexpectedly sweet words wash over me, soothing almost every part of worry and doubt niggling at me within a matter of moments. *Almost.* There's still the part of me that can't make sense of his evasive maneuvers when it came to answering the simple question that planted the seed in the first place. I trace my finger over the veins in his arm from his wrist to the inside of his elbow and back again.

"I have another rule, Dominic."

He gives a long, heaving sigh like he knows what's coming. "What is it?"

"No lies. If we're going to do this, we have to be honest with each other about everything."

The signal light clicks as we turn onto my road. Dominic's eyes flick between me and the street as we coast towards the house. "Are you suggesting I'm not being honest with you about something?"

I roll my eyes so hard they nearly fall out of my head, and warm amusement lights the corners of Dominic's eyes for a moment before being chased away by something darker. He pulls into my driveway and comes to a stop behind my car, letting the engine run.

I release my seat belt and nod towards his hand. "Tell me what's up with your hand, and please don't say you just cut it because *that* much is clear."

Dominic scrubs a hand over his face before turning to look at me, and I just know I'm going to hate whatever is about to come out of his mouth. "I wanted to wait until I got you home, so I could tell you this. Honestly, I didn't even know if I should've packed a bag because you might want some space from me tonight."

I frown. "Why would I want space from you tonight?" *Or any night?*

He rolls his head from one side to the other then grimaces as if his attempt to relieve the tension in his neck didn't work at all. "When I got to my place, Kristen was there."

As soon as her name hits the air, I want to burst out laughing. Kristen's behavior has raised every one of my red flags, but Dominic has been acting like it's not a big deal. Maybe whatever happened with them upstairs will be enough to change his mind. I cross my arms and nod for him to continue.

I'll let him finish explaining before I say 'I told you so.'

"When we were dating, I gave her a key. She never got around to returning it, after we broke up and I forgot she had it because she always used the doorbell when she would come over for—." The muscle in his jaw starts to jump, and I remind myself to breathe because hearing him even hint at their time together makes my stomach churn. "Anyway, she was in my bed. Naked."

My vision blurs, red creeping in from the corners until it tints everything. I fold my lips to keep the less than polite words crowding on my tongue from escaping and wait for him to continue. Internally though, I'm screaming. This woman is relentless. First, she interrupts

our dinner, then she caps off the night by propositioning my
—Dominic?

He clears his throat, clearly put off by my silence. Maybe he can
sense the storm gathering inside me. I'm not looking at him, but I can
feel his gaze, hot and heavy, on my face. "Nothing happened, Sloane. I
gave her some clothes and told her to leave. She threw my key at me
and stormed out."

I wrinkle my nose. "And your hand?"

He ducks his head like he was hoping I forgot about his mysterious
injury. "Before she left my room, she...threw a picture at the wall. The
frame broke, and I was in such a rush to get back to you that I wasn't
paying attention when I clea—"

Every emotion I've been feeling since he started talking boils over
and spills out of me with anger and disbelief at the forefront, mixing to
make a volatile cocktail I wish I could shove down Kristen's throat.

"She did WHAT?!" I gape at him, not caring one bit about how
ridiculous I must look with my mouth hanging wide open in outrage.
"Please tell me you weren't anywhere near the wall she *threw a fucking
picture* at!"

Surprise replaces every other emotion on Dominic's face as a
delighted smile curves his lips. I almost smile back at him, but I'm too
pissed off to do so. Kristen threw a picture at him because he wouldn't
sleep with her? Of all the ridiculous, outlandish, abusive, *toxic* things
for someone to do in the face of rejection...and it's especially gross
given the environment Dominic grew up in.

He reaches over and cups my jaw in his hand. A tender finger
brushes over my cheek. "Calm down, angel. I don't think she was
trying to hit me."

"Don't defend her, Dominic. Even if she wasn't aiming for you,
there's nothing okay about her throwing things at or around you. Who
does that?"

I'm seething. My blood boiling in my veins as I picture a glass
frame shattering against the wall, narrowly missing Dominic's head,
while Kristen sat in his bed with no damn clothes on like she belonged
there.

"I'm not defending her. Honestly, I'm just trying not to think about it. Kris can be intense, but I've never seen her like that." He shakes his head, worry flickering in the inky depths of his eyes. "As crazy as it sounds, I'm more concerned about her than anything. The stress from work must be getting to her."

I scoff. "You can't be serious right now. She broke into your apartment and propositioned you, and when you turned her down, she got violent. That's not stress from work, Dominic. That's a reason to file a restraining order."

He laughs and holds up his hands in mock surrender when I glare at him. "I'm sorry for laughing, but your reaction is just not what I expected."

"You thought I was going to be upset with you because of what she did?"

He shrugs. "I thought you were going to tell me to take my shit home because I've got too much going on."

"That would be pretty rich coming from the woman who had a full breakdown the first time you gave her an orgasm." I flush as the words leave my mouth. "We've both got stuff but, besides the stalker ex-girlfriend and your tendency to be an asshole sometimes, you're pretty perfect." *God, did I just call him perfect?* "I think I'm the one with too much going on. No one wants a heartbroken widow who..."

"Don't finish that sentence, Sloane." His warm hand covers my fingers, which are busy spinning my wedding band around in anxious revolutions. "Don't talk about your love for Eric like it's an obstacle someone has to overcome to be with you. You are who you are because you loved him. Anyone who doesn't understand that doesn't deserve to know you." Dominic spins my band back around to the front of my finger and brushes the pad of his thumb over the stone gently. "No real man is going to make being with you about erasing what you had with him, and a major part of that is helping you through those hard moments, not making you feel like shit because they happen."

The words are soft but there's no mistaking the command in them. The severity of his gaze is enough to devastate me, making my breath turn shallow as I meet it. Eyes the color of the night sky look right through me, and I feel paper-thin under his stare.

How is it possible for this man to see me so clearly, to say the things I need to hear even when I don't know I need to hear them?

Tears sting at the back of my eyes, but I fight them back because I don't want to cry, I want to throw myself in his arms and show him how much I appreciate him. And just like that, all of the irritation from the mess with Kristen falls away, leaving only an empty ache in my core.

Dominic catches the shift in my mood immediately, and he pins me with a lazy, sultry gaze that makes my whole body feel like it's blushing. Pinpricks of awareness have my skin tingling in every place his eyes touch. My face. The curve of my neck. My breasts. My belly. The bit of thigh peeking out from the slit in my skirt.

I'm about to spontaneously combust, so I dig through my purse and pull out my garage opener. "Okay. If you're done trying to make me cry, can we go in now? I can think of a few things I'd rather be doing."

He watches the door lift but the car doesn't move. "Are you sure you want me to stay?"

I don't even have to think about my answer. "Yes, I want you to stay. If I recall correctly, sleeping together every night was one of your rules."

His lips tip up into a smile as he pulls into the garage. "Since when do you play by the rules, angel?"

"Since doing so gets me orgasms and cuddles."

The garage door slams down, and Dominic cuts the engine. His dark chuckle fills the quiet around us and another rush of liquid heat gathers between my thighs. I'm so anxious to get in the house that waiting for him to get out of the car and open my door doesn't feel like a remote possibility. I flash him a smile and hop out before he can say a word.

I've already unlocked the back door and kicked off my shoes inside of the mudroom by the time Dominic catches up to me. The door slams behind him, and I hear the lock click into place mere seconds before his bag hits the floor and muscular arms circle my waist. He presses a kiss to my shoulder and trails more up my neck. I sigh happily and tilt my head to the side, giving him access he gladly takes advantage of, using the opening as a chance to breathe me in.

His warm breath tickles my skin. "You always smell so good. Like mango and tangerine with maybe a bit of coconut?" His hands go to my hips, spinning me around to face him, and I drop my purse and keys so I can run my hands down his chest. "I've spent every day for the last few weeks trying to nail it down, fighting the urge to ask you what the exact combination is so I can bottle it up and put it everywhere until my entire world is nothing but you."

The observation startles a laugh out of me, and I feel his smile against my lips. I want to tell him that he smells amazing too, like cinnamon, oranges, and clean soap, but I get distracted as he bends and plants a kiss on my collarbone. He makes his way down to my breasts and nuzzles them gently before pulling away.

I'm about to complain about the loss of contact when he starts tugging my camisole out of my skirt. It comes up easily, and I lift my arms to help him get it off completely. It's over my head and fluttering to the ground in a matter of moments.

When he finds me bare underneath my top, his gaze darkens. He backs away, finding a seat on the built-in bench by the door and spreading his legs wide. Both of his big hands are clasped together loosely, resting in front of his crotch but doing nothing to hide the growing bulge pressing against the seam of his jeans.

"Take the skirt off. I want to see all of you."

And I want to be seen. I've been dying to bare myself to this man all night, and him sitting here like an impatient king demanding my nakedness only makes me want it more. My hands go to the band of my skirt and start to tug the fabric down roughly. Eager to get rid of anything that's standing between me and satisfying his command.

"Slow down, angel. We've got all night."

Dominic sits back, his face schooled into the familiar mask of control and cold indifference I haven't seen in weeks. If it wasn't for the erection tenting his jeans and the muscle ticking in his jaw, I would think he doesn't give a damn about me stripping in front of him.

My breathing is unsteady under the weight of his stare, but I manage to squeeze out a calming breath and slow my movements. Pulling gently instead of tugging, until the fabric skims steadily down my body. Coasting over my stomach, revealing my soaked sex and bare legs to Dominic who watches without saying a word.

When the skirt falls to the floor, a wicked smile curves his lips. "Good girl. Now spread your legs and touch yourself. I want to see how wet you are for me."

Pleasure zips down my spine, and I feel myself flushing from the heat of his stare and the satisfaction coating his words of praise. Widening my stance, I hold his gaze and run a hand down my belly and over my cleft before slipping one finger through my slick folds. Between the orgasm in the elevator, and the need burning inside of me from whatever game we're playing right now, I'm soaked.

A breathless whimper escapes me as I dip a finger inside of my core. This doesn't feel nearly as good as having Dominic's hands on me, but I feel myself growing wetter anyway. Having his eyes on me while I touch myself the way he tells me to is so intimate, so carnal, so far from the lonely nights I've spent with my vibrator.

"Does it feel good, angel?" Dominic asks evenly. His erection is obscene now, and my mouth waters at the sight of the only part of his reaction to me he can't hide.

"It would feel better if it was you." I pant, swirling a finger around my swollen clit.

He arches a brow at me. "I'm sure it would. You make it sound like you *need* me. Do I have that right, Sloane? Do you need me to make you come? Am I the only one who knows how to take care of that perfect little pussy?"

A shudder moves through me, ignited solely by his words. I circle my clit once more and wonder when he's going to tell me to stop. The whole point of me doing this was to show him how wet I am for him, but I'm certain he can hear it. The filthy sounds of me pleasuring myself echo around us, proving my point.

"Yes." I moan. "I need you, Dominic."

"Show me." He says, leaning forward just a little. "Let me see how much you need me."

Reluctantly, I pull my hand away from the heat of my slit. My forefinger is glistening and soaked in my juices. Dominic watches as a drop runs down my hand, and I swear I see the exact moment dark brown gives way to molten obsidian.

He crooks a long finger at me, gesturing for me to come closer, and my feet move without question. Closing the distance between us in several strides that I try to make look sexy even though my legs are shaking. When I reach him, Dominic hooks a hand behind my knee and lifts my foot, setting it down to rest on the outside of his hard thigh.

I'm completely open to him. My soaked pussy is so close to his mouth I can feel the warm air from every breath that passes his lips. Ardent fingers run an incendiary trail up my leg, from my knee to my ankle, and then back again. Having his hands on me again feels like heaven, and I nearly sag with relief at the contact.

Why bother touching myself when he can make me feel like this in a matter of seconds?

A shiver rolls down my spine as he moves the hand I was just using to touch myself to his lips. He sucks my fingers into the scorching heat of his mouth and groans. It's a long and deeply sexual sound that reverberates through me as his tongue laps at my skin. Cleaning off my juices with long, hard pulls I feel in my core. When he's done, he places my hand back on my trembling slit and sits back.

"Finish."

"What?" My voice trembles, confusion, and hesitancy stamped across my face, while he waits patiently for me to follow his order. I want to resist, to fight back just a little, but even as disappointment claws at my chest, and the hope of handing over the reins to him dies, my body fights to obey him. The need to please him overpowering the need to have his hands on me.

I stare down at him, astonished by how quickly and subtly he's trained my body to respond to his commands. Mastering it without giving me so much as a hint of what it would mean to be conquered so completely. To be so desperate to please him that I'd go against my own best interest. To be so caught up in his spell that even when I'm standing over him in a universally recognized position of power, every part of me knows he's still the one in control.

"Finish. Show me how you're going to make yourself come when this is over and me taking care of your insatiable pussy is nothing but a memory."

My blood catches fire even as the thought of going back to a reality where Dominic touching me is no longer a thing breaks my heart. With a soft moan and the rough pads of his fingers trailing down the outside of my thigh, I slide two fingers through my slit before allowing them to sink into the warm wetness gathered at my core.

Dominic inhales sharply. "*Fuck.* Do that again but rub your clit when you pull them out this time." I do as I'm told, relishing in the sound of his ragged breaths. "Hold yourself open with your other hand, baby. I want to see all of you."

Again, I obey. My free hand reaches the apex of my thighs and holds my sex open, so he can watch my fingers disappearing inside of me.

"Touch me," I beg, sounding needy and breathless even to my own ears.

Dominic shakes his head but plants a kiss on the inside of my knee, and I want to scream. My body is on fire and there's a pounding need in my blood I know won't go away until his hands are on me.

"It's got to be you, angel. When these eights weeks are up, I want to be sure you know how to take care of yourself." His wicked lips curl into a sinful smile. "Think of it as my parting gift to you."

I lick my lips, pressing on the swollen bud with a firm but gentle pressure that leaves me panting but nowhere near release. Sweat beads on my hairline as my gaze sweeps over Dominic. He looks so cool and collected like there isn't a woman desperately fingering herself mere inches from his face. *How can he be so unbothered?* Agitation ripples through me, and suddenly I'm willing to do anything to get him as worked up as I am.

My eyes fall shut, and I shift my feet apart a little more, focusing all of my attention on my clit. "Maybe I'll get someone else to take care of my needs when this is done. Then I won't need your parting gift at all. Would that make you feel better? "

A sharp slap to my ass has my eyes popping open in surprise. Dominic's expression is a mixture of dark emotion—fury, desire, and possessiveness brimming in the dark pools. Pain spreads out from my right cheek, and my breath catches when Dominic rubs the sensitive skin with his palm, making pleasure mingle with it. The thrill of having his hands on me, even if it is to punish me for taunting him with my words, sets off sparks deep in my core. I whimper as I feel, more than hear, the long breath Dominic lets out.

His hand digs into my flesh, squeezing my ass hard, and I'm acutely aware of how close he is to where I need him. Just a simple shift and he could be sinking his fingers inside of me. But I know Dominic, and he's not going to let that happen, so I don't push it. I limit my movements to a small circling of my hips, and he keeps touching me. Staring up at me with blown pupils that tell me he's close to losing control.

"Well in that case..." He releases my flesh and drags his hand from my ass to my hip and then up my body, slowly unraveling me while he regains his composure. When he pauses to knead my breasts, my moan echoes around us, and triumph flashes in his eyes like I've just confirmed something for him. "Let's prepare for the inevitable moment where you let another man in your bed and realize too late that his touch does nothing for you because I've ruined you for anyone else."

I open my mouth to tell him I was only joking, that I already know he's ruined me for anyone else, *last night with Ash taught me that,* but the only thing that comes out is another moan. The early tremors of an orgasm start to move through me. I rock my hips into my hand, the filthy sounds of my fingers swirling around my clit, mingling with my heavy breaths. Sparks start at the base of my spine and spread out, blooming low in the pit of my belly. My core clenches hungrily around nothing, and I bite my lip, eyeing the erection straining inside Dominic's pants.

He catches me staring and blesses me with a dark chuckle that has no humor in it. "Stop thinking about my dick and focus on coming, angel."

"I'm trying." I pout, but my fingers have slowed down significantly. All of my thoughts on seeing Dominic's dick hard and throbbing for me. "But I want to see you. Take your dick out."

"You're not in charge here, Sloane." His hand goes back to my raised knee, spreading me out further. "Now be a good girl and come for me, so I can give you a reward."

It's a command and a challenge wrapped in one. Dominic's eyes are glowing with heated possession as he watches my fingers start to move again, the promise of a reward from him motivating me to hunt down the orgasm I abandoned. My mind is racing with hope and fevered desperation, anxious to find my release so I can find out what he has planned for me.

A hint of a smile touches his lips, and it tugs at the ball of desire forming in my womb, slowly unraveling it as waves of pleasure wrack my body. I reach up and grab my breast, rolling my nipple between my finger the way Dominic did in the elevator. My soft fingers don't feel half as good as his do, but I close my eyes and imagine that it's him touching me. Toying with the hard peak of my breast, pressing roughly into my clit and providing the perfect amount of friction.

"Oh, God." I cry out, my head falling to the side to rest on my shoulder.

"That's it, angel. You're so fucking wet. I wish I was inside you right now so I could feel your walls clamping down on me, rippling around my dick while you soak me in your juices. You're going to take every inch of me, Sloane. I'm going to pound into you, and I'm not going to stop until your greedy little pussy milks me for every last drop of cum."

Once again, Dominic pushes me over the brink with filthy words that speak to a fantasy I've only entertained in my head. My orgasm slams into me, a tidal wave of sensation washing me into a sea of pleasure that has my knees buckling. His hands go to my hips, spinning me around and lowering me gently to his lap with my back to his chest. He grips my chin, tipping my mouth up to his, so he can swallow my moans. My breathing is ragged when he pulls back and smiles at me.

"You're so fucking perfect."

I wiggle my ass over his erection. "Mhmm. Is this my reward?"

"Yes." He plants a soft kiss to my temple. "I'm going to let you take care of this for me."

A fresh wave of excitement blooms in my chest. I know sex isn't on the table, but just the idea of seeing Dominic's dick, knowing that I can touch and taste him, has the familiar hum of desire coursing through my veins. It's so fierce, so strong you would think I hadn't just found my own release.

Twisting in his lap, I catch his mouth in a slow, licking kiss that contains every bit of gratitude and excitement I feel right now. Then I pull away so I don't end up grinding on some other part of his body before I get the chance to collect my prize.

With a final kiss to his lips, I sink to my knees in front of him. The tile digs into my skin, and it's slightly uncomfortable, but I don't care. My hands shake as I undo his belt buckle and then the button on his jeans. I hesitate on his zipper for a second, my fingers brushing over the bulge in his pants. Part of me is nervous, seriously doubting my ability to fit all of him in my mouth, while the other part is screaming at me to stop fucking around and just try. Dominic makes a soft, amused noise in the back of his throat.

"Don't tell me you're having second thoughts, angel."

I peek up at him through my eyelashes. "Just giving myself a little pep talk. It's been a while since I've done this you know."

A hum of appreciation rumbles in his chest. "Yes, I know."

There's no mistaking the satisfaction coating his words, and suddenly all the years I spent alone, denying my body true intimacy and cultivating an extreme case of skin hunger, start to feel like a gift rather than a self-imposed punishment. Because all of those lonely nights, all of those awkward brush-offs and flat-out lies to get out of dinner invites, brought me to this moment right here.

Kneeling before a man who understands what this all means to me, who's as desperate to have all of my firsts as I am to give them to him.

I lick my lips and relish in the soft glide of his zipper coming down, putting me one step closer to my reward. Dominic hisses as I reach inside his briefs. His dick springs free, standing tall and proud, brutally erect and already weeping precum for me. He's so thick and impossibly long, I know I won't be able to take all of him in my mouth, but I'll be damned if I'm not going to try. I dive forward, wrapping one fist around his base and squeezing gently as I lap up the cum sliding from his flared tip down his shaft.

"God damn," Dominic says roughly, one of his hands fisting in my curls to hold my hair back from my face. "That's incredible. Do it again and look at me this time."

The rasp in his voice coupled with the taste of him on my tongue has me pressing my legs together, squirming desperately against the need building in the pit of my stomach. But it only worsens when I flatten my tongue against his shaft and meet his eyes. Our gazes stay locked as I explore every bulging vein and smooth ridge, committing it all to memory. The clean and masculine smell of him. The indescribable feel of steel sheathed in velvet. The sharp intake of breath as I flick my tongue around his crown, swirling it several times before opening wide and taking the first few inches of him into the wet heat of my mouth.

"*Fuck.*"

I pull back, hollowing my cheeks and sucking hard on the way up. I need both of my hands for balance, so I give his base one final squeeze before letting go and sliding my mouth back down his length. Letting him hit the back of my throat in one glide that still leaves several inches of him exposed. Dominic groans loudly as he stares down at me, his face twisted in a harsh mask of desire and fracturing control.

"Holy shit, Sloane." His hips stir restlessly, rocking up into my mouth on their own volition.

The unconscious movement sends a rush of triumph through me. I want to see him unravel, to be the reason he's falling apart, but it's taking every ounce of my self-control to hold still and let my body adjust to this invasion.

I shift on my knees, more from the building pressure in my womb than the feel of the hard tile digging into them, and pull in a breath through my nose. My eyes are starting to water, a tear falls down my cheek and hits black denim as my jaw burns and stretches to accommodate his girth.

Dominic's hand tightens in my hair and tugs, trying to pull me back up. I reach up and grasp his wrist, stopping him from moving me. When he stills, I remove my hand and take another deep breath through my nose before coming back up, tongue fluttering over his tip repeatedly before sliding back down again.

"Relax your throat, angel. You're almost there."

On the next glide, I do exactly as he says and manage to capture those last few inches. Dominic swears loudly, his free hand joining the other one at the back of my head as I take every inch of him over and over again. Out of the corner of my eye, I can see the veins in his arms straining under his skin. He's fighting to let me set the pace, to be gentle with me.

But I don't want him gentle, I want him half-mad with wanting me, too far gone to be a gentleman, too crazed with the need to come to remember to be careful with me. I want him to use me, to take every bit of pleasure he's denied himself since this started from my body. I want to ruin him for every other woman in the world just like he's ruined me.

More tears sting my eyes and my lungs burn, begging for a full breath, but I don't care. Nothing matters now except driving the man in front of me crazy. I bare my teeth, dragging them gently up his shaft with the next pull. And I don't know exactly how I expected Dominic to react, but the animal-like growl of satisfaction that rips from his throat is enough to make me moan. The sound vibrates around his sensitive flesh and finally sends him over the edge.

"Fuck yes, angel." He groans. "That's so damn perfect."

With both of his hands on the back of my head, Dominic takes over the rhythm. He pulls me up roughly, letting me get one full breath before driving me back down onto his dick. His hips buck up, meeting my waiting mouth and sliding down my throat in brutal glides that make me squirm. I'm so wet, so turned on from driving him to the point of no return, my arousal is coating my thighs.

My fingernails dig into his jeans as he continues his punishing rhythm, driving my open mouth down onto his dick over and over again. Hitting the back of my throat while I moan around him. I love every moment of it, and the power of owning his pleasure, of being more than his best friend's fragile widow, swells in my chest until all I can feel is it and him.

When Dominic's movements start to go unsteady, his hips jerking and fingers digging into my scalp, I know he's close. I smile to myself and suck harder, letting my throat constrict around him with small swallows that have him cursing and warning me he's about to come.

When the first burst of hot, creamy liquid shoots down my throat, I nearly choke from how thick it is. And I only get a second to recover from the warning shot before Dominic explodes in my mouth with a ragged grunt that almost makes me come again. I swallow every drop of it, feeling incredibly triumphant for a woman on her knees. And nothing, not even the ache in them, can take away the heady rush of power moving through me as I lick Dominic clean with his shaky breaths skating across my skin.

"Enough," he says harshly, reaching down and pushing me away.

I watch with a smile as he shoves himself back into his jeans before his dick gets completely hard again. He brushes his knuckles across my cheek, his eyes soft with wonder and an all too familiar wariness as they study me.

"I'm fine," I say, standing up and stretching to relieve the ache in my back. "You can't conduct a mental assessment every time we do something new, Dominic."

"Yes, I can." He stands too, gripping my waist and pulling me close. "Only you would get mad at me for being concerned about your well-being."

I wrap my arms around his neck and squeal when he picks me up. "I'm not mad. I just don't want to have to think about the *one* time I freaked out on you every time one of us has an orgasm."

"That's fair."

My brows lift in surprise at his easy agreement. "So you'll stop treating me like a ticking time bomb?"

"No." He laughs. "I'll just get better at conducting my mental assessments without you knowing."

"You're impossible."

24

SLOANE

Now

I forgot how good it feels to have regular orgasms that aren't courtesy of my vibrator or, in moments of true desperation, my own hand. For so long I thought the all-consuming, glowing from the inside out, walking on a cloud, feeling was lost to me forever.

But after three weeks of Dominic fucking me with his fingers and worshiping me with his sinful tongue on every available surface—my bed, my shower, the kitchen counter, and the now finished vanity in the bathroom of the Presidential suite—I can happily say I'm intimately familiar with the post-orgasmic haze and all it's pleasured filled glory once again.

I feel like my happiness is seeping out of my pores, broadcasting to everyone around me that someone is making me very happy at home.

And that would be a good thing if it didn't make Dominic stare at me like a loon, his chest puffed out proudly, causing me to blush through every Sunday dinner at Mama's in the past few weeks. If we weren't supposed to be acting like two people who are barely friends, I would grin back at him. I would let my feminine pride and never-ending desire for him shine in my eyes and gloss right over the other emotions I'm too scared to put a name to. Instead, I just smile into my phone and text him to cut it out before someone notices.

Not that anyone has noticed.

All of Dominic's heated gazes and casual touches while we were at Mama's on Sunday went unnoticed by Mal, and James, who sees us together multiple times a week, hasn't picked up on anything. *He would have to spend more than five seconds in a room with Dominic to do that, though.* Our apparent ability to fly under the radar has only encouraged Dominic and made me more anxious about us getting caught. He reassures me every night that things will be fine, even as shadows of something like uncertainty move behind his eyes. And once he's done using his words to comfort me, he spreads my legs and uses everything but his dick to make me come.

Last night, it was a combination of my vibrator and his tongue. The toy buzzing inside of my soaked channel on its highest setting while he lapped up my juices and sucked on my clit until I saw stars. I came three times like that and begged him to give me more as he rubbed his throbbing dick along my slit, lubricating himself in my juices before climbing up my body and holding my breasts together so he could fuck them.

I moaned and writhed underneath him while he used my body to get himself off, and the sounds he made as he came all over me are still ringing in my ears on Wednesday afternoon as I leave one of the smaller rooms on the seventh floor where Dominic's team has just installed crown molding. It's the only reason I don't realize the door to the storage closet is open until two warm hands grip my waist and haul me through it.

My surprised yelp is muffled by the hand over my mouth, and I immediately quiet as Dominic's face comes into focus. When he's sure I won't scream, he moves his hand to my chin, tipping my face up so he can brush his nose over mine. I smile at the sweet gesture that's quickly becoming my favorite non-sexual thing that he does.

"I'm sorry." He murmurs. "I didn't want to scare you, but I needed a minute alone so I could do this."

Hungry lips meet mine in a kiss that makes my toes curl. My lips part on a moan, and his tongue slips in. Licking into my mouth with slow, languid strokes that make me think of sex. Of his body on top of mine, the hard ridges of his abs slick with sweat and pressed to my stomach while he reaches the end of me with every thrust.

My arms go to his neck, fingers linking at his nape and pulling him down further so I can deepen the kiss. He lets me hold him there for just a minute before pulling my arms back down and ending it.

I'm pouting when his dark eyes meet mine. "That wasn't enough."

Dominic laughs. "It's never enough for you, angel."

I give him a playful jab in the chest that probably hurts my finger more than it bothers him. "Shut up. You're the one who pulled me in here. I was trying to get some work done while you weren't around to distract me. Little did I know you were lurking in a storage closet like a creeper."

His smile spreads and so does the warmth in my chest. I love making Dominic smile. Over the past few weeks, I've realized that putting a smile on his face is more satisfying than making him scowl.

"Are you happy with the molding in the rooms down here? It's not as ornate as the ones you selected for the suites upstairs, but I think it looks good."

I nod. "Yes, the guys did an amazing job with the installation. It went in a lot quicker than I expected."

Which worries me. Not for the project, anyone in real estate can tell you finishing a renovation early is a good thing, but for the relationship we've just started that we both agreed would end when the project does. I can't help but wonder if the deadline still stands if we wrap early.

It's your damn deadline, don't you think you should figure that out?

I should, but the truth is I don't want to think about ending things at all. Every time I've tried to picture going back to life without Dominic, my heart sinks inside my chest. It hasn't even been a full month, and I already can't imagine going to sleep without him by my side.

If Dominic catches the note of distress in my voice, he doesn't let on. Instead, he gives me another easy smile and nods in agreement, pleased that his team is moving through the remaining list of tasks so quickly. Maybe he hasn't thought about what this particular professional advancement means for us.

Or maybe he's not opposed to ending things early.

I shut that thought down, focusing on the handsome man in front of me instead. He's talking animatedly about some aspect of the project, completely unaware of the list of ways to slow this project down I'm currently compiling in my head.

"...but Andre can handle that because I have plans tonight."

My eyebrows raise in surprise. This is the first I'm hearing of any plans. "You do?"

"Yes." He states simply, hands cupping my ass through the fabric of my dress. "I'm taking you out to dinner."

"Oh really? How'd you manage to rent out the rooftop again so soon?" I wrinkle my nose to let him know I'm only half-serious. "Please don't tell me you sold your soul to Sebastian Adler."

He pinches my left cheek, and I gasp. "No, smart ass. We're going out in public, to a restaurant with other people."

"Dominic..." I can't bring myself to say the words because he *knows, he* knows this has to be private. We can't go out to dinner like a normal couple even if part of me wants to do exactly that.

"Two of those people," he continues, dropping a kiss at the corner of my mouth to erase the frown forming there. "Will be Mal and Chris."

"Chris?" My frown gets deeper. There's only one Chris I know and readily associate with Mal's name. A bastard from college who broke her heart into a million little pieces then went to med school on the other side of the country. "As in Mal's Chris from college?"

It's a dumb question and I already know the answer to it, but I'm holding out hope for a miracle. Dominic dashes it with a simple nod. "One in the same."

"I didn't realize you were still in touch with him."

Chris was the resident assistant on Dominic and Eric's hall during our freshman year of college. He was two years older and the object of Mal's affections well before they started hooking up during his senior year. They were only together for a few months before he pulled the rug out from under her. I don't even know everything that went down between them, but I do know he's the last person on Earth she would want to have dinner with tonight.

He shrugs. "Chris and I have always been cool. He just moved back to New Haven and he's been trying to get in touch with Mal for weeks, but she won't take his calls. I told him I would help him out."

"What does he have on you?" He gives me a confused look, and I laugh. "He must have something big on you to make you willingly participate in this whole charade. Mal will probably slice both of your balls off before she hears a word he has to say."

Dominic winces at the mention of a knife coming near his balls but looks otherwise unbothered. *Brave man.* "He doesn't have anything on me. I just...he wants to apologize to her, and I think it would do both of them some good to have closure after all these years."

"But if he's been reaching out and she hasn't answered, maybe she doesn't want closure. Maybe she's over it."

One of his hands slides up, resting on the small of my back. "Or maybe she's being stubborn and..."

"He really hurt her, Dominic." I search his face. "Do you know what it's like to have your heart ripped out like that? To be shattered by someone and left alone to pick up the pieces?"

The tortured expression etched into his features answers my question with a glaring certainty that steals my breath. *My God.* Who is the woman that hurt Dominic badly enough to put that look on his face, and why do I want to kill her for daring to own a part of him and throwing it away?

"Yeah, angel." His hands fall away from me as he takes a step back, schooling his features into a more neutral expression. "I have, and I know what it would mean to me to have that person own it. To hear them say they're sorry for hurting me even if they didn't mean to."

Emotion clogs my throat. My heart is breaking for Dominic, Mal, and all the people waiting on an apology that might never come. Except Mal's apology is closer than she thinks, and even though I don't agree with his tactics, Dominic's logic is sound.

An apology from Chris might go a long way towards healing the hurt I know Mal still carries with her. Years ago, when we were drowning our sorrows in wine and rom-coms at my house, she told me she still loved him, which means some part of her, buried deep under all of that resentment, might be open to hearing Chris out.

But the likelihood of me sticking my neck out for a virtual stranger is slim as hell, especially when I know I'm only one slip up away from blowing my entire relationship with her to smithereens.

I close the space between us with two short steps, wrap my hands around his waist and lay my head on his chest. Dominic stills then sighs and hugs me back. Everything is quiet around us, but I can't shake the feeling that something has fractured between us because of my words. And I'm desperate to fix it, to get us back to the playful moment we were having before.

His heart pounds underneath my ear as I search my brain for something to say or do to bring back the smile he had on his face just a few minutes ago. It takes me a second, but I finally remember the spark of amusement and satisfaction gleaming in his eyes when he teased me about calling him Dom at our first dinner. Inspiration strikes, and I lift my head. Batting my eyelashes and flashing him my biggest smile as I run my hands down his chest.

"Dom…" I say sweetly, loving the way his pupils dilate when he realizes the other two syllables of his name aren't leaving my lips. "All I'm saying is I think we should leave the Mal and Chris situation alone for now. He fucked up, and he should be the one to fix it. Not us."

The heat of his body bleeds into me, and his spice and citrus scent mixes with the clean sweat coating his skin and floods my nostrils. Taking me back to this morning when I woke up cradled in his arms with my face burrowed in his neck. The panty-dropping smile he gave me then is identical to the one he's giving me now.

"Resorting to playing dirty, huh?"

I shrug. "A girl's got to use every weapon in her arsenal."

His thumbs rub tiny circles on the small of my back, and I shiver under his touch. The way I always do when his fingers—which I know are capable of bringing me pleasure laced with the finest thread of pain

—are so gentle with me. It feels like being cared for, like being worshiped and revered, like being....loved.

Chill, Sloane. That's not what this is.

"Your arsenal is impressive, but I don't think it's fair for you to pull out the big guns to talk me out of doing a favor for a friend."

"Since when are nicknames considered the big guns?"

I really am curious because I don't know why it means so much to him for me to call him anything other than his given name. *He hates when people call him Dominic, babe.* Eric's warning from years ago rings in my head, and I don't know how to feel about using advice from my husband to navigate a relationship with his best friend.

"Since you're the only person in my life who's refused to give me one." His voice is a low murmur. "Now that you have though, and on purpose no less, don't think I'm letting you take it back."

My hands are busy now. Running over his chest, up his shoulders, and down the bulges in his biceps. He's so big—all muscle and masculine hardness that presses into my soft curves and makes me feel small and feminine in the best way.

"Fine." I concede, pretending for my own sake that I had a choice in the matter. "As long as you agree to shut down this dinner with Chris. It's a bad idea, and Mal will kill both of us for helping him ambush her, especially since we've been neglecting her lately."

A fact I feel bad about. Mal and I usually spend a few nights out of the week together, but I've only seen her for a few hours at work for the past few weeks. She hasn't complained or made any smart remarks —which still has me shocked—but I miss her and I'm sure she's missing me. And Dominic.

Dom. I remind myself. *You're supposed to be calling him Dom now.* Surprisingly, the nickname doesn't feel odd on my tongue. Like somewhere deep down, my mind knows this is right. The intimacy. The friendship. The warmth. All of the things I never dreamed of having with him, or anyone after Eric, wrapped up in three little letters.

He doesn't look completely convinced, but he still nods. "Okay. I'll text Chris and tell him dinner is a no-go."

"And I'll call Mal and invite her out for dinner." I stand on my tiptoes and offer him my lips for a kiss, which he gives me. "With me and you."

"Okay." He heaves an exaggerated sigh. "I guess that works for me."

I pinch his bicep, and he doesn't even flinch. "Don't make it sound like a hardship. You said you wanted to take me out to dinner and having Mal there was also a part of your plan."

"Yes, but that was when I thought Chris would be there to distract her." His eyes shine with warmth. "That way I could stare at you from across the dinner table without anyone noticing."

I blush. "You can stare at me tonight in bed."

"When you're drooling on my chest? I hate to break it to you, but it's not the most flattering view, angel." He laughs at his insult and holds me closer to him when I try to push him away.

My mouth drops open and a startled laugh falls out. "Shut up!"

Dom's answering smile is huge and playful, sending warmth radiating through me like sunlight. I want to stand here all day and bask in its glow, to let it soak into me and banish all of the worry and doubts—about what happens when this is all over and how I'm going to live without moments like these—that's hiding in the darkest parts of my mind.

* * *

"GOD! I NEEDED THIS!"

Mal grabs my hand from across the table, and the huge smile stretching her face makes me glad I talked Dom out of his plan to help Chris. She looks beautiful today, rocking a sassy black wig with loose curls and textured bangs that pair perfectly with her understated makeup and enhance her glowing amber eyes.

I squeeze her hand back and smile. "Me too."

It's not a lie. Even though I've loved spending so much time with Dom, I've missed Mal. Not being able to spend time with her is probably one of the major drawbacks of my current relationship. Missing out on little moments like this—meeting up at our favorite sushi spot

and laughing over drinks until our sides hurt—has left a Mal-shaped
hole in my heart. But I would rather go a few weeks without seeing her
regularly than lose her from my life forever, and that's exactly what
will happen if...

Stop worrying. Everything is going to be okay.

Pushing my guilt aside, I force myself to tune back into the conversation. Mal's hands are flailing around in the air as she fills me in on
the latest happenings since I've been working from home or La Grande
Nuit for the past few weeks to avoid lying to her about how I've been
spending my evenings. With Dom's face buried between my thighs.
With my lips wrapped around his dick. With his cum in my hair, on my
breasts, and down my throat. Honestly, I didn't know it was possible to
have so many orgasms without actually having sex.

Focus, Sloane!

"Yeah, I think we're going to have to let her go," Mal says, picking
up her glass and giving me an expectant look over the rim.

I clear my throat and take a sip of my drink to buy myself some
time to think up a response and hide the fact that I was only half listening. The last name she mentioned was Jeanie, the new office assistant
we had to hire when our regular girl went on maternity leave. Mal and
I were both excited about Jeanie at first. Her references were stellar,
and she had a great attitude.

But lately, she's been dropping the ball: failing to put consultations
on the office calendar, allowing clients to walk in and ambush team
members with new requests instead of going through the proper chan-
nels, leaving the reception desk unattended while she takes sporadic
breaks. Unless I missed something huge with one of our other team
members, Jeanie is the only employee we have that's walking on thin
ice. But what did she do this week that's got Mal all bent out of shape?

I sit my glass down on the table. "Okay, walk me through the situation again. I want to be sure I have all the details."

Mal plops her drink down and leans forward. "This girl told her
cousin she would make sure we designed her new kitchen for *half* of
our rate. She came in my office talking about her employee discount
should extend to her family members, and she had already sent the

quote to her cousin and was in the middle of drafting one for her aunt when I told her we absolutely would not cut our rate in half for her family members. I swear to God, if you would have been there, you would have lost it."

I have to remind myself not to act surprised because technically this is my second time hearing this information, but even if I was listening to Mal tell this story the first time around, my reaction would have been the same.

"Mal." I wheeze, trying to hold back the obnoxious laughter bubbling in my chest. "Please tell me she didn't really say employee discounts should apply to family."

She tries to keep a straight face, but it only takes a second for the dam to break. In a matter of moments, we're both doubled over the table howling with laughter at the ridiculousness of the situation. Neither of us is forming intelligible words as we try to talk through the fit of giggles and snorts. When we finally settle down, we both have tear-streaked faces and sore cheeks from laughing so hard.

"Oh my, God. I can't believe I missed that. What in the world was she thinking?"

"Child, I can promise you she wasn't thinking at all!" Mal snorts, sending us into another fit of giggles that's just as severe as the first one.

And that's how Dom finds us, bent over and gasping for air with stupid smiles on our faces that only get bigger when we notice him walking towards us. He folds himself into the interior of the booth beside Mal, and across from me, and his legs brush mine as he gets settled. He looks between us, and amusement shimmers in his eyes as they linger on me for a second longer than they should.

"Do I even want to know why you two are howling like a couple of hyenas?"

Mal bumps him with her shoulder. "Leave us alone! I was just telling her about this mess with our new assistant. She's behind on all the happenings in the office since you and James have been keeping her locked away in that damn hotel. She has other people that need her attention, you know."

Dom gives her a bored look. "Why are you saying it like I have any say in who Sloane gives her attention to?"

"I didn't mean it like that, jerk! I was just saying this hotel project has been keeping her so busy, I barely see her anymore. Thank God it'll be done in a few weeks."

I feel the weight of his gaze on my face as I study my menu. Mal's joy over the looming deadline lingers in the air between us. If she notices the awkward tension left in the wake of her statement, she doesn't say a thing about it.

"Yeah," Dom says casually. "Only a few more weeks to go. Then you'll have your best friend back."

Mal turns to face him, her lips tipped up in a happy smile. "*Both* of my best friends. I've missed you too, Nic."

"How nice of you to tack me in on the end there. What are you getting, Sloane?"

I lay my menu down, finally meeting his gaze. "Probably a stir fry. I need some vegetables in my life."

"She's still getting a dragon roll though, don't let her vegetable talk fool you."

I roll my eyes at Mal, but when the waitress comes and takes our order, I do get a dragon roll. Conversation flows easily between the three of us. Dom and I fill Mal in on the day-to-day on the hotel renovation while she regales us with more gossip. This time it's about Aunt Mary's son, Julian, who is supposedly sneaking around with the pastor's son.

"Personally, I think it's sweet J has finally found someone," Mal says, taking another bite of her fried rice. "I just think it sucks that Aunt Mary is going to try to disown him because of it."

"Does she know?" Dom asks. He's been quiet through most of the conversation, letting me and Mal talk while he frowns at his phone every now and again. I can't help but wonder if Kristen is the one texting him but asking him in front of Mal isn't an option.

Asking isn't an option at all.

"If she does, she hasn't said anything to anyone about it. Not even Mama."

Dom slides his phone into his pocket. "Well, hopefully, she doesn't lose it on him."

"Right." I dip part of my sushi roll into soy sauce. "The only thing she should care about is if her kid is happy."

But even I know that parents are more complicated than that. They spend their whole lives envisioning a certain kind of life for their kids, never stopping to think about whether they want it or not. Then they lash out when things don't turn out how they planned, which is why my mom felt so comfortable admonishing me for marrying Eric.

Pick someone in your league.

You need a man who can take care of you, Sloane.

Please don't embarrass your father and me this way.

"That's what I'm saying!" Mal exclaims, hands flying in the air. "But we both know how these older Black folks are though, they don't care if a man cheats on his wife or beats her, but as soon as two men show up holding hands, it's an issue."

"Maybe Mama can talk to her, help her not ruin her relationship with her son."

I smile at Dom's suggestion. He's always trying to solve problems, even if they don't involve him. Mal looks thoughtful for a moment.

"Yeah, I think I'll bring it up to her. If Aunt Mary will listen to anyone it'll be....you have got to be fucking kidding me."

My head snaps up at the strange ending to Mal's sentence and the sudden change in her tone. Both her and Dom are looking at a spot above my head. He's looking shocked and a little annoyed while Mal looks...well she looks pissed.

Oh, shit. I turn around to see what's caught their attention and nearly fall out of my seat at the sight of the man moving towards us. Six feet tall, short curly hair and light brown skin that sets off his chestnut eyes.

Chris Johnson.

He's at the table, sliding into the empty seat beside me, before I can pick my jaw up off of the floor and force myself to stop staring. He's still handsome, but the happy, smiling guy I always saw Mal obsessing over is gone. Replaced by a more serious man with small lines around his eyes, a hard set to his chiseled jaw, and a storm brewing behind his eyes.

"Sloane, Nic. It's nice to see you again." Chris offers me his hand, and my inner socialite won't let me ignore him. I flash Mal an apologetic smile as I take it.

"Chris. It's good to see you again too."

A lie. A flat-out lie. I pulled out every weapon in my arsenal to make sure I wouldn't see him tonight, so *how* did he end up here with us? I shoot Dom a questioning glare as I slide my hand out of Chris' grasp. He gives a subtle shake of his head to let me know he isn't the reason he's here.

"Mallory."

Chris says Mal's name like his entire reason for being is contained in the word. His tongue curls around each letter, caressing each syllable with soft, languid strokes that make me feel like I'm listening in on an incredibly intimate moment. *Shit.* No wonder she hasn't wanted to talk to him. He's only said one word to her, and *I'm* blushing. I can't imagine what it would be like to be on the receiving end of all of that intensity and have to pretend not to be affected. I flick my gaze to Dom as he shakes Chris' hand and heat creeps down my neck.

Okay, so maybe I can.

Mal sets her fork down on her plate and shoots daggers at Chris and Dom with her eyes. Her mouth is a flat line and there is a whirlwind of emotions playing across her face. Rarely do I see Mal like this: angry, hurt, eerily clam. Close to murder.

"Christopher, to what do I owe this displeasure?"

He sits back in his chair, crossing one leg over the other and smoothing a hand over the fabric of his very expensive suit. "You won't take my calls. Nic mentioned coming out to dinner with you, and I thought maybe you would be more amenable if we were face to face."

Dom coughs, his eyes flaring with panic when Chris mentions his name. And if it wasn't so damn awkward, I would be laughing my ass off right now. Lucky for him, all of Mal's attention is on the man sitting beside me.

"Well, you were wrong. Now you can leave."

Chris sighs. "I can't even have five minutes of your time?"

"You got that on the phone a few weeks ago, and just like now, that entire conversation was pointless."

A few weeks ago? Mal never mentioned speaking to Chris. I wasn't even aware he was back in town until this afternoon when Dom told me, but if making things right with Mal is his goal, it makes sense that he would try to contact her first. I rack my brain, searching for any instance where Mal was around me and in a similar mood. The only time that comes to mind is the day James hired Dom, and I came home to find her on my couch, her voice cold and sharp as she told the person on the other end of the line not to contact her again.

"That's because you won't listen to a word I have to say."

Mal narrows her eyes, and I almost feel bad for Chris because there's nothing even remotely welcoming about her right now. I certainly wouldn't want to be on the receiving end of this energy.

"Because it's too late, Chris! The damage is done. It's been done, and there's nothing you can say to undo it, so just leave me alone."

Chris shakes his head. "I can't do that, princess."

Mal shoots out of her seat. The movement is so sudden, it shakes the table a little. She tosses her purse over her shoulder as she fights back the tears shining in her eyes.

"Don't call me that. Don't call me that *ever* again."

Then she's storming out of the restaurant with the three of us shocked and staring after her. I throw my napkin on the table and start to get out of my seat, intent on going after her and making sure she's okay, but Chris stops me with a gentle hand on my elbow. I feel the weight of Dom's stare as soon as it lands on Chris' hand. He's not even trying to hide the possessiveness in his eyes. Chris catches it immediately and smiles at me as he removes his hand.

"Let me go after her, please."

Everything in me says letting him follow Mal will end badly, but there's an earnest and genuine need in his eyes that tugs on the part of me that wishes I would have gone after Eric the day he stormed out of our house. I don't know if Chris loves Mal like I love Eric, but I can't find it in my heart to get in the way of him trying to do the one thing I never got to do.

"Okay," I say hesitantly, watching Chris shoot out of his seat. Before he steps away, I grab his arm and pin him with a hard stare that I'm sure makes me look like my mother. "Dom says you're here to fix this, and I believe him *right now*, but if you're not serious about making things right then just leave her alone. Because if you hurt her again, you'll be dealing with me. Got it?"

Chris looks between me and Dom and then back at me again. An amused smirk curves his lips before he says, "Yes ma'am."

When I release his arm, he wastes no time running out of the restaurant. Dom and I watch him look both ways before he decides to turn to the left. It's a smart choice because Mal's apartment is a few blocks away in that exact direction. I wonder if he knows that or if it's just a desperate guess made by a desperate man.

Dom clears his throat, drawing my attention back to his handsome face. "Let's get the check, angel. I want to take you home."

"I'm worried about Mal. Maybe we should stop by her place and check on her."

He frowns. "And walk in on another scene like that? I'd much rather spend the rest of my evening with your thighs around my..."

"Dominic!" I laugh, looking around to see if anyone heard the beginning of that very inappropriate sentence. "How can you be thinking about that when you know how upset Mal must be right now?"

"Because Mal is a grown woman, and she knows how to hold her own with Chris."

He's right. I know he is, but it doesn't stop the sinking feeling in my chest. Even though I fought hard to keep Chris from this dinner tonight, I still feel like I betrayed Mal. Like somehow I'm still responsible for whatever pain she's feeling right now.

"I hope you're right."

He waves the waitress over and hands her his card. "I am."

"Okay." I stand and smooth my dress down. "I'm going to the bathroom. Please don't forget to box up my sushi."

By the time I get back to the table, Dom has all of our food, including Mal's abandoned teriyaki chicken and fried rice, boxed and in a bag. He hands me my purse and keys then puts his hand on the small of my back as we walk towards the doors. There's a slight chill in the air as we step out onto the sidewalk.

"Sloane?"

Dom and I freeze, his hand still pressing firmly on my back as we turn towards the sound and find Ash Strickland standing a few feet away. He's got a huge smile on his face that only gets wider as he moves forward and pulls me into a tight hug.

"Ash!" Panic slices through me as I try to relax into his hold. After a few awkward seconds, I pat him lightly on his shoulder and step back into Dom. His entire body is stiff as we collide, and I can feel the tension rolling off of him. "You remember Dominic right?"

"Yeah, of course." Ash offers him his hand, and Dom shakes it firmly. "How are you, man?"

"Good."

The one word is like a razor blade, cutting through the friendly smile on Ash's face in a split second. *Lord, he's not even pretending to be nice.* If I thought I could get away with it, I'd elbow him in the ribs.

"Ash, it's nice to see you again!"

My voice is high and threaded with anxiety. I'm so ready for this evening to be over. First Chris crashed dinner and upset Mal. And now I'm standing in front of the man I lied to in order to get out of a date with the one who made that lie, and all the ones that have followed, feel more than worth it at my back.

"It's nice to see you too. I'm sorry I haven't called. Work has been busy and…"

"You've been preoccupied with the other women you've been seeing." Dom cuts in, his voice still doing that razor blade thing. This time there's poison on the blade. "That's why you're here right?"

It's only then I notice the small bouquet of flowers in Ash's hand. He looks stunned, and once again I find myself wanting to laugh in the most awkward moment. I put my hand on his forearm and give him a soft smile.

"No worries. I've been swamped at work too. Actually, Dominic and I were just discussing the project we're working on over a quick dinner."

"Nice," Ash says, but his smile is gone and discomfort is etched into the fine lines around his eyes and mouth. "Well, it was good to see you."

"You too, Ash." I turn, happy to be done with this interaction. "Have a good night."

We walk back to the parking lot in silence, and I laugh when I see that Dom got a spot right beside me. I turn my head to ask him how he managed to do that, but he grabs my hand and pulls me between our cars before I get the chance. My shocked gasp hits the air as he presses me to the passenger side of my car and kisses the life out of me. Leaving me breathless and wet by the time he pulls away.

"Let me guess, you've been wanting to do that all night?"

He nips at my lips. "Yes, and seeing you in his arms again only made it worse."

"I sleep in your arms every night, and you're still jealous of a man I went on one date with?"

He pulls back to look at me and suddenly I'm drowning in a sea of dark desire that makes me feel like I'm melting. Every molecule of my body bleeding slowly into his with the kind of precision that makes it all feel inevitable. Like an invisible needle and thread is running between us, stitching us together with something much deeper than stolen moments, hidden desire, and a shared goal neither of us has mentioned since our first real night together.

"Angel." He plants a kiss on my lips. "I'm jealous of the wind that gets to blow through your curls." Another kiss, this time to my jaw. "Of the fabric that gets to hug your curves all day and the moonlight that streams across your skin at night." A licking kiss to my neck followed by a scrape of his teeth. "So yes, I'm jealous of a man you went on one date with because *he* doesn't have to hide how bad he wants you. Not even when he's about to take another woman out to dinner."

"Dom..." I breathe, but no other words come.

I'm flayed open by his words, by the emotion in his voice, and the gravity of his confession. I cup his face in my hands and pull him back up to me. Offering him my lips in place of the words I can't speak. He takes them with a fevered passion that makes the whole world fall away until there's nothing but me and him.

I hear the bag of food hit the gravel and then his hands are on me. His fingers hooking behind my knees and lifting me up so he can grind his erection into my core. And I want to cry because the contact is so perfect, the pressure so exact that the early tremors of an orgasm have already started.

"Unlock the door," Dom orders harshly, and I'm glad I still have the keys in my hand because digging through my purse is the last thing I want to do. The locks click and he steps back to pull the back door open. He lays me down on the seat and drops to his haunches in front of me. "Look at me. I want you to watch me while I take care of what's mine."

I sit up, using my elbows for support and not giving one single fuck about the fact that he's about to eat me out in a public parking lot. Anyone could walk by and find us like this, but that knowledge only makes his fingers pushing up my dress and sliding my panties to the side that much hotter. Two thick fingers slide inside of me, and it's all I can do to keep my eyes open and focused on the man in front of me.

He bites his lip and smiles at me. "Always so wet for me, angel."

"Yes," I say, even though it wasn't a question.

My back arches off of the seat, and my hips rock against the fullness in my core. Pleasure ignites in my veins, as another rush of arousal slips from me and coats his fingers. He curses through clenched teeth as he pushes in deeper. I buck against him, silently begging for more. He pulls back, then plunges back into me *hard*. I moan loudly and Dom bites the inside of my thigh.

"Be quiet or I'll stop right now. Is that what you want?"

I shake my head furiously, knowing that I'll die if he stops right now. "No. Please. I'll be quiet." I press my lips together, and he raises a skeptical brow like he doesn't think I can do it.

Challenge accepted.

But when he lowers his head and flicks his tongue over my clit, I almost lose it. Dom looks up at me, and the sight of my juices glistening in the hairs of his beard is so obscene I start to tremble. When he's satisfied that I'll keep my promise, he comes back to me. Flattening his tongue and giving me a long, filthy lick from the top of my slit over my clit. Then he pulls it into his mouth and sucks hard while his fingers plunge inside of me repeatedly.

There's nothing gentle about the way he's fucking me with his fingers, the pressure building in my core or the flames licking at my spine, but I don't need him gentle. I need him just like this. Filling me up. Stretching me out with the perfect balance of pleasure and pain. I writhe against his hand, amazed by the way this man is breaking me down, ripping apart every wall I've ever put around my heart.

Dark eyes find mine, and I feel his smirk against my sex. He can see me struggling to keep my eyes open, to keep the moans clawing up my throat from escaping. I can't tell if he's proud or annoyed that my lips are still sealed and my eyes are still open even though they're hazy with lust and desire. But it doesn't matter because I'm not going to lose this challenge. I *need* to see the pride and admiration shining in his eyes and hear the reverent, worshipful words he'll bless me with when I come without making a sound.

In a move I can only assume is meant to crush my resolve, Dom doubles his efforts. His tongue flutters wildly over my swollen bundle of nerves as his fingers pound into me. And I'm so wet the sound of them moving in and out of me echo in the car. I rock my hips, meeting every thrust, crushing myself to his sinful mouth and egging him on. When he curls his fingers inside of me, pressing into my g-spot and massaging it with expert precision, it sends me right over the edge. My nails dig into the leather, and I bite my lip hard as pleasure rips through me.

"That's it, angel." I hear him whisper in between soft licks directly to my clit. "You're so beautiful when you come for me. You're doing such a good job of staying quiet."

Oh, God! I scream internally. His words add another layer of desire to the liquid heat rushing down my spine and spreading throughout my belly. I pant desperately as I pulse around his fingers, my orgasm going on and on. When I come back down, I release a shaky breath and collapse onto the seat while Dom fixes my panties and dress.

He grips my hips and slides me down to the edge of the seat then helps me sit up. The smile on his face is almost as satisfying as the orgasm he just gave me, and I lean forward and kiss him.

"It's never enough for me either, angel." He murmurs against my lips.

It takes me a second to process what he just said, but when I finally realize he's referring to our conversation in the storage closet earlier today, I hum my agreement. Hearing that he can't get enough of me makes me want to drag him into the backseat of this car and have my way with him, but I know that's not going to happen.

"Well, once we get back to my place, you can have as much of me as you want."

"Hmm. You've got yourself a deal, beautiful." Dom stands and pulls me out of the car. "I'll be right over after I stop by my place to check my mail and get some more clothes."

"Are you sure it's safe?" I wiggle my eyebrows to hide the actual worry I feel at the thought of Kristen popping up on him again, and he laughs.

"Yes, I got my key back the last time I was ambushed." He reaches over and picks up the bag of food we dropped on the ground, inspecting the contents before setting it in my car.

"Still don't know why you would give a woman with crazy eyes the keys to your house, but I'm going to let it slide for now."

"You're very gracious, angel. I'll be sure to show you how much I appreciate it when I get back to the house." He leads me around to the driver's side and opens the door for me. As I climb inside, I feel his hand brush over the curve of my ass. "Have I told you how incredible you look in this dress today?"

"No, you didn't."

"Well let me say it now." He plants both of his hands on the roof of the car and looks down at me. "You look incredible in that dress,

Sloane, but I want it gone when I get back. I need you naked and waiting by the door with your pussy still soaking wet for me."

A fresh wave of arousal pools in my core, and I squirm in my seat because the way he's looking at me and the timbre of his voice as he issues another command I know I won't hesitate to follow speaks to a part of me that only exists with him.

The part that feeds on his praise and thrives on his satisfaction.

The part that flourishes when he gives me mind-blowing orgasms and then makes me feel like the most beautiful woman in the world for having them.

"That won't be a problem."

25

SLOANE

I didn't lie to Dom when I said being wet and ready for him wasn't going to be an issue for me. When I pull into my driveway I'm more excited than I was when I left him standing in the parking lot with my taste still on his lips. I park my car and damn near sprint to my front door, ready to get into the house and strip out of my clothes for another amazing night in his arms, but my steps falter when I see a familiar form perched on my front step with her shoulders hunched and arms wrapped around her knees.

"Mal?" I run up to her and drop down to her level, catching her face in my hands. "What's wrong? Are you okay?"

My heart is beating a mile a minute as I turn her face this way and that, checking for any signs that she's been hurt. When I see there are only tears streaming down her face, I calm down but only by a little bit. My relief at seeing she isn't physically hurt is quickly stomped out by white-hot rage at Chris. I told him to make this right. I warned him not to hurt her, but that's exactly what he did. And now, he's going to have to deal with me.

I pull her up from the steps and wrap my arms around her. "I'm going to kill him."

Thankfully, she laughs through the tears she's crying into my shoulder. The giggles just barely slip out between the soft sobs, but they're there, and hearing them makes me feel marginally better about staying at the table with Dom while Chris went after her.

Dom! I need to text him and tell him not to come over.

"Mal, sweetie. Let's go inside. I'll warm up your leftovers and you can tell me exactly what the hell is going on with you and Chris."

She doesn't say a word as I unlock the door and scan the living room for any evidence of the man who's practically moved into my house over the past few weeks. Luckily, Dom's pretty clean, and there's nothing downstairs that indicates his, or any man's, presence in my home.

Mal plops down on the couch as I go to the kitchen and set the bag down. I pop her food in the microwave and pull out my phone to text Dom.

> Sloane: Mal's here. She's in pretty bad shape and will probably stay the night. Tell Chris that I'm not in the habit of making empty threats.

I set the rest of the leftovers in the fridge and pull out a bottle of wine and two glasses. All the while, guilt blooms in my chest. Guilt over leaving Mal to deal with a man who broke her heart all on her own. Guilt over being kind of upset that she's here because it means I have to sacrifice a night with Dom when our time is winding down. Guilt over wanting him so much. Guilt over falling in—

The microwave beeps at the same time my phone pings. Both of them pull me out of my thoughts and back into reality where my brain remembers that my guilty conscience won't do anyone any good, but my actions will.

Dominic: Don't worry about following through
on your threat because I'm going to kill the
fucker myself. I'm going to miss having you in
my arms tonight.

I can't help but smile as I read his message. Something like delight flowing through my veins at the thought of him being equally miserable at the idea of spending the night away from me.

"Please tell me that's Ash making you grin at your phone like a fool and not some stupid TikTok," Mal calls from the living room. "My faith in my ability to pick good men has been shattered, and that would go a long way towards restoring it."

I don't know whether it's her voice or the mention of Ash's name, but I jump so hard I almost drop my phone. When I manage to catch it, I put it on the counter face-down and give Mal a tight smile, which she takes as confirmation that I was texting Ash.

"I knew you guys would hit it off." She yells from the couch. "So when are you two going out again?"

I give her a noncommittal shrug as I pull her food out of the microwave and grab a fork. As I head into the living room, I roll my shoulders back and try to look like I'm not about to lie right to her face.

"Mal, we can talk about Ash at any time." *How about never? That sounds good to me.* "I think it's more important for you to tell me why you were sitting on my front porch crying."

She takes the plate from my hand and frowns. "You threatened to take my key if I kept showing up unannounced."

"We both know that's not what I'm talking about." I roll my eyes at her obvious deflection and head back to the kitchen to grab the wine and glasses I left on the counter. Sitting down beside her, I fill them and set the bottle on the coffee table. "What happened with Chris? How long have you known he was back in New Haven?"

Mal picks up her wine and takes a long drink. "He called me like two months ago out of the blue, saying he was moving back and he wanted to see me. I told him I would rather wear the same wig for the rest of my life than spend a minute in his presence."

I snort. "How did he even have your number? I thought you guys hadn't spoken in years."

"He reached out to Mama when Eric died, and she gave him my number, talking about I would love to hear from him."

The days and weeks following Eric's death are a blur for me. Full of phone calls, text messages, notes, and cards from people I didn't know at all or hadn't seen or heard from in years. Death brings all sorts of people out of the woodwork, so it isn't surprising that Chris reached out.

"And were you happy to hear from him?"

She sets her plate on the table and lays her head in my lap. "Yeah, I was. He was there for me when I needed him."

Okay, now I'm confused. I thought Mal was still angry with Chris over the way he left her when we were in college. Now she's telling me there's a whole other layer to their story I missed when I was too out of my mind with grief to function.

"So what happened?" I run my fingers over her hair. "Why are you so angry with him now?"

"Because he left me again, and now he's back like it's supposed to make a difference. But I just can't…"

"Trust him." I finish for her, and she nods. "What did he say when he caught up to you tonight?"

"The same thing he said when he called me a month ago. He's sorry. It's different this time. If I give him another chance, he won't hurt me again."

I think back to the self-assured man who sat beside me at dinner tonight. The way he said Mal's name. The sincerity piercing through the storm clouds in his eyes before he went after her. I don't know if Mal can trust them, but I know his feelings for her are real. Whether or not that will stop him from fucking everything up again, I can't say.

"Do you think he meant it?"

Mal yawns and closes her eyes. "I think he thinks he meant it."

"You staying here tonight?"

She peeks at me through one eye. "Yes, but I'll take the guest room because I don't want to know what kind of shape your sheets are in right now. Jasmine once told me that Ash gets real messy when he comes." She giggles at my scrunched up nose. "Homegirl practically lived in the laundry room when we were suite mates."

"First of all, I don't know what's more upsetting: Jasmine sharing that information with you or you relaying it to me so nonchalantly. Second of all, I'm a bit bothered you think I would have unprotected sex with a complete stranger after one date. Third of all, and this is probably the one that has me most upset, how dare you suggest I don't change my sheets after sex?"

I mean technically I haven't had sex yet, but Dom made a point of stripping the bed down and putting on fresh sheets last night while I soaked in a bath he ran for me. My heart twists at the thought of going up to my room and laying in bed without him. I doubt I'll be able to get any sleep tonight.

It'll be good practice for when this is all over.

Mal sits up, cackling like a madwoman. "It was girl talk, Sloane! And there's nothing wrong with sleeping with someone after one date. Hell, I don't think it's an issue to have unprotected sex as long as you both can prove you're clean and you're on birth control." She pauses, looking thoughtful for a moment. "I don't have a response for that last one, but I'm glad your hygiene is on point."

I toss a pillow at her head and jump up off the couch. Her laughter echoes off of my back as I walk to the kitchen and pick my phone up off of the island. "You sure you need to stay the night? Seems like you and your smart mouth are okay to me."

She sticks her tongue out at me. "I'm okay, but I'd still like to stay over if you don't mind. Our dinner got cut short, and I want to spend some time with you."

"No, I don't mind at all."

"Then come sit your ass down."

Mal pats the cushion beside her. I sit down and laugh to myself because she and Dom both have a habit of bossing me around my house. She grabs the remote and turns on the TV, scrolling through the options before landing on some trash reality TV show I only watch with her.

I scoot into the corner of the couch and pull a blanket over my legs. "You sure you okay?"

"Yes." She slides into her own corner and stretches her legs out. "And that's the last time you're going to ask me."

"Fine, but just know I'm here if you want to talk. I'm also very serious about kicking his ass, for the old and the new, so just let me know when you want to cash in on that."

"As much as I'd like to see you try, I don't think that will be necessary."

"Try?" I put my hand on my chest, pretending to be appalled even though we both know the likely hood of me taking down a man Chris' size is slim to none.

"Yes, *try*. You're a lot of things, babe, but a fighter is not one of them."

I wave my hand dismissively. "Please, I still know all of the self-defense moves from that course we took in college sophomore year."

Mal snorts. "Shut up! We went to one class, and you left halfway through to go to the fair with Eric."

Now I'm laughing, remembering the way Eric peeled out of the parking lot when I came flying out of the gym, lured in by his promise of fried Oreos and funnel cakes. The only thing my brain retained from that class was how to get out of a front chokehold, but even that is fuzzy because I only saw the demonstration and never actually performed the move.

"Okay. Maybe I can't take him, but he gave me his word. He should be gentlemen enough to let me beat him up, especially since he was given a warning."

"Yeah. Good luck with getting that man to keep his word."

Bitterness shimmers in her eyes, and I can practically see her brain carrying her far away, back to the exact moment she realized she couldn't trust the man she loved. That she couldn't count on him to do the things he said or keep the promises he made to her. I turn my attention to the TV because it feels wrong to watch her relive another painful moment. My heart aches for her, for whatever future she pictured with Chris that will never come to pass.

When she finally snaps out of her reverie, I pretend to be engrossed in the mess playing out on the TV. Surprisingly, it's more of a disaster than the dinner we just had, and we sit quietly, watching rich women who remind me too much of my mother and her friends, argue at various high-end restaurants in their city. After a few episodes, both of us are yawning and half asleep.

"Alright." I stand up and stretch. "I'm going to bed."

"Me too, as soon as this episode goes off."

"Just remember to turn the lights off. Night."

I blow her a kiss and head upstairs for what I know is going to be a sleepless night. I close the door to my bedroom and head straight to the shower. I take my time washing, shaving, and moisturizing in hopes that the monotony of the tasks will distract my brain from the sad, empty feeling burning a hole in my stomach.

My bed looks as lonely as I feel as I climb into it. The side I didn't realize I've come to think of as Dom's is noticeably empty and cold, and it takes me several moments to get comfortable between the sheets. I roll my eyes, annoyed at myself for not being able to make it one night in the bed I've slept alone in for years without him. Part of me is starting to rethink agreeing to his rule about sleeping in the same bed every night because if sleeping alone is hard right now, I can't imagine what it's going to feel like when this is done. Everything is quiet around me, nothing but the sound of my own breathing is in my ears as I try to force myself to fall asleep.

"You can do this, Sloane," I whisper to myself. "You've done it before."

And I have. Four years ago when my sanity depended on being able to fall asleep without the warmth of Eric's body against mine and the sound of his breathing in my ears. But this is different because Eric was gone, lost to me forever along with all of the things I loved about sleeping next to him, and Dom isn't lost to me yet. We still have plenty of time together, and he's just across town in his loft, hopefully having as hard of a time sleeping as I am.

I roll over and grab my phone off the nightstand. My finger hovers over his name for less than a second before I press the call button and put it to my ear. After a few rings, he picks up.

"Missing me already, angel?" The smile in his voice is unmistakable as it filters through the speakers and washes over me, and even though I know he can't see me, I'm smiling back.

"Just calling to make sure you weren't ambushed again."

I turn on my side and close my eyes, pretending like he's in bed beside me, rubbing small circles on my back while he whispers in my ear.

"Ahh. Well, in that case, you'll be happy to know I'm perfectly safe and alone here. No exes lying in wait and no broken glass to clean up." Papers shuffle in the background as he sighs into the phone. "I miss you."

His admission lights me up from the inside out and erases the smart remark I was going to make about his ill-timed joke. A dumb smile stretches across my face, and I try to hide the quiver in my voice as I respond. "I miss you too. What are you working on?"

"Just looking over some plans Andre sent me earlier."

That must have been what he was looking at when I noticed him on his phone at dinner. The amount of relief I feel at knowing it wasn't a message from Kristen is surprising, even to me.

"For a new project?"

"Yes." He lets out an audible sigh. "Something like that. I'm just finishing up though, and I'm more interested in hearing about how much you miss me."

"Too much." I breathe, hating the amount of emotion I put into those two words.

I can hear him moving around now, and I picture him in his loft turning off lights, closing doors, and then finally, laying down in bed. There's a rustle of sheets and covers and then everything goes quiet again. Nothing but the sound of his breathing in my ear.

"Do you want to elaborate on that?" He murmurs.

"Nope." I yawn, and relief floods me when I finally feel my body relaxing into the mattress. Almost like I needed Dom's raspy lilt in my ear before I could fall asleep. "I'm tired, and I can't be held responsible for the things I might say to you right now."

"Oh?" I can see his eyebrow raised with humor and intrigue in my mind's eye. "Sounds like the perfect time for you to elaborate then."

"Dominic."

It's a flimsy warning I know will do nothing to deter him. His disapproving scoff at my use of his full name makes me smile. The man is really serious about his nicknames.

"What did I tell you earlier, angel?" Heat drips from every word, sending a current of electricity down my spine, and I wonder how he can have that effect on me from across town.

"Hmm. You tell me a lot of things, *Dominic*, so I can't be sure. Let me think." I'm playing with fire, but there's something so sweet about the promise of being burned by him. "Earlier at work, you told me you needed me to choose a new paint color for the accent wall in the eighth floor hallway. Then in the parking lot after dinner, you told me that I'm gracious and incredibly understanding…"

An amused growl interrupts me. "Are you sure you want to play this game with me?"

I bite my lip. "I don't know what you mean."

I was trying to keep my voice even, but there's no hiding the fact I've gone from relaxed and sleepy to turned on in a matter of seconds, and Dom's voice rasping in my ear like velvet wrapped sin doesn't help at all.

"You're about to find out. Reach into the nightstand and get out your vibrator."

Desire erupts in the pit of my belly, my entire body tenses with the need to obey him, but I hesitate. "Mal's here. I can't…"

"You can and you will, angel." He says darkly.

The words reverberate through me, breaking down every shred of my resistance. The same way he did when we were in the parking lot earlier tonight and in the elevator at Cerros. The same way he always does. Something about the command in his voice, the certainty in his words just makes it easy for me to forget the whole world. To care more about my own desire than the fact Mal is here. To want to know what happens after I take out my vibrator so bad it doesn't matter that having phone sex with my husband's best friend while his sister is just downstairs is so fucking wrong.

"Don't make me ask again."

Oh, God. I'm so far gone for this man, so completely and utterly in his control, that I would be disgusted with myself if I wasn't so damn turned on. My hands shake as I retrieve the toy from the drawer and pull it back into bed with me.

"I have it." I cradle the phone between my shoulder and ear and try to get comfortable. My heartbeat is pulsing between my legs as I pull my panties down. "But I don't think I can be quiet when I come, Dom."

His laugh is like dark magic, curling through the speakers and spreading warmth through my body. I want to ask him what's funny, but he doesn't give me the chance.

"Oh, now she knows my name." Fabric rustles on his end, and I picture him sliding down his briefs and gripping his dick in his hand. "You don't need to worry about being quiet when you come, angel."

Even his voice turns me on. I whimper as I slide a finger through my wetness, barely hearing his words over the blood roaring in my ears.

"Stop touching yourself and ask me why." He orders sternly.

I don't even need to ask how he knows I'm touching myself. The man knows everything about me. "Wh-why?"

"Because you're not going to come tonight, angel. Maybe going without an orgasm will help jog your memory."

My hand is frozen, hovering over my clit. "I was just joking!"

"Too late to turn back now, baby. This time is all for me." His breathing is ragged, and now I'm sure he's gripping his dick in one of his big fists, using the precum leaking from his tip as lubrication. "Let me hear you say it, Sloane."

"This time is all for you." I want to cry as the words pass my lips, but I say them because I know that it will please him.

And whatever pleases Dom, pleases me.

"Good girl. Now turn your vibrator on and get it wet."

I do as he says, sliding the toy through my juices repeatedly, letting it brush over the swollen and sensitive bud even though doing so puts me in danger of breaking Dom's rule. My breath catches, a soft moan slipping past my lips, and he groans.

"Slide it in because I need your hands free for this part. Tell me when it's done."

My skin is on fire, yet somehow covered in goosebumps, as I push the vibrator inside of me and nearly die from the sensation of the buzzing in my core. I close my eyes and try to concentrate on anything but the pleasure racing down my spine.

"Done."

I'm a breathless, panting mess as I wait for him to tell me how we're going to work together to get him to release. I love that he's being selfish, that he's using me for his pleasure without planning to give me anything but the gift of hearing him come in return. *Finally.* I think to myself. *He's finally done treating me like a fragile, breakable thing.* And I've never felt more powerful.

"Perfect." His voice has descended into the pits of hell, and I know his eyes are as dark as his tone. I can see the liquid pools of obsidian shimmering behind my lids. "Palm your breast in one hand and stroke that pretty pussy with the other. *Slowly.*"

I'm trembling as my index finger swirls around my clit. My back arches off of the bed, and I cry out softly. Dom lets out a groan that goes straight through me. Our moans mix with the faint sounds of skin slipping over skin. Me touching myself for him and Dom stroking himself off for an orgasm that's going to shatter both of us. My walls begin to clench around the vibrator with early warning signs of an orgasm I'm not allowed to have, so I slow my movements.

"Don't slow down."

I whimper. "I have to! If I don't, I won't be able to stop myself from coming."

"Figure it out, angel," he says between ragged breaths. "If you come tonight, I won't let you have an orgasm for the rest of the week."

"Dom!" I'm whining, desperate for something, anything to put out the flames licking up my spine. Growing hotter and climbing higher the longer I listen to him and touch myself.

"Pull the vibrator out and slide it back in. Let me hear how wet you are."

The toy slips out easily, coated in my juices and making the most filthy and obscene sound as I slide it back into me. He only told me to do it once, but it feels so good I can't help but do it over and over again. Imagining that it's his dick fucking into me, stretching me out with every glide. I don't even recognize the sounds pouring out of my mouth, some strangled combination of his name and the word 'please'.

"Fuck, Sloane." He shudders, and I can tell by the rough edge of his words that he's close. "You're doing so good, angel. Hearing you fuck yourself like that is going to make me come."

Unshed tears burn my eyes and my neck hurts from the awkward position it's in because of the phone, but it's all worth it for the sound of Dom unraveling on the other end of the line. I can hear his fist moving furiously, stroking his dick with a brutality that has my knees shaking and my walls fluttering against the constant quivering of the toy inside of me. I don't know how much longer I can hold off.

"Oh, God." I moan, biting down on my lip to stifle the sound.

"I wish I could see your face. See you struggling to hold it together, fighting back the need to come even as you work yourself over for me. Is it killing you to hold back, baby?"

"Ye-yes."

The one broken word is the only thing I can manage to say because all of my energy is centered on the inferno swirling in my veins. The tidal wave of pleasure threatening to break through the dam of my resistance at any second. I force myself to focus on something, anything else but the sound of skin slapping against skin. Of wet juices easing the glide of busy hands moving with a frenzied determination.

And just when I'm about to break, I hear it. The sharp intake of breath followed by a long, animal-like growl that rips free from Dom's throat and shatters me into a million tiny pieces. The vibrator is still whirling away inside of me, every inch of my skin is still drawn tight with the built-up pressure of my stalled orgasm, but somehow I feel satisfied. I mean, I'm still horny as hell, so turned on that even the slightest bit of friction will set me off, but knowing that I made it through the single most erotic phone call in my entire life without disobeying Dom's order is gratifying as hell.

I remove the toy from my pussy gingerly and toss it to the side. Then I pull my hand out of my panties and press my thighs together to relieve some of the ache. I can't help but smile to myself as I listen to him recover from his release.

"Shit." He says finally, still fighting for breath. "That was so— you're so damn incredible, Sloane. I ruined these fucking sheets. I need to clean up."

I can hear the sheets rustling as he starts to move, but I have one request before he gets rid of the evidence. "Wait! Send me a picture." And then because I know he won't be able to resist me if I beg a little. "*Please*, Dom."

Both ends of the line are quiet as he considers my request. Finally, he answers. "I suppose you do deserve a reward for being such a good girl tonight."

"I do," I murmur, mouth already watering at the thought of a picture of his dick, still hard but well spent, pressed against abs that are slick with cum. "It wasn't easy, Dom. You know how much I love to come for you."

The last part elicits a soft growl from him, and I fight back a laugh as I hear shuffling and the tell-tale clicking of the camera. Seconds later, my phone dings with a text notification, and my heart is in my throat as I open the picture.

"Oh my God." I moan. "How did you manage to make a dick pic sexy?"

It's even better than I expected. His dick is still hard, his long fingers wrapped roughly around his shaft like he was stroking it when he took the shot. Cum is everywhere, spilling from the flared tip, smeared on his fingers and in the fabric of the sheets wrapped around his powerful hips.

Dom laughs quietly. "I need to clean myself up and change my sheets, angel."

"I know." I pout, remembering the pressing loneliness that's waiting for me when we hang up the phone. It was what prompted me to call him in the first place, but I forgot it completely while we were talking. I sigh heavily, wondering if he'll think I'm weird if I ask him to stay on the phone with me tonight.

"When I get done, I'll call you back. I don't think I'll be able to sleep without your snoring rattling my bones."

My mouth falls open in outrage even as my heart soars with a joy that can only come from being known and understood by someone. From never having to ask for what you want or need but being given it anyway.

Of course, he knew I missed him.

Of course, he understood that I wanted to find a way to be with him even if it couldn't happen physically.

And of course, he knew I needed all of those things before I knew it myself.

Careful, Sloane. You almost sound like you're in love. I push the thought aside, refusing to give any credence to the ramblings of my tired brain.

"I do not snore!"

26

SLOANE

Now

On Thursday evening, I find myself home alone wrapped up in a rare group Facetime call with both of my parents. My dad is still at work and my mom is going through a large selection of evening gowns, looking for the one most likely to make her look like she has a heart.

"Sloane, darling. I happen to know that Ash is one of the bachelors being auctioned off at the Rockwell Foundation's annual charity event this year. Please tell me you'll be there to save him from the swarm of ladies who'll be bidding on him. Half of them are old enough to be his mother."

"Lauren." My dad says sternly.

I resist the urge to roll my eyes and tell my father that even his best lawyer voice won't stop his wife from trying to force me to talk to her about my non-existent relationship with New Haven's most eligible bachelor. Once again, that's not me talking. Ash was literally on the cover of *Harem*, an exclusive print magazine with a cult following, this week with those exact words in sharp, red letters above his head.

"No, Mom," I say instead. "Ash and I have decided we're better suited to be friends, so he'll have to fend for himself at the auction."

Or be rescued by whatever mystery woman he was meeting at Roku yesterday. Either way, his fate at the charity event doesn't have anything to do with me, and I refuse to act like it does. My mother gives a disapproving tut, but it's Dad who speaks.

"I'm sorry things didn't work out, Bean." His chestnut eyes shine with sincerity. "I hope my relationship with him didn't have any bearing on the decision."

I shake my head. "Of course not, Daddy. We're just looking for two different things."

Ash is looking for someone emotionally available, and I, apparently, am only looking for Dominic Alexander. The one man I shouldn't want but have given up on resisting.

"What a shame." My mother mutters. "You two made a beautiful couple."

"Uh—thanks?"

Oblivious as always, she flashes me her socialite smile. "You're welcome, love."

We chat for a few more minutes before I finally manage to get them both off the phone, so I can collapse on my bed in peace. I'm exhausted and grumpy because it's almost seven in the evening and the only person I want to see or talk to isn't here yet.

In fact, I haven't seen Dom all day. Between going to the office to handle the whole Jeanie situation with Mal and running around to check in on different projects being handled by my senior designers, I haven't had time to swing by La Grande Nuit to see him or a free moment to do more than shoot him a quick text.

Apparently, his day has been busy as well, and now he's stuck at the office going over details for the groundbreaking on a new project with Andre. It must be the same project he was working on yesterday because when he text me to say he was running late, his message had the same vague tone he used on the phone last night.

I settle into my pillows and pull out my phone. Scrolling through our messages and smiling at the only picture in our thread. Even in the light of day when most explicit things, but especially dick pics, look sleazy and low budget, Dom's picture is just....well, hot. I stare at it, examining it closely and letting the uncomfortable pressure that's been nestled in my core since last night build up until it reaches an impossible pounding that makes me feel like I'll die if Dom doesn't get here soon and relieve it.

The picture staring back at me sets off sparks of inspiration. In an instant, I'm considering doing something I haven't done in years — sexting. Normally, I wouldn't even consider sending a picture of myself to a man to grab his attention, but something about the photo staring back at me that makes me feel bold. *Oh, what the hell.* Sighing, I untie the string holding my wrap dress together, unveiling a lacy red lingerie set with a garter belt and straps identical to the one I had on the night Dom came here to claim me.

I position the camera just so, allowing it to capture the swell of my breasts, the smooth skin of my belly, and the lace cuffs on my thighs. When I'm happy with the way everything is lined up, I take a deep breath and snap the photo. Typing out the message takes a little more courage than taking the actual photo, but I manage to do it, and the whooshing sound of the text being sent steals my breath.

> Sloane: I miss you. Come home to me.

It's kind of ridiculous to be nervous about sending a simple text message to the man I've allowed to have me in bathrooms, elevators, and parking lots, but that's what I feel as I wait for his response.

Nervous. Vulnerable. Exposed.

And the feeling only gets worse as the minutes tick by. One after another after another. Passing slowly without so much as a peep from my phone. And when I can't take it anymore, I jump up from the bed and march downstairs to the kitchen, leaving it behind. I pour myself a generous glass of wine and wear a hole in the floorboards as I pace back and forth, reminding myself of all of the strategies Dr. Williams has given me for staving off panic attacks.

But deep breathing doesn't work. And focusing on one object is hard because the only thing I want to look at is my phone. Closing my eyes isn't an option because it'll make it hard to avoid stubbing my toe on the legs of the barstools I can't bring myself to sit on.

A knock sounding on my back door surprises the hell out of me, and I almost drop my untouched glass of wine when I hear it. My heart skips several beats as I turn towards the sound, realizing that only one person in my life uses that door. And then I break out into a sprint. My bare feet don't make a sound as I run into the mudroom, unlocking the door with a huge but uncertain smile on my face.

"Angel." Dom greets me. A heavy, slow gaze roves over my body, reminding me of the state of my clothing. My wrap dress is open, hanging on either side of my body and framing my curves. When his eyes snap back to mine, the fire burning in them is hot enough to brand me. "This is quite a greeting."

Then he smiles that wolfish smile, and I almost evaporate. *Almost.* Instead of disappearing into thin air, I launch myself at him. Knocking the breath out of his lungs and purring like a cat in heat when his hands slip under the fabric and grab my ass.

I rain kisses down on him. Covering his eyes, his nose, his beard, and finally his handsome mouth with the physical representation of my joy. Quickly, and without any protest on my end, he takes over the kiss. Slanting his lips over mine and dominating me so completely my thighs are quivering around his waist when he finally pulls away. I press my forehead to his and close my eyes, breathing him in with greedy gulps of air that make my lungs burn.

"You didn't text me back," I whisper, brushing my nose across his three times just like he always does to me. "I thought…"

I don't know what I thought, but I can tell by the way his fingers are digging into my skin that I was wrong. Whatever kept him from texting me back doesn't have anything to do with the panic that's been curled around my breastbone for the last twenty minutes.

"I'm sorry. I was working, but as soon as your text came through I left Andre's ass in the office and ran at least three red lights to get here and see this in person." His fingers caress me through the lace of my underwear. "That picture didn't do you justice."

He kicks the door closed and starts to move us through the house. Bypassing the kitchen and the living room to take me upstairs. Every step he takes makes his dick brush against me, pressing into my core through fabric I quickly realize isn't the denim he usually wears. Opening my eyes, I take a moment to actually look at him and nearly lose my breath when I realize he's wearing a suit. A sharp, black designer suit that hugs his broad shoulders and a graphite black tie against a smooth black shirt that gives his dark eyes an other-worldly look.

"You should have sent one back. I never get to see you in a suit."

The last time I did, I was too pissed off at James for hiring him— and too mad at Dom for existing—to appreciate how fucking incredible he looks in one. I smooth my hands over the fabric, wishing I got to see him in action today. Marching around the glass and metal offices of Archway Construction, going over plans, and ordering employees around in a refined, less carnal version of the king voice he uses with me.

Construction Zone Dom is hot, but I bet Conference Room Dom is infinitely hotter.

He smirks at me as he passes through the door of my bedroom, unraveling my legs from his waist so he can toss me on the bed. I squeal as my back hits the mattress and grin up at him as he steps back to lean against the dresser.

"Well, I'm here now, angel." His huge hands gesture towards his body. "Look your fill."

The invitation to openly gawk at him is unexpectedly sexy—but then again, so is everything Dom does. I sit up on my elbows and let my eyes roam over him, appreciating every inch of his incredible body and large frame. It's a thorough examination, my hungry eyes like fingertips skimming over his skin, but he doesn't even flinch. Instead, he crosses his arms over his chest and brings one of his thumbs to his mouth. Running it across his bottom lip, while he stares back at me. My nipples pebble and my skin tingles underneath the weight of his gaze.

I lick my lips. "Take the jacket off."

Both of his eyebrows raise in amused surprise. "Are you taking charge tonight, Sloane?"

I blink slowly, turning my options over in my mind. Part of me is shocked he's willing to hand over control, and the other part is scared to take the reigns, knowing that the fear of feeling silly for trying to boss around such a commanding man is still a very real thing for me. I study him, looking for any indication that he's playing with me, but his face is deathly serious even as desire starts to line his features. *What the hell,* I think to myself. *I have nothing to lose.*

"Yes," I say with more confidence than I feel. "Now, take off the jacket."

If being ordered around by Dom is sexy, then watching him follow my orders is downright erotic. He moves slowly, shrugging the jacket off of his shoulders and then taking one muscular arm out of each sleeve with practiced precision. I bite my lip as I watch him fold the fabric neatly and hang it on the chair by my dresser. His muscles shift and bulge under his shirt with the movement, but my eyes are drawn to his hands as they straighten his tie, smoothing the silk to make sure it's lying perfectly against his chest and abs.

"What's next?"

There's a huskiness to his voice as he asks the question, and it makes the sight of him deferring to me that much sexier. I squeeze my thighs together, acutely aware that I haven't had an orgasm since last night in the parking lot.

"Sleeves. Roll them up. *Slowly.*"

Again, he follows my order without a word. My eyes snap to his deft fingers, watching closely as they remove one silver cuff link and then the other. He sets them both down on the dresser with a soft clink before settling the dark velvet of his heated gaze on me. I hold it for only a moment then shift my attention back to his fingers. Riveted at the sight of him rolling the sleeves of his shirt up to his elbow, exposing the corded veins of his forearms one by one.

"Do you have any idea how sexy you are when you're biting your lip?"

I shake my head because I don't know, and I really don't care. All I care about now is how amazing it is to have him standing in my bedroom. How hard he is while he looks at me like I'm the only woman in the world and strips for me at my request.

"Loosen your tie and then unbutton your shirt, Dom."

My favorite fingers in the world go to his neck and yank his tie loose, leaving it hanging. Then he's pulling his shirt out of his pants and running his hands slowly up his stomach and chest until he reaches the button at his collar. I arch a brow, trying to appear unaffected even as liquid heat pools in my core.

"Are you teasing me?"

His eyes go wide, feigning innocence as he makes short work of the buttons. "I have no idea what you're talking about. I'm just following your orders."

"Mhm hmm. Following orders means leaving out all the extra steps."

"I'm sorry, angel. I'll be sure to follow your orders exactly next time."

God, I love this.

More than I ever expected to. Now I can see why Dom likes control in the bedroom. The heady rush of power as you watch someone bend completely to your will, obeying your every command just to please you. And it's even more intoxicating for me to know he's trusting me to run the show—to take control of his pleasure and my own—because it confirms what I thought last night when we were on the phone: he doesn't see me as the guilt-ridden woman who ran out on him just a few weeks ago because she couldn't stop her self loathing and fear from eating her alive.

I'm so different now, so much more comfortable with allowing myself to have this even though I'm still not fully convinced I deserve it. And as much as I hate to admit it, he was right about waiting. About giving me time to settle and feel secure in this relationship. I thought I was ready for everything before—and I *probably* would have been fine if he'd given it to me—but today there's no probably or maybe.

There's only the powerful, pounding certainty that even if everyone else in my life might look at this situation and say it's wrong, I know it's right. Because here in my bedroom, there's nothing we can do that won't feel predestined, inevitable, and impossibly right.

Suddenly, I'm dying to have him on top of me, anchoring me to Earth and the truth singing in my blood with the weight of his body.

"Come here."

I sit up a bit to reach for him, and he strokes his beard thoughtfully without making a move. "I would, but I'm not completely undressed yet. And I think you want me naked for this next part don't you, angel?"

Lust clogs my throat, stealing my ability to speak. I nod and watch him take the rest of his clothes off. First, he toes off his shoes, then his hands are on his belt. The veins in his forearms bulge deliciously as he undoes the buckle and unbuttons his pants. The quiet glide of his zipper is agonizing. Making my fingers itch to pull it down myself, but the power dynamic between the two of us has shifted back to normal.

It was nice to have the power, but I can't find it in me to be sad about giving it back to him. I *want* him in control, so I wait with bated breath while he undresses for me. Praying all the while that his comment about wanting him naked for the next part means what I think it means.

After what seems like an eternity, he's striding towards me in all of his naked glory. Every hard slab of muscle, shifting beautifully with each step. His dick is fully erect and the ever-present bead of precum leaks from his tip. Then he's standing over me and gripping my ankle to pull me to the edge of the bed. Reverent fingers stroke up my legs, caressing the lace cuffs circling my thighs as his lips go to my knee.

"Tell me about your day."

The words are a soft murmur against my skin, but an order nonetheless. He continues to press kisses to my leg, starting at my knee and moving down my inner thighs. I'm spread wide before him to accommodate the width of his massive shoulders and the small puffs of air from his nose skate across the flushed skin of my sex. I suck in a breath to help me concentrate on forming a sentence that isn't a plea for him to tongue my pussy through the lace of my panties.

"It was uneventful, certainly not as interesting as what's happening here."

Heat flashes in his eyes even as his mouth turns into a flat line of dissatisfaction. "Details, angel. I want to hear all about your day while I eat this magnificent pussy."

Oh, God.

He releases the clasps on the straps of my garter belt in seconds and places his hands on the band of my underwear. Rough fingers dig into my flesh as they grip lace and begin to pull.

"Lift your hips for me."

My body follows his order instantly, and Dom takes full advantage. Sliding the lace down my legs and tossing it over his shoulder. Our eyes meet for a second before his gaze drops off to inspect me. I spread my legs further, a shameless and wholly unnecessary invitation. I'm so wet I can feel the evidence of my arousal slipping out of me, taking every bit of my brainpower with it. Which is unfortunate because the man between my legs is still determined to get me to use at least some of it to recount the details of my day to him.

Dom puts both of his big hands on my ass and lifts me to his mouth. Then he gives me a slow, filthy lick with the flat of his tongue, starting at the end of my slit and dragging through my folds until he reaches my clit.

"Oh, God." My head goes back, my eyes close and the entire world falls away. "More. Please, Dom. I want more."

"I'll give you whatever you want, angel."

I don't even need to hear the 'but' because I feel it floating in the air between us. Hovering over me with its tongue sticking out, teasing me for not being able to think even though no woman in my position would be able to.

"My day was good, but I missed waking up next to you," I admit softly. "Mal was gone by the time I got up, but she asked me to come to the office today, so we could handle the situation with our office assistant together."

"Keep talking and watch me."

I lift my head and open my eyes just in time to see him lowering his head back to my body through a haze of lust. A moan rips from my throat as he laps at me with soft strokes of his tongue. Even though he's going slow, and seems to be in complete control, there's no mistaking the satisfied grunt that leaves his chest when he plunges his tongue into me.

"We—shit, Dom. That feels so good." I roll my hips to meet the thrusts of his tongue and he pinches my ass to remind me to keep talking. "We were going to fire Jeanie, but she sent in a letter of resignation this morning. We spent the afternoon reaching out to temp agencies to...."

He turns his attention back to my clit, sucking it between his lips and pulling rhythmically while his tongue flutters over the swollen bundle of flesh mercilessly. My hands grip the duvet as the force of my day-old orgasm descends on me. Another pinch, this time to my other cheek, reminds me to keep talking before I miss my chance to come again.

I bite back a moan and force myself to focus even though I don't know where I was in my retelling of the day's events. "We'll have someone new by next week. Mal and I went to lunch. I spent the afternoon checking on my senior designers and then—"

I feel it. The ripples of pleasure making my sex spasm. Languid heat pushing warm tingles through the base of my spine and out into the rest of my body. I hone in on the sensation, too afraid of losing it to do anything but freeze under Dom's busy lips and wicked tongue. But just as I'm about to fall over the edge, he pulls back.

"Then?"

I blink slowly at him, desire and need clouding my brain for long seconds until I finally regain control. "Then...I came home."

He drops my hips, snaking his hands around to my front until one is gripping my thigh and the other is poised to take his tongue's position. The skin of his knuckle is warm and rough as it brushes against my clit. Instinctively, I buck into his touch and silently thank God when he holds his hand steady, allowing me to create the friction I need to feed the pressure building inside of me, instead of pulling away.

"And—" His eyes are black as night. "—you missed *me*."

On the last word, he thrusts two fingers into me, pushing deep and curling upwards to massage my g-spot. I gasp loudly; the intrusion forces me to stretch to accommodate the width of his thick fingers, and it hurts just a little, but he doesn't relent. I arch up off of the bed as Dom repeats his words, this time phrased as a question.

"I—I already said that."

"You told me to come *home*, angel." His fingers are brutal as they pound into me, every stroke pushing me towards a meltdown of epic proportions. "Home. Like this house and the most precious thing in it belongs to me. Is that the case? Do you belong to me?"

I shake my head. Unable to form a coherent thought, let alone string together a sentence. Everything about him is devastating me— the gravelly rasp in his voice, the heat of his body bleeding into mine, the perfect way he's touching me—and I know he's done this on purpose, waited until the moment when I'm too far gone to think, or lie, to ask the question he wants the answer to most.

Truthfully, I hadn't thought much about the content of the message because I was so preoccupied with sending the picture before I chickened out. The picture was sexy, and so I wanted the message to be sexy and concise. Leaving no room for confusion or doubt about whether I wanted him here with me tonight. But why did I choose that particular phrase?

Because this place doesn't feel like home unless he's here. Because he's the only person who's felt like home since Eric. Because I belong to him in all the ways I never thought I could belong to anyone again.

All good, valid reasons.

All perfect things to say to the man who's crucifying me with his eyes.

All completely wrong things to say to someone who agreed to a casual relationship with an expiration date you insisted on having.

"It was just a text." I finally manage to say. Even in my altered state, I know I haven't even begun to answer his question, but I can't say any of the things I've just thought out loud. Hell, it's scary enough having them swimming around in my lust-addled mind, painting pictures of a future I can't have with him or anyone else.

"A text written by you, right?"

I'm writhing madly now, my hips churning desperately in search of release even as frustration claws at my chest. "You know that already!"

"So then you shouldn't have any trouble telling me what it meant." Something dangerous shifts behind his eyes. Fire singes the corners and creeps in further until it turns his devastating midnight gaze to the hardest, blackest form of obsidian. "Is it possible that I misinterpreted it, angel? Because I cut a very important business meeting short to come take care of you, and doing something like that based on a text only makes sense for a man like me if the woman who sent knows that she's mine."

Torture. Everything about this moment is torture—from the exquisite pleasure his wicked fingers are stroking into my body to the ruinous emotion playing across his features and laying waste to my soul.

"Dom, please." Beads of sweat trickle down my spine while the sound of his fingers gliding in and out of me fill the air. "*Please.*"

"Say it, Sloane."

He dips his head, dark eyes locking on mine as he sucks my clit into his mouth with ruthless precision. My thighs clamp down around him. They're quivering and weak from his ministrations, but I'm desperate to keep him here. To hold him hostage until I fall over the edge of the cliff he's dragged me to.

Dom lets me keep him there for a few seconds. Happy to feed into the illusion that I have any power over him just so he can be the one to shatter it with a quick shift of his shoulders and a beatific smile on his stupidly handsome face.

"Say. It."

"You know that I am…"

"I. Need. To Hear. It."

Each word is punctuated by a curl of his fingers and a jolt of pleasure zipping down my spine. I'm ready to fall apart around him. To detonate like the most lethal bomb. To say anything just to plunge into the ocean of sweet relief. And the bastard knows it too.

I shake my head furiously. Trying to resist the urge to obey the command skating across my skin as tears leak from the corners of my eyes. Dom lowers his head back to my body, raining soft kisses down my belly. And it's those gentle presses of his lips that break my resolve. I last all of five seconds before my lips part.

"I'm yours."

The words slip past my lips so easily I wonder why I even bothered to fight saying them at all, but then I remember being owned and acknowledging that ownership are two very different things. And of course, there's the issue of our deadline and the million and one things that will make Dom's name etched in my heart look insignificant in comparison.

None of it matters right now though. Right now I can pretend like my world begins and ends with the growl ripping from Dom's chest, no doubt prompted by my words, and the sensation of his fingers twisting in and out of me at a breakneck pace.

"Oh, God. Yes, Dom. Yes!"

My walls clamp down on him. A fresh wave of heat washes over me, and then I'm falling. Finally falling over the edge of the cliff I've been dangling from for ages. I arch off of the bed and scream, but the sound is swallowed by Dom's mouth when he moves up the bed to cover my body with his.

He's all gentle touches and whispered praises as I come back down to Earth, cradled in his arms with the flared tip of his dick nudging against my entrance.

27

DOMINIC

Now

Sloane Kent is going to be my undoing.

When I die and have my soul damned straight to hell, I'll know beyond a shadow of a doubt that the determining factor wasn't being too much like my bastard of a father, stealing five dollars from my mom's purse to buy candy on the way home from school, or cheating on a spelling test in fifth grade. Hell, it won't even be the time I stood beside my best friend in the whole wide world and watched him marry the woman we both loved.

No, it'll be for this moment right here.

Nine o'clock on a Thursday night in September, with my dick nestled between her legs, her juices running down my fingers, and the admission I pried from her body with my own ringing in my ears.

Yeah, this is the moment.

Because this is the point of no return, and even though I know it, Sloane doesn't have a clue. She's all wide-eyed and breathless. Her pussy already throbbing for me, clenching like mad to try and pull me in.

A good man would warn her. He would explain to her that as

soon as she takes the first inch of his dick into the welcoming heat of her body, he's never letting her go. But I'm not a good man. I'm the bastard who's been waiting a lifetime for this moment. The one who's too afraid of scaring her to fully explain the gravity of the situation. The one hoping like hell the constant reminders that she belongs to him will suffice. The one who's going to walk into hell with a smile because he'll get to relive the heat of this moment for eternity.

"Oh please, Dom," Sloane begs, rocking against me like she didn't just have an orgasm.

I brush my nose across hers. "What do you need, angel of mine?"

"You," she says in a breathless whisper. "I need you."

I lift up a little, balancing my weight on my forearms, so she can breathe. "You've got me, baby." Dipping my head down, I drop a kiss to her mouth and nearly bust at the sight of her licking her essence off of her lips. "Tell me what else you need."

"I need this, Dom." She lifts her hips a little, capturing a bit of my tip inside of her. We both moan. "Please, I'm ready. I'm so fucking ready for you."

And I believe her, but I'm not sure if it's because my dick is the closest it's ever been to the heat of her without fabric as a barrier or because I'm still reeling from hearing her say she's mine. Either way, I don't have a lot of time to figure it out because Sloane is trying to take matters into her own hands with another tiny rock of her hips. I have to pin her to the bed with a firm hand at her waist.

"And you'll have me, but I need you to slow down. Let me take care of you, okay?"

"Okay." She's pouting, but she's listening, which is good because it gives me time to think. Time to absorb the fact that this is happening. After years of waiting and wishing and struggling to focus on the world spinning around me when all I want—all I've ever wanted is her. In my arms and my bed to finally make sense of the place she's always held in my heart.

Pulling myself away from her body is the last thing I want to do right now, but I do it anyway because I need to get every stitch of clothing off of her so I can feel her skin against mine when I finally claim her. I kneel on the floor in front of her.

"Sit up."

Sloane reaches for me, and I take her hand, pulling her up off of the bed into a sitting position. My heart threatens to beat right out of my chest when she looks up at me with those half-lidded eyes.

I pull in a deep breath, steadying myself before I touch her. When I'm sure I won't bruise her, or shred the little clothing she's wearing, I reach out, brushing my knuckles over her cheek before sliding the sleeves of her dress off of her shoulders. Her bra and garter belt are next, followed by the lace cuffs circling her thighs. I drop all of the fabric onto the floor and take her in.

Holy shit.

This isn't my first time seeing her naked, or even my first time stripping her down, but it is the first time I've done it with the anticipation of being inside of her pounding in my blood. The air between us is thick, charged with lust, desire, and the scent of Sloane's arousal. I run one hand up her leg and watch as every inch of her skin pebbles with goosebumps. She's so fucking responsive, arching instinctively into my touch and letting little moans escape her lips when I get close to her pussy.

"Have you ever used a safe word, angel?"

I draw a light circle on the inside of her thigh, and she releases a small sigh as she shakes her head. Some part of me knew the likelihood of her ever having used a safe word was slim, but relief still floods me when she gives her answer. The selfish, most possessive part of me rejoicing in being able to take yet another one of her firsts.

Leaning forward, I capture one of her nipples in my mouth, pulling on the flesh until it's a hardened peak. I sit back and smile at my handy work, the brown skin tinged with redness from the light drag of my teeth.

"Well, I need you to pick one. Right now." I hold her gaze, seeing the worry and hint of annoyance flaring there. "Just so I can be sure you're okay, without having to ask you if you are. You said you're tired of me conducting mental assessments. This means I won't need to."

Because it'll be up to her to let me know if it's too much, and I trust her to do that. Sloane looks thoughtful for a moment and then she nods slowly.

"Fine." She runs her hands down my chest, making a beeline for my dick. I grab her wrist to stop her from going any further. "Are there any rules about what it can't be?"

I thread my fingers through hers. "No, as long as it's not something you'd usually say during sex. There can't be any confusion about whether you need me to stop or not. Pick something that reminds you of…"

"Noir."

The word pops out of her mouth and brings my sentence to a grinding halt. *Noir.* As in the club where I saved her and got to touch her for the first time in years. The place where my hands remembered what it was like to hold her and my heart decided I could never go back to a life where I couldn't. It was the first place where I dared to dream of more than an adversarial relationship with her. Where I thought of, but didn't dare hope for, nights like this one.

I stare at her with wonder and amazement, marveling at her ability to make everything, including choosing a damn safe word, fraught with meaning and a thousand unspoken wishes. *What does it mean for her though?* I try to keep the question from shining in my eyes, but she sees it.

She gives me a shy smile. "That night in the club, you made me feel like nothing in the world could touch me as long as you were there shielding me. And then when you brought me home and waited for me to turn on a light before you pulled off…it might sound weird, but you made me feel safe and cared for."

My dick throbs impatiently, spurred on by the emotion in her words. "It doesn't sound weird, angel. Not even a little." *It sounds perfect. Like your heart knew just like mine did that there was no turning back.*

All of her features light up in response to my words, and she bites her lip like she's trying to keep herself from saying something else. I raise a brow, letting her know I see her holding back.

She shakes her head. "You don't have to know everything going on in my mind."

"Yes, I do." I release her hand and push her back on the bed, covering her body with my own before her back hits the mattress. Her legs are still spread, and the heat from her core is making it hard to focus. "Tell me."

I'm not the only one having trouble focusing. Sloane's breathing has turned shallow. Her pupils are blown, and underneath me, her hips are churning involuntarily. I rock into her, letting the tip of my dick get coated in her moisture.

"I was just...." She exhales on a ragged breath, curling her legs around my hips. "My safe word also means black. I was thinking about how it's kind of our color."

I stare down at her, waiting patiently for her to continue even as my heart pounds in my chest and my dick gets impossibly stiffer at her words. Everything she says tonight is a perfectly poised dagger, piercing my heart and sealing her fate. How can she think I'll ever give her up when she says shit like this?

"You know," she continues, running her hands down my back. "Black like your eyes when you look at me like...well like you're looking at me right now."

Like I love you so much I can't fucking breathe? Like I might rip the world apart with my bare hands if my plan doesn't work and you walk away from me when this is over?

I know exactly the look she's talking about. It's the same look I've spent the past twelve years replacing with scowls and sharp words. The one that's been in hiding so long, it doesn't know how to do anything but flash like a neon sign whenever I'm with her, close in ways I never thought I'd get to be. I press my lips to hers and kiss her until I'm sure I won't ask her what *she* thinks the look means.

"Mhmm. Tell me more." I pull back from her slick heat and drag my dick up and down, sliding through her folds and grazing her clit with each glide. Torturing both of us just so I can hear the catch in her voice while she gives me a few more reasons to love the color black.

She gasps."I...I can't think of anymore."

I feel the sting of her nails digging into my back. My muscles tremble as every cell in my body aches, begging me to end this agony. Sloane arches into me, her nipples brushing my chest, and I drop a kiss to the corner of her mouth.

"Black like your heels when you stormed out of James' office and told him not to hire me."

Reaching between us, I take my dick in my hand and position myself at her entrance. Sloane's eyes go wide, and I remind myself to go slow. But she's so hot and wet, her pussy already throbbing for me.

"Black like that fucking skirt you wore that night." My arms shake as I push into her. That first, velvety inch feeling like heaven. Sloane's legs tighten around me, her body stiffening as she adjusts. "It kept riding up your thighs, teasing me with inches of golden skin I didn't think I would ever get to touch."

"Dom, please," Sloane begs. *"Please."*

I run my hands down her thighs and to her hips, giving the supple flesh a light squeeze before making my way to her ass and taking both cheeks in my hands. "Black like the lace thong you had on the first time you let me taste your pussy."

On the last word, I lift her hips and pull her forward onto my dick. Filling her with one single motion that steals the air from both of our lungs. Sloane screams, her head thrashing against the duvet as she writhes underneath me. I search her face for any sign that I've hurt her, but there's nothing but pleasure as she scratches at my back.

"Yessss," she moans, her eyes falling shut. "It's so perfect, Dom. *So perfect."*

Usually, I like for Sloane to look at me when she says shit like that, but right now I'm fucking glad she's not. Because hearing those words and looking into her eyes while her walls tremble around me would bring this whole thing to an embarrassing end.

With her eyes closed, I have a chance to pull my shit together. I take a deep breath and relish the feeling of being inside of her. Nothing, not even the past few weeks of fucking her with my tongue and fingers, could have prepared me for this moment. For the greedy little pulses of her cunt or the scorching hot heat of her wrapped around my dick. Sloane wiggles underneath me, a little whine escaping her, and I can't help but smile. She's just as desperate for me as I am for her.

I pull back out and slam into her again, grinding my pelvis into her clit and eliciting the closest thing to a growl I've ever heard from her. It's all the encouragement I need to keep going. Dipping my head, I take her mouth in a dirty kiss. My tongue plunges into her, matching the strokes of my dick.

Sloane's legs tremble and then fall away from my body, landing on the mattress, opening her up for me, and presenting an opportunity I can't pass up: the chance to see my dick disappearing inside of her. I pull back and sit up on my knees to sweep my gaze over the place where we're joined. I run my hand down her body, making her shiver as I trail my fingers from her stomach to the apex of her thighs. She shivers, her eyes popping open to pin me with a lazy stare.

"Look at you. Taking all of my dick like a good girl." I roll her clit between my fingers and angle my strokes to hit her g-spot. "Is this what you had in mind when you sent me that picture and told me to come home to you, angel?"

She nods, looking down her body to watch me drive into her with another thrust. The sound of my skin slapping against hers fills the room, but I still want to hear her. Usually talking is the last thing I want to do during sex. It's distracting and makes it impossible to stay in the moment, but none of that seems to apply when it comes to being with Sloane. I squeeze her waist with my other hand, intent on getting my answer from her.

"Use your words."

Heat flashes in her eyes as she rolls her hips to meet my thrusts. "Yes. This is exactly what I was hoping would happen when you got here, and it's better than anything I could have ever dreamed."

And just like that my body is covering hers again. I seek out her mouth and take her lips in a sloppy, wet kiss that reflects how desperate I am for this woman. To own her. To consume her. To love, and be loved by, her. I'm dying to tell her that twelve years of wet dreams and jacking off in my shower to the curve of her lips has done nothing to prepare me for how it feels to be inside of her.

But even if I had a thousand years to try, I would never be able to put this feeling into words.

Bracing my hands on either side of her head, I change the rhythm. Moving from furious strokes that make her breasts bounce to slow, deep plunges that make her eyes roll into the back of her head. Her skin is flushed from the orgasm she just had, but I can tell she's close again. Her breathing is ragged, and her smooth palms glide down my sides, so she can dig her nails into my hips.

Sloane breaks the kiss, leaning forward just a little to scrape her teeth over my jaw. I shrug her off with a shake of my head because I'm way too close to coming for her to be doing shit like that.

"Cut it out." I breathe, snaking a hand around her neck to grab a handful of curls.

It's not a gentle hold, but that only seems to make Sloane enjoy it more. She gives me a devious smile that sends a zing of pleasure directly to my balls. They tighten painfully in response, and I groan.

"Come here, angel."

Still fisting her hair in my hand, I sit up and pull her with me while I'm still inside her. Suddenly, she's straddling me. Her legs on either side of my body and her perfect breasts swinging in my face. I capture one nipple and then the other in my mouth, licking and teasing them, while Sloane pants above me. I'm so deep inside her that she's gone completely still. Her head is back, resting against the hand I have at her nape.

I press a kiss to the valley between her breast, inhaling her scent and waiting. For her to start moving or tell me it's too much by using her safe word. The seconds seem to stretch into hours, but I wait for her without asking if she's okay because I promised I would.

Finally, she exhales and lifts her head to meet my gaze. And the smile on her face is the best thing I've ever seen. Bright, and happy with a little bit of uncertainty around the corners of her mouth. Then she places her hands on my shoulders and starts to move, replacing all traces of doubt with a frenzied desire that makes her all the more beautiful.

Shit.

Releasing her hair, I let my hands go to her hips, but force myself not to take over the rhythm. This is her show, and I don't want to do anything to ruin this perfect picture. My eyes go to her face, committing every furrow of her brow, purse of her lips, and sweat-dampened curl to memory. I'll never get tired of looking at her. Of seeing her beautiful face swallowed up by lust and pleasure while she works herself on my dick. Using me to stoke pleasure into her veins, fueling the fire burning deep in her core.

I wrap my arms around her back, pulling her closer to me. "Tilt your hips forward, baby."

She does as I say, leaning forward and allowing her clit to grind into my abs. A sharp hiss escapes through her clenched teeth as her fingers dig into my shoulders. Her mouth is right by my ear, so I feel the warmth of her breath skating across my skin when she says, "I'm so close."

I turn my face into her neck and pull the tender flesh into my mouth, sucking with long pulls that make her walls tremble around me. Sloane's hips churn restlessly, a rolling grind that slicks my abs with her juices. Her legs circle my back as her movements become jerky and less coordinated. That's when I know her orgasm is getting closer.

Anticipation and lust expand in my throat, seeing Sloane come is my favorite sight. Something about watching her fall apart, and knowing she trusts me to hold her together, makes me feel like the luckiest man on the fucking planet.

"Then come, angel," I whisper, biting down on the spot that I just kissed. "I want to feel you milking my dick because I know that when you go off, I'm going right with you."

Sloane leans back, shaking her head when her eyes meet mine. "Not yet. I want to see you come first."

I pull her back to me, skimming my lips down her neck. "No."

There's no way I'm going to give in to the pressure building at the base of my spine before I feel her detonate around me. But there's a steely determination shining in Sloane's eyes that lets me know she has other plans. She pulls her legs back up under her and balances her hands on my shoulders. Then she lifts up, exposing several inches of my dick to the cold air before slamming back down, taking them back into the heat of her pussy and starting a punishing rhythm.

"Fuck, *Sloane,*" I growl, digging my fingers into her hips.

I don't know if I'm trying to stop her or help her finish us both off, but I keep my death grip on her waist until she pushes me back on the bed and forces me to let go. Her soft hands are on my chest, covering my thundering heart and pinning me to the bed while she rides me. And all I can do is hold on for dear life. I stare up in awe at the goddess hovering over me, capturing a perfect nipple in my mouth whenever she comes close enough.

She gives me a triumphant smile. "You look so good underneath me."

"Not as good as you look on top of me, angel."

"Good enough to make you come?"

I move my hand between her legs and start toying with her clit. She glares at me, but the moan that falls from her lips makes it worth it. "Absolutely."

There's no point in arguing about who's going to go over first because I can tell she's on the edge. Sloane lasts less than a minute with my thumb pressed firmly against her swollen clit, working at it with slow circles that match the swirl of her hips. The tremor starts in her core, every inch of her clamping down around my dick, then it spreads outward until she's nothing but a trembling heap of moans screaming my name before collapsing onto my chest.

And it's those broken shudders of unabashed pleasure, coupled with her pussy pulsing around me, that finally set me off. I come hard, wrapping my arms around her and thrusting up into her and flooding her pussy with hot ropes of cum that make my vision go black.

I hold onto Sloane while my ears ring and my blood pounds with the satisfaction of finally unleashing more than a decade's worth of love, hope, desire and need onto the only woman who was made to handle it.

28

SLOANE

"**B**abe, I have something I need to tell you."

Eric is sitting at the dining room table writing out our monthly budget, and I can't help but smile because he's done this every month since we've been married. Even now, when we're more than financially okay, he feels like it's necessary to have a written breakdown of our monthly expenses, and I think it's adorable.

I cross the room and stand behind him. He smells amazing, and he's just cut his hair and shaved, so he's looking extra good. I wrap my arms around his neck and place a kiss right under his ear, which gets his attention immediately.

"I know you aren't starting with me when I'm trying to get this budget right." He shifts in his chair, parting his legs so I can slide between them and sit on his lap. I happily take his offer and make an attempt to look innocent, shaking my head slowly, and he laughs. "What do you want?"

"Well, I just found out about an unexpected, but welcome, expense and I thought you would want to know about it sooner rather than later."

His brow furrows. "An unexpected expense?"

I nod. "Unexpected but welcome."

Pulling the positive pregnancy test out of my shirt pocket, I place it on the table in front of us, right next to his half-finished budget. His eyes turn into saucers as they register the two pink lines.

"Unexpected but welcome," he says quietly. He looks at me, and I can't quite tell what he's thinking because his expression is serious, too serious. My heart starts pounding.

"Are you mad?"

"No!" He chuckles, and I breathe a sigh of relief. "I could never be mad at you when you're telling me something like this." His thick arms wrap around me, pulling me into a hug. "You've made me the happiest man in the world, Sloane!"

Suddenly, his lips are on mine, taking my mouth in a gentle kiss with an underlying thread of passion. His muscular arms anchor me to him, so every inch of our torsos is touching. One of his hands has already found its way under my shirt and is slowly, but deliberately, heading towards my bra.

The possibility of more teases me as his tongue makes a quick, but incendiary, pass over my lower lip. It's an invitation. One I'm tempted to accept because despite feeling a little nauseous, I want him. My body is already reacting to him. The familiar throb of anticipation is starting to build in my core, and I am trying to surrender to it but my mind is racing.

We're having a baby. There's a tiny life growing inside me, and eventually, after months of morning sickness, sharing my body and hours of labor, they will come into the world and depend on me and Eric for everything.

And what if we're not good at this? What if we screw this kid up so bad they have to spend their entire life recovering from their child-hood? What if I'm like my mom?

I cringe, and Eric stops immediately. "Are you okay?"

His voice is gentle, and his eyes crinkle with concern. I shake my head. "I'm freaking out, babe. What if I suck at this?"

"Oh baby, you suck at a lot of things, but this won't be one of them."

He starts to laugh, and I punch him in the shoulder, hard. "You're an asshole." I try to stand up, but he tightens his hold on me, keeping me from going anywhere.

"Okay, okay. I'm sorry!" He holds his free hand up in surrender, all traces of humor now gone."Why are you freaking out?"

For some reason, the question makes me tear up. I shake my head. "I don't know. I'm just scared, you know?"

"Baby, it's perfectly natural to be afraid."

"It doesn't seem like you're afraid though." My voice is tiny, child-like. I'm jealous of his poise. Jealous of the way he can take life-altering news in stride while I'm losing my mind.

"Sloane." His voice is serious, filled with determination. "Of course I'm afraid. I don't know anyone who wasn't afraid when they found out they were expecting. It's a natural thing, but we can't let fear overshadow the joy of this moment."

The hand underneath my shirt snakes around to caress my belly. His touch and his words calm me significantly, but there's still one major thing concerning me.

"I don't want to be like my mom, Eric. I don't want to spend my kid's whole life making them feel like nothing they do is ever good enough for me. I want to be close to them, to make sure they always know they're loved and cherished."

Eric nods, understanding fully how my complicated relationship with my mom is playing into this meltdown. And at this moment, I'm so in love with this man, so thankful to have someone in my life who understands me even when I might not be making the most sense.

He kisses my forehead. "You're not going to be anything like your mom, Sloane. There's too much warmth and love in you for you to ever be as critical and cold as she is, especially to your own child. You're going to be an amazing mother, baby. I don't doubt it."

I search his eyes for any indication he doesn't believe what he's saying and find nothing. My favorite thing about Eric is I can always trust him to tell me the truth, even when it hurts, and right now I know he is.

He genuinely believes I'll be a great mother, and even though I don't quite believe it, I know for a fact he'll be a great dad, which means we'll be okay.

29

DOMINIC

I thread my fingers through Sloane's curls and gather them into a makeshift ponytail that gives me a full view of her perfect lips wrapped around my dick. She peeks up at me through her lashes and my grip tightens, the tips of my fingers digging into her scalp just enough to give her the bite of pain she seems to love. Heat flares in her eyes and she moans her appreciation around me; the vibrations making my dick pulse as a bead of precum slips onto her busy tongue.

Sloane arches a sassy brow at me. I'm not going to last much longer, and after nearly a week of doing this—having each other when-ever and where ever we can—she knows it. And I'm starting to think making me come within minutes of pulling me into the wet heat of her mouth was her plan all along. And it may be her way of getting back at me for yesterday when I fucked her in the shower and ruined her twist-out. She was so mad she didn't speak to me for the rest of the morning, and last night before we went to bed, she let me know in no uncertain terms that accepting the multiple orgasms I gave her after dinner, did not mean I was forgiven.

So this is it: my punishment that's not a punishment because I don't give a fuck about coming embarrassingly fast when her throat is constricting around my shaft, mimicking the way her pussy clenches when she's about to come, and driving me crazy.

"Fuck, angel." I hiss through clenched teeth. "You're going to make me come in your perfect mouth."

I'm still fisting her curls in my hand, and my grip tightens when the first wave of pleasure crashes into me, sending ripples of liquid heat to the base of my spine. My heart pounds wildly in my chest, matching the pulsing of my dick and the violent rush of heat threatening to explode out of me at any second. I let out a ragged breath and give myself over to the sensation.

Sloane chooses that exact moment to slow down, and her eyes dance with mischief and magic as she comes to a complete stop, releasing me with a loud smack of her lips and a kiss to my tip. She breaks my hold and a victorious smile curves her lips as she stares at her handiwork. My brutal erection, weeping precum and throbbing for the release she just denied me.

"Sloane…"

But I don't know what else to say because I have the strangest mix of pride and frustration swelling in my chest as I stare up at her. She just used one of my moves on me, and she looks so damn pleased with herself for doing it. She blinks at me innocently as she climbs off of the bed.

"Dom."

I wrap my fingers around my dick and give it a rough stroke. Sloane tries to hide it but watching me touch myself is turning her on, and I can't help but wonder if the sight is enough to break her resolve.

"Are we even now, angel?"

"Not quite."

"Tell me what I have to do to get back in your good graces."

Touching myself doesn't feel nearly as good as what she was doing to me moments ago, but I don't stop because Sloane can't take her eyes off of me. She's biting her lip and tracking every stroke with her eyes and when I squeeze another bead of precum from my tip, she makes a breathy noise in the back of her throat. I've almost got her, but then I fuck it all up by smiling at her reaction to me, and her gaze snaps to my face.

"Don't come."

My hand stills immediately. "What?"

"*Don't* come. After what you did yesterday, you don't deserve to."

"It's not like I did it on purpose!"

"Tell that to the curls you ruined."

I sit up and reach for her, but she's already backing towards the door. And by the time I untangle myself from the sheets, she's already bolted. The sound of her laughter echoes through the hallway as she rushes down the stairs.

Despite my neglected dick and the need for release pounding in my blood, I can't stop myself from smiling at the sound as I head to the bathroom to shower and get dressed for the day.

"That fucking woman."

* * *

It's close to two in the afternoon when I finally make it to La Grande Nuit. I was supposed to be here sooner, but the meetings I had scheduled at Archway ran longer than usual, and then I got caught up in an emotionally exhausting conversation with my dad, who only ever calls to make me feel like a bad son for not visiting him in the assisted living home I pay for.

Agitation simmers in my veins as I rush into the lobby, praying that being dumb enough to take that call hasn't made me miss the chance to see Sloane at work. When I left the house this morning, she said she'd only be in the hotel long enough to drop off some materials that got delivered to her office yesterday, but I'm hoping I can convince her to stay a little longer because a stolen moment in a remote corner would work wonders for my mood.

"Excuse me! You're Nic Alexander, right?"

I spin around and see a tall, curvy woman with smooth brown skin, dimples, and red hair that's cut closer to her scalp than mine is, approaching me. She looks familiar, and it takes me a second to realize she's one of Sloane's senior designers. I think her name is Sasha.

"Yeah, that's me."

"Great." She thrusts the boxes she's been holding into my hands. "Mal asked me to bring these by for Sloane because she's out sick today."

I look at the box of cabinet pulls I watched Sloane rush order from her tablet two days ago while I massaged her feet on the couch and try to hide my surprise. This isn't the first time she's sent someone else to bring my team a product they had to rush in. And it's nothing weird about her utilizing her team members to run errands when she doesn't have time, but it is weird for them to think she's sick when I know for a fact that she isn't.

She was perfectly fine when I left the house this morning, her cheeks still flushed with pride at sending me to work with blue balls. She even kissed me goodbye and teased me about still being hard. I smacked her on the ass and told her I would see her later and she hummed her agreement.

So what changed?

I take the boxes from Sasha's outstretched hands. "Thanks for bringing these in."

"No worries."

Then she turns to leave, and I have to balance the boxes in one hand just to pull my phone out of my pocket and text Sloane.

> Dominic: Playing hooky without me, angel?

Once the text goes through, I catch the elevator up to the eighth floor where my team is. Andre is working with another guy to grout some tile in the bathroom of a smaller suite.

"Hey," I call from outside the door. "I have to go handle a personal issue. You guys good?"

Andre answers without even looking at me. "Yeah, don't worry about us."

"Cool. Text me if you need something." I set the boxes on the floor. "We just got these in, can you make sure they get installed today?"

"Yeah, we'll handle it after we finish this up."

With that sorted, I head back out. By the time I get to my car, Sloane still hasn't texted me back. Part of me wants to call Mal and see if she knows what's going on, but I know she'll just drop everything to head over there to try and fix whatever the problem is.

And that's not what I want.

If something's wrong with my angel, I want to be the one to help her through it, to pull her into my arms and wipe her tears away while she just *feels*.

Because even if I am a bastard like my father, and all signs continue to point towards that fact the longer I spend in Sloane's bed without letting her know the truth about us, I know I can do this. I can be the man Sloane needs me to be. I can make her life easier, better, fuller in all the ways she lost when Eric died.

The ride back to her place stretches into an eternity, and the quiet in the car is exacerbated by the silence on my phone. The longer it goes on, the more worried I get. I pick it up again, looking specifically at the date because I know Sloane gets sad like I do when any date having to do with Eric comes around. But it's September 23rd, and the date doesn't ring any bells for me. I close the calendar, annoyed that it hasn't offered any additional information and my home screen is still glaringly absent of any notifications from the only person I want to hear from right now.

I swipe past a text from Kristen, a missed call from Chris, and an email from Seb. Getting back to any of them, but especially Kristen, is low on my list of priorities as I turn onto Sloane's street. When I pull into the driveway, her car is still parked in the same space. Even though I want to get to her as soon as possible, I still take the time to pull into the garage and use the key she gave me to open the back door. Everything in the house is quiet as I move through the mudroom and kick off my shoes, but I know she's here somewhere.

"Sloane!" I call out, moving through the kitchen where I see that her purse is still on the counter beside her phone, open laptop, and a pile of paperwork. Almost like she started working and then stopped abruptly.

Maybe she did get sick.

I drop my keys on the island and start towards the stairs but stop short when I see a tangle of wild curls peeking out from underneath a blanket on the couch. She's curled up in the corner, practically in the fetal position, with tears streaking down her face.

"*Angel.*"

30

SLOANE

Before Eric died I didn't know what it was to truly grieve someone, to mourn the life you had together and the future you envisioned with them. Up until four years ago, I was one of those lucky people who had never been touched by catastrophic loss. My parents were healthy, only children of wealthy couples who passed away before I was born, so when I lost him, I was unfamiliar with the way grief worked.

The ebb and flow of waves crashing into you on the days your brain associates with that person. The sting of tears at the back of your eyeballs that force their way out regardless of where you are and what you're doing. The way those tears taste exactly the same every time they fall. Like heartbreak, devastation, and open wounds that will never heal.

That's the only thing I taste today.

The unique flavor of grief sticking to the roof of my mouth and making it impossible for me to speak even as Dom walks into the living room, eyes filled with fear and the truest, deepest concern for me, and kneels in front of the couch. His brow is furrowed as I look right through him, unable to focus on the handsome curve of his lips or any of the other million things I've come to love about his face.

His face. The face I've fallen asleep to every night for over a month. The face I gazed up at when I was on my knees for him just a few hours ago. The face I was thinking about when I looked at my calendar this morning and got the niggling feeling I was forgetting something. And not just a small something. Something huge. Something important.

Something pre-Dom Sloane would have never forgotten.

"Angel." Dom breathes again, putting his hands on my shoulders and sitting me up so he can take a seat beside me. I barely breathe as he hauls me and my blanket cocoon into his lap. He presses a gentle kiss to the top of my head. "What's the matter? Tell me how I can fix it."

His voice is so tender, his words soothing to match the circles he's rubbing on my back, and I want to lean into his touch, to take the comfort he's so readily offering me, but I don't deserve it.

I don't deserve any of it.

The happiness I've gotten from being with him for the last few weeks. The joy I've found in being cared for and desired. The reprieve he's given me from the demons lurking in the shadows of my mind, reminding me that I'm the cause of all the pain our loved ones have experienced in the wake of Eric's death.

Because I'm the one that sent him to it.

A sob breaks free from my chest, ripping through me with enough force to make me crumple in Dom's arms. He wraps them tighter around me like he can hold me together with the sheer force of his will, and I let myself take comfort in the feeling because it might be the last time I get to have it. That might sound a little melodramatic, but I know Dom isn't going to let this go. He's going to keep pushing and asking until I tell him what's wrong. And once I do, he's going to hate me. For real this time.

"I'm here, Sloane. I'm right here with you, just tell me what you need."

A time machine. I think silently. *Except I'm not even sure I want*

*that because going back in time to fix my mistake would mean I don't
get to be here with you.*

Instead of answering, I just cry harder. Endless sobs wracking my
body repeatedly until even Dom's large frame is shaking with the force
of them. And through it all, he never lets me go. Never once complains
about the tears falling from my face and gliding down his neck,
seeping into his shirt and soaking his skin.

He just rubs my back and rocks me like a parent would rock a fussy
baby until I finally quiet down. When my sobs dissolve into softer, less
gross, sniffles, I wipe my nose and take a deep breath, preparing to tell
him a truth I've never shared with anyone about the day we lost Eric.

"I was pregnant." I feel his entire body stiffen underneath me and
know immediately that this is news to him. Honestly, it kind of
surprises me, given how close he and Eric were. "This was the year
before Eric died. We found out in July, and we were waiting until we
got out of the first trimester to tell anyone. You know...in case
anything happened."

A broken piece of a smile crosses my lips as I think about how
happy we were in those few blissful weeks. Ecstatic about the life
growing in my belly. Our baby. A secret that was just for us.

"Then one night in September I woke up in the most excruciating
pain and bleeding like crazy. Eric rushed me to the hospital, but I
knew." My voice cracks, and Dom's hold gets impossibly tighter. "I
knew I was losing the baby, and the doctors confirmed it."

I barely remember the trip to the hospital, but I do remember the
doctor telling us we were lucky we waited to tell our family and friends
because having to notify people about the loss could be just as trauma-
tizing as experiencing it.

Lucky.

There was nothing lucky about being one of the only two people in
the world grieving the life we created.

There was nothing lucky about being so devastated, *so broken*, I
could barely get out of bed.

Eric tried to be there for me, but I pushed him away. Choosing to
lean into the guilt and despair that said my doubts, my fears about

being the kind of mother I had, were the reason my baby was gone. None of it made any sense, but it wasn't long before the thoughts swallowed me whole, carrying me so far into the pit of despair I'd do anything to claw my way back out.

"Eric never told me."

I swipe angrily at the fresh tears slipping down my cheeks. "I don't think either of us talked about it with anyone. For a while, we didn't even talk about it with each other. Then in January, Eric said he wanted to try again. You know how he got around the New Year, feeling all hopeful about life."

"Yeah," Dom laughs softly. "He was always the first one to make his resolutions."

"Exactly. He was sure we could try again and everything would be fine, but I—" I lay my head on Dom's shoulder and look at my hands, watching my fingers twirl my wedding band around. "I was scared. For months, I put him off with excuses about how busy work was for both of us and how hard it would be to have a baby while we were renovating the house. Just all kinds of stupid shit to not have to tell him I was terrified of getting pregnant again."

"Sloane, you—"

I shake my head to stop him from finishing his sentence, from trying to comfort me before he knows the worst part of all of this. The culmination of the tragic last months I spent with my husband. The moment Eric realized how far I'd sank, how determined I was to suffer, to sit in my grief instead of leaning on the partner who loved me and would have gladly carried me out of it if I'd just let him.

"The day Eric died, we got into an argument. We were eating breakfast, and he mentioned that Mama was starting to ask him about grandbabies. Then he launched into this adorable speech about how badly he wanted to have a family with me, and I just lost it." My lips are trembling, and everything in me is screaming for me to stop, but now that I've started, I can't. "Before I knew it, I was screaming at him about not being over the miscarriage and then I said babies were off the table for at least another couple years because I got an IUD."

Truthfully, I could have gotten the implant taken out whenever I wanted, but I didn't want him to know that. I just wanted to put an end to the conversation, to stop feeling like I was being stabbed in a wound that hadn't healed.

I close my eyes and let those last moments with Eric wash over me. "He was so mad he couldn't speak. I don't even know how long we sat there staring at each other before he grabbed his stuff and headed for the door."

Dom pulls in a sharp breath, and his fingers dig into my skin. I wonder if he's picturing it too. His best friend's last moments on Earth, how hurt and angry he must have felt in the minutes before a drunk driver T-boned him on a road he wasn't supposed to be on in the first place.

"Angel, you don't have to say anymore."

I laugh, and it's a twisted, bitter sound that makes him flinch. I wish I didn't have to say anymore. I wish I didn't have to let him know how completely fucked up I am, how unworthy I am of the comfort I'm drawing from his body at this exact moment.

"He said he never thought I could be so selfish and if I felt like I couldn't talk to him about things like this then maybe we didn't have any business being married. Then he slammed the door and left. And I remember being *happy* he was gone, relieved I didn't have to keep seeing the hurt in his eyes. But I had no idea, Dom. I had no idea that would be the last time I'd see him."

With the last of my confession out in the open, I brace myself for the inevitable moment when Dom stands up, dumps me unceremoniously onto the floor, and walks out of my life. But seconds pass and then minutes and he doesn't do any of that. Instead, he turns the tiny circles he's been making to sweeping passes that go from my lower back to my nape and back again.

Confused, I extract my face from his neck and look at him. I need to hear his voice, even if it's so he can tell me how much he hates me. "Say something, please."

"Today is the day you lost your baby."

He drags his gaze to mine, and the storm of emotions I see there *destroys* me. He blinks and a single tear skates down his cheek. I've never seen him cry before, not even at Eric's funeral, so seeing him shed real tears for me, for Eric, for our baby—it makes my heart twist uncomfortably in my chest.

"Yes, but please don't let that make you feel like you have to stay." I look down, fiddling with my ring again. "I understand if you want to go. I know you probably hate me now, and I can't blame you because I hate myself."

His long fingers grip my chin, lifting it so I can't miss the raw grief and pure compassion playing across his features. Two things I don't deserve from him or any person who loved Eric.

"Hate you? Why would I hate you?"

My brows fall together. "Did you hear what I just said, Dom? Eric is dead because I was too selfish and cruel to let him see that I was afraid. If I would have acted like an adult and told him how I felt, he never would have been on the road that morning. He would have been home with me."

"No!" I flinch at the sharpness of his tone, and Dom pushes out a rough breath through his nose. "I'm sorry for raising my voice, but how could you think telling me this would make me hate you?" He scrubs a hand over his face, and I just stare at him, too stunned by his words to come up with any of my own. "I could *never* hate you, Sloane."

"You should."

"Don't tell me how to feel about you." It's a gentle warning wrapped in that commanding tone I've grown accustomed to, and it brooks no argument. "Angel, what you and Eric went through—the things that were broken between you that you never got the chance to fix—it all breaks my fucking heart for you and him, but you have to know that your chance to heal together was stolen from you because some asshole couldn't be bothered to call an Uber while he was getting shitfaced at seven in the morning, not because you got into an argument and he left for work early."

"But—"

"Eric might have been upset about the birth control thing," he continues, ignoring my feeble attempt at protesting. "But I think we both know he was more hurt that you didn't talk to him about it than anything. He loved you, Sloane, and if things didn't happen the way they did, he would've come home with flowers and an apology. He would've held you in his arms and made you tell him everything you were keeping bottled up inside. And he would have listened to all of your fears and told you, *like I'm telling you now*, there was nothing wrong with being afraid."

Fresh tears stream down my face as I listen to Dom, allowing him to paint me a picture of resolution and peace with his words. I've never imagined what it would have been like if Eric had made it home that day, but it feels nice to let the alternate reality wash over me, easing the ache in my heart with hypotheticals that are far more comforting than the memories I've been torturing myself with all day.

But I don't deserve it.

I destroyed my life, my happiness because I was afraid, and for years I've honored my vow to never forget it. But this morning I realized that's exactly what I've been doing, losing myself in Dom and this relationship that's doomed to fail, allowing the heat of his body and the solace I've found in his arms to quiet the truth screaming in my veins. *People only get one chance at happiness, one shot at real love, and I threw mine away.* I wipe away the tear falling from his eye before it disappears into his beard.

"I don't know why you're being so nice to me."

"What did you expect me to do, Sloane? Let you bare your soul to me and then leave you here, hurting and alone?"

That's exactly what I expected, but it all sounds so ridiculous coming out of his mouth. Probably because the incredulity coating each word makes it sound perfectly unreasonable for me to be craving his fire and rage while he pins me with a sorrowful gaze that sees down to the depths of my soul.

Anger and frustration claw at my chest, and I push against him, struggling to break his hold. I need to put some space between us before I allow myself to find comfort in his arms that I don't deserve. He releases me, and even though I'm the one who wanted space, as soon as I leave the heat of his body, I'm left with the distinct feeling of being set adrift.

Dom stares up at me, watching me pace back and forth in front of him like a caged animal. He's calm, completely in control of his emotions, while I'm spinning out in front of him.

"I expect you to be disgusted that I've been so caught up in you I forgot what today is!" I narrow my eyes at him. "For four years, I've felt the onset of grief surrounding this day in my bones. There's been no escaping it, no denying how completely I fucked up everything because of what happened to me on this day. It cost Eric his life. It cost Mama her son and Mal her brother." The tears are back, blurring my vision so I can't fully see his face. "It cost you your best friend. And I *forgot*. I woke up this morning and I was happy… "

"You deserve to be happy, angel."

"No, I don't!"

I'm glad I can't see myself right now because I feel positively feral. Chest heaving, hair flying in every direction, a blanket half wrapped around my body while tears stream down my face. There's nothing remotely attractive or sexy about this moment, and despite Dom looking like there's nowhere else he'd rather be, it's not lost on me that this isn't what he signed on for.

He's here for my body, not my shattered heart.

Wiping my tears away, I push out a ragged breath. "You should go. This isn't…dealing with my grief isn't a part of our arrangement. Just go back to work and I'll—"

"Shut up, Sloane." He grabs my wrist to pull me back into his lap. I land on top of him with an irritated scowl.

"Did you just tell me to shut up?"

"Yes, because I didn't want you to waste your breath on the rest of that sentence when we both know I'm not going anywhere."

"You're not?" I ask in a voice so small I can barely hear it.

"No." He shifts my legs so I'm straddling him and slips his hands under my shirt. Over the past few days, he's had me in this position countless times, but right now there's nothing overtly sexual about us sitting like this. Nothing to suggest his interest in me is solely in my body, but then again, I knew that. "What do you know about my dad?"

All of my irritation fades away at the random question, replaced by confusion and a little bit of uncertainty. Every bit of information I have stored in my brain about Gabriel Alexander was given to me by Eric, Mal, or Mama. None of it, not a single thing, came from Dom, and I don't know what I'm *supposed* to know or where he's going with this line of questioning.

A deep laugh rumbles in his chest. "Relax. I know you've probably gotten an earful about my piece of crap father from everyone with Kent as their last name."

"Yeah," I say slowly. "But I think they were all just trying to help me understand you."

Dom nods solemnly. "I'm sure they were. Luckily, it means I can skip over the part where I bore you with all of the details from my tragic childhood and get straight to my point."

I frown, still confused. "Which is?"

"My dad was a bastard, Sloane. He's still one, except now he's old, dying and getting all the toxic shit he put out into the world back tenfold. You know how he treated me, how he treated my mom?" I nod. "*That* is the kind of person who deserves to never be happy, to never know peace or joy or love. Everything he did—every hateful word he said, every punch he threw—it all came from a dark place he *chose* to go to. Did you choose to hurt Eric?"

His eyes widen a bit to drive home the point he's trying to make. I shake my head, finally understanding. "No. I wasn't trying to hurt him, but none of that matters because I *did*. I hurt him and he died, Dom. I can't ever forget that, I —"

Dom grabs my hands, stopping me from digging my nails into his chest. Stunned, I blink down at where his long fingers wrap around mine. I didn't even realize I was doing it, and I can't tell if I was fighting to get away from him or latching onto him like a lifeline.

"You're hurting right now, angel, and that's okay." He murmurs, waiting until my fingers have relaxed to let me go. "You lost a lot in a short amount of time, and I don't know anyone who would be completely whole after that. But this idea you have in your head about not deserving to be happy is ridiculous. If anything, life owes you some good, joyful moments to give you a break from the grief you've been carrying around all by yourself."

Every word that comes from his mouth—coated in understanding and compassion—feels like a physical blow to my body. I can feel my muscles tensing with every breath he takes, knowing that it will come with another kind word I don't want to hear.

"No."

"Yes," Dom growls, his eyes burning into mine. "Being happy doesn't mean you've forgotten what you've lost. Grief doesn't work that way, Sloane. Human emotion is more complex than feeling one thing at a time, and happiness doesn't erase grief, it enhances it. It makes the knowledge of what you've lost more acute, but it also makes it possible for you to open yourself up again, to make room for what you've lost to come back to you in a different way."

I open my mouth to respond to him, but the only sound that comes out is a strangled sob that cracks my chest wide open. In some distant part of my brain, I wonder if I should be embarrassed about this. About being reduced to a blubbering mess of tears and sobs with my face buried in the crook of my husband's best friend's neck while he holds me like he's never, ever going to let me go.

Yes, you absolutely should.

I'm almost tempted to believe the small voice screaming in my head, but then Dom kisses my temple and it's swallowed whole by a wave of tender emotion that rushes through me and stops my tears in their tracks before they begin anew.

Only this time they're tinged with happiness, soaked in the familiar, yet foreign, feeling of love swelling in my chest, clogging my throat with a painful knot of realization.

Love.

I love him.

I'm in love with Dominic Alexander.

Except I can't be. Not just because I still feel like I don't deserve this, but because there's nothing I can do about it. This relationship we're in has an expiration date on it. One that I put there to keep this exact thing from happening, to keep myself from falling in love and dreaming of doing something stupid like blowing up my life and destroying my relationships with Mama and Mal.

This is my husband's best friend we're talking about, and he's the last man on Earth I should ever *want,* let alone love.

But here I am.

Wrapped around the only man who's felt like home to me since Eric died, heart thundering in my chest and bones sagging with exhaustion. Dom rubs my back, crooning softly in my ear and telling me to breathe. To settle. To relax because he's here with me and he's not going anywhere.

Against my better judgment, I follow his gentle commands, letting myself relax into his hold until my eyelids grow heavy and fall closed.

31

SLOANE

Now

When I wake up, my mind is fuzzy and still clinging to the slivers of a dream about meeting a guy whose face I never see at my first college party, dancing with him all night long, and connecting on a level that shouldn't have been possible for strangers. I haven't had it in months, but I've always thought of it as my subconscious attempt to rewrite the parts of the night that were ravaged by alcohol. Still, I can't imagine why my brain would choose today of all days to call that particular fantasy up. I stare at the wall and try to figure it out, then decide not to dwell on it because a tired, grief-riddled mind can't be trusted to adhere to logic.

Groaning, I turn onto my back and realize I'm in bed alone. There are beams of orangish-red light streaming through the windows, letting me know it's early in the evening. I sit up slowly, bracing myself for the throbbing pressure behind my eyes that indicates the start of the headache I always get after spending hours crying.

Surprisingly, the pain doesn't come, and I'm able to go to the bathroom and make myself presentable without any issue.

When I'm satisfied with my appearance, and completely over the puffiness around my eyes I can't do anything about, I head back down-stairs to find Dom. Everything in the house is still, golden rays of sunlight stream in through all the windows, and there's no sign of him anywhere. I'm almost convinced he left, but then I see that the light in my home office is on.

As I pad down the hallway, his gravelly baritone filters out through the slight opening in the door and calls to me on a cellular level. I stop short, waiting for my heart to slow to a more manageable rhythm—something that doesn't feel like I'm about to go into cardiac arrest—before tapping on the door and pushing it open.

Twin pools of midnight greet me, looking both surprised and delighted to see me standing in the doorway. I hold his gaze and hope like hell I'm not as easily read as he is right now because my heart hasn't slowed down one bit. In fact, it's galloping at warp speed, trying to beat its way out of my chest and take its rightful place in the palm of his hand.

God, I forgot how devastating it can be to stare into the eyes of the man you love.

Because that's exactly what this is. Love. Can't eat, can't sleep, can't breathe without you, love. Your smile lights up my world, and your arms feel like home, love. I could stand here all day and watch you do the most mundane task without ever getting bored, love.

I am so fucking stupid and have set myself up for the heartbreak of a lifetime, love.

"I'll have to get back to you." Dom is saying into the phone, closing his computer, and shoving the papers in his hand back into a folder, all with his eyes on me. "Bye, Seb."

He crooks a finger at me, beckoning me to him, and I don't think he cares about what the person on the other end of the line—Seb? As in Sebastian Adler?—is saying because as soon as my feet start moving, he hangs up the phone and sets it down.

"Were you working?" I round the desk and slide onto his lap.

He pulls my legs up and drapes them over his hard thigh. I lay my head on his shoulder, pulling in a deep breath just to flood my nostrils with that spicy, masculine scent that's uniquely him.

Warm fingers ghost over the bare skin of my legs. I was wearing yoga pants when I fell asleep on him, but he must have taken them off when he carried me to bed because he knows how much I hate sleeping in anything more than Eric's old t-shirt and a pair of underwear.

"Just going over some permit applications."

I press a kiss to his neck. "Are you ever going to tell me about this mystery project you've been working on?"

He sighs. "Eventually. I think I'll need your expertise at some point."

"Mhmm." I sit up and smile at him. "If I didn't know any better I'd say you like working with me."

"I *love* working with you. You're my favorite interior designer."

"You're only saying that because I put out."

Amusement shines in his eyes, but he doesn't refute my statement as he brushes his nose over mine. Once again, that keen sense of deja vu hits me, layering on top of the dream still lingering at the edge of my mind. My eyes narrow as I try to hone in on the details, but they just won't come.

Dom looks concerned as he searches my face. "What is it?"

"Nothing." I shake my head. "I just got the strongest sense of deja vu."

No way am I mentioning the dream. This man has already seen enough of my crazy for one day. There's no need to show him anymore.

"Deja vu?" He asks, a smirk tugging at the corners of his mouth.

"Yes." I roll my eyes when he lets it take over. "Sometimes when we're together you'll do something, like brushing your nose over mine, and I'll just get this distinct, unshakable feeling we've done it before. Like we've lived that exact moment, but I just don't know when or how. Do you ever feel that way?"

Just as suddenly as it appeared, the smirk goes away, replaced by a look I can't quite discern. I stare at him, feeling awkward and confused by his silence and the sudden change in his mood. Finally, he shakes his head.

"No, can't say that I have." He tightens his hold on my waist, and it's the only warning I get before he stands up and my feet meet the floor. A shadow of an emotion passes behind his eyes as he looks down at me. "Are you hungry?"

I nod slowly, examining him to try and determine where his head is. "I could eat, but I didn't take anything out for dinner. Not that there was anything to take out. My fridge is disturbingly empty."

The past few days have been nothing but cuddle-filled mornings and sex-filled evenings, and it hasn't left me with a lot of time to do anything that doesn't involve being around the man standing in front of me. We've spent every night holed up here, devouring each other and pretending nothing outside of the edges of my bed, and an array of food delivery apps, exists.

"Good thing I had some groceries delivered."

Dom takes my hand and pulls me out of the office, leading me into the kitchen and gesturing for me to take a seat at the island. At some point, probably while I was sleeping, he managed to clear the countertop. Putting away my sketches, computer, and paperwork and leaving them in a neat stack with my phone on top.

"Thank you for cleaning up and ordering food."

"You don't need to thank me, angel."

He doesn't even look at me as he says it, and I tell myself not to read too much into it. Instead, I focus on studying the broad planes of his back and the way his muscles shift underneath the soft cotton t-shirt he's wearing as he moves around.

But staring at him only makes the sinking feeling in my gut worse because I immediately notice the muscle in his jaw jumping as he starts to remove the skin from the salmon filets he's just pulled from the fridge. I shift in my seat, feeling restless and awkward in my own kitchen.

"Do you need some help?"

"Oh, yeah." He chucks his chin at the refrigerator. "There's stuff for a salad in there if you want to throw it together."

"I think I can do that."

Working on dinner with Dom, even on something as simple as pan-seared salmon with a salad, feels nice. Familiar and easy in a way I haven't had in such a long time. We work in coordinated movements that say everything about the time we've spent together over the past few weeks. The mornings making coffee, the evenings spent shoveling take-out onto plates, eating as quick as we can, and loading the dishwasher before ripping each other's clothes off.

Too bad it won't last. My heart squeezes at the thought.

But even as we move around each other, doing our parts to finish up dinner, something feels weird. An awkwardness hanging in the air that doesn't dissipate even as we eat. Dom is still deep in his head, and I'm still feeling self-conscious and vulnerable after my breakdown earlier today.

All of the tears, the weight of my confession, and Dom's absolution have left me exhausted. Turns out, laying the ugliest parts of your soul at someone else's feet and being washed clean by their words and compassion can take a lot out of you. None of that tells me why he's so quiet though. It does nothing to explain the antsy tension rolling off of his body in waves.

Maybe it was all too much for him. Maybe he's spent the last few hours thinking about what I said and is wondering how to tell me he can't do this anymore. Because even though he gets where I was coming from, he can't stand to be with the woman who....

Stop it. Just ask him what's wrong, and he'll tell you.

I set my fork down, preparing to do just that, and my phone starts vibrating on the table to announce an incoming Facetime call from Mal. I pick it up and start to press the decline button, but Dom's voice stops me.

"Don't. She probably just wants to check on you since you called in sick today."

He stands up and grabs my plate, stacking it on top of his and moving to the sink. I stare after him. Everything in me wants to ignore this call so I can go wrap my arms around his waist and fuse myself to his body until he makes me believe everything is okay.

"Answer the phone, angel."

Something in his voice, the quiet reservation in his tone, makes the

worry brewing in my soul even more acute. But my phone is still ringing, loud, incessant, and impossible to ignore.

Pushing out a frustrated sigh, I hit the accept button and school my
features into something more friendly for Mal...and Mama. Both of
their faces are squeezed into the small screen, beaming at me with
identical smiles that remind me of Eric more and more every day.

My lips curve into a real smile as I listen to them talk over each
other, telling me something about a new dress Mal bought for Mama
that she refuses to wear. After setting me up with Ash, Mal has been on
a matchmaking spree, and Mama is her latest victim. She's been
nagging her about updating her wardrobe, so she can attract some
'sexy granddaddies.' *Mal's words, not mine.*

"Just let her see it, Mama!" Mal is saying now. "I'm telling you
that you look amazing. Step back a little."

Mama huffs but backs away from the screen. "I don't care what
neither one of you say. I'm not wearing this little slip of nothing
anywhere."

The camera flips around, and Mama comes into view. Her slender
curves are wrapped in a strapless black dress that hits around her knee
and hugs every inch of her. My eyes stretch wide and my eyebrows
nearly hit my hairline.

"Wow." I breathe. "Where have you been hiding all of that body,
woman?"

"In clothes, where it belongs!" Mama hisses, trying to pull the
fabric down her legs and getting annoyed when it reveals more of her
cleavage.

Mal flips the camera back around, and I can see her fighting back a
laugh. Her amber eyes are shining with amused tears. She's getting a
kick out of this, but I know it's only a matter of time before Mama
starts getting snappy and sends her, and that sexy little dress, packing.

"I think you look incredible!" Mal says as Mama comes back into
the screen. "We might have to take you out on the town the next time
Ash lets Sloane out of the house."

Two things happen the moment Ash's name comes through the
speakers: my heart drops into the pit of my stomach as I watch a hint of

sadness move across Mama's face and the sound of glass breaking pierces the air around me. One makes me jump out of my skin while the other breaks my heart in two.

I haven't mentioned dating to Mama since the first time Mal blabbed about it—mainly because Ash and I were done before we started and there's no real way to tell my mother-in-law I'm sleeping with her son's best friend—and she's clearly caught off guard by it being brought up again.

My panicked gaze finds Dom's apologetic one, making sure he's okay before flying back to the screen to see if the two women on the phone heard what just happened on my end. Four amber eyes look back at me—two of them attempting to disguise the sadness shimmering in their irises while the other pair dances with amusement.

"Oh, shit," Mal whispers. "Is he there right now? So, *that's* why you missed work today!"

Mama shakes her head, looking disappointed with her daughter. "Mallory Pearl! That's none of your business."

"I—"

Fuck, what do I say? There's no way I can tell them Ash is here. It's one thing to let Mal think he's the reason why I've been unavailable lately, but it's a completely different thing to insinuate it while Dom is standing right there. Things are already weird enough between us, and the thought of lying about us makes me feel sick to my stomach.

What's the alternative? Telling them it's not Ash, but Dom, standing in your kitchen right now? Yeah, that'll go over really well. Look at how devastated Mama is! If she ever finds out about you and Dom, she'll be outraged.

And I'll deserve it. Every angry look and harsh word. Every second she'll spend wondering how I could ever claim to love her son when it took nothing but a few orgasms and cuddles for me to fall in love with his best friend. Because I *am* in love with him. But no one, not even Dom, can ever know.

"You don't have to finish that sentence, but you can tell me all about it when you buy me lunch tomorrow. Okay, love you! Bye!"

Mal ends the call in a rush, and both of their faces disappear before I can say anything more. I drop the phone on the table and rub my eyes with the heel of my hands. Suddenly, everything hurts. My eyes, my head, my *heart*. The weight of all of the lies—spoken and unspoken— crushing me like boulders.

I don't hear Dom move, but I feel the moment he comes up behind me. That familiar tingle of awareness zipping down my spine just seconds before his hands go to my shoulders and start massaging them gently. Working the knots out of my muscles with firm swirls and presses that make tears prick in my eyes. I force them back down. We don't have a lot of time left together, and I don't want to spend any more of it crying over things I can't change.

"Are you okay?"

I pull in a deep, calming breath. "Yes. I'm just not okay with lying to them like that. It feels gross to deceive someone you care about on purpose."

Dom sighs. "I know exactly what you mean."

The words shock me, but I don't know why. He cares about Mama and Mal as much as I do. They've been his family for a lifetime—the people who protected him from his abusive father when his mom couldn't and the ones who comforted him when she died—it shouldn't surprise me to hear lying to them is taking a toll on him too.

And actually, I don't think it does surprise me. It just breaks my fucking heart. Because I love him and this is the first time I've felt like he's more anxious to get out of this relationship than I am.

So what if he is? You can't be angry with him for sticking to the terms you both agreed on.

Unfortunately, the voice in my head is right. Dom and I made a deal and my sudden realization about the depth of my feelings for him doesn't change it. We've got four weeks left together, and even though the thought of letting him go feels impossible right now, at least I won't have to keep lying to the people I love. Funny how that now includes him.

"Guess it's a good thing we only have to do it for a few more weeks then."

His fingers stop moving, frozen over the knots in my shoulders that have come back in full force. It hurts to even mention the little time we have left together. Since our first dinner when I set the date, we haven't discussed it much. I guess neither one of us wanted to ruin a good thing with talk of it ending, but now I see why we've been avoiding it.

I reach behind me, lacing my fingers through his. Dom squeezes my hand lightly before pulling away. "I should finish cleaning up this mess from dinner."

The line of his shoulders is stiff with tension as he makes his way back to the sink. He takes his time washing the pan he cooked the fish in, scrubbing it from top to bottom with a painstaking thoroughness that tells me everything I need to know about his mood right now.

If I had to guess, the muscle in his jaw is jumping like crazy again. Indicating that his mood has gone from bad to worse. I stare a hole in his back as I try to figure out what to say or do, but after five minutes of listening to him scrub my pan within an inch of its life, I've had enough.

I slide out of my seat. "I'm going to take a shower."

Dom gives me a half-grunt, half-nod, but he doesn't turn around or make a joke about helping me get dirty before I clean myself off like he usually does. Anxiety and worry swirl in my gut as I climb the stairs. They stick to me like a second skin, refusing to be moved by the scalding hot water, the suds running down my body in the shower, or the shampoo and conditioner I scrub into my scalp even though I never wash my hair at night.

By the time I finish detangling my curls with my fingers, the bathroom is covered in steam, and the glass of my shower is just foggy enough to distort the large frame leaning against the vanity, watching me. I cut the water and step out, giving Dom a full view of my soaking wet body. It's not a new sight for him, but his eyes still turn molten as they study me. I can't help but smile to myself as I dry off and put my hair in a wet bun that's going to be a mess to deal with in the morning.

I saunter past him and throw him a saucy look. "Like what you see, Mr. Alexander?"

He arches a dark brow, looking more like himself than he has all night as he follows me into the bedroom and settles himself on the edge of the bed. "Always, angel."

"Well are you going to do anything about it or are you just going to sit there and stare at me?"

He crosses his arms and runs a thumb over his bottom lip. A gesture I've come intimately familiar with. One that I know means he's trying to decide exactly how he wants me.

Because with me and him, it's never a question of if.

32

SLOANE

There's something to be said about the way desire can sweep in and erase every other thought in your head. The way lust can curl low in your belly and suddenly make you forget just moments ago you felt bereft, helpless, and on the verge of heartbreak. And when it happens, when the doubt and confusion are replaced by the all-consuming fire of wanting and being wanted, you'd be a fool to choose to ignore it.

To opt for the uncertainty of reality when you can dive headfirst into the arms of your lover and be swept away by the decadent fantasy of nothing in the world mattering more than the invisible string linked between your heart and his, pulling you together with the kind of natural inevitability that only happens with magnets.

As I stand in my bedroom, naked as the day I was born, waiting for Dom to tell me how he wants me, all of the things I was worried about seem to move further into the back of my mind. Beaten back by the need humming in my veins and the fire burning in the dark eyes boring into mine.

Finally, Dom's lips curve into a sinister smile, and my heart starts to pound in my chest. *He's decided.* The knot of anxiety in my belly begins to unravel at the sight, relaxing into a languid spiral of need that has a slow rush of arousal moving through my core.

"Get over here," Dom says.

His legs are open, relaxed into that king's pose that makes my heart skip a beat and exposes the erection tenting his pants. I cross the room and slip between them, my breasts bouncing in his face when I finally reach him. His hands go to my hips, caressing the skin there with a gentleness that makes me shiver because it's in direct contradiction to the gravel in his voice when he says, "Kiss me."

I don't hesitate. Dipping my head down and taking his lips in an embarrassingly clumsy kiss that makes him laugh. I close my eyes, letting the sound wash over me, and lower myself onto his lap. Dom wraps his arms around me, crushing my body to his until it's almost hard to breathe. Every pass of my lips over his is a hungry glide that doesn't even begin to touch the need building inside of me.

Not just the need to find my release or help him find his, but the need to be close to him. To climb inside of his skin and never come out. To etch myself in his veins until my name is written in his blood. To brand him with my touch the same way he's branded me. To be as necessary to him as oxygen. To make him love me as much as I love him.

To ensure that he's as wrecked by this ill-advised relationship as you are? What a recklessly desperate thing to do to someone you claim to love.

I break the kiss, startled by the agonizing truth of my thoughts, and Dom groans underneath me, clearly frustrated by how suddenly I pulled away from him. His eyes crinkle at the sides while confusion glitters in his nearly-blown pupils.

"I'm sorry," I murmur against his lips. "My mind is just every-where right now."

"Angel, if you're thinking about anything besides what we're doing, then I'm not doing something right." He lays back on the bed and gazes up at me while I straddle his hips. "I know how to get you out of your head."

I wiggle my ass over the bar of steel nestled between my cheeks and arch a brow. "You're right. Sitting on this does always seem to do the trick."

"You can sit on that later. Right now I want you to take a seat right here."

He gestures towards his handsome face and offers me a devilish smile. Immediately, I'm transported back to that first day in the Presidential Suite at La Grande Nuit when he told me I could say I hated him and he'd still want me to sit on his face.

That day I knew I didn't hate him, but I could have never imagined just a few weeks later we'd be here. Me, hopelessly in love with him. Him, completely oblivious to the emotions rioting inside of me.

When I don't start moving immediately, Dom sits up and grips my hips, yanking me up his body as he lays back down until my pussy is hovering over his face and my hands are gripping the headboard. Both of his hands are on my ass, and he uses them to urge me closer until the entire lower half of his face disappears into my sex. I can feel the heat of his breath coasting over the sensitive flesh, making me quiver.

"Your pussy is so perfect, Sloane." He breathes, every word making his lips brush over my clit. "So perfect and so fucking mine."

The first lash of his tongue has me crying out and fighting the urge to come even though my orgasm is a raging storm cloud, full and overwhelming with the need to be released. My hips roll into his mouth of their own volition, and Dom lets out a masculine grunt of satisfaction when I start to fuck his face. His tongue flutters over my clit, and my walls start to tremble.

I know I'm not going to last long like this. It's all too much. The emotions swirling in my chest and the desire pounding in my veins. Dom's hands on my body and the greedy, reverent noises he's making as he devours me. Like burying his face in my pussy is the only thing he's ever wanted to do.

Like using his body to worship mine is his sole reason for existing.

Then two of his fingers slip inside of me from behind, plunging into my core without a bit of resistance thanks to the wetness slipping out of me, sliding down my legs and coating Dom's chin and chest.

The pressure from his fingers inside of me is delicious and resisting the urge to rock into them is impossible. I lift up a bit, angling my hips forward so my clit is directly aligned with his busy tongue, while his skillful fingers move in and out of me in a steady rhythm.

I grasp at the edges of the headboard desperately, letting my eyes fall shut as I give over to the sensation of being feasted on by the most incredible man. Then Dom pulls my clit into his mouth, sucking in steady pulses that force open the floodgates, and I come with a thready cry as pleasure courses through me. Every muscle in my soaked channel clenching desperately at his fingers, my tender flesh quaking over his tongue for long moments.

My brain doesn't even register that he's flipped us over until my back hits the pillows and Dom's gentle lips are raining kisses over my face and down my neck. My scent is all over him, my juices glistening like dewdrops in the hairs of his beard. I relish every kiss, letting every sip he takes from my skin soak into my soul while my eyes fall shut.

"Open those eyes, angel," Dom whispers, planting a final kiss against the corner of my mouth before pulling away from me. "I'm not done with you yet."

The loss of his body heat leaves my damp skin exposed and vulnerable to the cool air. Goosebumps break out across every inch, and I moan in protest as I open my eyes to see where he's gone. I find him standing on the side of the bed, ridding his body of every stitch of clothing in record time. When his erection springs free from his briefs, hard and throbbing, I hum my appreciation and lick my lips.

"I want that in my mouth."

Dom smiles as he grips his dick, squeezing it with the kind of roughness I'd never be brave enough to use for fear of hurting him. Mischief swirls in the never-ending pools of obsidian as he pumps himself with long, thorough strokes that make my mouth water.

"I *could* put it in your mouth. I could fuck your face until I come down your throat and you swallow every last drop…"

"Yes, *please.*"

My pussy throbs incessantly at the thought, hunger, and need mixing with the urge to please him. To keep us in this moment where everything feels right, instead of that weird and awkward place we've been suspended in for the last few hours. I start to sit up, eager to get my hands on him to do exactly that, but he shakes his head and climbs back onto the bed, settling his large frame over mine. I spread my legs to make space for the span of his hips and stare up at him.

"But I'd much rather look into your eyes while I sink into you." He hooks a hand behind one of my knees and bends it back, holding it in place while the other grips my hip, so I'm pinned down and held open for him in the most exquisite way. "I'd much rather memorize every line of your gorgeous face when I'm so deep inside of you the only thing you feel is me."

All of the air leaves my lungs in a woosh that has nothing to do with the weight of his body on top of me and everything to do with the desperate way I wish he knew he's been the only thing I've been able to feel since the moment he grabbed my hand in Club Noir.

His eyes on my face.

His fingers in my hair.

His lips on my skin.

Completely unaware of the way his words are devastating me, Dom continues. "I love fucking your mouth, Sloane, but nothing compares to being inside you. Feeling every pull and squeeze of your pussy while you come all over me. Hearing you say my name through those soft, breathless moans while you beg me for more. That's what I want right now. Can I have that, baby?"

The last part is a gentle question, whispered to me as he searches my face, and I'm almost annoyed by it because we agreed having a safe word would mean no more mental check-ups on his end, but I think him getting me through today earns him a pass.

"Yes." *You can have whatever you want from me.*

He releases my hip and slides his free hand up to grab my left one, lacing his fingers through mine. Then he starts to kiss me. Gentle glides of his lips over mine that are somehow still firm and demanding. When his tongue sweeps over my bottom lip, I open for him instantly. Hungry for his taste, desperate for any part of his body to invade mine.

And when he finally slides into me, with one heavy thrust of his dick that's met with no resistance from my soaked core, I moan into his mouth. I don't know that I'll ever get used to the feel of him inside of me, the delicious stretch of my walls that balances neatly on the edge of pleasure and pain.

How fitting that I would discover my need for both in his arms. In this relationship where pleasure could only ever exist with pain.

Dom swallows the sound with a groan of his own and starts a painfully slow rhythm. Every drive of his hips is a maddening swivel that grinds his pelvic bone over my clit and makes my breasts bounce. He breaks our kiss just to watch the movement, his eyes growing impossibly darker as I squirm beneath his inspection and prepare for an increase in tempo, a variation in the force of his hips that never comes.

Instead, he returns his dark gaze to mine and brings our joined hands to his lips. Laying a soft kiss to each one of my knuckles, lingering just a moment longer on my ring finger before moving on to the next one. When he's done, he presses them back into the pillows and brings his forehead down to mine. We're both panting, our sweat-slick skin sticking together, as he drives into me at that same even pace until I climax without warning, catching us both by surprise.

"That's it, angel." He murmurs against my lips, nipping at the broken sounds spilling from my lips. "Give it up to me. Let me hear you."

Honestly, I don't have a choice because short of biting down on my tongue, there's nothing I can do to quiet my moans or stop the tears leaking out of my eyes as I writhe underneath him and whisper a mixture of his name and a phrase I think is supposed to be 'Oh God.' Moments later, I feel him tensing above me and his movements grow jerky. He drives into me once, twice, and then a third time before grunting my name and exploding inside of me.

Dom brushes his nose over mine, pride shining in his eyes along with something so tender it almost looks like love. *Don't project your feelings onto him.* I shake the thought away and force myself to stay in the moment.

When this is all over, I'll have all the time in the world to break my own heart by replaying moments just like this one and dreaming of what could have been, but for now, I just need to focus on this.

On the feel of Dom sliding out of me and collapsing on the bed beside me. On the way his heart is racing when he pulls me close to him and I lay my head on his chest. On his fingers trailing up and down my spine as we both recover from the rawest, most intimate sex we've ever had.

33

SLOANE

Now

"Don't you look pretty!"

Mama stands up from her seat at the table and pulls me into a tight hug. I hug her back just as fiercely, breathing in the familiar scent of her. She always smells like home to me. Like the creamy, buttery goodness of fresh baked cakes and pies. I love hugging her. Love being enveloped in the bubble of security that is her orbit.

It's the best place to be, especially when you feel a little off-kilter and anxious, which is exactly what I've been since I woke up on Tuesday morning and realized the swell of tender feelings pressing against my rib cage, and making a mockery out of my promise to never feel this way for another man, hadn't gone anywhere.

In all honesty, I didn't think that they would.

But if they had, ending things in a few weeks would be a lot easier. And I wouldn't have spent the last two days biting the hell out of my tongue to keep myself from confessing my love to Dom every time I spoke to him. And he isn't making it easy. With his impossibly handsome face, body built for sin, and heart made of gold. Every time he touches me, every time he looks at me, every sweet word he whispers to me while he's buried inside me feels like it's tailor-made to rip the words from my soul.

And Lord, am I tired of fighting.

That's why when Mama called me today and asked me to grab an early dinner with her, I texted Dom to say I would be home late and jumped on the opportunity. Plus, getting some one-on-one time with my favorite mother-in-law is an added bonus. I squeeze her a little bit tighter before letting her go so we can sit.

"Thank you!" We both beam at each other from across the table. "You look beautiful as well."

She's decked out in a burnt orange sweater and a pair of dark-washed jeans. The sweater is a little more form-fitting than she usually wears, and I force back the comment about her taking Mal's advice to spice up her wardrobe because she'd never admit it anyway. A petite Black girl with a sweet smile comes over and takes our food and drink order. When she's gone, Mama fiddles with the napkin in front of her before meeting my eyes.

"I'm so glad you didn't have dinner plans today, sweetheart." She grabs my hand. "I've been missing you."

Guilt slices through me as I squeeze her hand back. Outside of Sunday dinners, I haven't spent much time with Mama lately. Usually, I make a point of stopping by to see her at least once or twice a week, but since Dom and I started up, I've been going straight home. All too eager to lose myself in him.

"I know. Things with work have been really busy, but I haven't meant to be missing in action. We're almost done with this project, so I'll be able to come by more."

"Oh, honey. I'm not trying to guilt-trip you. You've got a right to live your own life. I don't need y'all stopping by my house every day out of the week getting on my nerves." She rolls her eyes at my lifted brow. Everyone knows that Mama loves to have a house full of people around. If we don't stop by on our own, she'll call with a reason for us to come over. "And I think we both know that work isn't the only thing keeping you busy."

Now it's her turn to arch a brow at me, and my heart sinks into my stomach. I should have known this was the reason she didn't include Mal in our dinner plans. She wants the chance to tell me exactly how she feels about me starting to date again without anyone else around.

"Mama, I—"

She holds up her hand to stop me from talking, and I close my mouth because I don't know what I was going to say anyway. I expect to see her face harden like it has in the few rare moments I've seen her angry, but it doesn't. Her features remain schooled in that soft, open expression she always wears. The one that makes you feel like you can tell her anything.

"I didn't mean it like that, Sloane." She chuckles, patting my hand softly. "That was just my awkward way of trying to broach a subject that's going to be uncomfortable for both of us to discuss. That is if you want to talk to me about it at all."

Relief trickles down my spine, and I give her a smile that's already turned watery. Her kindness, the gentle way she's cradling my fingers in her hand, it's all too much. And so much more than I deserve. I slide my hand out of hers and pretend to straighten my blouse.

"You don't have to dance around the subject. I know Mal's already filled you in."

Mama laughs. "She did tell me, but I figured I could get the more dialed back version from you. That girl gives too much information."

"Yeah, she does."

The waitress comes back with our food, and we fall into an awkward silence. I push my pasta around on my plate and wait for Mama to tell me exactly what she wants to know. *Please don't let her want to know about Ash.*

"Sloane," Mama says, finally breaking the silence. "All I want to know is are you happy? This man you're seeing...Mal told me he's nice, says one of her friends used to date him, but I don't care about him as much as I care about you. So just answer that question for me and I'll try not to ask anything else."

Oh, thank God. Now, this I can do. I can reassure her, tell her how happy and okay I am without going into any specifics about my non-existent relationship with Ash or revealing anything about my forbidden relationship with Dom. I'll be cutting it close, balancing my words on the fine line between a lie and the truth, but I'm willing to do it to give her some peace of mind and hopefully banish the sadness that was in her eyes on our call the other day.

I take a sip of my drink. "Yes, I'm happy, but it's not like I was miserable before, Mama. I was just..."

"Lonely." Mama finishes for me, filling in the blank I left open.

Her amber eyes shine with a heartbreaking understanding that can only come from losing the person you love too soon. I know she knows that pain, having lost Mal and Eric's dad when they were babies, and it's comforting to talk to her like this. Widow to widow instead of bereaved wife to devastated mother.

"Yes, after Eric I just never saw myself wanting anything with anyone else. He was my person, and no one will ever take his place in my heart, but I just felt like maybe it was time for more than the lonely little bubble I'd resigned myself to."

She nods. "That makes perfect sense to me, honey."

I search her eyes for the sadness that was there before and come up empty. Her expression doesn't look anything like I expected it to—no hidden hurt or anger, no judgment or accusations about not loving her son enough lining her features — just the kind of love and under-standing you'd expect to see from a mother. It soothes something deep inside of me, wrapping me in a sense of comfort and peace that makes me want to pour my heart out to her.

"I think I might love him." I blurt, slapping my hand over my mouth when I realize what I've said. *Nice work, Sloane. You're supposed to be downplaying the relationship, not letting her know how far in over your head you are.* "Oh, God. I shouldn't have said that to you. You're here to check in on me not hear about me falling in love..."

Dammit. Why did I say that again?! Mama's eyes go wide, stretching with amusement. Despite my ramblings, she doesn't seem at all bothered by what I've just said. Almost like she doesn't see a problem with me being in love with another man.

Maybe she doesn't.

"I'm happy to listen to anything you want to share, baby. Just don't be like Mal and start giving me all the details about your sex life. I don't need to know that."

She scrunches up her nose, shaking her head in disgust as if she's recalling a particularly explicit moment Mal shared with her. Between the look on her face and the relief I feel at her willingness to listen to me talk about things I haven't spoken about with another living soul, I feel like my heart is about to explode.

"Trust me, the last thing I want to do is talk to *you* about *that.*"

"Good. Now, did you mean what you just said? Do you really think you might be falling in love with this man?"

I meet her eyes and nod. Guilt twisting in my chest at the knowledge that I'm not giving her the full picture. I don't want Mama to think I'm talking about Ash. Dom and I already spend so much time lying about what we are to each other, and I don't want the first time I talk about my true feelings for him to be under the guise of a relationship with another man.

"It's not Ash, though." I bite my lip, fiddling with my wedding band anxiously. "Please don't say anything to Mal. She doesn't know yet, but I started seeing someone else. He's a former client, so it's kind of against my rules, but we just sort of fell together in this inevitable way. He's kind, and he takes care of me in a way no one has since Eric."

"And he knows about…" Her eyes flick to my wedding band as she clears her throat, stumbling over the words. "He knows you were married before?"

He was at the wedding.

"He does, and he's so understanding about everything. Me wearing my ring and sleeping in Eric's old shirt from high school. He doesn't make me feel weird when random things remind me of Eric and make me sad. He just gets it. He gets me. When I'm with him I don't feel like I have to erase the part of me that will always love Eric. And I didn't think I'd ever find that with someone."

It's not the full truth, but it's the closest I can get to it without crossing over the line I've been so carefully toeing since the first time me and Dom kissed. Mama reaches for me, grabbing my hand again and squeezing tight, so I can't pull away.

"That's incredible, Sloane. All I've wanted for you since Eric has been gone is for you to find someone worthy of all the love you have to give. Eric would want that for you too, baby girl. He'd want to see you smiling again, the way you have been for the past few weeks." A lone tear leaks from the corner of her eye, and she swipes it away. "Don't think I haven't noticed you trying to live the rest of your life for everyone else. For me. For Mal. For Eric and his memory."

I open my mouth to protest, but she shuts me down with a firm shake of her head.

"You can't lie to me, baby, because I know the truth. That's exactly what you've been doing, and I'm telling you right now to stop it. If you love this man, if he's as special as you say he is, then you make sure you hold on to him. Grab this second chance at love by the balls and don't let go until it stops feeling like a gift straight from God himself."

Her face is so serious, her fingers gentle but insistent as they squeeze my hand, that I have no choice but to push back the laugh bubbling in my chest as a result of her using the word 'balls' and the Lord's name in the same sentence. I squeeze her hand back.

"Okay, Mama."

"Alright, now. You better mean it because if you lose this good man over some misguided notion that you have to be sad for the rest of your life just because we lost Eric, I'll have to break out my belt."

I roll my eyes and laugh at the ridiculousness of her threat to spank me. It feels good to let the seriousness and emotion of the moment melt into something else. Something easier and closer to the light and airy banter we usually have with each other. I'm glad to be back to normal and happily let Mama guide the conversation into safer territory— mostly family gossip—while we finish our meal.

While we talk, I can't help but think about how much lighter I feel after getting it all off of my chest. Managing to do so without a huge blowup happening or one of us dissolving into tears feels *amazing*.

Like kicking off a pair of heels after a long day of work. I feel happier, freer, and more hopeful than I've ever been about my future with Dom.

I'm ready to admit that I love him, and I don't want to let him go. And if he feels the same way, then maybe we have a shot. I could go home tonight and tell him how I feel, and we could develop a plan for coming clean to Mama and Mal. I've already laid the foundation here tonight, easing our way for telling the truth to the people we love most, but I know it's still going to be tough.

Mama will wonder why I lied about seeing a client and Mal...Mal will flip her shit, but I'll have Dom by my side and he'll help me sort it all out. I trust him to do that, to be my safe place, my shelter in the storm.

* * *

As I HUG Mama goodbye at the valet station, my heart is beating a mile a minute. I'm anxious to get back home and talk to Dom. To see his face when I tell him for the first time that our relationship doesn't have to end when the renovation does. That I want something more than a temporary fix to my skin hunger, I want to build a life with him.

I tap my foot impatiently, scrolling through my messages while I wait for the valet to pull my car around. I've got a few texts from Mal, James, and Sasha, but the only one I care about is from Dom.

> Dominic: Please tell me you're on your way home to me. I miss you.

> Sloane: Hmmm. That depends.

> Dominic: On?

> Sloane: Whether or not any of the cookies I hid from you last night are left.

He likes to tease me about my sweet tooth, but I've quickly learned he's not opposed to enjoying a baked good now and then. Last night I had a major chocolate craving—thanks PMS— and baked some cookies from scratch. He had his greedy fingers in the pan before they even cooled off, scarfing them down like a starved man.

I had to jump on his back just to stop him from eating them all, which resulted in some very dirty counter sex. And then, while he was in the shower cleaning flour and sugar off of his skin, I stashed some away in an old cereal box.

It was a good hiding place, but no part of me believes he's been in the house alone for hours and hasn't found them.

> Dominic: Don't know anything about any hidden cookies, but I've got something better for you.

> Sloane: Your dick is not a sufficient substitute for homemade chocolate chip cookies, Dominic Alexander.

> Dominic: True, but maybe this is.

I double-click on the image he's attached to the thread and find a bag from Twisted Sistas sitting on my counter. I'd bet my last dollar he has a slice of double chocolate cheesecake in that bag. He must have stopped by after work just to get it.

My heart swells in my chest, that increasingly familiar bubble of tenderness expanding until emotion clogs my throat. This is why I love him. Not because he buys me chocolate cheesecake just days before my period is about to start—though the timing really does make it more meaningful—but because he's always thinking of me. Always trying to find new ways to make me smile and laugh.

It's almost like he's addicted to seeing my eyes shine with joy and happiness that's aimed squarely at him.

> Sloane: Is that what I think it is?

I hit send on the message just as the valet pulls up in my car. I run around to the driver's side and press a tip into his hand before sliding into the seat. Another message notification pings as soon as I pull away from the curb and flashes on the display screen in the car.

Dominic: Come home and find out.

I'm not that far away from the house, so I don't text him back. Besides, using the short drive to get my emotions under control seems wise. I want to go into this with a clear head and heart, with nothing but the absolute certainty of my feelings for him driving me forward.

By the time I make it to the front door, I'm practically vibrating with excitement. The thrill of knowing everything in our relationship is about to change for the better makes my hands shake as I slide my key into the front door. Before I can turn it though, it swings open and Dom is there. Standing in front of me with a warm smile curving his lips and his arms open wide.

I fall into them immediately, and he walks us backward until I'm in the house and then slams the door shut. I'm pinned to it in the span of a heartbeat, and my breath catches as he picks me up so we're eye to eye. I wrap my legs around his waist and let my purse and keys fall to the floor so I can grip his face and pull his mouth down on mine.

The kiss is slow and luxurious like we have all the time in the world, and Dom lets me guide it. My fingers flex in the soft hairs of his beard as I explore his mouth with my tongue. He tastes amazing. Like cinnamon, oranges, and mint. And I lick into his mouth like a woman starved; my tongue tangling with his in a carnal swirl that leaves us both panting and wanting more when he pulls away.

"I guess it's safe to say you missed me."

I brush my nose across his, loving the way his eyes flutter closed before opening again. This time they're a little less focused and a few shades darker, that rich brown slowly giving way to black.

"I did. Apparently, I've grown accustomed to spending my evenings by your side. How terribly inconvenient."

I scrunch my nose up as if being used to spending my nights with him is the worse thing that could happen to me, and he rewards me with a pinch to my ass before carrying me over to the couch and throwing me on the cushions. His body comes down over mine immediately, covering every inch of me with the exquisite pressure of his weight.

Dom buries his face in my neck and inhales. Pulling in a long, deep breath and then kissing me there until I squirm underneath him. He chuckles darkly against my skin, and I pretend to be annoyed by shoving half-heartedly at his chest. I'm just about to wrap my legs back around his waist when his phone starts ringing in his pocket.

"Shit." He shifts and pulls the phone out of his pocket to look at the screen. Whoever is calling must be someone he needs to talk to because he jumps off of the couch and gives me an apologetic look. "Sorry, angel. I've got to take this."

I wave my hand at him and smile. "It's fine, Dom. I need to run upstairs and change out of my work clothes anyway."

"Sounds good. I should be up in a minute." He offers me his hand, which I happily take, and pulls me off of the couch, smacking my ass before heading down the hall to the office.

I hear the low rumble of his voice as he answers the call, and I can't help but smile to myself as I head upstairs. My hopeful brain conjuring a vision of a million nights just like this.

Dom and I home together.

His noise and warmth filling the house where chilly silence used to be.

34

SLOANE

Now

Changing out of my work clothes quickly turns into a whole ordeal that includes taking a long shower, completing all the steps of my neglected skincare routine, and putting on something other than Eric's t-shirt to lounge around in for the rest of the night.

I almost shed a tear when I bypass the worn cotton shirt and choose a silk negligee that barely covers my ass, but telling Dom I want a future with him while I'm wearing a very real representation of my past seems kind of wrong. I know it doesn't bother him—all of the little reminders of my love for Eric—but this moment is for us, and I don't want anything to make him doubt the depth of my feelings for him.

I'm settled on the edge of the bed, rubbing lotion into my skin, when Dom comes sidling through the door with a fork, a canister of whipped cream, and a plate holding a slice of double chocolate cheesecake in his hands. The smirk curving his lips tells me everything I need to know about where his mind is right now: so far in the gutter there's no hope of fishing it out, and I narrow my eyes at him and shake my head.

"I just want to eat my cheesecake in peace." *And tell you I love you before we have sex, so you don't think I'm only saying it because of the mind-blowing orgasms.*

"Then we're on the same page." He drops down to his haunches in front of me, setting the plate and fork in my hand. I watch as he uncaps the canister and adds a generous dollop of whipped cream to the top of the slice. "I just want the honor of watching you while you do it."

I wrinkle my nose at him. "You see me eat all the time."

"And yet somehow it never gets old." He watches me intently, and those dark eyes, glowing with desire and interest, make my skin tingle. "Eat, angel. I want you to taste like chocolate the next time I kiss you."

The order strikes a chord deep inside of me, throwing gasoline on a fire that's always burning for him. Heat rushes down my spine, a tightening deep in my core making me grow slick with need. My hand shakes slightly as I grip the fork and break off a piece of the dessert I no longer want because every cell in my body is distracted with wanting him. Still, I manage to take a bite; my eyes falling shut a little to savor the tangy, sweet flavor of the cheesecake and whipped cream on my tongue. Dom groans under his breath, and one of his hands goes to my thigh.

Our eyes lock, and I search his face to see if he wants me to continue. Personally, my appetite has shifted and the only thing I want in my mouth right now is him, but I'll keep going if he wants me to because I know it'll all work out in my favor anyway.

He gives me a slight incline of his head, and I hide my disappointment as I ready my next bite. This one is more whipped cream than cheesecake and some of it slips off and lands on my breast. I start to use my other hand to wipe it up, but Dom stops me with a wolfish grin.

"Please, let me."

Then he leans forward and opens his hot mouth against my skin. He licks the spot clean with one lavish stroke of his tongue, but he keeps licking and sucking at me like he can't bring himself to pull away. I moan and rush to sit the plate down beside me, balancing it on the edge of the bed so it doesn't fall onto the floor. Both of my hands come up, taking the back of his head in a firm hold that's my only recourse for keeping him there.

When he's done laving at my breasts, he trails kisses up one side of my neck while his deft fingers push the straps of my negligee down. The cool air has my nipples tightening immediately, the sensitive peaks brushing against the fabric of Dom's shirt with my every breath.

"Lay back." He growls.

But he's pushing me back onto the mattress before I even have a chance to process the order. His hands grip the hem of the silk and pull, sliding it down my body to reveal my naked skin. I see him toss it somewhere behind him, but I don't know exactly where it ends up because all of my attention is on the show he's putting on for me. The way his muscles flex and bulge as he strips himself down. The hungry look in his eye as he plucks the canister of whipped cream from the floor and uncaps it before climbing onto the bed with me. His large frame hovers over mine, his full lips just inches from my face.

I lift my head for a kiss, and he gives me a maddening shake of his head. I don't even try to hide my pout when he chooses to press a kiss to my jaw instead, licking and biting his way down my neck to my chest. He stops when he reaches my breasts and grins up at me as he brings the cold tip of the canister up to my nipple.

A light spray of cool creaminess coats my overheated skin, and I arch off of the bed. A moan falls from my lips when the wet heat of his mouth descends. His tongue is the first thing I feel, curling around the cloud of sweetness and pulling it into his mouth, leaving him with nothing but my increasingly sensitive breast to suckle on. He doesn't seem to mind though, lavishing attention on my nipple and the swell of flesh surrounding it with an almost single-minded determination. The hairs of his beard scrape against my skin with every flex of his jaw, and it hurts but not enough to make me want him to stop.

But eventually, he does, pulling back to give my other nipple the same treatment. Covering it in the light and fluffy foam then using his tongue to lick the bud clean. Torturing me with the hot suction of his mouth for long moments before moving to another part of my body to do it all again. He makes a show of licking whipped cream off of both of my breasts, my stomach, and each one of my fingertips, while I writhe on the bed. Pressing my legs together in a desperate attempt to appease the throbbing there and begging him to put an end to the madness.

Finally—when I'm mere seconds away from taking matters into my own hands—he puts the top back on the canister and sets it on the nightstand along with my abandoned slice of cheesecake. I watch his dick, fully erect and pulsing brutally, bob up and down as he walks back around to the foot of the bed. He catches me staring and gives me another wolfish smile that sends a flood of arousal through my core.

"Like what you see, angel?"

I nod, biting my lip and watching with increased interest as he takes his dick into his hand and strokes himself. Dragging the precum leaking from the tip down to the root of his shaft, hitting every ridge and bulging vein as he does it. I'm breathless, and turned on beyond belief, but I still manage to nod.

"Yes. It just might be my favorite sight in the world."

Satisfaction flares in his eyes at my words, and I feel a surge of feminine pride. Loving that speaking from my heart can make those pools of molten desire harden into obsidian. I sit up to reach for him, but he comes down on me first. Nudging my thighs apart with his knees and settling his weight over me. He's stretched over me completely, his long fingers wrapped around both of my wrists to keep me from moving.

Although I'm already spread wide for him, I open myself up a bit more. Allowing the hard ridge of his pubic bone to sit against my clit while his dick slips between my wet folds. I let out a contented sigh as Dom brushes his nose against mine. Even in moments fraught with desire and need, he still finds a way to be gentle with me. To remind me that I'm safe and cared for.

Yet another reason why I love him.

Thinking those words with Dom just seconds away from filling me just feels right. For the past few days, I've been fighting back every thought of love, terrified to admit the depth of my feelings for him to myself. Horrified at letting them show on my face in vulnerable moments like these, but tonight I don't have to do any of that. I don't have to worry about my heart shining in my eyes, because I finally feel brave enough to put words to what he might see there. To let the truth expanding in my chest hit the air and change everything for the better.

Dom presses a kiss to my lips. "You know what my favorite sight in the world is?"

Each word is spoken between the wet glide of his lips against mine while his hips start to rock, teasing my entrance with the tip of his dick and stealing my breath.

"No." I pant, rocking my hips to meet his. "Tell me what it is, *please.*"

Dark eyes bore into mine as he pulls back, withdrawing from me completely. He was barely inside me, but I whimper at the loss anyway because I'm desperate for him. Desperate to have this conversation over with, so he can ease the pressure building in my core. My hips churn restlessly, seeking him out to no avail, and a shudder rolls down my spine when I see his abs tighten at the same time his hips swing forward on a harsh thrust that allows him to bury himself inside me in a single stroke.

I'm wet and ready for him, but the shock of being filled so quickly and completely has me arching off of the bed. My face crumples into an expression that's half surprise, half pleasure as Dom starts up a punishing rhythm that threatens to shatter me in moments.

"That." He drops a kiss to the corner of my mouth and groans. "The moment when I'm so deep inside of you we both know you'll feel it tomorrow. *That* is my favorite fucking sight in the world. Your whole face just transforms, and I get to watch your brain process the fact that it's *me* taking you, *me* owning you, *me* reminding you that your body and your pleasure belong to me."

My heart. Don't forget my heart.

I fight against his hold, wanting more than anything to wrap my arms around him and hold him closer to me—to let him feel how much I agree with what he's just said—but his grip is too tight, so I opt for words instead.

"*Oh, God.* Yes, Dom." I breathe into his ear as he rests his head in the crook of my neck. "It all belongs to you."

The responding growl he lets out is deep enough to rattle my bones, and I close my eyes just to absorb the feeling. The raw, animal power moving through him as he slams into me over and over again. Each thrust drawing me closer to the edge of my release. Dom's mouth is everywhere. Lips blazing a trail of pleasure from my jawline to my collarbone. Teeth nipping at my earlobes and grazing lightly over the sensitive space between my shoulder and neck. And I feel like I'm surrounded, completely deprived of any touch, taste, or smell that doesn't come directly from him.

It's the best feeling in the world.

When my walls begin to clamp down on him—little ripples indicative of an incoming wave of pleasure—Dom releases me and pulls out. Ignoring the slight ache in my wrists from being restrained for so long, I lunge at him, showering him with kisses and pressing my sweat-slicked skin to his. He lets that go on for five seconds before grunting at me and flipping me around so that my ass is in the air and my cheek is pressed to the mattress.

Rough fingers grip my waist and yank me onto his waiting erection, and we both moan at the change in position. Sparks of pleasure skitter along my skin as I start to rock back onto him with slow, lazy strokes that drag his erection over my g-spot with every movement. I hear Dom suck in air through his teeth, a tell-tale sign that I'm driving him crazy, and hide my satisfied smirk by pressing my face into the mattress. But a sharp slap to my ass lets me know I didn't do a good enough job.

"Hey!" I push up on my elbows and glare at him over my shoulder. He fists a hand in my curls and uses it to pull me up and back until I'm practically sitting on his lap. I turn my head and kiss his jaw. "What was that for?"

"You already know."

He wraps his arm around me and pulls me closer until there's no space between the hard planes of his chest and my back. His hand is on my waist, guiding my movements as I grind down on his erection and drive both of us closer to the edge of the cliff with every roll of my hips.

"I just like to see you come, Dom," I whisper, biting back a broken moan. "Is there something wrong with that?"

"It is if you haven't already."

One of his hands slides down my body and comes to rest between my thighs. I glance down and stare, riveted at the sight of his fingers parting my folds to find the needy bundle of nerves throbbing for him. As soon as he does, my head falls back to rest on his shoulder and my eyes fall shut. I surrender myself to the sensation washing over me, to the pure, unadulterated pleasure being given to me by the man I love.

Dom times every swirl of his finger perfectly with the movement of my hips, both of us working as one until I finally fall apart. Stars shoot behind my eyelids as the orgasm slams into my body, setting off tremors deep inside me that trigger Dom's release almost instantly. He bites down on my shoulder, still working my clit with an expert's touch, as he floods my core with the heat of his cum.

We both collapse onto the bed and Dom takes special care to keep his weight from crushing me into the mattress until he finds the strength to roll over onto his back. Once he does, he pulls me into him, and I plant a kiss on his chest, smoothing a palm down his side. My fingers brush over the small tattoo on his ribs and pause to trace the numbers: 08. 24. 09.

The month coincides with the death of his mom, but the year is wrong. Marie Alexander died in August of 2008, while this tattoo suggests the event significant enough to make him mark it on his skin, happened a year later, around the time we started college.

I've been curious to know what it means ever since the first night he stayed here, but I've never felt like it was my place to ask. I didn't want to stumble upon some open wound and end up making things in our supposedly casual arrangement awkward, but things are different now. I love Dominic, and I've bared all of my scars and ugly truths to him, and he gave me nothing but the gift of his acceptance and understanding.

Maybe I can do that for him too. Maybe being the one listening, instead of the one always opening up, will help me be brave enough to put words to the emotions swirling around in my chest.

"What's so special about August 24th?"

His fingers stop moving, and I know in an instant asking him that question was the exact wrong thing to do. I sit up and find him already looking at me with an expression I can't read.

"I'm sorry. You don't have to tell me." *Really, you don't. I have something more important to tell you anyway.*

Dom blows out a long breath. "You remember when you asked me if I had any idea what it felt like to be shattered by someone and left alone to pick up the pieces?"

"Yes."

His mouth turns into a flat line, and his eyes go empty and dark while his brain takes him to someplace far away from me. "Well, that's the day I learned what it felt like."

Shit. I should have known the only tattoo on his perfect bronze skin has to do with the woman who broke his heart into a million pieces. My heart twists in my chest, the ugliest, most bitter jealousy coursing through my veins for this nameless, faceless woman who owns more of Dom than I ever will.

She broke him and he still carries her in his heart.

She hurt him and he still wakes up every day with a reminder of her etched into his skin.

The way I want to be because I love him.

"Oh." I lay back down, this time on the pillows beside him instead of on his chest, and he doesn't even notice the change in my position. His eyes are still dancing with shadows, his mind in some far-off place where the memories of the woman he actually loves live. It hurts to watch him—to see him long for someone else when just seconds ago, I was about to risk everything to have him—but I can't stop myself from soaking in the sight of him. Memorizing every crease in his forehead as he relives the love he lost and wondering if that's what I look like to him when I think of Eric.

Probably not, because Eric is gone forever and for all I know the woman in his mind is still alive and well, waiting for another chance to claim his heart.

Suddenly, laying in bed beside him with his cum dripping out of me feels like the worse thing in the world. Seeing love light his handsome features and knowing with a sickening certainty that I've seen a lot of emotions play out on his face—annoyance, irritation, compassion, amusement, lust, pleasure, desire, need—but I've never seen love. Not if it looks like this haunted, tender emotion that makes his eyes glow and rips my soul to pieces.

There's no way I can tell him now. I'd just be setting myself up for heartbreak.

I sit up slowly, way too aware of the mixture of our orgasms leaking out of my body, and swing my legs off the bed. When my feet hit the floor, it takes every ounce of self-control I have to take slow, steady steps to the bathroom. I close the door behind me and lock it, allowing myself one minute to cry and grieve for the future that had seemed like such a clear possibility to me just moments ago, then I clean myself up and wash my face without looking at my reflection in the mirror.

When I emerge from the bathroom, wrapped in a robe, Dom is out of the bed and fully dressed. Even though my heart is broken the stupid thing still stutters at the sight of him, pausing for a beat before flying into a full-blown gallop that only increases when his eyes meet mine.

"I have to go."

He stands and walks over to me. Both of his hands go to my hips and he squeezes me lightly in a gesture that does nothing to soothe the jagged edges of my heart. *He's leaving.* We agreed to spend every night in bed together. It was his rule and now he's breaking it because of *her*.

This is worse than if he was rushing off to deal with Kristen and her non-sense. At least I know who she is. At least if it's her, I know who and what I'm up against. But how do I compete with this phantom of a woman who, from what I can tell, no one has even heard of? *Get a grip, Sloane. There's no point in competing for a man you can't keep. And only an idiot would try.*

I wrap my arms around his waist and bury my nose in his chest, inhaling his scent like it's the last time I'll ever get the chance to experience it. "Why?"

Dom's arms envelop me, holding me close to him as he presses a kiss to my messy curls. "There's some time-sensitive things that need my attention. I was going to try to handle them tomorrow, but they can't wait."

I tense as the lie hangs in the air between us. The knife in my chest twists deeper, and I pull away from him before the tenderness of his hold sets the sob building in my chest free.

"Right. Got it. Of course, you should go take care of your business."

His brow furrows, confusion etched into his features over the quiver in my voice. "Are you okay?"

I wave a dismissive hand at him as I walk towards the bedroom door. "I'm fine. I'm sure I have some work I need to catch up on too."

I don't mention that we could work on whatever things we need to get done together. That we have spent more than one evening on my couch working and watching television while I sketched and he reviewed reports from his subcontractors and checked in with vendors.

Dom trails me down the steps, and I start counting the seconds until he's out the door and I can finally release the avalanche of emotion swirling inside of me. He breaks off, heading into my office to get his things, and I swipe angrily at a tear that slipped out without my permission. When he comes back, I busy myself with fixing a glass of water I don't want or need while he throws his stuff into his bag and grabs his keys.

"Walk me to the door, angel."

I sit the glass of water on the counter and follow him into the mudroom. I watch him lace his boots and wonder if it's appropriate to use a safe word outside of the bedroom. If it's still a valid way to indicate to your partner that something they're doing hurts beyond belief and you need them to stop everything to comfort you. He stands and his keys jingle in his hand. The sound transports me back to the day Eric walked out on me and an overwhelming wave of shame and grief washes over me.

On Monday, Dom lulled me to sleep with promises, whispering that everything was okay and he wasn't going anywhere. He said life owed me some good for all the pain I've lived through, and for a moment, for a life-changing, heartbreaking moment I thought that maybe he was right. That maybe our relationship was life finally deciding to pay up.

But as I watch him throw his bag over his shoulder, I know he was wrong.

This is what I deserve. Not happiness. Not a second chance at love in the form of my husband's best friend. But a reminder of my selfish habit of hurting people I claim to love without even realizing it.

When I decided to get an IUD, I didn't know how bad it would hurt Eric. I just knew I was afraid of getting pregnant. When I decided to ask Dom about the tattoo, I didn't know it would remind him of the woman who broke his heart. I just wanted to prove to myself I could be a safe space for him the same way he is for me.

And maybe in some deeper, darker part of my mind, I was hoping I would find out that he isn't perfect. That he's just as broken as I am, so I could feel a little more confident in telling him how I feel. Because if he's broken too, then maybe he won't scoff at my love and throw it back in my face.

How fucked up is that?

All my life I've grown up thinking my mother was the most selfish, destructive creature I've ever known, but it turns out I'm just like her. So caught up in my wants and needs, I'll completely disregard the feelings of the people around me to have them met. Happy to exploit someone else's pain just to satisfy my insecurities.

My feet are heavy, dragging like they have cement blocks attached to them, as I make my way to the door. Dom grabs me the moment I'm within reach, bending down and grazing his lips over mine before giving me a soft kiss. Absently, I wonder how he's doing it, how he's managing to act like he's still into this when I know his mind is with the woman who branded herself on his heart long before I thought to want him.

"Goodnight, beautiful." He says softly, releasing me from his grasp.

"Goodnight."

I offer him a weak smile, hoping my face isn't revealing anything about the pain curling around my breastbone. I must be doing a good job of hiding it because Dom just gives me a soft smile before walking out of the back door. I don't even wait for him to get in the car before I slam it closed and lock it.

Slowly, and with tears blurring my vision, I walk back into the kitchen and start to turn off the lights in the house. I grab my phone off of the counter and head back upstairs to climb into bed alone. I shrug off my robe, plug my phone into the charger and fall into bed with nothing on.

My bed smells like him, which only makes the tears fall faster when I bury my face in the pillows just to stifle the sobs wracking my body.

35

DOMINIC

E very dog has its day.
That was one of my mother's favorite sayings, and out of all of the words she's ever spoken to me—all of the loving murmurs, corny jokes, and polite euphemisms—this is the one stuck in my mind as stare at Gabriel Alexander. My father. My tormentor. My big bad wolf who's lost all of his teeth and traded his claws for cable-knit sweaters that make him look like a harmless sheep.

But I know better.

Leaving Sloane's bed to come and check on him of all people set my teeth on edge, but he's been asking to see me for weeks. And according to his nurse Angie, who called for the sole purpose of shaming me into rushing to his bedside, he just found out the lung cancer he's been fighting for years is no longer responding to treatment. Thankfully, Sloane was in the bathroom when the call came through, so she didn't have to see me feel nothing when the words '*maybe* a few more months' and 'palliative care' filtered through the speakers.

I don't want her anywhere near that version of me. The angry, bitter

man who shed the last vestiges of childish love for his father somewhere between relapses one and two when the diagnosis became
another weapon in his arsenal, an aid in his manipulation, a license to
unleash his inner-demons whenever and where ever he pleased.

Yeah, subjecting her to that would be disastrous, and so much
worse than being weird and evasive when she asked about the tattoo I
got to remember the day she walked into my life and changed it
forever. I hated avoiding her question, hated the way it sounded like
there was someone else for me when there's only her.

I could see that's what she was thinking, and before I could tell her
the truth, or figure out why the idea of there being someone else looked
like it devastated her, she went to the bathroom and I got the call that
changed the entire course of our night.

Now I'm here—walking into the living room of a man who looks
surprisingly chipper for someone who's just been given a few months
to live—wondering what would have happened if I'd just told her the
truth.

"If you came to spit on my grave, you're a couple of months early."

"I'm not here to spit on your grave." *It'd be a waste of saliva.*

"Well sit down, boy. Cancer ain't contagious, you know."

"Yeah, Pop. I know."

He peers at me over a pair of reading glasses as I settle into the
chair beside him. "Sure as hell can't tell by the way you been ignoring
my calls. Angie had to tell you I was dying before you could be bothered to come across town."

"I've been busy."

"Too busy to come and see your dying father." He shakes his head.
"Selfish. *Just selfish.* I don't know where you got that from. Certainly
wasn't from your Mama, that woman was an angel. She didn't have a
selfish bone in her body."

I give him a pointed look. "Guess that only leaves one other
option."

"It always comes back to that, doesn't it? I'm the bad guy. I'm the
selfish, mean drunk who was unlucky enough to raise a bastard of a
son that thinks he's so much better than him."

The muscle in my jaw starts to tick, and I want to laugh at the ridiculousness of this entire situation. Me, coming down here to see him out of some misguided sense of obligation, leaving Sloane by herself to draw all sorts of conclusions about the things I didn't say. Him, not being able to go five minutes without laying into me.

"Think? I've never laid a hand on a woman, Pop. Can you say the same?" His mouth falls open as he flounders for an answer, and I wave him off with my hand. "Don't answer that because we both know the truth. I saw you hit Mom. I saw every slap across her face, and every tear she cried while she covered up the bruises yo—"

"Shut up!" He jumps up from his seat to stand over me.

Once upon a time, I would have been frightened by his raised voice and the anger stamped across his face, but today the sight just makes me want to laugh. Because I could stand up right now and tower over him. I could knock his ass back in his seat without breaking a sweat.

And we both know it, but I'm the only one smiling about it.

"You think it's funny?" He snarls. "You're not any different than me, boy. Don't think for a second there aren't people in the world you've hurt. Some of them on purpose, some of them by mistake, but either way you hurt them. And that makes you a piece of shit just like me."

I watch him shuffle over to his kitchen. "I'm nothing like you."

He's spent his whole life letting the monster in him run the show, but I've dedicated mine to fighting it off. Building an impenetrable fortress around it to ensure it never got out.

"You can keep telling yourself that, boy, but know this: being slow to strike, doesn't make you any less deadly."

His words land like a physical blow, finding the weak spot in my resistance that's been splintering since the first night Sloane let me touch her—when I felt more like him than I ever have. I let my guard down and my monster slipped out, baring its teeth and clawing at anything that came close enough to hurt her.

And it wasn't the last time I let it come out to play.

I threatened James with bodily harm. I fantasized about the way

Ash's teeth would feel shattering against my fist when I saw his hands on her and regretted not getting the chance to find out.

Until this instant, I hadn't thought about it. I've been too preoccupied with Sloane to pay attention to the moments, which seem harmless on their own, but together suggest a pattern of behavior. A dangerous list of exceptions made for a part of me that hasn't been able to stretch its legs fully in decades.

"Don't act like you know anything about me."

A sly smile curls his lips as he heads towards the freezer and pulls out a bottle of liquor. Bile rises in my throat as I stare at him, and I fight it off. Consoling myself with the knowledge that unlike the bastard I'm currently sharing air with, every time I've given in to my more primal instincts, it's been to keep the woman I love safe. It's never been fueled by alcohol and certainly never meant to hurt her.

But his words are buzzing around inside my head, niggling at me until even I can't deny that despite my best intentions, and her not knowing it yet, I *have* hurt Sloane. I hurt her every day when I keep the truth from her. And tonight, I let it steal the light from her eyes to protect the future I'm trying to build on an unearthed past.

Nausea turns my stomach and my lungs constrict, every revelation is another pound added to the millstone around my neck. The one I thought I'd put down when I finally claimed my angel.

"I know that look." He says, twisting the top off and pouring himself a drink. I watch him toss it back, too stunned by my realizations to wonder how he has alcohol here. He puts the top back on and grabs the bottle by the neck. "It's the same one your mama used to get when she realized she was wrong about something."

I stand. "I'm leaving, Pop."

"Fine, but don't go before you tell me what finally made realize you ain't as perfect as you made yourself out to be." He crosses his arms and studies me. The look in his eye makes me feel like a five-year-old boy cowering on the floor beside his mother while she begs to take the blows meant for him. "If I had to guess, I'd say it's got something to do with a woman. Now I know you ain't a cheater because you made a whole speech about how you would never do a thing like that when you were about ten, so it's probably something small. Got in a fight with her and made her cry? Made some promises you couldn't keep? Come on now, boy."

My stomach churns harder with every word he speaks. It doesn't even surprise me that he's managed to hit the nail on the head once again. After all, monsters recognize monsters.

"I'm not telling you a damn thing." I breathe through clenched teeth. "*I said* I'm leaving."

"Guess you can't stand to be in the same room with me when I'm speaking the truth, huh?"

He shuffles towards me and presses the bottle into my hand with a sickening smile stretched across his face. I stare down at it absently, holding it closer when I should be pushing it away. The glass is cool against my skin, a welcome respite from the self-loathing burning me up from the inside out. The bottle is smooth and narrow with clear liquid swishing around inside. Vodka. His preferred weapon of mass destruction, and now he's giving it to me like some rite of passage.

Give it back, Dom.

My fingers close around the neck. "Are you even allowed to have alcohol here?"

"I'm a dying man. No one gives a damn if the alcohol takes me before the cancer gets a chance. Take it, *son*. You look like you're gonna need it."

He steps back and looks at me, still holding the bottle of poison even though he's no longer making me, and those wolfish eyes flicker with the satisfaction of finally catching its prey after a lifetime of giving chase.

* * *

EARLY MORNING SUNLIGHT filters through the bottle of vodka, shooting shards of light throughout my living room. The sun is high in the sky, bathing the loft in multiple hues of gold that make me think of Sloane's eyes. It's been over twelve hours since I've seen her and held her in my arms. When I left my dad's last night, I couldn't bring myself to go back to her place. I didn't want to face her with his words swirling around in my head and the bottle of poison he gave me clutched in my hand.

So I came back here and tried to replace his vitriol with facts and common sense, which felt damn near impossible with the things I realized about myself at the forefront of my mind. I've never been dramatic enough to think Gabriel Alexander was out to destroy me. Never painted the dysfunction and violence I lived through as a child as some intentional, meticulous plan for the person I was supposed to admire the most to tear me apart piece by piece so he could rebuild me in his likeness.

But after spending the night reliving the moment he pressed the bottle into my hand, I think I might have to reconsider.

I push a breath out through my nose and roll off of the sofa, leaving the bottle on the coffee table, so I can get ready for work. Going through my morning routine without Sloane by my side is weird, and it just drives home the knowledge that I have to come clean with her about everything. There can't be any more lies of omission or evaded questions. I can't claim to want a future with her and keep the information that changes everything a secret.

And she's not the only person I owe an explanation to.

As much as I hate the way she acted the last time we spoke, I have to reach out to Kristen and do my best to explain why our relationship was always going to fail without breaking the promise I made to Sloane to keep our arrangement under wraps.

It's the least I can do after all the years I spent wishing I could love her enough to make the pain of watching Sloane with Eric fade into the background, so I pull out my phone and send her a text.

> Dominic: I need to talk to you. Can you meet me for coffee around 12?

She responds almost immediately.

> Kristen: Yes! Come to the cafe by the courthouse.

A few hours later, I'm sitting at the only free table in the coffee shop across from the New Haven Courthouse, waiting for Kristen to show. From her message, I thought she was excited about meeting up, but I've been here for fifteen minutes and still haven't seen her. I take a sip of my coffee and decide to check my email. There's a message from Alex that he's marked urgent, which can only mean it's about the project I've been working on for weeks without anyone, but especially not Sloane, knowing.

Underneath that is a progress report on the La Grande Nuit renovation from Andre to me, Sloane, and James. My heart does a free fall into my stomach as I open it. We've been ahead of schedule this entire time, but according to Andre's message, we're on track to finish the renovation next week.

Fuck.

James has already responded to the thread thanking everyone for their hard work and requesting a meeting with me and Sloane this afternoon. I type out a short response, confirming I'll be there, and then pocket my phone. When I look up, Kristen is floating through the cafe with her eyes on me. She's smiling brightly, and it's kind of weird to see her so happy, especially given the way we left things, but I don't question it.

"Nic!" She takes a seat across from me. "I'm so glad to see you."

"It's good to see you too, Kris."

I smile back at her and find that it's genuine. I am actually happy to see her, even though I know this conversation probably won't end well. "Thanks for meeting up with me. I wasn't sure you would want to."

"Honestly, I'm surprised *you* wanted to meet after how we left things."

"Yeah, that was a pretty rough day."

She laughs. "That's a huge understatement, Nic. I was horrible to you, and I completely disrespected your boundaries. I don't even remember half of the shit I said, but I know none it was okay. I just got it in my head that we had to work because there was no real reason why we shouldn't. We had all the ingredients, you know? But none of that excuses my behavior, and I'm sorry. Especially about the picture frame. I promise I'll buy you a new one."

Shock courses through me. I wasn't expecting this conversation to go like this at all. I run a hand over my head.

"Thank you."

"Of course. When I told Ash what I did, he said I needed to apologize immediately, but I haven't had time to reach out because I've been super swamped at work."

"Ash? As in *Ash Strickland*?"

"One in the same." She flicks her hair over her shoulder. "We ran into each other at Roku one night and just hit it off. We've been inseparable ever since—" She pauses, taking in the surprise I know is stamped across my face. "Oh no, Nic. You weren't looking to get back together were you?"

I shake my head furiously. "No, I'm just surprised that's all. And happy for you of course."

"Okay." She doesn't look convinced. "What did you want to talk about?"

For a second I consider not telling her because there's this happy glow around her and she finally seems to be moving on from us. But I know backing out isn't an option. Kris came here and owned her shit, and I have to do the same. With a deep sigh, I cross my arms and launch into her long overdue apology, being sure to leave Sloane's name out of it.

At first, I can tell that things aren't sinking in because she still smiles fondly when I start talking about how we met. But then I get to the part about using her as a distraction from the pain I was in over a previous relationship, and her entire face falls.

"Who was she?"

I bristle at the question. "It doesn't matter, Kris. Just know I understand how wrong I was for letting you think we could have had a future together when I knew my heart belonged to someone else. It was selfish, and I'm truly sorry for how it hurt you."

"That's such a cop-out, Nic. You're telling me our entire relationship wasn't real, and you think I don't deserve to know the name of the woman I was competing with for all these years without even knowing it?"

"You were never in competition with her, Kris."

"Well excuse me if I don't feel that way." She glances at her watch then stands. "I have to get to court, but thank you for this...enlightening conversation."

I stand to walk out with her, but by the time I finish sliding on my coat, she's gone. Sighing, I drop a tip on the table and head towards the door, hoping my conversation with Sloane will go better than this one did.

36

SLOANE

Now

On Friday afternoon, I make my way to James' office on leaden feet and less than two hours of sleep. Every time I closed my eyes last night, I was hit with the image of Dom's face as he lied his way out of my house. It kept me up all night, forcing me to replay the entire day with him—the good and bad parts—pinpointing the exact moment everything went wrong. My tired mind was desperate to blame everything on the tattoo, but this fracture is about more than that.

It's about me being in love with him, and him willingly walking out on me even though he promised to stay by my side. It's about the ghost of a woman looming between us, making it impossible for his heart to recognize the love in mine. It's about this stupid arrangement and the deadline approaching quicker than either of us thought it would.

And by the time I get to James' office for the last-minute meeting he called this morning, I'm well and truly exhausted from thinking about it all.

Both men are already in the office, quietly discussing some new resort being built in California, and it's the most I've heard them talk in weeks. James seems more relaxed around Dom than he's been since he kissed me, though it's probably just a byproduct of the project wrapping early and saving him money. They both look up when they hear me coming, and it reminds me of walking in here all those weeks ago and being told I had to work with the man I thought hated me.

That day Dom looked right through me —his face a careful mask of cold indifference and thinly veiled annoyance. And today I expect... well I don't know what I expect, but it's not this. The shadows from yesterday still slithering around like dark tentacles that reach out to grip my soul. The haunted look he wore when he walked out the door overpowering the friendly, but disconnected, smile he gives me when I sit down beside him.

Our legs brush like they did that first day, and I'm so aware of him. So aware of the love coursing through my veins, fierce and strong even in the face of the doubt swirling in my gut. I don't know how we're going to work our way through this hole I dug us into, or if it's worth the effort when we only have a week left together.

"Has anyone ever told you two how incredible you are together?" James clasps his hands and leans forward in his chair, a huge grin stretching across his face. "Actually, it doesn't matter because I'm saying it now. You guys are incredible together. The best damn team I've worked with in years."

"Thanks." Dom and I say at the same time.

I cast him a furtive glance, but he doesn't look my way. This is the first time I've seen him since last night, and I haven't even talked to him besides the text he sent me this morning to say he hoped I slept well. I bite back the bitter laugh creeping up my throat as I study his features, horrified amusement blooming in my chest at how far away this reality is from the optimism of his message.

Did he know our clock had run out when he sent it?

My blood freezes in my veins as I consider the possibility then push it away, so I can listen to what James is saying. "I want to give you and your teams bonuses for being so dedicated to my dream. We've had some bumps along the way—" He gives me and Dom

knowing looks. "—but I couldn't have done this without either of
you."

"That's very kind of you, James. You can submit the bonus with
your final payment to Studio Six."

"Same for Archway."

"Excellent. Now that we've got that out of the way, let's talk about
the opening. My event planner has advised me to keep the same date,
so you still have a month left to send my assistant the....."

Just like the first time we met in this office, James and Dom's
voices float around me while the sound of my heartbeat pounding in
my ears drowns them out. I'm half-listening, but I still manage to catch
all the pertinent details when I'm not obsessing over the absence of
Dom's eyes on my face.

Why won't he look at me?

James turns his attention to me. "You okay, Sloane?"

I shift in my seat, stealing another look at Dom to see him typing a
message on his phone. Those fingers that were just threaded through
mine last night flying over his keyboard while the eyes I long to have
on my face stay glued to the screen.

"Yes, just digesting the good news."

James nods, practically glowing with excitement. "I'll be honest, I
didn't know how things were going to pan out after that first meeting.
When you stormed out of here like a bat out of hell, I thought this
project was going to go to shit, but Nic assured me you guys could put
your differences aside and, as always, he was right. You two seem
more friendly than ever."

My eyes go wide, stretching until they're nearly the size of saucers.
I had no idea Dom spent the moments after our first meeting assuring
James we could get along. An awkward silence fills the space where
my response is supposed to go, but I'm too busy hoping neither one of
them can see the way his words slice into me.

Each one is like its own individual form of torture as it pierces my
heart. Dom had faith in us before he knew the possibility of more
existed, but why?

"We've come a long way," Dom says as he pockets his phone. "But I'm sure Sloane will be back to plotting my murder in no time."

"I think you'll be safe out in California."

"California?" The word pops out of my mouth so quickly it surprises me. I turn and see Dom finally looking at me. "What's in California?"

"The Cerros Resort," James says cheerfully. "Nic got the contract before he signed on with us. They've been waiting for him to wrap up here, so they can break ground."

"*Archway* got the contract," Dom corrects him; his tone is even despite the fact his eyes have gone a bit wild. Like someone's just spilled his biggest, most important secret in front of the one person he didn't want to know. "They can do the job without me."

"But they don't want to. It's going to take at least two years to get it all done, and I doubt Adler is going to leave a project like that in the hands of one of your henchmen. I certainly wouldn't."

Two years. Dom has a signed contract that will require him to be in California for two years. All at once, the pieces start to click together. The secret project he won't tell me anything about, the plans he won't let me see, the increasingly frequent phone calls with Sebastian.

It all makes sense now.

He's leaving, and he knew he was leaving when we started this. When he came to my home and begged for me. When he swore to take care of me and made me say I was his. When he held me in his arms and let me lay my soul at his feet.

When he made me fall in love with him in a million different moments that meant more to me than they ever did to him.

I dig my fingernails into the palm of my hand, pressing so hard I might draw blood. *I have to get out of here.* Both men look up when I shoot out of my seat.

"Sorry to cut this short, but I'm suddenly not feeling well. Good luck with California, Dominic."

James nods and says something, but I can't hear him over the sound of my heels slapping into the marble floor. The tears don't come until I'm speeding out of the parking lot, and I let them fall freely while I wrap my mind around the mess I made.

Mal said working with Dom on this project wasn't a big deal. She said it wasn't the end of the world, but I knew that day. I knew with a certainty I couldn't explain, that this collaboration was going to turn my whole life upside down, and I've never been more devastated at being right.

But devastated is the last thing I should be right now because I knew this was coming. Our ending was determined before we began. And of course, it sucks that we're ahead of schedule, but there's no arguing with the fact this is for the best. An unexpected way to expedite the process of recovering from a relationship with a man who's in love with someone else.

"Yes," I whisper to myself. "This is a good thing."

Then why the hell does it hurt so much?

* * *

DOM'S NAME flashes on my phone for the third time in the last five minutes, and I send the call straight to voicemail, managing to slip my phone back into my purse just as Mal pushes a shot glass into my hand.

"Take this shot and come dance with me!"

She sways her hips to the beat of the music and waits for me to comply, completely oblivious to the fact almost every man in the club is watching her. Even I can't take my eyes off of her body, clad in an olive-green halter dress that hugs every curve and breathtaking gold stilettos that snake around her calves, making her impossibly long legs look even longer.

She's gorgeous.

And I'm so glad she was willing to come out with me tonight. I had to lie to her and say Ash and I were through, and I just wanted to blow off some steam, but it still feels good to be here with her. It's the most honest moment I've had with my sister and best friend in the last month.

That's right, Sloane. Focus on the silver linings of having your heart broken by your husband's best friend.

My eyes stretch wide as I watch her down her fifth shot of the night. I have no idea how she's still going, between the drinks we had at dinner and the shots we've taken since getting to the club, I can already feel the hangover I'll have tomorrow.

But Mal says a carefree night out is the only cure for heartbreak, and she's been through more breakups this year, not to mention whatever is happening with her and Chris, than I have in my entire life, so I kind of have to trust her on this. If the resident break-up expert says we need to get drunk and dance our asses off, we're getting drunk and dancing our asses off.

Hangover be damned.

Returning her mischievous smile, I toss back the shot she's given me. The vodka burns as it goes down, and I relish the feeling, hoping the searing pain will cauterize the gaping hole in my heart.

"That's my girl!" Mal exclaims. She's still dancing around me, holding her hand out and wiggling her fingers at me—inviting me to leave all of the hurt and anger bubbling in my veins on the dance floor.

So that's exactly what I do.

We dance for hours, screaming the lyrics to all of our favorite songs and moving our hips in time to the beat, being rowdy and ridiculous and a lot like the girls we used to be in college. The ones who never left the dance floor and didn't know a thing about the heartbreak lurking in our futures.

Mal and I are catching our breath, drinking water, and resting our feet when two men who've been eyeing us from the bar finally get up the courage to come over. They try to look casual as they pause in front of our booth.

"You two are easily the most beautiful women in this place tonight," one of them says. He's taller than his friend, with black and blonde locs flowing over his shoulders. "Can we join you?"

I look at Mal, trying to gauge her reaction and figure out how I feel about opening up our girl's night to these two. Her eyes are bright, latched onto the guy with the locs, and a welcoming smile takes over her face when he smirks at her. Just as she's about to open her mouth and say they can join us, a deep voice cuts in from behind them.

"These two are spoken for."

All eyes turn to the source of our interruption, but I already know who it is. *Dom.* I don't know how or why, but somehow he's here and despite my determination to get a jump start on grieving us, my heart still tries to pound its way out of my chest at the sound of his gravelly baritone.

The two friends spin around then step to the side as Dom moves towards the table, sliding into the booth beside Mal while another person, Chris, takes a seat beside me. *Wait, what?*

I blink slowly, my head swiveling between the amused expression on Chris' face and the unreadable look on Dom's. How are they even here right now?

"Mal texted," Dom says, answering the question I didn't know I had spoken out loud. *Damn you, Drunk Sloane.* "She said you two were out drinking to get over your breakup with Ash and were going to need a ride home."

I press my lips together to keep any other thoughts from passing between them without my permission, but I swear I see a flicker of pain flash behind Dom's eyes as he says the word 'breakup.' Like he's angry I'm trying to accept the inevitable.

Mal's face contorts into something between a scowl and a smirk as she looks at Chris. They exchange a heated glance that makes me blush. Clearly, things between them aren't as done as she wants everyone to believe they are. She bites her lip as she holds his gaze.

"Christopher, how nice of you to come to our rescue."

"I'm always happy to be of service, princess."

I cringe inwardly, suddenly wishing to be very far away from whatever sick game of seduction the two of them are playing because there's nothing remotely cool about witnessing your sister-in-law decide if she's going to sleep with her ex. Judging by the sparks of energy shooting between the two of them, Chris is going to get lucky tonight.

He rises from his seat and smiles at me. "Sloane, always a pleasure to see you."

I finish off the last of my water. "Yes, it was nice to see you too, Chris."

Dom stands up and lets Mal out of the booth. She gives me a wave and a half-apologetic look before blowing me a kiss and disappearing into the crowd with Chris chasing behind her. I stare after them in disbelief, my sluggish brain having a hard time processing what I'm seeing.

"Grab your stuff, angel." Dom orders, the inky black depths of his eyes glittering with the promise of trouble if his command isn't followed immediately. He extends his hand to me. "I'm taking you home."

37

SLOANE

Now

I ignore his hand as I grab my purse and slide out of the booth, but that doesn't stop him from placing it on the small of my back and ushering me out of the club like a drunken toddler, which, in all fairness, I kind of am. By the time we hit the parking lot, I'm teetering on my heels, the alcohol in my system making me struggle to stay upright. The fourth time I stumble, Dom swoops down and picks me up, and I immediately start to fight against his hold.

"You don't need to carry me."

He scoffs. "I'm not watching you break your neck in these ridiculous shoes."

"Then look at something else!" I kick my legs, and his fingers dig into my thighs. "You don't get to swoop in like some knight in shining armor, saving me from myself. I didn't ask you to come here, and I certainly didn't ask you to carry me around like a damn caveman, so put me down, Dominic!"

He makes a rough sound in the back of his throat, something like disbelief mixing with obvious frustration, but he keeps walking without saying a word. I fight him every step of the way, thrashing wildly against his body and swatting at his chest until the hem of my dress rides up my thighs. By the time we make it to the car, I'm exhausted and frustrated, but Dom looks no worse for wear. He deposits me in the passenger seat and reaches over me to latch my seat belt.

And I'm either too tired or too caught up in absorbing the strong line of his jaw—and the distracting way the muscle in it is jumping—to fight him off. But as his hands work at securing me in my seat, I don't breathe a word. I don't think I'm breathing at all because my lungs feel like they are on fire from the lack of oxygen.

The burn is preferable though. Better than inhaling his scent and letting the smooth, spiciness of his skin flood my altered senses. Dom turns to look at me, and his eyes are dark and full of shadows when they find mine.

"Wherever you are, is where I'll be." He says, a deep frown causing his brows to dip inward. "I'll walk through Hell for you, angel. You *should* know that by now, but I guess you're too busy healing from our apparent breakup to acknowledge all the ways I've shown you."

He pulls away from me suddenly, slamming the passenger door so hard I jump. By the time he slides into the driver's seat, I've recovered fully from his little speech and am glaring at him with a steady gaze that's quite impressive for the amount of alcohol I've consumed.

"Are you going to break all of our rules before this is done?"

"What rules have I broken, angel?"

I cross my arms over my chest. "I'm not spelling it out for you."

"You will if you want me to respond."

"I don't *want* anything from you, Dominic." *Except for your heart.* I swallow the thought, not wanting him to know I'm desperate enough to take whatever scraps he has left to give, as long as there's some piece of him that belongs to me. His gaze hardens, and I know it's because I keep calling him by his whole name.

"Are we doing *this* again?"

"No, we're not doing anything anymore."

I turn to look out of the window, and Dom reverses out of the parking spot with a sigh. Soon we're sailing down the empty streets of East New Haven towards my house.

"You're not being fair, angel. I can't fix this if I don't know what the problem is."

"Fine!" I throw my hands up in the air, hating how all of the pain from the last day has managed to bleed into the one word. "I'm upset, Dominic. Is that what you want to hear? I'm hurt because I had to find out, from James of all people, that you've had an exit plan in your back pocket this entire time. A one-way ticket out of New Haven and away from—"

"Andre is going to California," he cuts in, the words balanced on the fine edge of a razor blade. "You would know that if you'd bothered to answer any of my phone calls today."

"I didn't want to talk to you."

"Right, because giving me a chance to explain would probably ruin your plan to push me out of your life for no damn reason."

"Giving you the chance to…." I roll the words around in my mouth, tasting the bitter irony coating them, and laugh. "You don't explain things, Dominic. You deflect. You distract. You get up and walk away even if it means breaking your promises."

He scrubs a hand over his face. "I told you I had to deal with something time-sensitive last night."

"And maybe you did, but we both know something changed the minute I asked about your tattoo. You left so you didn't have to lay in my bed and pretend to want me when all you could think about was *her*."

I spit the last word at him and then turn my head, so I don't have to see the moment he realizes all of this—even my reaction about California—is because of an ex whose name I don't even know.

Because that's what's at the root of all of this: jealousy. Hot and bitter jealousy coursing through me, searing my veins because some woman from a million years ago has slipped in between us. Disrupting the steady rhythm we've fallen into and derailing my plans to tell him how I feel.

She doesn't even know it, but she's stealing precious time from me.

Time I don't have to spare. Time I need to figure out if it matters that we're both broken when we make each other feel whole. Time I'll have to spend committing every inch of Dom's body to memory, and soaking in enough of his heat to last me a lifetime, if I can't ever bring myself to say the things I need to say to find out.

Silence stretches between us, chafing against my skin and making me even more agitated.

"You're not going to respond to me?"

"I'll respond when you say something that doesn't sound like you think I'm cheating on you. We have an arrangement, Sloane. And until you look me in the eyes and tell me it's over," his gaze scorches the side of my face, but I don't turn to meet it. "There is no one else for me."

I bite my lip, forcing myself to swallow the hope bubbling in my chest. I wish I could believe that, but the look in his eyes last night told me everything I needed to know. There is someone else out there for him, someone who's probably a lot less complicated to be with than his best friend's widow.

"No lies, Dom. That was part of our agreement too, and I don't know if you even know you're doing it, but you are lying to me. Whoever this woman is, she owns you in a way I never could. And the look you had on your face when I asked you about the tattoo....I'd know it anywhere. I see it every day when I look in the mirror."

Except lately, I've been seeing it less and less. The haunted look of missing a part of my soul has been replaced by joy, happiness, *love*. I still can't believe I did it. That somehow I managed to move aside all the hurt, self-loathing, and thoughts of not deserving happiness to nurture the love blooming in my chest for him. But he doesn't want it.

"Stop talking, Sloane."

I scowl at him as he turns into my driveway, the hurt churning in my gut transforming to anger in a split second. As soon as he puts the car in park, I unlatch my seat belt.

"Fuck you, Dominic."

I hop out and slam the car door, digging my keys out of my purse while his dark laughter rings out behind me. I glance over my shoulder and see him hot on my trail, tracing my clumsy footsteps with his perfectly steady ones.

I'm still struggling to dig out my keys when the heat of his body covers my back, blocking me from the chill in the air. His warm breath skates over my skin as he reaches around me and slides his key in the door.

"Let me."

The door swings open, and I let out a frustrated groan when he walks in behind me and closes it. Without another glance in my direction, he heads into the kitchen and starts rummaging through my medicine cabinet, probably searching for something to stave off the headache we both know I'll have tomorrow.

And instead of being touched by his forethought, I'm pissed off. I want to shout at him, throw something at his head and tell him my impending hangover isn't his problem, because *I'm* not his problem anymore.

But instead of doing any of that, I stomp up the stairs and jump in the shower to delay the inevitable. The moment where I'll have to look at him say what I've known since the shadows in his eyes killed the hope in my heart: this is over.

* * *

WHEN I'M DONE with my shower, I towel off and walk back into my bedroom, half expecting Dom to be waiting for me, only to find that I'm completely alone. Again. The silence in the house stretches on endlessly, pressing down on me and knocking loose another shard of my shattered heart.

Exhausted and heartbroken, I crawl into my unmade bed with nothing on. My sheets still smell like Dom; I pull them over me and close my eyes, telling myself not to listen for any sounds that might suggest he's still here because they won't come.

But then the doorknob turns and heavy footfalls that are trying to be soft move towards me, and my stupid, treacherous heart swells with joy and screams, *"He's still here! Maybe there's hope."*

I can feel his eyes on me, sweeping over my body for long seconds before he sighs and sets something on the nightstand with a faint click. For a breathless second, I wait for him to turn and leave. And my brain and heart are at odds, one wanting him to stay so we can have one last night together and the other hoping he'll leave because settling for his body when I want his heart is a unique kind of hell.

In the end, the decision is made for me by the rustle of Dom's clothes as he sheds them and leaves a messy heap on the floor. By the shifting of the mattress as he climbs into bed beside me. By the contented sound he makes in the back of his throat when he wraps his arm around my waist and pulls me back into his chest.

By the stupid smile that curves my lips when I realize he's completely naked, and every inch of his skin is pressed to mine.

Warm lips graze my neck, sending shivers down my spine that make me squirm against his lengthening erection. "Be still, angel. I just want to hold you."

"What if I want more than that?"

"You're drunk."

Of course, he thinks I'm talking about sex. He hasn't even considered the possibility I might want more from him than that. That I might want everything. And why would he? This entire relationship has been based on physical need, on lust and desire neither one of us tried to fight.

"Not anymore. Some guy with a bad attitude and caveman tendencies crashed my *break-up celebration* and sobered me right up."

"A caveman, huh?" His laugh rumbles in his chest and reverberates through me. I can't help but smile to myself. Our relationship might be at the end of its road, but I'll always love being able to make him laugh.

And despite myself, I can't deny how good it feels to let him hold me. To let the pain of the end of our book fade into the background while we focus on the sweet perfection of the current chapter.

"Yes." I pick up his hand and pull it to my lips, so I can press a kiss to his palm. "He growls and everything. Some people think he's an ass, but I put up with him because he does such a good job of taking care of my needs."

My fingers thread through his, and I drag our linked hands down my body. Past the swell of my breasts, over my belly, and then finally coming to a stop at the apex of my thighs where I am already slick from wanting him too much.

"Sloane." My name is a warning issued in a voice that belongs to a man standing on the edge of control and deciding whether or not to leap. He flexes his fingers, nudging my clit ever so slightly and eliciting a moan from me. "An hour ago you were throwing back drinks to try and get over *our breakup*, which by the way, I had no idea about, and now you want this. *Now* you want me?"

My heart splits open because how can he not see that I've always wanted him? How can he not know all of this—the downward spiral of emotions and disconnect between the things I do and say—is because I want him too much?

Enough to convince myself that right now it doesn't matter if he's in love with someone else because tonight, he's mine.

And in the darkness of my bedroom, I can pretend he's giving me more than his body. I can squeeze my eyes shut, surrender to the need humming in my veins, and forget about the woman who left him with enough shadows to smother the fire he once burned for me.

"Think of it as saying goodbye," I whisper. Dom pulls his hand away and starts to sit up to leave the bed. I turn over quickly, wrapping my fingers over his bicep to stop him. He stills, letting me hold him there with a grasp he could easily break. "Please, Dominic. I need it."

I need this last time with him to happen while the minute amount of alcohol in my system is still dulling the pain of having my heart ripped from my chest. And this is the only way I can do it. The only way I don't break apart and say all the things I should have said before I asked about that damn tattoo.

In an instant, I'm flat on my back with a glowering Dom over top of me. The position is familiar, every inch of his body pressed against mine, but the tender way he's holding me doesn't match the anger in his eyes at all.

He looks ready to tear something apart with his bare hands, while those same hands—one under my head and the other lifting my hips to meet the flared tip of his dick—cradle me with a deference that makes tears well in my eyes.

"Do you need *it* or do you need *me*?"

The question takes me back to our first night together when I said something similar. He'd brushed his nose across mine and asked me what I needed. There was a softness to his eyes then that I appreciated because it fit perfectly with the vulnerability I felt.

Right now his eyes are glowing, outrage and maybe confusion charring the corners and matching the rough edge of his question perfectly. I close my eyes, savoring the way each word settles against my skin with a cutting accuracy that makes me bleed.

I wrap my legs around his waist and rock up into him. I can't answer his question because the answer is both, and I don't want to have to explain that to him. Dom realizes what I'm trying to do immediately, and he moves his hips back when I move forward.

"Answer me, Sloane. Tell me what the hell is going on."

"We're saying goodbye, Dominic. Think of it as your parting gift."

He moves his hand around to my hip and pins it to the bed, making my legs fall away from his body. Flames dance in his pupils as he leans in close and skims his lips over mine.

"If you want this to be over, you know exactly what you need to do."

I bite my lip, willing myself to do the reasonable, mature thing and say those words. But when I look at him all I see is the future I was prepared to risk everything for and a man who'll never know how much I love him. And I'm raw. Cut open and guts spilling out, bleeding too profusely to behave like anything but the wounded animal I am.

"You're right. All I have to do is ask you about this, and you'll go running for the hills again."

He sucks in a breath as my fingers brush over his inked skin. "I didn't leave because of the tattoo, Sloane."

"You want me to believe that?"

"Yes."

"Fine." He breathes a sigh of genuine relief before I continue. "I'll let it go if you tell me something about her. You can choose anything you want. Her name. How you met. How she broke your heart."

"Jesus, Sloane." He pushes off of me and moves to the side of the bed. "Why can't you just let this go?"

I sit up, crossing my arms over my chest as I watch him start to put his clothes back on. "Because you won't tell me the truth, Dominic! Even though I already know it."

"You don't know anything!" He roars, prowling towards me with a wildness flashing in his eyes. When I flinch at his sudden advance and harsh tone, he stops short. Just barely reigning in the fury rolling off of him in waves. "If you did know, I wouldn't have to tell you that you're the only woman who has ever owned any part of me. And it's always been you, Sloane. For twelve fucking years, you've walked around with my soul clutched between the same fingers you wear Eric's rings on. You're the ghost I've been chasing. Now look me in the eyes and tell me you already knew that."

Every one of his words sends a thunderous wave of shock coursing through me. This can't be true. *It can't.* There can't be a version of this life where Dominic has been in love with me for *twelve years.* Where he stood by and watched me fall in love with his best friend.

It just can't be.

"What are you—" My voice is shaking, every word a warbled version of itself, so I clear my throat and try again. "That's not possible. You haven't liked me from the first moment we met."

His lips curl into a bitter smile. "That day in the dorm wasn't my first time meeting you, angel."

"Yes, it was, Dominic. Otherwise, I would have recognized you when you walked into the room. I would have remembered meeting you. I would have remembered."

"You were drunk, Sloane. It was the first party of the year, and it felt like everyone who moved on campus early was packed into that one small house. There were so many fucking people there, but the moment you walked in, all I could see was you—"

"Stop!"

My stomach rolls as I process Dom's description of a night I've seen in my dreams many times over the years but have never fully remembered. I try to pull the pieces together in my mind, to force myself to remember something that could refute his story, but I can't get anything to stick.

"You wanted the truth from me, angel. This is it. This is our truth."

"Dom, *please.*"

I hold up my hand because I need a moment of quiet. Just a few seconds to get the gears in my brain to start turning. He presses his lips together as I begin to mumble through my recollection of that night, more to myself than him.

I remember the hours before the party he's talking about. My mom and I argued on the phone. She called me a constant disappointment, and I finally accepted I would never be good enough for her. Then I decided to fit eighteen years' worth of teenage rebellion into one night.

And, because I had no idea how to be a rebel, I made a trouble list.

Back then, the worst thing I could imagine doing was wearing a dress that barely covered my ass, getting drunk at a frat party, and....*oh no.* The very last item on my list was something about spending the night in a guy's bed, but the next morning, I woke up in my own. Nothing but hazy images and the distinct feeling I was forgetting something important.

I curl my arms around my middle, attempting to hold myself together as the most impossible truth seeps into my bones. "It was you?"

Dom is silent, and I have to look at him to see if he heard my question. He stares at me with eyes so soft, so tender, I find it hard to believe just moments ago he was a raging fire.

"Yes."

"But I...I didn't even check that off my list. I woke up in my bed. Alone."

"Because I took you home, angel." The words are soft with the slightest bit of heat coating them. An accusation. "I left a note."

"No."

My entire world tilts on its axis as disbelief swirls in my gut. Even though he's confirmed it, I still don't understand how this can be true. For years I thought I dreamed up the person I spent the last part of my night with. Crafted him and our soul-deep connection, forged in a matter of hours, in the depths of my mind.

Now Dom wants me to believe he's the mystery man from my dreams and I belonged to him before I belonged to Eric. Which would mean our seemingly random connection—the one I never understood on his end—wasn't sparked by the night at Club Noir. It was reawakened.

This is too much.

"Sloane—"

"Please don't say anything else." I clutch myself tighter, rocking back and forth. "I need you to go."

Dom stares at me, and I force myself to hold his gaze. He presses his lips into a hard line and nods like this played out exactly how he expected it to, and he's mad at himself for thinking it could have gone any differently, but he doesn't say anything else.

And when the door shuts behind him, I'm left with nothing but silence and the regret of asking him to leave when all I wanted was for him to stay.

38

SLOANE

Then

"*Call me in the morning, okay?*"

The words ring in my head and press against my skull, making the already incessant pounding happening behind my forehead even worse. I groan and rub at my temples, wondering whose voice it is and why I can't remember anything more than a few snippets of my first college party.

"Sit up straight!" My mother whispers through clenched teeth, and I glare at her. Any chance at remembering the details of last night were lost the moment I woke up to find her standing over me. Her face pinched in disapproval as I wiped the drool off of my chin and tried to remember how I got home.

She took one look at me and launched into a speech about my lack of decorum and respect for myself and the Carson name. Then she dragged me out of bed and forced me to get dressed for the breakfast being hosted by her sorority for legacy pledges.

We've been here for hours, mingling with people I have no interest in getting to know, and listening to endless droning about sisterhood and community service initiatives everyone knows are more about optics than they are about service.

I feel the gentle prodding of my mother's elbow in my ribs and finally give in. She looks pleased when I lean back in my seat and cross my legs but frowns when she sees my face.

"Would it kill you to smile?"

"Probably."

She purses her lips, and I turn my attention to the podium where the chapter head is wrapping up her speech about pledge week. "Thank you so much for being here today. We look forward to seeing you ladies in the coming weeks."

The crowd starts to disperse immediately, and I'm one of the first ones out of the building. My mother is hot on my heels as I start the short walk back to my dorm.

"Sloane Elise Carson!" Her heels click on the sidewalk as she struggles to match my pace. "I swear I've never been more embarrassed in my life. You know better than to behave that way in public."

"If this is another one of your 'you're a constant disappointment, I'm ashamed of everything you do' speeches, you can save it. We just did this yesterday, and I'm done with it."

"Oh, young lady, we are far from done." Her fingers wrap around my elbow, forcing me to stop. "Your father and I did not spend the last eighteen years giving you the world, just for you to come here and piss your entire future away by becoming a drunken party girl with *loose* morals."

The emphasis she places on loose makes my spine stiffen, and her eyes snap with a sick satisfaction once she realizes implying that I'm a whore has captured my attention.

"It was one party, Mom. I went to one party." *And despite my plan to spend the night with someone, waking up in my bed this morning tells me my morals are perfectly intact.*

"It doesn't matter! You're not here for boys and alcohol, Sloane. You're here to solidify your place in society as a well-bred, educated woman of value and substance. That is the only way you will secure a husband and future worthy of the sacrifices we've made for you."

"Is that what your sudden obsession with being a mother is about? Making sure I marry well?"

Her shoulders go back. "Don't act like my interest in your life is new. You've had the very best of everything…."

"Except a mother!"

The slap across my face catches me completely off guard. Tears well in my eyes instantly as I cup my cheek with the hand not being held in my mother's bony grasp. She doesn't even look remorseful as she leans in close to me.

"I am *done* with your disrespect. Your little friends might get away with this kind of behavior, but I won't have it." She releases my arm and straightens her blouse. "I knew letting you room with a bunch of random girls would be a mistake. They're bad influences on you."

I blink through the tears blurring my vision. "What are you talking about?"

"I'm talking about removing you from an untoward situation. If this is what you're like after one night of living with those girls, I shudder to think what you'll be like after an entire year."

My gut clenches as I realize what she's saying, and she smiles at my horrified expression. Every bit of the small amount of joy I got from my moment of freedom dies on the curves on her lips.

"You're going to make me move back home."

She tilts her head, both of her brows lifting in amusement. "And subject myself to you sulking around day in and day out? I don't think so. I'll contact my friend in Housing tomorrow and have you moved to a single room. Maybe having your own space will help you remember how to conduct yourself."

"Why are you doing this?"

"Because someone has to save you from yourself, darling."

Except this doesn't feel like being saved. This feels like being punished for daring to live my life outside of her terms. This feels like yet another entry on her never-ending list of my failures and short-comings.

And it hurts to watch her take so much joy in penciling it in.

"Well, I'd better go." She pats me on the shoulder. "You should get back and start packing your things. I'll send you the details for your new room as soon as I have them."

I manage to nod and watch her glide down the sidewalk happily. Like ruining my life has just made her entire day. Once she's disappeared into a group of students and parents carrying boxes, I turn and start walking in the other direction with no particular destination in mind. Somehow, I wind up on the steps of the library watching a campus tour for incoming freshmen head into the lecture hall across the street.

"Oh damn, was that the midday tour?"

Startled, I turn to find a tall guy with smooth, brown skin, dark brows, and a strong jawline towering over me. His eyes—the most arresting shade of amber—dance with humor as he fixes me with a mind-melting smile.

"Yes," I say when I finally manage to find my words. "They just left though. I'm sure you could catch up to them if you run."

Instead, he plops down on the step right beside me, and his arm brushes mine ever so slightly. Then he's looking at me again, smiling as if leaving this step is the furthest thing from his mind.

"Nah, I think I'll just catch the next one. Is it okay if I sit with you?"

"Why would you want to do that?"

He shrugs. "You look like you're having a bad day."

"Something like that. I don't want to talk about it with a stranger though."

Both of his dark brows rise and for an instant, he looks like he's second-guessing his decision to abandon the tour, but then he smiles again and extends his hand to me. "I'm Eric Kent."

I stare at his proffered hand hanging almost awkwardly from his arm while he waits for me to do or say something. After a beat, I place my hand in his, allowing his long fingers to wrap around mine. His skin is warm, and he clears his throat gently when another second goes by without me telling him my name.

"Sorry," I say finally. "I'm Sloane Carson."

"Nice to meet you, Sloane." More of his perfect teeth come into view as his smile grows wider. "We officially aren't strangers anymore."

39

SLOANE

Now

Day One without Dom started with me watching the sunrise through swollen, puffy eyes I hadn't closed for more than a minute all night. I dragged myself out of bed at five in the morning and sat in the bathtub for long hours, soaking in all of my regrets and wishing I gave Dom a real chance to explain before I asked him to leave.

I was overwhelmed by what little information he gave me, but all the questions I was too scared to hear the answers to in the moment kept me up last night. I stared at the ceiling and tried to picture the details of the night he remembers so vividly, that have evaded me for years.

Me walking into a party and seeing him. A tall, impossibly hand-some stranger with smooth, bronze skin and trouble in his eyes. I wondered if the connection was immediate. If I was drawn to him the second his midnight stare locked on me and whether I gave in to the urge to be close to him as soon as I felt it.

And then I obsessed over all the different ways we could have ended up *here*.

But no matter how many times I turned it over in my head—the list, the party, the note Dom says he left that I never saw—I just couldn't put it all together. Once I realized I wouldn't be able to do so without the help of the one person who would probably rather lick an un-sanded piece of plywood than talk to me, I gave up trying and decided to distract myself with work.

I've been sitting at the island choosing materials and adjusting project budgets for over three hours when my phone starts vibrating. I grab for it instantly, hoping stupidly that it's Dom, and see my dad's name flashing on the screen. I consider not answering, but I haven't talked to him all week, so I paste a smile on my face and accept the call.

"Hey, Daddy."

"Bean!" He bellows. "I'm so glad I caught you. How would you like to join us for brunch at the club? Your mother says you usually have plans with Mal and Annette, but I wanted to extend the invitation anyway. We haven't shared a meal since…"

Since your wife told me I needed to get over the death of my husband and find a rich man to marry.

"Thanks for the invite, Daddy. I don't know if I'll be able to make it though I've got to—"

Mom.

Suddenly, the memory of my mother's visit the morning after the party hits me. She was in the room when I woke up because my room-mate let her in, and I have no idea how long she was there before the weight of her disapproving stare woke me up.

It's wholly possible she could have seen Dom's note and gotten rid of it before I ever laid eyes on it. That would certainly explain the way she acted after the legacy pledge breakfast: the speech about me having loose morals, the implication that I was boy-crazy and more concerned with partying than getting an education.

My mother has never been a nice woman, but that day she was especially cruel. And I guess now it makes sense. She saw me acting out in all the ways that went against her code of perfection and wasted no time nipping it in the bud.

Isolating me in a single dorm on the opposite side of campus from my friends. Threatening to tell my father about finding me hungover after my first night of freedom. Stealing my only chance at remembering Dom and changing the course of my life forever. But would she do something like that?

There's only one way to find out.

"Actually, I think I will take you up on that offer. What time should I meet you guys there?"

Dad rattles off the details, and as soon as we're off the phone I race upstairs to get dressed. My stomach is in knots as I pull on my clothes and force my curls into submission. Just the thought of speaking to my mother about that day makes me want to throw up, but I know I have to do this.

For me and Dom.

For the future I dreamed of having with him just days ago.

For the one that was stolen from us, but ultimately gave me Eric.

* * *

"ARE you expecting a phone call from someone special?"

My mother's eyebrows dance whimsically as she says the last two words, but her smile is still stiff and cold around the edges, reminding me of the ugly curl of her lips on that day. We've just finished eating and are sipping mimosas by the bar while my father chats with some colleagues across the room. The moment he left us alone I started feeling anxious and pulled out my phone just to have someplace to redirect my energy while I figured out how to broach the topic.

I turn my phone over in my lap and hold in the laugh that's building in my chest. The irony of her using our first moment alone in weeks to meddle in my personal life is almost too much. She still hasn't apologized for the hurtful things she said at that dinner, and now I'm about to ask her to own up to yet another horrible thing she's done to me.

"No. Just waiting on some important news for one of my projects."

She frowns at my mention of work on a Saturday. "You work too much, Sloane. When do you make time to live your life?"

I set my glass on the bar. "I love my job, Mom. I work hard because I'm good at it, but in no way does it stop me from living my life." *Certainly didn't stop me from making a mess of it.*

Her lips are pressed into a tight line. And I can't help but wonder if she's physically restraining herself from making some smart remark about me being good at making a rich man happy if I put my mind to it.

"Darling, you haven't been in a serious relationship since your marriage ended, and I don't need to remind you how hard dating is after a woman turns thirty."

My mouth falls open. "My marriage didn't *end*, Mom. My husband died. There's a huge difference. "

She waves a dismissive hand at me as she takes another sip of her drink. "You know what I meant, Sloane. Honestly, do you always have to make me out to be some kind of monster who doesn't appreciate what you've been through?"

"You don't appreciate what I've been through. You constantly minimize my grief, just like you minimized my marriage because you *never* liked Eric. Once you realized he didn't come with a trust fund or private school education, you wrote him off."

I'm shaking and my voice is shrill, but thankfully low, as I hurl the words at her. All of the things I've thought but never said because I didn't think her view of the world could ever impact my relationships in any real way. But today I know that's not true, and I'm pissed at her for all of it.

Not because I regret Eric—I could never do that—but because it had to have torn Dom apart to watch us together, to love me, and let someone else have me. I spent twenty-four hours thinking he loved someone else, but he lived that reality for twelve years. And it must have been hell for him.

A hell my mother crafted with her own selfish hands.

One of those hands wrap around my forearm as she leans towards me. "Lower your voice."

"Oh, I'm sorry." I snatch my arm away from her. "The last thing I want to do is embarrass you by making a scene in public."

"You're an adult, Sloane. The only person you'll be embarrassing is yourself."

"I don't give a damn what these people think of me, but you do. And you've always cared more about perception than anything else."

Annoyance flashes in her eyes as she looks around the room to make sure no one is watching us argue. "Do you have a specific grievance you want to air out with me or are you just ruining brunch for no good reason?"

"Actually, I do have an issue I want to talk to you about." I cross my legs and angle my body towards her. "The day after I moved onto campus, freshman year you came to visit me. Do you remember?"

"Finding you in your bed drooling and hungover from a night of underage drinking? Yes, I remember it."

"Do you also remember taking a note from my desk and never mentioning it to me?"

Her brows lift, and she takes a short sip of her drink before she answers. "That was so long ago, Sloane. I can't recall every single detail of the day."

"Either you remember the day or you don't."

"Fine. I *might* have seen a note on your desk with the name and number of a young man scribbled on it asking you to call him in the morning."

I chew the inside of my cheek to keep myself from exploding on her. I can't believe it's true. "What did you do with it?"

"I haven't the slightest clue, Sloane. It was twelve years ago."

"Mom."

Another flash of annoyance, this one born solely from being pushed to tell the truth for once in her miserable life. She picks an invisible bit of lint off of her dress. "I put it in the trash where it belonged. Any man you met while you were dressed like a slut and behaving like some around the way girl wasn't worthy of being associated with the Carson name."

My heart pounds, and I struggle for a response as I absorb this new layer of truth. "Why are you making it sound like you did me some kind of favor? You went through my things and made a choice for me based on what you wanted not what I needed!"

"What you needed, little girl, was someone to save you from yourself. You think you know everything, Sloane, and you always have, but I know more about this world than you ever will. Maybe if you'd let me make more choices for you, you wouldn't be a thirty-year-old widow who works on *Saturdays*."

Several seconds tick by and I stare at her, wondering, not for the first time, what I ever did to make her hate me so much. Mothers are supposed to be kind, loving, and supportive of their children, but mine has only ever been *this*.

Throughout my entire life, she's taken a sick pleasure in hurting me, in reminding me nothing I did was good enough for her, and I've always laid down and taken it. Allowing her to mistreat me because of a biological connection she's never valued or protected.

And I'm over all of it.

"I'm done, Mom." I grab my purse and slide out of my seat. "With this toxic relationship, your snide little comments about my marriage and my choices, all of it. And I'm done with you."

"Another dramatic exit." She scoffs. "You're not going to guilt me into apologizing by storming out of here, Sloane. I stand by all the things I've said and done. One day when you're a mother, and you find yourself making the same choices as me, you'll understand."

The last sentence sends me over the edge, and I'm in her face in the space of a heartbeat. My teeth are clenched, and I feel like a wild animal as I sneer at her.

"You are not a mother. You're a self-centered narcissist who cares more about status and perception than you've ever cared about me. I don't expect you to apologize because I know you wouldn't mean it. And for the record, if I ever have a child, I'll never be the kind of mother you were to me."

For the first time in my life, I believe it. And my heart aches for the version of myself that doubted it for so long. For what that doubt cost me and Eric.

"Lauren! Sloane!" A voice says from somewhere over my shoulder, and I turn around to see my mother's friend, Ella Hamilton, sauntering over to us. "How nice to see you two together!"

My mother's smile is fraught with tension as she stands and embraces Ella. "Yes, we're so glad Sloane could join us for brunch, but she was just leaving."

"Oh, that's unfortunate." Ella gives me a fake smile. "I guess you won't mind if I steal your mother away for a moment then?"

"Not at all."

We all know stealing someone away for a moment is just code for saving them from an unpleasant conversation, but I don't care because I've said everything I need to say to my mother. Our conversation has answered some vital questions for me about what happened the day after I met Dom. Now I feel like I have an important piece of the puzzle, but I still don't have all the facts.

And I know there's only one way to get them.

40

DOMINIC

Now

Sloane: I need to see you.

The words of Sloane's latest message swim around the screen, and I blink slowly to try and get them to stand still. When my phone buzzed an hour ago the last name I expected to see was hers, but there it was. My brain refused to believe I wasn't imagining it, so I stared at the first message, and the ones that followed, and took a swig of the vodka my father gave me every time one came through.

Deciding to take that first drink was easier than I thought it would be, but then again, it's easy to give in to the monster inside of you when life has already snatched away every reason to keep it locked away. When I got back from Sloane's place last night, my resolve was already waning, but when I woke up this morning without her in my arms, it broke completely.

And the bottle I left sitting on my coffee table yesterday called to me, promising the gift of numbness and the ability to forget how incredibly wrong I was about everything.

I thought I could rewrite history. I thought I could claim Sloane's heart with lies and keep it without dealing with the consequences of telling them, but I was wrong. And now we're both bleeding out, gutted by the truth I waited too long to tell.

Hurting Sloane was never my intention, but there's no amount of alcohol that can make me forget the horror on her face when I finally told her the truth or the way her eyes flashed with steely determination when she told me to leave. As if everything we shared over the past month meant nothing to her at all.

And maybe it didn't.

At our first lunch together, I heard her say she took a vow to never fall in love again, and despite the brief moment I spent thinking her jealousy over the tattoo meant something more, it seems she's determined to keep that promise. Eric will be the last man she loves in this life, and it doesn't matter that her heart knew mine first.

I've done everything I can to change her mind, and now I'm back to a life of craving her and knowing I'll never have her again. And unlike last time, when I'd only had a sip of her skin, trying to recover from the weeks I've spent surrounded by her in every sense of the word is going to be impossible.

There won't be a single moment I'm around her where I won't be utterly devastated by her presence, paralyzed by the curve of her neck, and envious of every breeze that gets to thread itself through the curls I love so much.

Which is why I had to call Seb this morning and agree to oversee the Cerros Resort build.

Hopefully two years out of New Haven will be enough time to learn to live without her. Sadly, that's the best I can hope for because there is no getting over Sloane for me. I knew it the moment she walked back into my life, connected to my best friend by heart and hand, and the only thing I wanted to do, besides punch a fucking wall, was kiss her.

So this is my punishment for coveting an angel, for daring to want an ounce of her goodness for myself: being exiled to my own private

hell where I'll try, and fail, to forget what it was like to watch my
dream slip through my fingers.

I toss back the last of the vodka and promise myself never to drink
again. Admitting to being reckless and selfish like my father is one
thing, but developing an alcohol addiction is something completely
different. The bottle makes a hollow clinking sound when I set it back
on the coffee table, and the strongest wave of shame ripples through
me as my doorbell rings.

Pushing out a breath through my nose, I drag myself out of my seat
and head towards the door. The last thing I want right now is company,
but I'm thankful for a reason to get out of the seat I've been slumped in
for hours. Once I get rid of whatever uninvited guest is at my door, I'll
throw that damn bottle away, take a long shower and start preparing for
California and a life without….

"Sloane?"

"Where have you been?" She pushes past me, barging into my
place with a determined look on her face. "I've been calling and
texting you, and you never answered."

"I've been busy."

Both of her hands are on her hips as she makes her way into my
living room. I follow her, watching as she catalogs the changes I've
made over the last six years, noting every single difference from when
Eric lived here.

Of all the things I expect to feel when I look at her standing in my
home for the first time in years—golden skin scrubbed clean of any
makeup she might have worn today, black curls pulled into a messy
bun on the top of her head, hazel eyes swimming with anxious concern
—bitter is not one of them.

But that's exactly what I am.

Bitter because seeing her here reminds me of the conversation we
had at Cerros when she said this place would always make her think of
Eric. I hate myself for allowing my mind to linger, for even a second,
on how the specter of his ghost robbed me of nights with her in my
bed. For resenting her loyalty to him in death. For being angry with her

for deciding that today of all days was the right time to prioritize me over his memory.

My chest tightens as jealousy, fueled by the sparkle of Eric's ring on her finger and the memory of her asking me to leave last night, courses through my veins.

Jealous. Over her dead husband who, let's not forget, was also your best friend? That's low, Dom. It is low, even for me, but it's also a reminder of how completely wrong I am for her no matter how hard I tried to convince myself otherwise.

"Is that a bottle of vodka?"

She looks mildly terrified at the presence of alcohol in my home, and I hold back a laugh as I sit down. I wonder what she would think if I told her where I got it from. If it would help her realize sending me away last night was the right choice because I have too much of my father in me to be any good for her. Too much of his bitterness, too much of his chaos, too much of his selfishness.

"It *was*."

Even as resentment pounds in my veins, I can't get over how good it is to see her. To watch her move around my space, leaving her scent in the air as she walks over to the couch and takes the seat closest to the armchair I'm sitting in.

"But you don't drink, Dominic."

"Things change."

Concern shines in her eyes, and it pisses me off. I don't want her concern, not after I tore my heart out and put it in her hand, only for her to hand it back to me. Still pounding, still gushing blood with every beat.

"I know you're probably upset about last night, but I didn't think —" Her eyes bounce between me and the bottle. "Did you drink that *entire* thing by yourself?"

I stare at her, keeping my expression blank. "Does it matter?"

"Yes." She looks stunned by the question. "Of course, it matters."

"Why?"

The fingers on her right hand find the rings on her left and start to spin them around. Sloane doesn't have many nervous habits, but this is definitely one, and I've only seen her do it in moments of extreme distress.

"Because you've been ignoring my texts and calls, and I didn't expect to come here and find you drunk. I mean why would you..."

I lift a brow. "Drink an entire bottle of vodka?"

She nods, guilt flickering in her eyes. "Yes. You've always been so adamant about not having the same vices as your dad."

"That was before I accepted the truth about myself."

"Dom, you have to know you're nothing like him."

"How would you know, Sloane? You've never met him."

"And I don't need to. I've heard the stories, and I know you're a better man than he could ever be."

I cross my arms, fighting back the swell of emotions her words elicit. For so long, all I've wanted was to be known by her. For her to look at me and really see me. Not her enemy. Not her husband's best friend who she barely tolerates. *Me.*

The man who braved a thousand hells just to let her continue to dance through the clouds of heaven.

"He would disagree with you." I see the exact moment she puts it all together. The vodka, the self-loathing, the thinly veiled rage eating me alive. She leans forward in her seat, inching closer to me.

"When did you see him?"

My fingers tap along the arm of the chair as I consider whether I want to answer her question. We haven't talked about my dad since the day she told me about the miscarriage and her fight with Eric, and I've been determined to keep it that way. To protect her from the ugliest parts of me. But we're done now, and there's no point in hiding anymore.

"On Friday night when his nurse called to tell me he only has a few months to live."

Her brows raise in surprise, and I know she gets it. She accused me of leaving her bed that night because of the tattoo, and maybe her asking about it did scare me, but it wasn't the whole reason I left. And I never got to explain because by the time I got back to her, we were in crisis mode and everything, including her, was spiraling out of my control.

"Dom, I'm so sorry."

She starts to reach for me then thinks better of it and pulls back, tucking her fingers into her lap. Every inch of my skin aches for her, desperate for the touch she's suddenly so reluctant to give. And I'm hit with the realization that this is what the rest of my life will be like: the almost touches, the awkwardness of pulling away when all you want to do is move forward.

I drag my gaze back to her face. "Why are you here?"

"I told you I needed to see you." There's a gentle waver in her voice that calls to me, tugging at my need to protect her. To do whatever it takes to make the uncertainty lacing her features go away.

Hard to do that when you're the one who put it there.

"Yes, but you never said why."

"I want to talk about last night. I have questions, and maybe some answers, about that day you might be interested in."

My jaw flexes as I stare at her, and I watch her trace the sharp line with her eyes. She's probably trying to gauge my mood based on the movement of the muscle there.

"You think there's something about that night *you* can tell me? I remember every second of it, Sloane. From the dress you were wearing to the exact words you said when you walked up to me and sat on my lap."

I bark out a laugh when her brows raise further. How can she give me answers about that night when she still doesn't remember the most basic details of our time together?

She shakes her head. "I don't have any answers about that night, but I do have some about the morning after."

Now my interest is sparked. I've spent twelve years wondering what happened the morning after I left her, and I've imagined all sorts of scenarios, including one where she saw the note and threw it in the trash because she woke up regretting everything.

"What about it?"

"Like I said last night when I woke up the next morning I didn't remember anything besides making the list and going to the party, but I did keep feeling like I was forgetting something. There was this voice I kept hearing, telling me to call them in the morning, and I thought it was from a dream because I couldn't remember anyone *actually* saying it to me." Her tongue darts out, swiping over her bottom lip. "I even asked my friends to help me figure out what happened, but they never saw us together, and no one could figure out why you wouldn't save your number in my phone if you were real."

Something like joy goes through me as I listen to her describe making some attempt to find me even when she wasn't sure I was real, and it makes me a little more willing to walk her through the details.

"When you found me on the back porch, you said they left you to go hook up with some guys. By the time we left, they were nowhere to be found. I walked you back to your place and put you in bed. You asked me to stay, but I was afraid you wouldn't remember anything in the morning and didn't want to risk freaking you out. I wanted to give you my number, but your phone was dead, so I left the note instead."

I can't keep the pain out of my voice because I did everything I could to protect our connection. I thought ahead, I considered all the possibilities, and I still lost her. The thought of finding out why after all these years has my throat tight.

Sloane's eyes go soft. "I never got that note, Dom. My mom took it. She was in my room when I woke up the next morning, and she saw it on my desk."

"How do you know?"

She bites her lip, like she's not sure she wants to talk about it right now, then launches into a lengthy explanation about the visit with her mom the day after we met and the confrontation earlier today at brunch. When she's done, there's an angry spark in her eyes that matches the one burning inside of me.

And I recognize it immediately.

Our siren song of destruction.

The familiar invitation to join her in setting flames to everything, every circumstance and choice, that kept us from each other. But I can't accept it, not this time. "She was right."

Her brows pinch together. "What?"

"Your mom." I clarify. "She was right. She did you a favor by throwing the note away."

"How can you say that? The note was our only chance at finding each other. It would have helped me realize you weren't just a figment of my imagination!"

I hate the vehemence of her tone—the outrage she seems to be feeling at having a future with me stolen by her mother—because it makes a stupid amount of hope surge through me.

Hope I can't afford to feel when I know that no matter what I'm going to have to let her go.

"And it all worked out the way it was supposed to. You and I were never a good idea. We wouldn't have worked."

I push to my feet and walk over to the window, pacing back and forth in front of the glass I want to put my fist through. Having this conversation with Sloane right now feels like the purest form of torture.

"You don't know that, Dom. We never had a chance. *You* didn't give us one! You saw me with Eric, and you didn't say anything. You just treated me like shit. Why?"

"Because he was my best friend, Sloane. My brother. What was I supposed to do? Steal you away from him? Tell him about our night together and beg him to let me fuck you first?"

She flinches, but I can tell my crass words are pissing her off, not hurting her. Her mouth opens, working to craft a response to my comment, which is so far out of line I want to snatch it out of the air. She rises from her seat, and for a second I think she's going to walk out, but instead, she comes over to me.

"Don't be an asshole, Dominic. That night was about more than sex, and it wasn't fair for you to make such an important decision for all three of us!"

She's right. The decision I made did impact all of us, but I'm the only one who carried it. I'm the one who shouldered it every single day. I stare down at her, letting her see the weight of the past twelve years crushing me like boulders. A lifetime worth of wanting something I could never have. A thousand days of torture and pretending, making choices that left everyone happy except for me.

Dropping the act should be a relief, but I'm just pissed at her for forcing me to relive the night I hate her for forgetting. *This conversation needs to end now.* I scrub my hands over my face.

"You said you had questions. Ask them, so we can be done."

41

SLOANE

Dom looks at me, and I wish for the first time in weeks that his eyes were somewhere else. Because one glance into the liquid pools of midnight shows me the fire raging inside of him. The darkness and shadows and ghosts that can only be conjured by reminders of things you'd rather forget.

His words are sharp, reminding me of all the times over the years when he's used this exact tone to make me believe he hated me. It hurts to be taken back to those moments, to that feeling, but I see it for what it is now.

Deflection.

Him trying to make me retreat when I should be advancing. And I'm so lost in bearing witness to him in his own private hell, that it takes me a full minute to think of my next question, which is just an extension of the conversation we've been having.

"Why didn't you say anything? I mean we were alone for a few minutes when we met in your room. You could have told me then or any of the other times we were alone."

Dom exhales harshly. He's frustrated that we're still on this, but I just have to know. "What would it have changed, Sloane? At that point, Eric was already in love with you. And when I saw you with him, I *knew*. I fucking knew he was better for you than I could ever be. You were so happy, smiling and looking at him like he was the only person in the world for you."

"But that night…"

"You weren't yourself. You were angry and drunk, and I saw your fire and felt my entire world shift. I looked at you and thought 'Finally, someone who's just as ready to burn the world down as I am,' but I didn't question why you wanted to."

I frown. "It wasn't your job to ask."

No one would expect a college freshman to assess the mental state of a stranger at a frat party. And while I don't remember much, I can say with some certainty that if he would have started asking questions I didn't want to answer, I would have found someone else to help me check the items off of my list. Truthfully, I was lucky I ran into him and not some other asshole who would have gladly taken advantage of me.

"Maybe not, but I didn't have to dive into the madness head first, with no plan and not a care in the world about how it was going to turn out as long as I got to have you." Both his nostrils flare, and he pushes out rough breaths that make his chest heave. "Eric wouldn't have done that. He would have taken one look at you and gotten you out of there."

My heart aches at the longing in his words, the jealousy in them wrapping around my lungs and squeezing as I listen to him compare himself to his best friend. Eric was the other, better, side of my coin. He always gave me so much comfort; his presence was like a calming salve, soothing away old hurts, providing steady support and quiet words of reassurance that didn't stop coming until he was sure he'd kept me from going off the deep end.

There's no denying Dom is different, mainly because he's always the one sending me off the deep end, but also because in the weeks we've been together, he's shown me he's willing to jump off the cliff with me if talking me off the edge isn't an option. He always gives me space to be angry and a little unreasonable.

Before we were us, I thought he got a sick satisfaction out of striking the match and watching me burn, but now I know his fascination with my fire is because of how closely it resembles his own. Eric was my better half, but Dom is the mirror image of my soul. The place where all my shadows and every burst of flame are known, understood, and loved.

Of course, there are differences in my relationships with both of them, but I don't think one is better than the other because the result is the same. With both him and Eric, I've felt supported, protected, and safe to be any version of myself.

"Don't do that. We have no idea how Eric would have handled that situation, and we never will."

His lips curl into a sarcastic smile. "I guess we'll just agree to disagree."

"Dom."

"What's your next question, Sloane?"

Even though I know exactly what I want to ask next, my lips don't part. Suddenly, I wish I didn't come here because seeing him be this man—this brooding, drunk asshole who reminds me so much of the person I used to call my enemy it hurts to look at him—is ripping me apart.

This isn't my Dom. The one who sent Mal to check on me when I freaked out. The one who comforted me after I got into it with my mom. The one who went out of his way to save me before I even thought to call him mine.

I take a deep breath. "Why did you get the tattoo?"

Tension lines his shoulders, and the muscle in his jaw starts to tick rapidly. He shakes his head. "I don't know."

"Yes, you do. You don't do anything without a reason, so tell me why. If you were so convinced you were bad for me, so determined to believe I was the best version of myself with Eric, why would you get a permanent reminder of that night?"

"So I could remember to hate you!" He roars, throwing his hands in the air like he's physically releasing the truth. "You forgot me. And out of all the men on the planet, on that *fucking* campus, you found Eric. The one person I could never try to steal you away from. Not even if it meant watching you fall in love with him or standing beside him while he made you promises I never got the chance to. I watched you build a life with him, and it hurt. Wanting you. Loving you. Being yours when you were always his. It all hurt, and so I decided to try hating you instead."

"And did it work?"

He hesitates, just for a second. "Yes."

The words hit me like a physical blow. Each one landing its punch until I feel broken and bruised. I don't even flinch at his raised voice, don't even care about the resentment coating his words as he talks about watching me with Eric. What hurts the most is hearing him say he did hate me. After weeks of believing the words he whispered to me that first night in my bed—*I never hated you, Sloane.*—the confession has tears leaking out of the corners of my eyes.

"Dominic..."

"Tell me you regret it, Sloane."

I search his face, confused about what exactly he wants me to say I regret. The night we spent together? The past few weeks where I've allowed myself to think of him as my home?

"What?"

"You're asking me why I made the choices I made. Why I didn't break you and Eric up, so we could be together as if you wanted things to go differently, so *tell me*. Tell me you regret falling in love with him." He's stalking towards me, and with every step he takes forward, I take one back. "Tell me you regret marrying him. Tell me you regret letting him kiss your pretty mouth and claim every inch of your body. Tell me you regret building a life with him and wearing his ring every day. Tell. Me. You. Regret. It."

I put my hands on his chest to stop him from coming any closer. "No. I don't regret it."

And it's the truth, while I'm actively grieving the future Dom and I lost, I can't bring myself to regret what I got to have with Eric. It's just hard for me to think of all of our happy moments together without considering what it must have felt like for Dom.

"I know you don't, angel. He was your Prince Charming, your knight in shining armor, and all I am is the jealous asshole who fucked his best friend's widow after years of fantasizing about her. The piece of shit liar who used you to make the dreams of a college freshman come true."

Our faces are so close I can practically taste the vodka on his breath. My heart pounds in my chest, and I can't even begin to think about what to do with all the fury building inside of me. Incited by the ugly, nasty words spoken by the man I love who seems determined to hurt me.

"You don't mean that."

"Like hell, I don't." He barks out a gruff laugh, eyes flaring as he wipes a tear from my cheek with his index finger. "I'm surprised you're so upset, weren't you just trying to end this last night?"

I lift my chin. "That was before...." *Before I knew I was the woman who put that haunted look on your face. Before I knew I was the woman you loved enough to carry the pain of losing her with you every day.*

I don't say any of those words, but Dom sees them. He sees them etched in my features, stamped across my face like I've put them on display just for him. I suppose in a way I have. I know how easily he can read me, even when he's experiencing the first alcohol-induced buzz of his life, and I wouldn't have started that sentence, or thought those thoughts, if I didn't want him to know about them.

The dark eyes I've spent weeks falling in love with laugh at me.

"I don't know what you came here for, angel. This was never supposed to be more than a casual arrangement, and you got what you needed out of it. Your skin should be well and truly sated until you find your *next* husband." He's speaking through clenched teeth, forcing each word out of his mouth. "And don't worry about anyone finding out about this. I might be a selfish bastard, but I never break a promise."

He hovers over me for a second. His handsome face twisted into a mixture of self-loathing and anger that would break my heart if I wasn't so pissed off at the things he's just said to me. Then he pushes off of the wall and moves back to the couch, shoulders sagging like letting the most hurtful things he's ever said to me fly out of his mouth have brought him great relief.

In that moment, I hate him. Only a little, not more than I love him, and not enough to lessen the sting as his words settle against my skin. The comment about finding my next husband cuts especially deep, and I think maybe that was the point. I've sparred with him enough times to know he's always precise and intentional with his blows.

Tears swim in my eyes, and I just let them fall. I don't even care if he knows he's hurt me. Some part of me wants him to know because it's still stupidly hoping the sight of them will cause my Dom to resurface and send this monster back to whatever cage it's been living in.

It feels dumb, trying to reach my Dom when the man in front of me is so eerily familiar to the person I used to dread spending more than a minute around by myself, but I can't stop because I love him, and I don't want to believe *this* is how we end.

Him, drunk and lashing out like an animal with a wound they won't let anyone see, let alone fix. Me, reaching for him even when he keeps pushing me away. I know this is just pain. This is just him acting out the same way he did when I thanked him after Club Noir.

That was about his father, and I don't know how exactly, but this is about that old bastard too.

Sometimes I forget about the parallels between my childhood and his. Both of us grew up with one parent whose unconditional love wasn't enough to shield us from the damage of their narcissistic partners. And as a result, we grew around the shadows they gave us, walking around like open wounds looking for any excuse to turn a spark into a flame. It's no wonder he took one look at me that night and felt relieved. We've always matched each other's energy. Sometimes in the worst ways, but sometimes—especially over these last few weeks —in the very best ones.

I don't want to lose that. I don't want to let his father or my mother

Restore Me   441

take another thing from us. And the only way to prevent that from happening is to make him accept that we're nothing like them.

"You're so full of shit." I force the words past the lump in my throat. "All of this talk about not being good enough for me because you're like your dad or you're not like Eric. It's all bullshit, Dominic. You gave up the chance at something great because you saw that your best friend was happy. Selfish men don't do that."

I move over to him, sitting on the coffee table and taking his hands in my mine. Dom's head snaps up, his brows furrowed together in surprise. For a second, I think I see his expression soften in reaction to my tears, but it's gone in an instant so I continue.

"I can't say I understand why you didn't say anything all those years ago, but I'm thankful you didn't because it gave me a chance to love Eric before his life got cut short. It gave *you* a chance to love him too, even in the moments you were bitter and jealous and hating both of us for having each other. I don't know why things worked out the way they did for us, but I'm not sorry. Because in some way I know I couldn't have been yours if I wasn't his first."

Letting go of his hands, I reach up and cradle his face between my palms, forcing him to look at me for this next part. "And I am yours, Dom. I'm so fucking yours, and you don't even know it because all of the stuff that's happened over the last few days has stopped me from being able to tell you the one thing I've known for a while now: I love you. I love you so much, and you can try to scare me away, but I'm not going anywhere unless you look me in the eyes and tell me this is over."

The first time I say 'I love you' his eyes fall shut, and his face morphs into a pained expression. The second time he shudders as if he's literally revolted at the idea of me loving him and shakes his head until I release my grip on his face. And when I'm done talking my heart has left my chest and made a new home in my throat.

I feel like I'm going to throw up as I wait for his response. Seconds seem to stretch into hours as I wait for the familiar warmth of that midnight gaze to caress my face, and all the while, I hold my breath.

But when he finally opens his eyes and looks at me, I know I'm not about to get the reaction I was hoping for.

"This is over."

* * *

I DON'T KNOW how I make it from the tenth floor to the sidewalk in front of Dom's building. But one second I'm on my knees in front of him, telling him how much I love him, and the next I'm swiping at tears that refuse to stop coming as I walk towards my car.

Every step I take seems to make the crack in my chest splinter more, and I have to force myself to keep moving. Putting one foot in front of the other even though I think I can feel myself actively dying. But every beat of my heart reminds me that it's not *me*. It's the hope—for me, Dom, and our future—that was bursting out of me on the drive over. It felt like a flower in full bloom, shifting from tight buds to beautiful, unfurling petals reaching towards the sun.

And now the edges of the petals are turning black, curling back onto themselves before breaking off and floating away.

My eyes are on the ground, tears blurring my vision, as I make my way to the parking area for visitors. People are walking around me in both directions, everyone too busy or caught up in their own world, to notice the heartbroken woman moving at a snail's pace on the sidewalk.

Not that I'm complaining. Running into anyone, but especially someone I know, while I'm crying outside of Dom's building would be embarrassing and weird. I probably wouldn't even have the capacity to come up with a good lie about being here, which would mean risking people finding out about us when everything is already done.

Knowing I don't want to deal with the heartbreak of losing more of the people I love, I open up my bag and start to dig for my keys. I've just put my hand on them when my shoulder collides with someone else's, almost making me drop everything. Startled, I look up with an apology already on my lips.

"I'm so—" The words die on my tongue as my mind puts a name

to the familiar face staring back at me. Thin lips curled into a scowl masquerading as a smile, brown eyes filled with displeasure, flawless, tawny skin over cheekbones that are more prominent today than I've ever seen them thanks to the sleek ponytail she's wearing. "Kristen."

My heart sinks as I try to imagine what I must look like right now. Eyes puffy and swollen from tears that are still falling, clothes wrinkled like I've just rolled out of bed, hair in a messy bun that's probably got more than a few loose strands flying around.

I hate the idea of running into her looking like this, but my ego has to take a backseat to the panic coursing through my veins. I rack my brain for something to say, thinking maybe I can play it nice and distract her from the fact I have no reason to be outside of Dom's place on a Saturday evening looking like I'm doing a walk of shame.

"Sloane." She crosses her arms over her chest. There's a small gift bag dangling from her fingers, and I wonder absently if it's for Dom. "*This* is the last place I'd expect to run into you."

"I know right?" I glance back at the building and force out a laugh. "Dominic needed me to bring some papers by for the hotel renovation we're working on together. Did he tell you about it?"

"No. I don't think he mentioned it." She looks me up and down, and I shift my weight to my other foot. "Forgive me for staring, I just don't think I've ever seen you dressed so...*casually*."

I bite my lip. Letting her take such an evident dig at me is pissing me off, but I know I have to play it cool because acting cagey and defensive will only make her more suspicious.

"I know!" My voice is a little too high and overly friendly as I spit out the first thing that comes to mind. "I was on my way back home from Ash's when he called. Hence the sleepover clothes." I gesture awkwardly at my outfit and laugh again. "You remember Ash right?"

She studies me for a second; her eyes snapping with frenzied energy that reminds me of the look the doctors on Grey's Anatomy get when they finally crack a case, and for a second I start to get nervous. Then she throws her head back and laughs, and my worry dissipates.

"Of course! He's such a nice guy." Her lips quirk. "Please tell him hello for me the next time you guys talk."

"I definitely will." I move around her, rifling through my purse for my keys. "See you later, Kristen."

"How was he?"

The words reach my ears just as my hand lands on the keys at the bottom of my purse, and I drop them again when I spin around to face her, wondering if I imagined the double entendre.

"Excuse me?"

"I said how was Nic?" She takes a few steps forward, her ponytail swishing as she closes the distance between us. "Was he in a good mood? I mean, I know you two haven't always gotten along, but I'm sure you know him better now after working with him for so long. In your expert opinion, is it safe for me to go up, or should I turn around now and give him his gift later?"

She dangles the bag in front of me, and I struggle to keep my face neutral. The idea of her going up there and being with him when I can't makes me want to throw something.

"Um. I didn't pay much attention to his mood, but I'm sure he'll be happy to see you." I finally pull out my keys and wave them at her. "I've got to run. See you around."

Kristen waves and gives me a smile that's supposed to be friendly but feels all wrong because it doesn't match the triumphant glint in her eye that makes me feel like she's just caught me in a lie.

"Later, Sloane."

42

SLOANE

Now

Mal takes one look at my shower cap, ratty old sweats and the half-eaten bowl of ice cream clutched in my hand and frowns. "What the hell is wrong with you?"

It's a good question, but I can't even begin to answer it truthfully. Which is why I've been hiding out at home all week, wallowing in my grief and trying to check at least one item off of my heartbreak recovery list.

It was a lofty set of goals—fix my broken heart that only wants to be put back together by the hands that destroyed it in the first place, cleanse my mind of all thoughts and images from the last four weeks, find a way to hate the person I love—but I set them so the next time I came face to face with someone who knows me as well as Mal does, they wouldn't be able to see the pain written all over my face. I guess I failed at that too.

I move aside to let Mal in the door. "Nothing."

She steps inside gingerly, almost like she thinks moving too fast might cause me to break, and I appreciate it because I honestly believe it might. Since I walked out of Dom's place, I've felt like a shell of myself. Fragile like a piece of glass that's already got a crack running down the middle. One sudden move, one more bump, and I'll shatter into a million little pieces.

"Sweetie, you answered your door in a *shower cap*."

"I'm deep conditioning my hair."

"On a Wednesday night?"

"Yes." I throw myself back onto the couch cushion I've been stuck to since Saturday. "There are no rules against deep conditioning on a weeknight."

Mal plops down in the opposite corner and tosses her hair over her shoulder. Today she's wearing a red wig with blunt bangs and bone straight tresses that reach the center of her back. This is my first time seeing her all week, and it's good to have something else to focus on besides the image of Dom looking at me and saying it's over that's been playing in my head on repeat.

"Not officially, but I for one have no interest in spending a week-night suffering through an in-depth wash routine."

I shrug and set my bowl on the table. "It's not like I have anything better to do."

"You're not going to find it sitting in this house." There's a sad sparkle in her eyes as she studies me. "I know you're sad about things ending with Ash, but that doesn't mean you have to give up completely. He was just one man, there are plenty more where he came from."

The smile I give her feels brittle and forced. "Thanks, but I'm not sad about Ash."

"You're not? Then what's with the 'I just got my heart broke' look you're sporting?" Her eyes light up with a mischievous glow. "Were you dating someone else?"

I shake my head. "No, Mal."

But it's too late. She's already grabbed the bone and started to run with it. A happy little squeal hits the air as she bounces in her seat like a child and points at me. "You were! You totally were! Who was it?"I open my mouth, but she waves me off. "Oh, no. Let me guess. James?"

"*No.*" I push to my feet and head towards the kitchen. "I wasn't seeing anyone else."

"Liar!" Mal calls from behind me as she follows me into the kitchen and takes a seat at the island. "Oh my God! That reminds me. I ran into Kristen at Twisted Sistas yesterday, and she told me the craziest thing." I start to rummage through the refrigerator, examining a jar of pickles way too closely just to avoid letting her see the panic on my face at the mention of Kristen's name. "She said she ran into you outside of Nic's place over the weekend, and you looked like you had just rolled out of bed. Then she launched into this whole theory about you guys sleeping together because Nic broke up with her around the time he took the job at the hotel."

I freeze and the jar of pickles slips from my hand and hits the floor. Mal is on her feet in an instant, rushing over to me and grabbing me by the shoulders.

"Sloane! What the hell?"

She spins me around, and the feel of her fingertips pressing into my shoulders is the only thing anchoring me to Earth. *How the hell did Kristen figure it out?* Mal walks me over to one of the bar stools and urges me to sit. I watch her clean up the mess with the same stunned expression on my face.

"Are you okay?" She sits back down beside me, her forehead creased in clear confusion. "Don't worry about what Kristen said, girl. Nobody would ever believe you and Nic would be together, I mean you two barely—"

"It's true."

Her mouth snaps shut. Then falls open. Then snaps shut again. And it would be comical to see Mal struggling for a response if it didn't feel like I just ruined our entire relationship with two little words. When I get the courage to look at her, she's still speechless, so I launch straight into the apology I've been preparing for weeks just in case this moment came.

"Mal, I'm so sorry. We were only together for a few weeks. It was a stupid mistake, and it's over now." I grab her hand and squeeze it. "*Please* don't hate me."

The creases in her forehead deepen as I stare at her, pleading with my eyes for her to say something, anything, in response to what I've just confessed. When Dom and I first made our agreement, I lived in fear of this moment—dreading the dip in her brows and the tears in her eyes that would make the hurt there more evident—but none of it is happening the way I thought it would. Mal is deathly still beside me, her features frozen in surprise and the corners of her lips twisting into something between a smile and a horrified scowl.

"Mal, please say something."

"I just—" She shakes her head, a small laugh bursting from her mouth. "I mean I don't know what to say, Sloane. Honestly, I think I might be in shock."

"Okay," I say slowly. "I'm sorry to just spring this on you. Do you want me to get you some water or something stronger?" I start to rise from my seat, but she pulls me down and stares at me with wide eyes.

"No! You already have the whole kitchen smelling like pickle juice." Her lips quirk like she's fighting back another laugh. "Sit your ass down and tell me what the hell is going on with you and Nic."

This time it's me struggling for words. Out of all the things I thought she would say when she finally got her brain working again, this isn't it. I sigh. "Nothing. Nothing at all."

She rolls her eyes. "Don't get all technical with me. Nothing is going on now, but something *was* going on and it's still affecting you."

Her lips push out into a surprisingly sympathetic pout as she glances at my shower cap. I press my lips together because I'm not sure if the next thing that passes through them is going to be a sob, laugh, or weird mixture of both.

"Why aren't you mad right now?"

"I didn't say I wasn't mad." My face falls, and she gives me a light bump with her shoulder. "Calm down, girl! I'm mad at you for not telling me what was going on. We're supposed to be best friends, and you're out here keeping major secrets from me."

All of my breath leaves my body in a relieved woosh. "But not because I was in a relationship with Dom?"

"DOM?" She makes a gagging sound. "Ugh. Why do you call him

that? Never mind, don't tell me. I don't want to know anything about your sex life."

"Mal."

"Sloane." We stare at each other, and I let her see all the worry and doubt I'm feeling. "No, I'm not mad at you, and I could never hate you. Do I think it's weird you and Nic somehow ended up in a situationship? *Yes, I absolutely do.* But you're both grown, consenting adults. Why would I have an opinion about what you guys do?"

"Because I was married to your brother."

Having this conversation with Mal right now is incredibly surreal. I thought I would have to keep this secret for the rest of our lives, carrying the biggest lies I've ever told her with me to the grave. But here we are, talking about me and Dom like it's no big deal.

"True, and you made him very happy for the entire time you two were together. Unless you're about to tell me you and Nic had an affair before Eric died, I don't know why it would be an issue."

My throat constricts when she says 'affair' because it immediately makes me think about the feelings Dom had for me before I even knew Eric. We never acted on them, but just the fact they exist could spell betrayal in Mal's eyes.

"Sloane," she says slowly. "You guys didn't have an affair right?"

I shake my head wildly. "No! Mal, of course not. We would never do anything like that to Eric. I mean I didn't even like Dom until we started working together on this project."

"And what about him? Did he think of you that way before then?"

The question makes my stomach churn. Answering Mal without telling her about the night Dom and I met feels impossible, but broaching the subject while he isn't here to explain his side of things feels wrong, especially when I don't fully remember everything.

"I don't know how to answer that."

Mal leans forward, obviously intrigued and a little concerned by my hesitance. "Can't go wrong with the truth."

Her eyebrows wiggle, and I give her a weak smile before telling her everything I've pieced together from the night Dom and I met. The party, the list, the way he described our connection, and how those underlying feelings came back to life that night in Club Noir.

Shaking her head in disbelief, she rises from her seat and crosses over to the cabinet. I watch her pull out a bottle of wine and two glasses. "What are you doing?"

She looks at me like I've grown two heads. "Pouring wine. We both need some after that story."

I snort. "Pretty sure alcohol is what got me into this mess to begin with."

"And *I'm* pretty sure you weren't pounding back glasses of sauvignon blanc at a frat party."

"How are you taking this so well?"

Asking her this question again feels like tempting fate, but I just can't get over her nonchalant reaction. The entire time Dom and I were together, I worried about how this would go, and it's just shocking to know I got it so wrong.

"Wow." Mal rounds the island and hands me my drink as she gets settled beside me. "I think I might be a little offended at how little faith you have in my ability to be reasonable."

"It's not that I think you're unreasonable, I just know you're sensitive about seeing me with someone else. When I went out with Ash, you said it made Eric being gone feel too real."

"Right, but that doesn't mean I don't want to see you happy!" She wrinkles her nose at me. "Please don't tell me that's the reason you and Nic didn't work out."

I take a short sip of my wine. "No. That's not it at all. I mean we talked about it, at length, but that's not what tore us apart."

"Okay, so what happened?"

"Mal, you don't want to hear me cry about Dom."

"Yes, I do." She sticks her tongue out at me when I glare at her. "Come on, Sloane. You know you've been dying to hash this out with someone besides your therapist."

With another long-suffering sigh, I decide to give in because I know she won't leave me alone until I tell her everything. In some ways, I feel like I owe her this truth after weeks of lying. And once I start talking, it all just flows out. The surprising beginning of us, the perfection of the middle, and the devastation of the end. I don't realize I'm crying until Mal presses a tissue into my hand.

"Fuck, Sloane. I'm sorry." She wraps her arms around my shoulders. "Do you want me to kill him? Because I've spent some time researching how to dismember a body, and I think I can do it."

Somehow I manage to laugh through the sobs, and it reminds me of the day I found her on my doorstep crying over Chris and threatened to murder him for her. I wrap my arms around her and hug her back; my heart swells with gratitude, overflowing with relief that my confession hasn't shattered our relationship the way I always thought it would.

"I don't want you to kill him any more than you want me to kill Chris."

We pull back and look at each other. Her eyes shine with the kind of understanding that can only come from a woman who's living with a broken heart as well.

"Well," she sighs. "I guess the bastards get to live another day."

* * *

THE LAST HALF of my week is infinitely better with Mal by my side. After our talk on Wednesday, she spent the night and has stayed close since. I was determined to grieve this relationship on my own, but to my surprise, she was just as determined not to let me. And there aren't enough words in the world to explain how thankful I am for her constant support.

On Friday afternoon, I'm heading out of the house to meet her and Mama for dinner when I see a familiar midnight black Range Rover parked in my driveway. I stop in my tracks and watch in slow motion as Dom steps out of the car. Excitement and apprehension spring in my chest at the same time. *He's here. He came to see me.* But I also can't forget the last time we were face to face. When he managed to rip my heart out with three little words.

A shiver rolls down my spine as I take him in, studying every line of his handsome face as he closes the car door and stares at me. His

J.L. SEEGARS

expression is unreadable, and his eyes rake over me slowly, making me feel the weight of his gaze as surely as if he's touched me. I close my eyes, relishing in the moment, in the feeling of being seen by him after going so many days without it.

When I open them back up, he's standing in front of me. A heady swirl of emotion moves across his features as we breathe each other in. I want to throw my arms around his waist, to bury my face in his chest and make him swear to never, ever leave me again, but I don't. I just look up at him, letting him see it all. The hurt, the fury, the rage, *the love.*

"Sloane."

He reaches for me, but I step back. I don't want him to touch me yet. Uncertainty and fear flash in his eyes, and I can't help but feel triumphant. Good. Let him doubt himself. Let him be afraid of me rejecting him like he rejected me.

"Why are you here?"

"I needed to see you."

I frown. "Why?"

Dom reaches for me again, this time managing to capture my wrist in his long fingers. And, *oh, God.* His touch alone threatens to unravel me. "Let's go inside and talk."

A bitter laugh breaks free from the hollow space inside my chest. Of course, he would just come here and act like everything was back to normal. Like we're still the same Sloane and Dom we were before he let a lifetime's worth of bullshit break us. I snatch my hand away from him. "You can say whatever you need to say to me right here."

He clenches his jaw and nods. "Okay. Then let me start with I'm sorry. I fucked this all up, Sloane. I told you when we started this that I wasn't worthy of you, but I promised I would try my best to be, and I broke that promise a million different ways on Saturday."

Just the mention of Saturday makes my heart twist painfully in my chest, but I can't let him take all the responsibility for the mess we made together. "You didn't get there on your own."

"But I drove us over the edge, and you deserve to know why." Both of his hands ball into fists. "I already told you I went to see my dad the night you asked about the tattoo." His eyes flash with anger like he's still upset with himself for doing that. "Our visits always go left pretty quickly, but this one dissolved in a matter of moments. It ended with him telling me I was a selfish bastard who hurt people just like him. Then he pressed a bottle of vodka in my hand and sent me on my way."

I bite my lip, willing my anger to stay. To not be drowned out by the sadness and compassion for the little boy in Dom constantly being victimized by his father. "I'm sorry you had to go through that, but I still don't understand why you would let him get in your head."

"Because when he said it all I could think about was how not knowing the truth about us was hurting you, and then Friday happened..."

Hearing how I helped his dad niggle his way into his head, allowing the poisonous seeds he'd planted to grow, breaks my heart, and I have to cross my arms over my chest to keep myself from reaching for him.

"And I freaked out about California and made you leave when you told me the truth about everything." Heat creeps up my neck when he settles his gaze on my face. "I'm sorry for reacting that way. It was just a lot of information to process, and I was over-whelmed."

"And I took your reaction as confirmation of my deepest fears and spun out." He grimaces, still angry with himself. "My therapist says it was classic self-sabotage."

"You're in therapy?" This is news to me. I haven't heard him mention he was seeing someone before, but I know how private mental health care can be, especially for Black men. He shrugs like it's no big deal.

"I just started back."

"That's amazing, Dom."

He grabs both of my hands in his. "I'm trying to work through my mess, so I can be better for you. What happened on Saturday, the things I said, the shit I did. It wasn't okay. I hurt you *again*. And I know I don't deserve it, but I want a chance to make it up to you. More than anything I've ever wanted in my entire life, more than my next fucking breath. Will you please let me do that?"

He pulls my hands up to his mouth, brushing his lips over my knuckles while his eyes break my heart. He's pleading with me. A vulnerability swirling in his irises I haven't seen before.

And God, do I want to give in to him. It would be so easy to let the ice surrounding my heart melt away and fall into his arms, but I can't do it. The hurt is too fresh. My hands are still bleeding from picking up the pieces he left my heart in, and I just need more time.

"I can't."

43

SLOANE

> Dominic: The first time I saw you, you took my breath away. Standing there in a white dress at a frat party, like an angel that came down to Earth for the sole purpose of claiming my heart. You succeeded. I won't say those words to you now because they're too important to put in a text message you won't ever read, but I feel them, angel. I've always felt them.

It's been three weeks since I've laid eyes on Dom, but I've heard from him every single day. Text messages I won't allow myself to read. Notes that are always attached to flowers or other gifts he has delivered to my house. Voicemails and audio messages I have to force myself to delete because I know the moment I hear that smooth, dark rasp I'll be a goner.

They started the day after I left him standing in my driveway and haven't stopped since, and every time I get one, my resolve cracks a little more. Usually, I dismiss them as soon as they come in, but today is the opening for La Grand Nuit, and I miss him. Which is why the second his name popped up on my phone, I opened the message and ended up reading the most devastating one he's sent so far.

And now that I'm in the thread, I can't stop scrolling, reading every single thing he's written to me over the last twenty-one days, and trying not to ruin my makeup.

> Dominic: I did try to hate you, Sloane, but I never succeeded because hating you was even more impossible than loving you.
>
> Dominic: Tried to get on a plane to California today, but I couldn't do it.
>
> Dominic: You were in my dreams last night. I wish I could have stayed asleep.
>
> Dominic: They're using a new crust on the double chocolate cheesecake at Twisted Sistas. Have you tried it yet?
>
> Dominic: I just watched the episode of Grey's where Meredith asks Derek to choose her. He was a bastard for walking away.

Some of the messages make me laugh, but mostly they make me want to cry. I turn my phone face down and pull in a few deep breaths through my nose, willing the tears to go away so I can finish getting dressed for the launch party. Mal and I spent the entire morning pampering ourselves. Getting our hair, nails, and makeup done before coming back to my house to get dressed.

She's agreed to be my date, promising to stay by my side for the entire evening just like she has for the last month. We haven't talked much about Dom over the past few weeks, but I know they still talk and see each other at Sunday dinners when I'm not there. And I'm honestly glad their relationship hasn't suffered because of me. Dom needs all the family he can get, and Mal can't afford to lose another brother.

Skipping a family dinner every now and then to keep things from being weird seems like a small sacrifice to make.

"Hey," Mal calls as she walks into my bedroom. "I got something for you!"

There's a large white box with a black bow in her hands, and she's smiling wide as she sets it on the bed and gestures for me to come over. I eye the box warily as I walk over. Mal has never bought me anything that's required an actual gift box before, and I don't know what to expect.

"Mal, what is this?"

"Open it and see!"

I run my fingers over the bow and glance at her. She's bouncing happily on her tiptoes, and her face is split into a wide grin that makes her dimples pop. The excited energy pouring off of her is contagious. I tug on the bow and it comes loose easily. Mal makes an excited little squeal in the back of her throat that has me laughing as I open the box to reveal a black dress with a sheer corset bodice and beaded straps.

"Wow." I give her a puzzled look as I pull the dress out of the box completely and rub the tulle skirt between my fingers. "It's beautiful, but you didn't have to do this."

"I know I didn't, but you've been through a lot the last few weeks, and I wanted you to feel beautiful tonight."

"Aww, Mal. That's so sweet."

She waves a dismissive hand at me. "Yeah, yeah. I'm the best sister in the world. We already know that. Now shut up and put it on!"

"And just like that, the moment is gone."

"Get a move on, Sloane. We have to leave soon."

"Fine," I mutter as I slip out of my robe and into the dress. "I do appreciate it though, Mal. Not just the dress, but everything you've done over the last few weeks. I couldn't have gotten through this without you."

"I know, Sloane." She sighs as she zips me up. "I'm the best thing that's ever happened to you. Besides this dress."

I stare at myself in the mirror and realize she's right. This dress is perfect, so much better than whatever I was going to pull out of my closet. Even though the color makes me think of Dom, I can't help but love how the soft fabric hugs my curves and accentuates my waist. The corset makes my cleavage look amazing, and the two front slits in the skirt give the slightest peek of my bare legs underneath the tulle.

"Wear these." Mal hands me a pair of simple diamond studs. "They'll pull the whole look together."

This is how she's been all day, standing over me and making suggestions that are really orders. Telling me to go with a neutral color for my nails, and a softer look for my makeup, talking me into getting a halo braid so I wouldn't spend the night fighting with my curls. I don't think she's ever been so opinionated about my appearance, but so far she hasn't led me wrong, so I take the earrings and put them on.

Mal smiles like a proud mom when I'm done and helps me pick out a pair of heels before forcing me down the stairs, out the door, and to her car. Within minutes, we're heading downtown towards La Grande Nuit, and I'm trying not to feel anxious about seeing Dom for the first time in weeks with the words from his messages in my head.

"He's not going to be there."

My gaze snaps to Mal's face. "What?"

"Nic." She says, cutting her eye at me. "He's not coming to the opening."

"Oh." I try to keep the disappointment out of my voice. "I guess that's for the best."

Mal nods but doesn't say anything as she pulls in front of the hotel. We both hop out, and I smooth my dress out while she gives the keys to the valet. Then she's beside me and bumping me with her hip.

"Ready?"

I slap on my best socialite smile. "Ready."

* * *

THE EVENING PASSES IN A BLUR, and even though I know he's not going to be there, I spend a good part of it looking for Dom and being heartbroken every time I don't find his dark eyes somewhere in the crowd.

Despite her promise to stay by my side all night, Mal abandons me as soon as James pulls me into a conversation with a group of real estate investors looking to build some luxury condos a couple of blocks away from Twisted Sistas. While we chat about design and budget, she stands off to the side laughing with members of our team and texting on her phone.

By the time I manage to disentangle myself from the conversation, leaving the gentlemen with one of my business cards and a promise to schedule a meeting next week, I'm ready to go home. Celebrating the completion of the project that brought me and Dom together without him has taken all of my energy.

I find Mal in a corner still typing away on her phone and wonder if it's Chris she's talking to. When she sees me walking up, she slides her phone back into her clutch and gives me a soft smile.

"Time to go?"

"Yes."

She links her arm through mine and leads me back through the crowd, completely dismissing everyone trying to come up and chat, until we're at the entrance. Right before we open the door, she slows down. "Alright, I don't want you to be upset with me, but there's someone outside who wants to speak to you."

The moment the words hit the air, my heart starts to pound in my chest. Suddenly I understand why she was so adamant about my fashion choices today, she knew Dom was going to show up and wanted me to be looking my best.

"Mal…"

She tugs on my arm, forcing me to look at her earnest expression. "Sloane, just listen to what he has to say okay? You guys have both been miserable for the last few weeks, and I'm tired of watching you pout. You love him. He loves you. Don't let anything get in the way of that."

"I don't —"

"Don't tell me, tell him." Then she's opening the door and shoving me out of it with a maniacal laugh. I stumble onto the sidewalk with a shocked gasp that turns into a full-blown yelp when I collide with the hard planes of the chest I've been dreaming of for weeks. A familiar set of warm hands go to my waist, steadying me in an instant.

"*Angel.*"

The warmth of his tone lights a fire in my belly, and it only burns brighter when I look at him. He's wearing a black-on-black tuxedo that somehow matches my dress and makes his eyes look impossibly darker. I bite my lip, feeling myself softening for him immediately. All of the ice around my heart finally melts away and leaves nothing but the love I've been trying not to feel for so long.

"You're here." I breathe, my hands going to his chest so I can feel his heartbeat underneath my palm. "Mal said you weren't coming."

"Like I said before, wherever you are is where I'll be." He searches my face. "Are you upset that I'm here?"

"No."

The smile that stretches across his face makes my knees weak, and I can't stop myself from smiling back. He lets go of my waist and brings his hands up to cradle my face. My breath catches as he rests his forehead against mine. "Tell me you've missed me as much as I've missed you."

Desire swirls in my veins as I let the command in his reverent tone wash over me. And in this moment I can't deny him anything, especially the truth. "I've missed you more."

He makes a disbelieving sound in the back of his throat just before he brings his lips down on mine. I moan into his mouth, arching into him desperately while my hands run over his chest. Kissing him again feels like finally coming up for air after a lifetime of being underwater. Every breath I pull in is full of him, and I relish it, hating every second I've had to go without it. I never want to be without him again, and I try to convey it with every glide of my lips over his.

"Okay. I need to stop now." Dom pulls back with a groan. "I have something to show you. Will you take a ride with me?"

I'm almost afraid to move, to do anything that takes us out of this moment. Things with us are so precarious, so fragile, it feels like moving an inch will send us spiraling into madness again. Dom senses my hesitancy, and he rubs small circles over my jaw with his thumbs.

"It's all out there now, angel. Every truth I've hidden from you, everything I've wished I could tell you for as long as I've known you. You know it. There's nothing left that can break us. Tell me you believe it."

I place my hands over his. "I believe it."

His answering smile is enough to quell every doubt I've ever had about us. He leads me to the car with his hand on my back, and it's the only thing keeping the rapid flutter of the butterfly wings in my stomach from carrying me away.

Once we're in the car, I don't bother asking where we're going because I know he won't tell me, but I can't help but notice how nervous he is as he maneuvers the car through the streets. I tap my fingers on my knee and study him. I've missed him so much, and it's good to see him, especially in a tux that somehow matches my dress despite Mal having just bought it for me....

Wait a minute. I knew there was something weird about how Mal showed up out of nowhere with a sexy dress for me. She knew Dom was going to be waiting outside the door for me, so it's not crazy at all to think she might have helped him plan our coordinated outfits.

I narrow my eyes at him. "You look nice tonight. I can't help but notice your tux matches the dress *Mal* bought for me."

"She went to the store and picked it up." A smirk plays on his lips as he glances at me. "But I ordered it for you weeks ago."

My heart does a little flip. "She's such a little liar. I should have never believed her whole speech about wanting me to feel beautiful tonight."

"Don't be mad at her. She was just helping me out, and you do look beautiful tonight, angel."

I blush. "Thank you. For the compliment, the dress, and everything else."

"You don't have to thank me. It's the least I could do." He glances over at me, eyes lingering on the swell of my breast. "I was probably being a little selfish when I chose the dress though."

"Why do you say that?"

"Because it's our color. I wanted you to see it and remember you belong to me."

Liquid heat rushes down my spine, and I shift in my seat, unable to speak past the lust clogging my throat. It's been weeks since we've been together and the hungry possession coating his words is making it hard to focus. I turn my attention back to the road. I thought we were heading towards my house, but Dom bypassed the turn for my neighborhood a while back.

Moonlight bathes the winding road in front of us, illuminating a sign for Medford Hills—a quiet area that became popular when the family that's owned it for over a hundred years decided to section it off and sell the lots to the highest bidder. Most of the land has been bought up by developers looking to build luxury homes and sell them for a nice price tag, or homeowners looking to cut out the middle man and have their dream homes built themselves. There's been tons of competition for the lots that are left, huge plots with plenty of trees and space to build.

Dom's leg starts bouncing, his jaw going tight when he turns down a freshly paved driveway lined with trees. I try to hide my smirk, but I think it's cute how nervous he is about me seeing whatever it is he has to show me. He stops the car before we reach the end of the drive and hops out, coming around to open my door.

"Close your eyes, angel." I look at him, surprised by the soft rasp in his command. He reaches over and cups my jaw, keeping my gaze trained on him. Whatever is at the end of the road, he doesn't want me to see it just yet.

"Fine, but this better not be the part of the night where you murder me and bury my body in the woods."

He rolls his eyes, and I can't help but laugh as my eyes fall shut. He grabs my hands, helping me slide out of the car and fixing my skirt when it gets tangled around my legs. I suck in a breath when his fingers sneak under the tulle and brush the skin bared by the split in the fabric. Dom laughs softly and the sound soaks into my skin. "We've got a short walk, but it's a relatively easy path. It shouldn't take long, even in your heels."

"Okay."

He closes the car door behind me then places one of his hands on the small of my back while the other stays in mine. I squeeze his fingers as we walk. There's a gentle breeze blowing, and I can hear the leaves on the trees around us rustling. I wish I could open my eyes and see where we are because I'm sure it's beautiful.

"Right here is good," Dom says, slowing his steps. "Don't open your eyes yet though." He lets go of me, and it's a struggle to obey his command when I don't know where I am or what's going on around me. I can feel that he's still close though, so I keep them shut.

"Look at me."

When I open my eyes, my jaw drops. Dom is a few feet away from me—dashing as ever in his tuxedo and giving me a wolfish smile—but it's the scene behind him that steals my breath.

There's a grove of trees with lights wrapped around their trunks and branches surrounding an expansive clearing. And in the middle of the clearing, right in front of where Dom and I are standing, is a foundation for what's going to be a huge house. The sun has already gone down, and there isn't much light coming from the trees, but every inch of it is visible thanks to the lit candles outlining it.

Oh, God. My heart stutters to a stop when I realize what he's done. It's the house of candles from my favorite episode of Grey's Anatomy. Dom and I watched it one night while we were cuddling on my couch. I told him how romantic I thought it was, and the glow in his eyes as I gushed over Derek's reaction to Meredith's vulnerability was so intense I jumped his bones before the scene was over.

Out of the corner of my eye, I see Dom moving towards me and reluctantly drag my eyes from the amazing sight in front of me to him. And thank God I do, because otherwise, I would have missed my chance to see him sink down on one knee in front of me with a ring box he must have pulled out of thin air open in his hands.

"Dom…" I don't even know what to say because I don't know what it means yet. I know what I *think* it means, but I want him to say it. "What is all of this? What are you doing?"

"Making it up to you."

"With a *house*?" I can't even mention the ring, haven't even been able to bring myself to look at it yet.

He laughs. "Yes. One I hope you'll share with me for the rest of our lives. I want you in my bed every night, Sloane. In my arms, in my home. You said we couldn't be us in my place, so I thought maybe we should have our own place. Something we built together, something that belongs to us."

A tear falls from my eye without my permission as I take in the glowing lot again. "*This* is the secret project you've been working on. The one you wouldn't give me any details about. You were never going to California."

"I was never leaving you, and I *told* you I would need your help with it." He seems content to let me drive the conversation even though I know he has a lot of things he wants to say. "And I will need it. I can build the house, but you'll have to tell me what to put in it. Sloane, look at me."

Following his command is easy even though my frayed nerves have me moving in slow motion. I lose my breath again at the sight of him on one knee. By what it means. A life with Dom. Not just a few weeks together. Stolen nights, hidden desires, lingering touches—all the hallmarks of forbidden love reversed by a question I already know the answer to.

"You're *really* doing this."

"Every moment in my life has led me to this moment, angel. *Of course*, I'm doing this. Now, are you going to let me?" And there it is again, the inevitability that's defined us from the moment we first laid eyes on each other. That invisible needle and thread linking my heart to his. For so long I've thought that thread, and the way it moved, was just a result of our connection. A by-product of the electricity racing between us, but now I know it wasn't just acting of its own volition. There was a hand holding the needle.

The same one that's steadied me with firm pressure at my back countless times, wiped my tears when I cried over things I couldn't change, and spelled love in my skin with gentle strokes of fingertips.

Dom was the one holding the needle that stitched my heart back together. And he'd done it quietly, carefully, and at great cost to himself because he knew there was no hope in finding the piece of my heart I'd lost four years ago when Eric died, so he gave me pieces of his instead. Using them to put mine back together again, to make me whole. To restore me.

I put my hand on his cheek, letting my fingers sink into the soft hair of his beard. "Yes. Sorry. Please go ahead before I start crying."

"Sloane Elise Kent, I've loved you for a lifetime, pretended to hate you for over a decade, and spent more than my fair share of time thinking the only thing I was destined to do in this life was want you. I used to look at it as a bad thing, but now I know it's not. Because wanting you is the only thing that's gotten me through living without you. It's gotten me to this moment right here, where I can look you in the eyes and tell you that I love you and I can't live without you. That I want your messy hair, your bare feet, your anger and heartache, your smiles and cuddles, your kisses and your moans. I want everything, including the honor of calling you my wife. Can I have that, angel?"

My throat is tight, constricting around a ball of emotions I can't even begin to name, but I manage to push past it because this answer is too important not to put words to.

"Oh my God, Dom." I laugh through the tears. "Yes." I don't even let him stand all the way up before I'm launching myself at him and showering his face with kisses. He catches me with a grunt and kisses me back, both of his hands going to my waist to steady me. The ring box digs into my skin, and panic grips me as I finally think about what saying yes to Dom means for the rings Eric gave me: taking them off, setting aside the symbol of my love for one man to make space for the claim of another.

Dom sets me on the ground and straightens his tux as I start to fidget with my wedding bands. I don't want him to be the one to pull them off to place his ring on my finger. I've just started to slide my engagement ring off when his hands cover mine. "What are you doing?"

My brows fall together. "I have to take these off, so I can wear the ring you got me." *The one I haven't even bothered to look at.*

"No, you don't." He opens the box back up. "Did you even look at the ring, angel?" I shake my head, which makes him laugh even harder as he puts the box in the interior pocket of his jacket. "What kind of woman doesn't look at the ring before she says yes?"

"One who's more excited about the man she's saying yes to than the ring itself."

My comment wins me a tender smile that sends liquid heat through my veins. Dom reaches for me, pulling my left hand into his and fixing my rings. Liquid pools of obsidian swallow me whole as he strokes his thumb over the stone in my engagement ring.

"Did you know Eric and I picked these out together?"

I blink, trying to remember if that was information I'd ever been made privy to. Not likely, since Eric went out of his way not to mention Dom to me when it wasn't necessary. "No. He never told me. Probably because he knew I would have chucked the ring at his head if I had known."

"Probably," Dom smirks. "Anyway, since I was with him when he bought these, and I know how much they mean to you—how much he means to you—I was able to contact the jeweler and have this made."

The metal is cold as he slips it onto my finger, but it's the band that stops my heart. It's silver, like the other two rings I've worn every day for the last six years, with alternating diamonds that sparkle brilliantly in their individual settings.

He pushes the band all the way down until it's flush with the tip of the pear-shaped diamond of my engagement ring. It slides into place perfectly, enhancing the already impressive set and making a gorgeous stacked trio.

My chest swells with the tenderest love for him, and I stare at it in disbelief for long seconds before throwing my arms around him. He holds me while I cry the happiest tears I've ever shed in my entire life. Only he could find a way to honor what Eric and I had while doing something as life-changing as asking me to marry him.

"It's perfect. It's so perfect. I love it, Dom." I pull back and look at him. "And I love you."

He leans down and brushes his nose over mine three times.

Like he's always done.

Like he'll do for the rest of our lives.

"I love you too, angel."

44

DOMINIC

Six months later

The heat from the sun bleeds into my skin as I walk the path through the cemetery, looking for the beloved mass of black curls that will lead me to my angel. She insisted on visiting Eric's grave today, for the first time in four years, and I pretended to forget the flowers we bought for him just so they could have some time alone.

When I find her, she's kneeling in front of his headstone, talking quietly. I slow my steps, not wanting to make her feel embarrassed or silly for having the same kind of one-sided conversations I have with him when I come out here on my own.

"Anyway, I just want you to know that I miss you so much." Her fingers brush across the granite, tracing over each letter in his name. "We should have had a lot more time together, and I'm sorry I wasted so much of it being afraid. I promise I don't do that anymore. I always try to choose love over fear, and I think you'd be proud of me for that."

She raises her hand to wipe away a fresh tear, and I'm hit, like I always am, with an endless swell of pride at the sight of my ring entangled with the ones Eric gave her. It's not traditional by any means, but it's right. A perfect encapsulation of my love for her blended with his. Two things that shouldn't be able to exist together, but somehow do.

"He would be."

Sloane jumps up and scowls at me. She's trying to look upset about me sneaking up on her, but all I see is the tender love shining in her eyes as she walks over.

"Jesus, Dom!" Her tiny fist collides with my chest. "You don't sneak up on a woman in the cemetery."

"Sorry, angel." I hold out the flowers to her, and her expression lets me know she's not buying my apology or my excuse about forgetting the flowers. "Did you have a good talk?"

She leans down and places them in the built-in vase in Eric's headstone. When she's done, I hold my hand to help her up, and she takes it, letting me pull her into my side.

"Yes."

I press a kiss to the top of her head. "Good. He'd be so proud of you, baby. I think he would be most proud of the work you've done to forgive yourself and find the happiness you deserve."

"I think so too." She says quietly, wrapping her arms around me. "Thank you for saying it though. It makes it easier to believe."

"Anytime, beautiful."

My phone vibrates in my pocket, signaling an incoming text message, at the exact moment Sloane's does. We both sigh and pull them out, knowing the simultaneous notifications can only be coming from the group chat Mal started after we told her and Mama—who swore she knew something was going on with us— that we were getting married. I unlock my phone and sure enough, there are multiple messages from her on the screen.

Mallory: This venue is perfect! You guys need to book it TODAY!

Mallory: Ugh. Nic, you didn't have to send Chris. He doesn't know anything about wedding venues.

> Mallory: Are you guys on the way because if I have to spend another minute alone with this man, you're going to be short a best man and maid of honor.

I roll my eyes and put my phone away while Sloane laughs and types out a response. Those two are the most confusing couple on Earth. One minute they're flirting and doing a shit job of hiding the fact they're sleeping together, and the next Mal is acting like she wants to kill him.

I just hope they can get it together for the ceremony because I don't want my wedding to turn into a crime scene.

Sloane puts her phone away and grabs my hand, leading me down the path and back towards the car.

"Let's get going before we have to postpone this wedding to help Mal beat a murder charge."

"You sure you don't want to elope?"

The sound of her laughter echoes around me, but it's the smile she turns on me that stops my heart. I remember the days I used to pray for her smiles, and now I hope I never get used to her looking at me this way.

With the entire world in her eyes.

With love shimmering in dapples of gold.

With shadows and flames and the promise of a lifetime filled with the best kind of trouble.

The End

ACKNOWLEDGMENTS

There are so many people in this world who never get to live their dreams, who never get to fulfill their purpose for being on this Earth. I don't know if writing is my purpose, but I know for sure that it is, and has always been, my passion. The one thing that's made my heart light up and my soul burn with the brightest, most consuming fire.

Even though that love has always been inside me, I've spent a lifetime running from it, hiding behind my fear and hoping for a calling that felt less devastating, that required less vulnerability, less of my heart and soul out in the world for people to read and judge. But one day, and because of a bunch of different people I'm going to try to name below, I decided to stop waiting and start doing.

And, well, here we are.

If you're here, I hope it's because you have loved reading Sloane and Dominic's story as much as I have loved writing it. These two have been in my head arguing for years, and so I guess it's only fitting for the first thanks to go to them.

To my husband- KD, you've already got the whole book dedicated to you, but I have to say thank you once again. From the moment I told you about this book idea—which was YEARS ago—you've been nothing but a constant source of love and support. Thank you for always believing in me, even when I didn't believe in myself.

To my son- Eli, you have no idea how much you've helped Mommy while she was writing this book. Thank you for always being patient and willing to postpone our X-box play dates while I worked through these chapters. You're the best son ever.

To Quinn- My beautiful angel baby, thank you for making sure the sun always shined on Mommy when she needed it most. I miss you more than life.

To my sisters- Dashia, Naya and Mandi, I'll never have enough words to say how much I appreciate you three. All the love, all the hype, all the excitement and encouragement to never be ashamed or afraid. I love y'all so much. Thank you for putting up with me and my made up words and stories for all these years.

To my Mommy- I've always believed I got my love of words from listening to you talk and tell stories—even though most of them were about me and my shenanigans—thank you loving the girl I was and believing in the woman I've become.

To my baby bro- Dee, I think you were the first person to ever look up to me, and something about your unshakable belief in my ability to do anything has always made me feel like I could take on the world. I hope you know I believe in you that much too. Maybe a little bit more. I love you.

To my BookTok Babes- There are no words for how grateful I am for all of you! From the moment I shared the first snippet of this book —back when I didn't have a title, a release date or any belief in my ability to finish—you guys WANTED in this story. And you harassed, threatened and pushed me to make it happen, so this is just as much for you as it is for me.

To my ARC squad- You guys are truly the best to ever do it, and I won't hear otherwise. Thank you for being the first people in the world to give Sloane and Dominic a chance. They wouldn't be here if it wasn't for your feedback, your close reads and all around openness to something new.

To my high school besties- Alexis, Angelique and Tina, y'all have literally been riding with me and my writing for well over a decade. I can't even think about my work now without thinking about the days y'all had me hand writing B2kfanfiction with you as the main characters. Lol. My original hype squad. I'll always be thankful for you.

To the messy, emotionally complex humans who raised me, loved me, and sometimes, hurt me. You were never perfect, and I'm still finding ways to remember the best parts of you while I heal from the worst. I'll always love you, will never stop missing you and will always carry the best of you in my heart.

Thank you.

ABOUT THE AUTHOR

J.L. Seegars is a dedicated smut peddler and lifelong nerd who's always had a love of words, storytelling and drama. When she isn't writing messy and emotionally complex characters like the ones she grew up around, she's watching reality TV, supporting her fellow authors by devouring their work or spending time with her husband and son.

ALSO BY J.L. SEEGARS

Again: A Marriage Redemption Novella

Revive Me Part One: The New Haven Series (Book #2)

Revive Me Part Two: The New Haven Series (Book #2)

Made in the USA
Middletown, DE
29 August 2024

59963357R00275